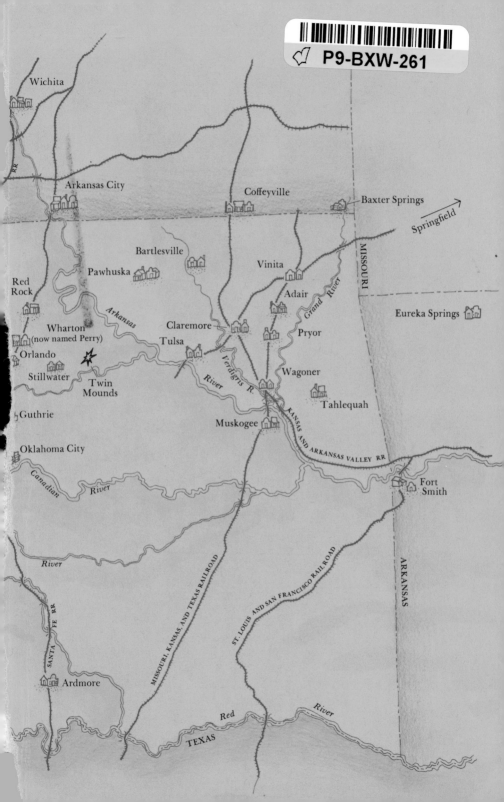

Wichita

Arkansas City

Coffeyville

Baxter Springs

Springfield

MISSOURI

Bartlesville

Pawhuska

Vinita

Red
Rock

Arkansas

Adair

*Grand River*

Eureka Springs

Wharton
(now named Perry)

Claremore
Tulsa

Pryor

Orlando

*Verdigris R.*

Stillwater

*River*

Wagoner

Twin
Mounds

Tahlequah

Guthrie

Muskogee

KANSAS AND ARKANSAS VALLEY RR

Oklahoma City

*Canadian*

*River*

Fort
Smith

*River*

ARKANSAS

SANTA FE RR

MISSOURI, KANSAS, AND TEXAS RAILROAD

ST. LOUIS AND SAN FRANCISCO RAILROAD

Ardmore

*Red*

*River*

TEXAS

RR

# DESPERADOES

# DESPERADOES

## A novel by
# RON HANSEN

Alfred A. Knopf    New York    1979

THIS IS A BORZOI BOOK
PUBLISHED BY ALFRED A. KNOPF, INC.

Library of Congress Cataloging in Publication Data

Hansen, Ron. Desperadoes.

1. Dalton family—Fiction. I. Title.
PZ4.H2496De    [PS3558.A5133]    813'.5'4    78-15273
ISBN 0-394-50350-3

Manufactured in the United States of America

FIRST EDITION

Most of this novel is based on verifiable fact. The characters in it represent my interpretation of people who actually lived not long ago. But though care has been taken not to contradict historical testimony, I have not hesitated to distort or invent situations and descriptions whenever it seemed fictionally right to do so.

I should like to acknowledge a rather large debt to Harold Preece and his biographical study *The Dalton Gang*, without which this book could not have been written. Besides many original newspaper sources, I have made extensive use of information from *When the Daltons Rode* by Emmett Dalton and Jack Jungmeyer; *The Dalton Brothers and Their Astounding Career of Crime*, reputed to have been written by Edgar de Valcourt-Vermont; and *Last Raid of the Daltons* by David Stewart Elliott, the editor of the Coffeyville *Journal*.

My thanks also go to the Dalton Defenders Museum in Coffeyville, Kansas, the Western History Department of the Denver Public Library, and to Stanford University and the Wallace Stegner Creative Writing Fellowship, which enabled me to complete this novel.

R.H.

*For my brother, Rob*

Of that marauding band I am the sole survivor. The rest have gone these many years, with their boots on. In fact, I am one of the very few yet alive of that whole elder school of border outlaws whose kind rides no more. And now that I am dry behind the ears I have a yearning to tell truthfully the tale of the Daltons and others of the old-timers whose lives and exploits have been so often garbled, fantastically romanticized, or vaguely related . . .

The tale will recount contacts with many of the less exploited desperadoes, as well as some of the more widely celebrated figures of the last frontier.

It will have dreadful and sinister things in it, of course: swift foray, desperate encounter, and the ultimate tests of reckless manhood; hot saddles, cracking guns, and last stands in a fated hour; fantastic courage and inglorious defeat—splendid things and mean, on both sides of the law's deadline. The sowing of black oats, and the terrible harvest.

And to leaven the wild antic of hair-trigger men in hair pants, the story also will have the romantic presence of women, gentle, stoic, and tempestuous, whose lives were entwined with the destiny of outlawed Daltons.

—Emmett Dalton,
*When the Daltons Rode*

# DESPERADOES

1 When Marshal Frank Dalton was murdered by whiskey runners in 1887, the federal government shipped him to Coffeyville, Kansas, in a mahogany box filled with ice. His face and hair were waxed by undertaker Lape and the body was hauled to Elmwood Cemetery in a quality black carriage with windows that did not warp what was looked at.

When my brothers Bob and Grat Dalton were shot dead in 1892, the bodies were handcuffed and stood in their stocking feet so photographs could be taken and the outlaws lay all night on a Coffeyville jail-house floor with blowflies crawling over their faces. Women came by with pinking shears to snip away bits of their hair and clothes, and the cartridges that were left in their belts sold for a dollar apiece.

And when Bill was gunned down by a marshal's posse in 1894, he was displayed in a coffin covered with window glass until he was badly decomposed. Spectators journeyed by train from Kansas and Texas and Oklahoma, and thousands of people crowded the mortician's parlor so they could file past and solemnly stare at the last of the notorious Daltons.

But I have spent these last years in Hollywood, California, where I suppose I will sleep one night and pass on to glory in striped pajamas, with my mouth open, and with a dozen medicine bottles on the bedside vanity. It is 1937 and I am sixty-five years old and not the kind of man I started out to be, but a real-estate broker, a building contractor, a scriptwriter for Western movies; a church man, a Rotarian, a member of

Moose Lodge 29, which is a true comeuppance for a desperado of the Old West, for the boy Emmett I was, and something to consider as I stood at night on my kelly-green lawn, a tinkling glass of ginger ale in my freckled, shaking hand.

A girl I didn't know was alone in the pool swimming slowly back and forth in satin underwear while in the dining room a combo from Havana played its trumpets and castanets in slick black hair and frilly sleeves. A week ago my wife and I returned from Coffeyville, Kansas, where I was the favorite son, where I was famous, so this was a welcoming party of sorts; but it was a celebration too, because my second book, *When the Daltons Rode,* had just been sold to a film studio here and I was made richer by quite a little. So male movie stars slouched around a billiards table in white flannels and sweaters tied at their necks and a makeup man was perched on our white corduroy couch with my stout and mankind-loving wife, hooting at Julia's comments, saying how precious she was.

If I went inside that grand stucco house with its South American look, women with platinum hair and clinging gowns and perfume strong as onions would beg to see my velvet-wrapped pistol or inquire about the Dalton gang and expect me to enchant them, become the gabby sidekick, confess about how it really was, as if those years of robbery were no more than a yarn about a blue ox or some carnival geek who chewed glass. If I went back inside I could see a houseboy carting drinks and a tray of bread squares smeared with black fish eggs, see a studio vice-president nuzzling the neck of another man's wife or a gaffer in a red cummerbund learning the rhumba with a girl from the typing pool. And I could see myself in an old silent movie that was flickering against the living room wall, see Emmett Dalton in middle age jabbing a six-gun at a bank teller's face as jostling dancers interrupted the screen, my holster strapped over a woman's back, a drawer of coins on someone's tuxedo shoulder.

The past was closer to me then than the sweating glass in

my hand and it seemed not long ago that I was a boy slumped against a sod house in the Indian Territory, watching Bitter Creek Newcomb wade through high yellow grass out to the buffalo wallow where he'd stare at a pane of water there with the white moon wafered in it. I could hear pool water slap softly in the skimmer as some girl in satin underwear glided to the ladder near the diving board, but all I saw was my brother Grat as he slapped the Navaho blanket up and sagged a shoulder against the mud wall, a pottery jug of white alcohol hung from his middle finger. Horses would nicker at the pole fence and he'd look at the empty night and scratch himself. "Ain't had this much fun since the circus."

I walked back toward the house and saw that on the screened breakfast porch newspapermen were taking photographs of Julia hugged like a shy, baffled mother by four of her merry party guests: Andy Devine, Frank Albertson, Broderick Crawford, and Brian Donlevy; Hollywood's latest version of Grat, Bill, Bob, and me. The stars clowned and made pistols of finger and thumb and Julia looked as amused as she could in her pearl necklace and navy blue party dress, a pretty hostess at sixty-four but less like the half-starved grand ladies here than a grocer's wife or a good farm woman who each morning scatters feed to the chickens.

The newspapermen saw me and called me up onto the porch to pose with my wife and then to stand alone next to a movie-house poster framed under glass on the wall. I suppose they fancied that I'd grin for their cameras with a knife in my teeth and a pistol in every hand, that I'd fan a roaring gun at a coffee can to make it whang and hop across the patio, but I was forty-five years away from the boy who wanted to be famous; I didn't want to be news anymore. The only picture they got for their rolls of black film was that of a tall, haggard man with a drink in his hand: Emmett Dalton in a charcoal suit, a rich executive with a needle of pain in his hip and a fourteen-year prison education, a man who golfs with bankers and stumps for good causes and talks to the governor on the phone.

alked into the kitchen and put my glass in the sink and garette. Julia came out of the dining room with a tray of lettuce and quivering gelatin dessert that she slid onto a shelf of the Frigidaire. She wiped her hands on a towel and asked, "Why are you frowning?"

"I ache."

"I have some aspirin."

"Maybe I'll just suffer for a while."

"Think how much they're enjoying this," she said.

My wife left with a dishrag she'd wrung out and I took the oaken stairs up to my locked study while a musician named Fernando lugged the combo's drums out to a school bus. I used my key and closed the study door behind me and stood in a dark brown room that smelled of old newsprint. I sat at a library table with maybe fifty books about the Dalton gang marked with yellow paper scraps or weighted open with bricks. Framed under glass on the walls were browned reward posters, red-and-blue billboard paste-ups for some of the Dalton movies, and three newspaper front pages dated October 5, 1892. In one mahogany cabinet were magazine articles, mostly false, and in the other I had the more reliable files of Deputy Marshal Christian Madsen, manilla envelopes once wrapped in twine and printed on each a name: Broadwell, Bryant, all four Daltons, Doolin, McElhanie, Eugenia Moore, Newcomb, Pierce, and Powers.

I switched on a study lamp and opened a cardboard box containing the clipping file on me. I unfolded my pocket bifocals and hooked them on an ear at a time, just as my brother Bob had when he said, "I can see clear to Nebraska with these." Then I sat in a stuffed chair for most of an hour, turning the pages over onto the carpet after I'd read what they said.

I heard my wife's high heels in the hallway and turned to see Julia in the room, a cup of hot milk and a saucer in her hands.

"Is it over?" I asked.

"There's still a girl asleep on the floor of the bathroom and a barefoot man at the piano playing 'Swanee' with his left hand. The houseboy's taking care of them."

"Was I missed?"

She smiled. "They make allowances for you. They think you live in a foreign country. A reporter asked about you."

"Did he use the word 'truculent'?"

She ignored that and said, "There's a young man here who's read your book," and in the doorway there appeared a boy in a green zigzag sweater and a white shirt with the collar spread out to his shoulders. I put him at twenty. I said, "What do you want?"

"I'm not sure. I drove all the way from San Bernardino."

I flicked my hand out. "Drive all the way back."

But Julia said, "You could at least visit for a minute, couldn't you, Em?"

The boy stood next to the coat tree with a tablet in his hand. "I read your book," he said. "It's fascinating."

I removed my bifocals and pulled up from the stuffed chair with pain. "Do you want to see my gun? I'll show you my gun and you can go back to San Bernardino and brag in some soda shop."

I limped to a mahogany cabinet where the pistol, a .44–40 Colt, was wrapped in red velvet and stuffed between some manilla files, a protection against common house thieves. I heard Julia say, "He's not really such a grouch; that's just his way of teasing."

I suppose the boy wrote that down.

Then Julia left and the boy and I sat at my library table next to the study lamp. He weighed the pistol in his hand, aimed it at a streetlight, folded the velvet cloth over it. I showed him a black bullet big as the top knuckle of his little finger. "That was dug out of my shoulder in Coffeyville. I was awake and face down on a mattress and rifles were held to my head. I remember it dropped in the doctor's pan like a marble."

He slouched in the chair, amused. "That must've hurt."

I squinted and asked him if he knew anything about the Old West.

"Not much, I'm afraid."

"You've heard about Jesse James."

"Yes."

"The Younger brothers?"

"I think so."

"Cole Younger was my cousin; neighbored the James boys in Kearney, Missouri. The James-Younger gang was our inspiration. They robbed stagecoaches, trains, the Kansas City Fair, a bank in Northfield, Minnesota, that did them in; shopkeepers took after the villains with shotguns, spade handles, and rocks they'd picked up in the street."

I was boring the boy; I could see his eyes stray. But I kept on and talked about other things: the Coffeyville reunion that Julia and I were just back from, about the movie Hollywood was making; about Eugenia Moore with her wing chaps, the law books my brother Bill read, the rifle called the Yellow Boy that Bob used once on a man; and the horses we rustled, the Mexican cantina we robbed, the locomotives big as shoe stores. I storied long enough to burn a candle down and when I quit the boy just sat there and frowned. He said, "You don't seem very sorry about any of this."

I stared at him.

"I mean, you murdered all these people."

"*I* didn't."

"Okay, your brothers then. I sort of expected you to repent more than you do."

"I was in a Kansas prison from 1893 to 1907. Penance is something I've already done."

"But you don't even—"

"Get out."

"Excuse me?"

"Get out!" I pulled up onto my shoes and stood there with

my hands quivering at the red velvet that covered the pistol, cocking back the hammer with both thumbs.

Then I was alone in the house except for my sleeping wife, and I sat at the foot of our bed in the dark, smoking down a Camel. I went into the bathroom and turned on the light and hung my suit and shirt on hangers. And I looked at my back in the long door-mirror, at the eighteen wicked scars of double-ought shot that were like cigarette burns on the skin, at the scar on my hip left by a rifle slug, that still registered rain and cold and too much time in my shoes with twinges sharp as cat bites. I peeled away a yellowed square of gauze taped to my festering right shoulder and squeezed a cream medicine from a silver tube into the ugly red eruption of skin, the result of a rifle shot that shattered the bone when I was twenty years old, that is still uncured forty-five years later. I tore the paper wrapper off a clean bandage and fixed it on. I buttoned on pajamas and tied my robe and with a glass of water swallowed three pills from three bottles, then carried my wife's cup and saucer downstairs to the kitchen sink where I left them for the maid.

And I stood in the living room next to the movie projector with its motor switched to reverse. I lit another cigarette and waved out the match and squinted through smoke to see the film collect off of the take-up reel, but after several hundred feet I stopped the machine and flipped the switch from rewind to forward and turned on the projector lamp, so that I could view my nickelodeon film: *Beyond the Law*, a movie starring me and written by me, produced by myself and John B. Tackett, adapted from the reminiscence I serialized in *Wide World* magazine. Tackett and I toured the country with it in 1918 and made a boodle of money even though it was pretty awful. I'd stared down dangerous men in my time but I was scared in front of Tackett's camera, the scowliest character ever on film. I flung my hands around, I slapped my shooting iron out of a polished black holster, I dressed like a buckaroo; and I was forty-six years old in that film, not the boy of my adventures; I looked ridiculous. Tackett was a fine showman, however, and he'd stand on movie-house stages in strange cities to deliver a stirring narrative about the Dalton gang, what trains we robbed and the way my brothers blazed to their deaths, ending with a list of the men we murdered:

"Charlie Montgomery, bushwacked over a woman. Then a Wharton ticket agent. Bill Starmer, after stealing his horse. Marshal Ed Short in a railroad car. An innocent bystander named Dr. W. L. Goff. And on a sunny morning in October, Lucius Baldwin, Charles Brown, George Cubine, and City Marshal Connelly; all of Coffeyville, Kansas."

And then as a surprise, an added attraction, I'd walk onto that stage with him and stare over the footlights to the farmers and clerks and secretaries who gasped or hushed or whispered to each other while the children slunk down in their seats like I was an ogre that feasted on noses and toes. Maybe I'd wave my white hat, maybe I'd autograph a program that was pushed at my fancy lizard-skin boots; then Tackett would signal the projection booth and I'd sit on a chair next to the curtain cables offstage, my back to the screen while three vicious, two-gunned bandits crouched out of the Condon bank and scurried across the bricked street to a dirt alley where two other glowering outlaws in frock coats fired pistols at clerks in a hardware store.

It was two in the morning in my Hollywood house and I saw myself with a boot in a stirrup and a money sack wrapped around the saddle horn, my damaged right arm hanging down in its sleeve as my eyes slid to take cues from the director behind a ratcheting camera. I jerked my skittering horse around and it balked at the artificial blue smoke and the hammering gunfire while actors with shotguns and sleeve garters stalked out into the street. I rode into a cross fire and I leaned down for my brother Bob without stopping my horse, bent as far as I could to pick him up, with blood dripping off of my fingers.

I stayed with that streaked, brown film to its slam-bang end and then the projector lamp flashed a square of white and I sat there hearing the film feed through the sprockets and onto the take-up reel.

Jesse James was shot in the back and Bob Younger died of tuberculosis and his brothers Cole and Jim were paroled from a Minnesota prison after twenty-five years on a life sentence. Jim took a job as a traveling salesman and committed suicide in 1902. Cole spent his last years with carnivals, lecturing on the evils of crime, and just before Frank James died of consumption in 1915, he was paid to stand by a theater door and tear children's movie tickets in half.

And Emmett Dalton spent his last years in Hollywood, California, or walking the streets of Coffeyville, Kansas, with a crowd shoved around me, adults and children gaping at the picket fence with pea vines on it where getaway horses were once tied to a pipe, and then at peach crates stacked at the rear of a restaurant that had been the barn where my brother Bob lay dying.

Bob is dead; that's what I'm sorry about. Sometimes it seems I return for him over and over again.


**2** All the notorious Dalton boys served as peace officers in the Indian Territories at some time. The best of us was my brother Frank who was murdered by whiskey runners on a Sunday morning in November of 1887. He was a marshal working for Judge Isaac Parker in the Choctaw and Chickasaw nations of what would become Oklahoma, and he was paid a paltry two dollars for every criminal he hauled into the federal court at Fort Smith, Arkansas, with any necessary burials being deducted from his paycheck. So he could not have been anticipating much extra spending money when he and Deputy Jim Cole got word that the Bill Smith bunch were selling hard liquor to the Indians out of a nester camp in the Arkansas River bottoms.

They rode through canebrake from three in the morning till five. Marsh fog splashed away from the horses' shoes. Then the sun lifted and they saw in the green morass a white tent with walls of mud and hickory logs. My brother Frank and Deputy Cole picketed their horses and crept up so close to the camp they could burn their hands on the cooking embers, and there espied the bootlegger Lee Dixon in a sleeping bag and Baldy Smith himself, in a black suit on a stained mattress with a chub whore out of Tupelo who called herself Mrs. Smith. The officers did not notice young Bill Towerly squatted down near the horse tie-ups drinking a cup of grainy coffee.

Frank stood up and walked toward the tent with a warrant in his hand that charged Smith with larceny and introducing. He stomped his boot heel on the board floor and Smith raised up his head from sleep and the two men talked for a minute and Lee Dixon got up on his elbow and rubbed his eyes and stared at Jim Cole.

Then Smith fired a derringer at my brother's stomach. Frank groaned and dropped down to his knees, holding the front of his coat, and he cocked his Peacemaker and shot Smith in the neck, and cocked it again and shot Smith's whore in the heart and Deputy Cole shot the man in the sleeping bag as he was hunting for the Dragoon he kept hidden under his pillow.

Blue gun smoke hung in the trees and Dixon was writhing with pain in his sleeping bag and Cole walked up to the tent with his pistol hanging by his leg, and out of nowhere that teenaged kid, Towerly, shot a hole in the deputy's chest just above his right nipple, knocking Cole backwards over a tent rope. Cole bellied through sump mud into the trees and slumped against his saddle. My brother Frank was on his knees and so bent over in his agony that his face was in the dirt and Cole thought Frank was dead until Towerly walked up to the tent in his gray long johns and hip waders and pushed Frank over to his back.

My brother had tears in his eyes as he rasped, "Don't. Please don't shoot. Let me be." But Towerly cocked his pistol and shot Frank in the mouth, and he cocked his pistol again and blew the top of my brother's head off.

I mention that miserable episode because it meant a lot to my brother Bob. He was seventeen years old at the time and he'd just been hired as a Cherokee policeman under the half-breed John W. Jordan, and it was Bob who escorted the body home in that mahogany box filled with ice.

He hunkered down out of the cold next to my brother's coffin, which was transported in a slat-sided cattle car. Bob wore a sheepskin coat and a broad hat that was pulled down and tied close to his ears with a wool scarf, but he didn't have gloves so when the train stopped for water and coal somewhere south of Chelsea, my brother got off and poured a brakeman's coffee on his fingers to take the bite away. And when he returned a railroad inspector had the coffin lid unlatched and leaned against a slat wall, and the man gazed at Frank's corrupted remains with a cheek of tobacco that he was spitting on the floor. "Lookit the fearsome holes in this man," he said. "Isn't it pitiful?"

So my brother stared at the body of a man with no more face than a plate of food and he puked into the straw and swore God's own vengeance on the wicked, much like a boy steeped in the romantic adventures of *The Wide Awake Library* and Beadle's *Half-Dime* novels. But I think he also made some other resolutions because he was very different after that.

I can recall very little about Bob from childhood when he and I slept in the same white iron bed. I'd see him call sooey at the pig trough with a basket of black apples and table garbage; see him combing his hair in the speckled mirror in the kitchen, experimenting with parts; see him in a wool shirt and knickers at the front of a one-room schoolhouse, parsing sentences on the blackboard. I remember him sitting on a milk pail stabbing a bowie knife at a plank between his boots. I remember him trying to stand on his hands and older brother

Frank squinting from tobacco smoke and holding Bob's feet, saying, "Up! Up!" I remember that he pissed against the barn in the cold and the gray steam floated up like seaweed. Those must not seem very special recollections of the Dalton who was to become the most famous, but Bob was the brother next to me, barely two years older than I was, and I envied him too much to pay close attention to his various attainments.

Bob was as handsome as Hamlet was when played by an actress (which was the fashion in those days), and he got tapped for Lady's Choice every time it occurred at hoedowns. His brown hair was cut very short and his sideburns were shaved off at the top of his ear. He had blue eyes that slanted a bit and white teeth that he took good care of, brushing them with baking soda four or five times a day. He remembered whatever he read and he could multiply like a banker and spell any word backwards, and one of the schoolmarms had it in her head that he'd attend Cornell Medical School. He paid attention to what women said; he listened so hard he frowned; and if he couldn't think of a proper answer he'd come up with something charming. He was six feet tall and maybe one hundred sixty pounds in his boots, all hard sinew and skeleton under his clothes, with skin as white as library paste. He was considered under the standards of that day to be friendly and suave and dashing. You cannot tell it from John Tackett's authentic photograph of Bob Dalton bootless and dead.

Soon after Frank's funeral my older brother Grattan was named to replace the bereaved hero. Grat was glorified in legend for a while because a rustler named Felix Griffin shot him in the stomach as Grat attempted an arrest, but my brother kept walking at him unvexed and used his hat to slap the man down to his knees. The bullet had split a wooden button on his shirt and Grat squeezed the slug out of his belly like a cinder. Some people claimed Grat had it in him to become as great a lawman as Heck Thomas and the talk about him became so exaggerated that when the Osage Indians created a tribal police force, they selected the great man's younger brother, Robert Renick Dalton, then eighteen, to be the new police chief, the youngest in the history of the West.

That year I was a cowpuncher at the Bar X Bar ranch near Pawnee where I mixed with bad company in the bunkhouse— Dick Broadwell, Bill Powers, Bill Doolin—and my brother Bob soon got the inspiration to save my soul by hiring me as his posseman.

I was the ninth son in the brood of fifteen kids who were Lewis and Adeline Dalton's, and when I left that measly, cramped, hardscrabble farm for sixteen-hour days on a horse, kicking cattle into pens, I was as happy as I'll ever be, like I'd been released from sufferance and began my life all over again.

But there was a pull to be with my brothers again that lured me away from that ranch. And I can recall the grin on the face of the sixteen-year-old Emmett Dalton who stood on the steps of the Methodist church for his official swearing-in. I was six-feet-two inches tall and long for my clothes and twenty pounds to the better of Bob, wearing a cardboard collar and a paisley tie and big-roweled spurs on my boots. My hair was slicked back with rose oil and cut close about my ears with a bowl so that the white of my scalp showed through. And my father, who was then seventy-three, sat on a split-bottom chair in a knee-long velvet-trimmed coat he wore over the scrubbed gray top of his long underwear, staring at me and smoking a corncob pipe, trying to place me among his children while the wind blew his white hair around.

Grat stayed on in the Cherokee legislative territory with an office in Tahlequah, and Bob worked the northern Osage nations out of an office in Pawhuska, the capital, with his warrants originating from the federal court in Wichita, Kansas. He hired twenty Osage men as peace enforcers; murderous, brown-looking men with black-looking hands, who wore greasy buckskins and feathered black hats and smelled worse than city sewers. I had rank over them and a desk job for a couple of weeks, but I got tired of that and soon I was riding with Bob, taking schooner wagons of criminals up to the federal court.

Bob and I walked down the mud alleys of boom towns with serious faces and hands on our pistol butts and older men sat on onion crates smoking pipes outside of their tents, snickering at us like we were children, like we ought to be wearing short pants. Bob stopped a lumber truck on a main street to check the driver's bill-of-sale and the carpenters hammering up the storefronts quit work to nudge each other or straddle a roof peak and shout jokes down at the brand-new marshal. But there was never a nineteen-year-old as sure of himself as Bob was. He seemed to think he already had Wyatt Earp's mean reputation. He pushed giant men out of his way on the streets; he shut down a saloon on a Saturday night because there was gambling going on; he was a stickler for licenses and paid-up fees. He arrested every drunk he saw; he'd handcuff a woman for stealing potatoes; he'd walk against a man's drawn gun and twist it out of his fist like nothing bad could happen to him. He was as unscared as a lawman can be.

He was dedicated then. I'd wake in the morning before sunup and see Bob crouched by the fire drawing up law enforcement inventions in his diary: gloves with hinged metal fingers, a contraption that locked a man's legs to his saddle, a mace; a vest of a hundred pockets that would hold a hundred iron plates so a lawman couldn't be gutshot. In his right boot he carried a .32 caliber pistol on a heavy .45 caliber frame so he could quick-draw on a miscreant simply by lifting his knee. Sometimes he'd lag behind me and I'd turn to see him muttering arguments with someone imaginary. Then he'd slap his pistol up.

"Keeping amused, are ya, Bob?"

"Heck, they don't have a chance against me. We're almost out of work."


After the Louisiana Purchase, displaced eastern Indian tribes were moved west of the Mississippi to the Indian Territory, which then took up most of the plains states. Farmers and railway companies worked on Congress to reduce the land area over the years until it was only the Ozarks and badlands of what is now Oklahoma. The property was considered inviolable and owned "until the rivers cease" by a strange collection of Indians, but chiefly by what were called the Five Civilized Tribes: the Cherokee, Chickasaw, Choctaw, Creek, and Seminole; nations with their own executive, legislative, and judicial bodies, their own laws and schools. The Indians leased their grassland to cattlemen for grazing and they traded with sutlers, but otherwise ignored the pioneers and immigrants as much as they could.

So if a cowhand woke up one morning with blood on his knife and sleeve, or if a boy stole the receipts from his uncle's cooperage, or a woman poleaxed her husband as he snored with a two-dollar chippy, the territories were where they got away; a vast, rugged section in the middle of the United States where your name was what you called yourself at the time, where a man could ride a horse for three or four days and not see another human being.

But Bob's Osage deputies could stalk a man who'd spent a week sloshing up rivers. They could root a child out of muskrat pits and smell a woman in the leaves she'd brushed against. I once locked ankle clamps on a man who'd been on the run so long he never stopped gasping, and another time I walked into a cave to discover a convict still in his prison stripes, squatted down and scratching himself, the smell of vomit near him. "You're a sight for sore eyes," he said. "Only thing I've tasted for a month now is gopher. And I got chilblains from the cold."

I'd drive an ox team with a stern Osage riding shotgun, and Bob would crouch in the back of the police wagon interviewing prisoners like that was his occupation. He'd ask, "What got you started in crime?" "What was your crucial mistake?" "Why aren't you repentant?"

He asked, "Did you like the life of a cowboy?"

The man said, "Yes sir, I did."

"Emmett seems taken with it."

"Well, it's outstanding education for the youngster and it's a worthy and stable livelihood. Cowboys are going to be riding herds for eons. I've got myself a bunk and three squares a day and I'm paid thirty dollars a month, and by God that's enough for a howl on a Saturday night and a savings account in a bank if I want it."

"Then why were you rustling livestock?"

The waddy scratched his chin. "Forgot my upbringin', I guess."

Bob sat next to me on the bench seat. "I hope you heard that," he said.

Or my brother Bob would ride through undulating prairie grass on patrol and he would rhapsodize: "When Dad first came to the territories, he was swapping brood mares and Army mules under government contract and this whole countryside was wild savannah and savages and prairie chicken and bears. There were buffalo then by the hundred thousand. Ground would shake nine miles away whenever they stampeded. Indians would climb inside the bleeding hides and skulk right into the midst of them, spear bulls so big it took two men just to carry the head. Twenty years later and his Great Plains were chockablock with sod houses and barns; squaws had all turned into oily nags; weather went sour and rivers dwindled; snakes dangled from branches of trees. Dad used to claim he traveled the entire Louisiana Purchase on twenty cents a week and he recalled neither hunger nor want. He was refreshed like the Israelites. Now he sits in a chair and forgets himself and the Army sends him six dollars a month in pension for duty in the Mexican War."

I said, "I onetime put salt into the sugar bowl just so's it would ruin his coffee. I once put a note in his shaving mug that said, 'Why don't you die!' I used to shove his left boot under the sofa and watch him thump through the house hunting it down. You never seen anyone so creased."

And Bob said, "Must be that you and I have different ideas about the Fourth Commandment."

The two of us would camp at sundown and he'd chop brush with a machete while I cooked pinto beans and sorghum in an old lard bucket. Then I'd lie with my head on a saddle, learning songs on the harmonica, while Bob rubbed his deputy marshal's badge with silver polish and made entries in his diary with a carpenter's pencil.

Mostly he commented on sunrise and sunset, the direction of the wind, and the relative temperature: "balmy and pleasant," or "chilly, frost on the grass until late morning, could see my breath when I talked." About every two weeks he'd take stock of himself and then there'd follow a list of commandments: "Resolved: to be more charitable in my speech; to be generous to those less fortunate than I am (for example, a meal, or an unexpected gift); to conduct myself like the knights of yore; to sit tall in the saddle." He wrote on January 11th: "Why am I so quick to ridicule and criticize others, yet so eager to hear flattery and praise of myself? Am I trying to deprive them because my need is so great? How can I mend the fences I've broken? These questions revolve in my brain as I gaze up at the galaxy of stars, and I have no satisfactory answer."

In many ways my brother was a stranger to me and for several months working with him I wasn't sure that I liked him very much. But there was an innocence and good faith to him that was convincing. He could be very sincere and intense about things and you discovered yourself seeing the world through his eyes and forgetting everything else. Sometimes we'd leave the Wichita jail and pound down a board sidewalk with suit pants stuffed inside our boots and Bob would announce, "I picked out a hotel room and got us a table at the Ambassador Grill; then we'll go play snooker. How would that be?" And I'd try to object but my mind would go blank; there didn't seem any alternative. If a night went his way he'd reward me with fantastic smiles and charitable speech; if he saw me bridle a bit he'd say graciously, "But why don't you do the thinking, Emmett. No reason I should have the vote on every dang thing," and like as not I'd botch it, the night would be miserable.

He was paid at the same rate that Frank was, a pissant two dollars a prisoner and six cents per mile traveling expenses, from which he paid room and board for himself, his assistants, and his suspects. After he rendered his accounts to the federal court, thirty-five percent was deducted as the marshal's fee and the bill sent on to Washington where the money could be delayed for months; so some weeks the only meals we had were what we took at farms we visited, and I scrounged a quarter a day sweeping out a saloon in Pawhuska or stacking cords of firewood for some widow in Ponca City. The two of us were stung so bad at times that we started administering our own fines for the smaller infractions and we put the money straight into our pockets.

I discovered two of the cowpokes I'd known at the Turkey Track ranch were rustling cow ponies for a race-horse trainer named Charlie Pierce, and I caught them in a copse of sycamores burning alterations on the brands. That would've been Bitter Creek Newcomb and Blackface Charley Bryant. Newcomb threw his hands up but Bryant extended a pistol at my face and I nearly cashed in right there but for the fact that we started conversing. I told them I couldn't see jail for them since they were buddies, but they convinced me they ought to be penalized something just to keep my conscience unsullied, and they paid me thirty dollars in silver coins that I split with my brother that evening.

Bob and I had a big restaurant supper of ham hocks and beans, during which he wiped his mouth with a napkin and concluded that what I'd done was almost legal and the sort of simple justice that he'd recommend in the future.

Maybe he thought I needed the salve but my conscience hadn't even tingled, whereas I think Bob got beat up by his. He denied himself the next day and that night; before he gazed up at the galaxy of stars, he probably took stock of himself in his diary and listed three or four more resolves.

**3** He used to claim that he knew secrets about women that no other man did, and there were rumors late in his short life that prostitutes would take him upstairs for free just so they could be schooled; and more than once I saw Bob straddle a chair opposite a strange woman at a café or train depot and, after some brief talk, stroll out the door with her arm engaged in his.

I never had his knack but I was jealous of it. I was common as toads to women. To work up even the faintest glimmer from them took everything I had and I'd sleep that night plumb worn out.

Julia Johnson was my sweetheart then and twenty years later I married her. She was sixteen when I first saw her practicing hymns on a church pedal organ that had a small mirror on the music stand so she could see the altar and pulpit. I rode up so close to the church window that my horse sunk down to its fetlocks in a spaded flower garden, and in the mirror Julia saw me leaning in with my elbows on the sill and my fists making my eyes slant like a Chinese rube, and her eyes dispatched me with one of those glances that girls have the handle on, which said I was boring and simple and big-eared and she'd just as soon I disappeared. I was seventeen and sold on myself in those days, however, and I couldn't countenance disregard, so I clomped inside that vacant church in my brown plow boots with red mud sliding off them in dollops and with two months' worth of smoke and unpleasant smells in my coat, and I slumped in a pew fairly stupefied as she worked through every song she had, from funeral to wedding march.

She had sun-browned skin the color of gypsies, and blue-black hair that was dark as a raven's wing and spilled down her back almost to the bench she was sitting on. I recall to this day that she wore a light-blue dress with a bow at the waist that had come untied, and she wasn't wearing shoes, just knee-high white socks that seemed new. And I believe the first sentence she used on me in that church was, "I hope you're not going to make a nuisance of yourself."

She was born in Kentucky and lived for some years in Texas where her father was a stockman. She had one sister, Lucy, and four brothers, two of them sheriffs. The Johnsons had moved only months before to a farm in Bartlesville twenty miles south of the Kansas line, and I commenced courting her there almost every night, making a nuisance of myself, until I broke down her resistance and she began thinking of Emmett Dalton with some fondness.

I shorthand that romance because it seems to me now so usual. I'd show up on her porch with a red bandana around my neck and my boots shined with tallow, a clutch of peonies in my hand, and I'd have supper with the Johnson family and try not to shovel my food. She'd do chores and I'd tag along. She'd wash the dishes and I'd dry; she'd ride the bell cow in from the pasture and giggle as I stumbled backwards over calf puckey, spouting about myself, and she'd sew my initials on white handkerchiefs while I pumped a frenzy in the butter churn.


My brother Bob was involved at that time with a girl of the same last name, Minnie Johnson. She was no relation to Julia but she was to Bob and me: a cousin, the daughter of my mother Adeline's dead sister. She was a pretty girl just turned sixteen, with green eyes and sausage-curled brown hair and skin as fair as white bread. She'd once let Bob unbutton her in the barn and he said she was as fine in the shingle light as the naked French actresses on postcards. And when she was thirteen she had allowed Bob to sneak into her bedroom on Christmas night and have his way with her.

She stayed off with my sisters Eva, Leona, and Nannie Mae most of the years that she and I shared the Dalton farmhouse, and after I left I hardly saw her at all except when she was hugging Bob's sleeve in a stroll down the Coffeyville streets, or at the contest booths under the shade trees at the Fourth of July picnic.

My brother wore a straw boater and a wrinkled white suit with his deputy marshal's badge pinned to his pocket. He'd deign to pitch a baseball at wooden milk bottles or toss pennies into teacups, but most of the afternoon he spent tipping his hat to ladies and carrying on like a boulevardier with his adoring cousin latched to him.

Whereas Julia and I took twenty nickel rides on a mule-pulled merry-go-round that had a fiddler turning with it for music. We drank lemonade from washtubs and reclined with Bob and Minnie on a patchwork quilt at night to gawk at the fireworks that whined and popped over the Caney River.

Bob sat back on his elbows and whispered to Minnie, "What's that one look like?"

She gazed at a red explosion dangling pink. "I don't know."

"A spider," he said. "What about this one?"

This time she just looked at his upturned profile and his glazed eyes.

And he said, "An elephant. See, there's its trunk."

She frowned. "Where are you getting all of this?"

He continued staring at some bursts of Roman candles. He said, "You just missed an orange tulip."

She said, "I don't think I understand you."


I spent more time in Pawhuska that autumn so I could be close to Julia, and Bob mixed·more often with our older brother Grat at the eastern border, where they made do on pretty skimpy paychecks by selling liquor to the Indians and engaging in graft against the pioneers. My brothers would stop ox-pulled Studebaker wagons and lean on their saddle horns shouting questions at the driver: "Where you from?"

"Haven't I seen you somewhere before?" "You ever been arrested for introducing?"

The canvas tops would be jagged with bureaus and desks and tapestried sofas that always seemed to get dumped in a sutler's ravine before the boomers got west of the Cimarron, and a woman would sit next to her husband with a blanket so much around her she hardly had a face.

Grat would plant unlabeled whiskey bottles in the flour sacks and accuse a farmer of bootlegging, or they'd demand an axle toll for a bad clay road that Bob insisted was a turnpike, and they'd trot away from the schooners with coins jangling in their pockets. One woman said, "We are three weeks out of St. Louis. We are used to hooligans by now." Squatters were sport in those days.

Bob mailed my mother twenty dollars a month, and to Minnie he sent boxes of frilled blouses, silk scarves, and long white gloves that buttoned past her elbows. And I'd receive letters recounting Grat's wild schemes for pocket money.

Bob was astonished by Grattan then, before Grat became alcoholic. He was twenty-seven years old, five-feet-ten inches tall, and weighed over two hundred pounds; broad and hard as a desk he was, with hands the size of telephones and too little imagination to ever be scared of anything. He could break through doors with his forehead. He could throw barrow hogs onto a porch roof. He was a bully throughout his school days, and after he flunked sixth grade two years in a row, he never returned. If someone snickered at his reading, he'd make the kid's mouth bleed at lunch. If someone fired him for letting a cow get mired during calving, Grat would sneak back at night and castrate the rancher's best seed bull. But Bob got a kick out of him. He'd write, "Good old Grat. Never smiles. Trims his mustache with lighted match sticks. Seen him peel the ears off a drunken Indian. The doors slam on churches when he rides past. He's an original Grat is. Tough as a night in jail."

I don't believe I saw Bob or Grat three times until December 1888, when my fourteen-year-old brother Simon died.

He'd always been puny and crouped, but that autumn he kept shoveled-up in his bed and withered away and turned the sheets brown with his fever.

I'd already arrived at our Labette County farm in Kansas when the undertaker drove his black carriage up. It was cold enough that the road out was jagged with frozen horse tracks and the saddle stock tied up to our white picket fence were shaggy with winter hair. I stood on the porch with my hands in my jeans, staring at a Christmas wreath of pine needles and cones that had been dipped in black paint and nailed to the front storm door, and when the hearse stopped I fetched four large men out of the whitewashed farmhouse, all kin to Simon and me, each with mustaches and suspenders and their pants shoved inside their high boots. We wobbled some as we carried the coffin up two steps and into the living room where we set it down on two chairs, picked our plates up, and ate lunch standing up, not saying a peep to each other.

Later I sat at a window and heard the screen door bang and saw Minnie in the backyard, taking down the gray laundry that flapped on the line. Red leaves swam around her on the grass. I saw her shade her eyes and stare across the cornfield to the pinkish woodrows and then I saw Bob and Grat on their horses, ducking under the colored trees. Minnie looked into her apron and walked back inside the house.

I saw Bob throw off his coat and hat in the tack room and I crossed the backyard rubbing my arms. Despite the cold, he knelt on the slick boards under the pump and jerked the handle till water gushed over his head. Goose bumps spread over his back.

"What say, Bob."

He grinned. "Well, hello there, doorknob." He reached a cold wet hand out and I yanked it once like a homespun farm boy.

I needled, "The saints still call you one of their own, or have you yielded unto temptation?"

He gave me a quizzical look, as if he suspected I'd been

reading mail meant for him. Then he said, "I've got change in my pockets. That's all I care about." He washed with hard yellow soap and I changed the subject to medicine and Simon's demise and I humped Bob's saddle and blanket into the barn while he brushed his pants off with a currycomb and buttoned on a stiff flannel shirt that was like cardboard on the clothes-line.

He said, "Did you notice how peculiar Minnie was?"

I said, "I don't think I've spoke three words to her. She's stayed pretty much to herself."

He said, "It's like I haven't arrived yet."

He stomped the dust from his boots and joined the family in the living room where tallow candles were out on the tables and a glass bowl heaped with rust-colored leaves sat on the head of the coffin. Minnie was sitting with my sisters but look-ing out a window that had started to frost. Bob stood by the oil lamp where the wallpaper was peeling down, combing his hair flat, staring at his sweetheart, wiping the water trickle from his neck.

"She's lost heft too," he whispered.

I said, "Why don't you be quiet about her."

Some visitors arrived for viewing after their Thursday night chores and with my brothers Ben and Charles and Henry and their wives and children, plus my sisters who were still at home, we had to take turns at the dining-room table, eating bowls of pork-belly stew and corn biscuits. Bob was still observing things about his loved one, and Minnie's eyes were avoiding. When she spoke at all it was about cooking. She thought pound cake was too heavy with four eggs.

Vespers were at seven. Julia bowed her head next to me and we clenched hands as a Methodist minister with a marled eye read from the Good Book and Grat slunk in from the kitchen and dug at his teeth with a thumbnail. After prayers were finished, everyone just sat around and looked uneasy and drank coffee. The cups clacked loudly in the saucers. The women comforted my mother until she began to cry, and then they took her to a back bedroom. "Lean on the Lord, honey," they said. Mom sat on a spring bed and wiped her eyes while a woman professed that Simon had been taken unto his heavenly Father's bosom and to that special place where the righteous know not fear.

I left Julia cutting chocolate-frosted cake and discovered Bob in the master bedroom with my father, who sucked at his pipe and spit into an empty peach can by his chair. "Your mother wants to divorce me, did you know that?"

"Yes," said Bob.

"The doctor says I should drink castor oil for my liver." He tapped his pipe into the peach can. "Minnie's been seeing a boy with a criminal record. That's news, I'll wager."

Bob leaned forward from his seat on the bed. "What's his name?"

"Charles Montgomery. Good manners, about thirty years old. Has a prominent nose that carries a wart. Served time for burglary, introducing." Dad blinked in my direction. "Which one are you?"

"Emmett."

"And you're Bob?"

My brother said, "This is the hired hand, right? Sleeps in the loft of Ted Seymour's barn?"

My father tossed his pipe onto the bed quilt. "I'm seventy-four years old and I don't care if I'm married or not. When I was a boy we used to poke heifers. You know what Simon loved most in the whole world? Licorice. I remember him better than I do either of you two fellas."

I think Bob closed Minnie's bedroom door behind him and had violent words with her while the assembled drank milk that my twelve-year-old sister Leona poured straight from the pail. Along about nine o'clock those people not family left and Ben took a kerosene lamp to the outhouse with him and I took Julia to a widow's house where she was being put up until the funeral. I played three games of pinochle there and returned to see that drapes were blowing out through Minnie's shuttered bedroom window.

I hung my coat on the hall tree and heard Bob and Grat

whispering in the front room so quietly all I could make out were the consonants, the k's and p's and t's. It was like hearing a fire snap and hiss and fall apart in a far-off kitchen stove. I walked into the front room. Grat said, "I believe that's what I'd do," and Bob shoved past me into the kitchen and let slide out of its brown suede case a Winchester 1866 carbine that was then called The Yellow Boy for its brass. He slammed the back door behind him.

Apparently Minnie had crawled out through her window and plunged through cornfields to Seymour's in her Sunday dress in order to deliver a warning to her lover.

I asked, "What's Bob going to do?"

"I make it a point not to meddle," said Grat. And I sat in a stuffed chair ruminating, staring at the coffin, while my brother snapped cards over into an upended hat.

I fell asleep shortly thereafter and woke to see Bob in the kitchen, opening pantry doors and closing them. He got a handful of oatmeal cookies and piled them on the kitchen table where he was cleaning his unused rifle. I straddled a chair and ate one.

"The lovers flee," he said.

I brushed cookie crumbs off my shirtfront. "How does that make you feel?"

He oiled the trigger mechanism and ignored me until I left.

Simon's funeral service the next day was fairly well attended. Children scrunched at the house windows, staring in, and farmers stood reverently in the yard while the minister read from the Psalms in the front room. Then participants and grievers alike mounted buggies and buckboards and clucked their teams in a slow walk to the Elmwood Cemetery and a plot next to Frank's where Grat had dug the grave himself, swinging a pick so hard the ground chipped up like arrowheads.

There was a lunch at a neighbor's farm and then Bob rode with Grat into the Coffeyville business district to help him lay in winter supplies. They bought deviled ham and raisins and boxes of dried figs to stuff in their saddlebags, and flour and lard and beef jerky to store in the Tahlequah office. Then Grat threw up his arm in a wave good-bye and Bob crossed Union Street to have his boot heel restitched by Mr. Brown.

Bob put a penny down for a paper and saw Charles Montgomery walk into Rammel's drugstore and walk out again with a paper bag. He was riding a horse with the Ted Seymour brand. Bob read the newspaper through with coffee in a café. The Kansas State Grange and Patrons of Husbandry were meeting in Olathe, it said. Ted Seymour had taken his wife with him to the Armour stockyards in Omaha.

I guess Bob then went to the city marshal's office where he reviewed the conviction record of Charles Montgomery, and instead of riding on to the Indian Territory, as he'd planned, he returned to the Dalton farm where he harnessed a dark brown team to a gray board-wagon and drove them to a ditch of sunflowers beside the Santa Fe Railroad tracks.

Bob loaded his rifle and crept across the Seymour backyard to squat in the empty chicken coop and stare at the barn and empty house. Sparrows had their nests in the coop and they chased and screeched a while. Snow began to fall and the temperature dropped to ten degrees, but Bob just huddled down in his mackinaw with the rifle cradled warm inside his coat and the barrel against his cheek. It was eleven o'clock at night and the ground was thick with snow when Montgomery pounded out of the Seymour house with dresses draped over his shoulder and two pair of ladies' shoes in his hand. When he was inside the barn he shouted to someone, "Look what I got for you."

Then he came out of the barn and swung a working saddle up to the top board of the fence. He went inside and brought out another saddle by the horn and Minnie Johnson stood in the doorway in Mrs. Seymour's shawl and watched Montgomery tug over a horse by its rope bridle. They spoke to each other and she shivered and went inside.

Bob told me this years later when we were on the porch stoop at Hennessey and Eugenia Moore was in the kitchen with a creaky ironing board. He said he had cocked his rifle four hours before so he did not do that then. He stood up and slowly pressed open the chicken coop's wire mesh door. He stood still a minute, then walked toward the barn. The falling snow was a grainy sound in the trees; otherwise it was silent night.

Montgomery was reaching under the belly of the horse to bring the cinch through the brass loop. Bob brought his rifle up and stood twenty yards away as Montgomery lifted up hard on the cinch strap. Minnie came out with one of Montgomery's coats and a carpetbag. She saw Bob and it so shocked her she couldn't say a thing. Montgomery turned his head just a little and there was gunpowder noise and a rifle bullet ripped into his neck, splitting his throat like a swamp root. He smacked against the saddle and the horse changed its hooves; he lifted a yellow-gloved hand to his neck, his mouth open like he was yelling or had just burst through the surface after touching the mud in a deep lake. He pawed for balance on the horse but it reared away and yanked the reins from their wrap on the fence. Minnie Johnson's hands were in prayer at her face as she sank down to her knees, and Montgomery fell off and died on his back in the snow.

Bob stayed where he was and looked at Minnie who was jerking with tears and still fairly far away. The night made everything blue. He yelled, "I'm a deputy marshal. That bag there isn't yours. Those clothes aren't. Same with the horses and bridles. So you're both thieves. I could shoot you in the face."

"Don't," she said.

"*What?*"

She shouted, "Please. Don't make me scared, Bobby. Please don't shoot me."

He left her there and whipped the team out of the ditch with a weed and lifted the heavy body of the man into the back of the gray board-wagon.

Cousin Minnie was gone when he returned. So was the saddled horse. No one ever heard of her again.

Bob stopped at the Dalton farm and stomped his boots on the porch and came back out of the house with me. I was buttoning up my long coat and shoving my pants inside my boots when I looked at Montgomery and saw the pockets of snow where his eyes were and a mustache white with ice. A blood-sopped scarf was stuffed around the man's neck.

"He'll be heavy as a tree," I said.

I slumped deep in my coat against the wind, my cheeks and nose stinging with cold, holding the reins as Bob sat stolid on the front box with me, his Winchester cradled in his mackinaw coat and snow on his hat brim, eyelashes, and shoulders. We'd been on the road to Coffeyville for ten minutes when Bob said, "Soon as I found out Frank was dead I swore I'd be the best dang marshal the West has ever seen, and I've really applied myself; you know that. But I never want to let myself get shot in the mouth for a lousy two dollar reward. I feel bad, Emmett. Miserable. But I'm not going to forget what I promised myself. I don't want to die poor like Frank, and I don't want to croup up in bed like Simon, and I'm never going to be so stupid in love that I can be bushwacked while I'm cinching a horse, like the corpse in the back of this wagon."

I just clucked the team and didn't say anything, but then I saw that my brother was staring at me, waiting for some kind of reaction. I don't think I had a single opinion in those days; I didn't have a comment in me. I said, "I can't improve on that at all, Bob. You took the words right out of my mouth."

"Shut up."

It was after midnight when we reached Coffeyville. Bob woke up undertaker Lape in his brick-basemented house on Ninth Street, and Lape crouched in the back not saying a thing as we rode down Walnut Street to the sign on the

wooden awning that read: LANG & LAPE, FURNITURE DEALERS
AND UNDERTAKERS.

Lape said, "There are reports I'll want to fill out. Questions I'll have to ask."

"That's fine," said Bob; then he and I unloaded the body
and propped it to a slump on the board sidewalk while Lape
dug out his keys. The undertaker bumped his way to the back
of the store and lit a grimy lantern over his embalming table.

My brother removed his gloves and brushed snow from the
dead man's face and coat; then he just squatted there, staring
at him. He said, "He was caught burglarizing Seymour's stable
and house; then all of a sudden he was dead. I don't know if I
meant to kill him or not. I took myself by surprise."

I could see Lape in back in a rubber apron and gloves,
limbering some hose. I said, "That's the amazing thing about
guns."

4 Much of what I know I owe to the letters Eugenia
Moore and I exchanged during my first years in prison.
Mine to her were unsigned and brief as the notes on
Christmas cards, all mailed to post offices in small
towns I'm sure she never lived in. Her letters back were long,
nine or ten pages of history and recollection that I marveled
at. She wanted to know everything about my brother Bob before she met him in Silver City, New Mexico, and she supplied me with stories about him thereafter.

I once wrote Miss Moore, "Horse stealing was how we occupied ourselves in 1889 and 1890," and then rambled with
suspicious detail for seven pages of cramped pencil writing on
prison stationery.

She replied, "It seems rather headlong, doesn't it."

Rustling, it was called, and it paid well. A brood mare might
fetch forty dollars, a gelding fifteen, and we could stay in ho-

tels with plumbing and spend on ourselves like faro dealers. So we kept on as pretty good lawmen but at night we picked the hated Indian ranchers to pieces. We'd rope a stray or hobble the last of a string of ponies and generally take what we could without risk. The more comfortable white ranchers we'd deprive in a larger way, opening up corral gates sometimes and simply stampeding the stock.

For example, once on a bitter February morning, the three of us rode up to a ranch before daybreak. Bob stayed in his saddle on the road, like a general, hunched out of the wind in a white slicker and blowing on his fingers. Grat broke through crusts of drifted snow as he walked through a skimpy windbreak of fall-planted trees: apricot, apple, and pear. It was a plank house with mud mortar and a sod roof. There were yellow stains in the snow where the woman had thrown out a slop pan. Grat pressed his bare hand to the frosted window till the glass was glass again and spied through it. Red burnt logs were fizzing in the fireplace. Man and wife were asleep in twin beds. He waved his left arm up and down and I scurried out of the barn with rope halters and a feed bag of oats, my hat squashed down with a wool scarf for my ears.

The corral was made of tree limbs that were almost straight. I lifted the poles of the gate and shoved them away and walked inside with the oats in the palm of my glove. The older horses were sleeping on three hooves with their heads hung out of the wind. Two mares blew air hard and clopped away from me on frozen ground, but a gelding came up to sniff my hand and raise his lips for the oats. Then another horse nosed him away and the gelding balked and made believe there was grass in the snow. A three-year-old with a blaze on its face took what I had in my hand while Grat climbed the fence behind the other horses. They were insulted and shied away but by then I had the lead horse walking forward to shovel at the feed bag. I backed outside the corral and wiped my nose on my sleeve and shook the bag. The horse looked at me like I was stupid and it had better things to do, but some others in the corral were smelling the air and murmuring and pushing each other out of the way, and the leader consented to walk into the feed bag and a bridle. Grat slipped a bit on a filly and we pulled them out to the road as the sun rose.

Bob was hunkered up in his coat on the road. "My feet have turned into stones," he said.

The two of us waited for Grat who came riding up last, having propped a spade against the front door; then we ran up the road in a racket.

We galloped toward the river and broke through the ice and waded the stolen horses east to the bowl of a dry creek bed that was all yellow leaves and snow. There we built a roaring fire and warmed up under blankets and I tampered with the brands where I needed to, burning new letters through a wet towel.

By afternoon, Grat and Bob were riding into Annie Walker's tent camp where rustlers and buyers congregated. A dog slept in the breath of some tied-up horses. A blood-smeared man was ripping his knife through a milk cow, butchering. Her stomachs fell out like laundry and steam rose up in the cold. A man stood under a tent flap in long brown bear hides, smoking a pipe. He was the middleman for the transactions, and he acknowledged Bob by backing inside.

As peace officers, we covered ourselves by bringing in minor offenders for trial at Fort Smith and Fort Scott, even garnered some reputation as enforcers, but we didn't worry much about petty crime, so except for Grat, who waded into brawls with a stocking full of lug nuts, we mostly retired and let the Osage deputies administer law in their nation. I got bored diddling with paperwork and spent more time around the bunkhouse of the Bar X Bar ranch, pitching pennies with Dick Broadwell and Bill Doolin, while Grat and Bob rode their horses on fake patrols with scowls on their faces. But soon they got just as tired of the sham as I did, and they spent their afternoons in porch chairs with their boots on a bannister, waiting to be fired. It would take more than a year.

The territories then were in the midst of the Homestead Run of April 22, 1889, which allowed sixty thousand settlers strung along a hundred miles of Kansas border to swarm across into newly opened Indian land at the sound of cavalry bugles. The price to those claiming land at the federal offices in Guthrie, Kingfisher, and Oklahoma City, was merely $1.50 per acre with an assessor's fee of $14.00 for entering 160 acres. Property within the city limits of Guthrie that cost $258.00 at the time of the run was four years later worth from one hundred thousand to a quarter of a million dollars. When I hired on as a cowhand, Guthrie had two wooden buildings, the land claim office and the stagecoach depot, and that was about it; after the run it had a population of thirty thousand people in a city of white tents spread out as far as you could see.

The federal government hadn't prepared for any of that, nor for the passions that come from bargain land, and there were too few peace officers to stop the claim jumpers and thieves and murderers, so most of those lawmen assigned to the territories stayed loose of the wars just like we did, until Congress established a United States Court for the Oklahoma Territory with the organic act of 1890.

My brothers and I pooled our money and claimed a fine section of land for our mother, and the Dalton family, lacking my father, packed up and moved southwest, which seemed a change of luck to Mom. Ben was prosperous, Charles and Henry were getting a little ahead, and the girls all took beaus. Only my brothers Bill and Littleton were still in California, and Bill was on his way to owning a wheat farm and about to stand for the California Assembly. The divorce action was brought before the courts that year and my father, who was by all accounts insane, stayed behind in Coffeyville where he died in a woodshed, banging from wall to wall in the night, spewing vomit and blood. Mice got to him before the neighbors did.

That was summer 1889. And it was summer too when Grat was caught by a rancher named McLelland, moving among his bunched horses with rope leads and tack and the squint of a stock show judge. McLelland and two hired hands tried to take Grat into jail but they found he was hard to wrestle as a piano and lashed him to a McCormick reaper until they collected more company. They then tied Grat face down on a shaggy, swaybacked mare and he spit at the men and hollered like Satan and one of the Cherokee dropped off along the trail, he was so spooked.

"I'm going to put an end to this rustling," McLelland said. "And a deputy marshal! I can't believe it! What I ought to do is take an ice pick and scar your face like Cain."

"I'd catch your children skipping home from school and break off their teeth with a chisel."

The rancher looked so horrified my brother smiled and rubbed his nose on the horse's hide. "Never mind what I say, McLelland. It's just talk."

When Grat didn't return with the animals to our morning fire, Bob and I took off after him and caught up with the McLelland party while they were still a few miles out of town. They were too many for our guns, however, and we weren't yet too inclined that way, so we hung back like wolves and skulked around the jail house the whole three months Grat was locked up.

Grat would sway at the bars, grating his belt buckle against them until the jailer had to hold his ears, and Bob and I would plunk ourselves down in the hard wooden chairs of the office and shine our badges on our pants legs. I'd write in a ledger the name of every man who walked through the sheriff's door. If they sat around drinking coffee, Bob would say, "Isn't there something you could be doing?" like he was a government inspector. He got a letter from Marshal Jacob Yoes, Grat's superior, asking, "What's going on over there?" And Bob sent back a long document stressing constitutional guarantees.

Soon after that Grat was set free without a trial and with the prosecutor maintaining that no one had mustered real evidence that theft had been intended. It would seem that we had survived the arrest, but it cast suspicion on the Dalton brothers and resulted in the dismissal of Bob and me from the Osage Tribal Police Force by the scrupulous merchants of Pawhuska.

That wasn't much of a blow because the federal government was still anxious for trained deputy marshals in the territories, so Bob simply transferred operations to Claremore in the Cherokee nation. There my brother and myself tried to make good and clean up our besmirched reputations, but Bob set out after a drunken Indian named Alex Cochran, who'd gutshot a deputy marshal, and accidentally fired his rifle at Alex Cochran's son, striking him so hard in the back at two hundred yards, it looked like the boy had been hit with a shovel.

We gingerly walked our horses to the body while the boy's mare looked down at her rider and then began chewing ditch grass. Then my brother discovered that the violent man he'd been pursuing had no more size to him than a smallish paperboy, and Bob moaned, "Oh my God," and jumped down from his saddle. The bullet had nearly degutted the boy. Bob tore off his shirt to pack him in and rolled a saddle blanket in under the boy to heft him up. The boy was puking blood on Bob all the way in to town, and soon every Cherokee there knew about it.

Bob sat gloomily on the stairs up to the doctor's office while I watched the surgery and handed the old man his sponges and clamps and silver tools. In the streets people talked among themselves and pointed at my brother, and twenty Indians stood on the porch across the street from Bob, staring and threatening and keeping their hands on their pistol grips. A girl in a gingham dress stood on the sidewalk and said, "A man paid me a nickel to ask you a question."

Bob hardly lifted his eyes.

"He said to ask if you were the same Bob Dalton who gave Charlie Montgomery not the chance of a suck-egg dog."


Nevertheless, we stayed on in Claremore for the winter, pitching a Confederate tent outside of town. Grat had ceased being

a deputy marshal after a letter of reprimand signed by Judge
Isaac Parker was mailed to Grat's office in Tahlequah, and he
frittered away his time while Bob and I kept the peace. He
bought a pint bottle of whiskey every morning and leaned on
a pool cue most of the afternoon and every night about ten
you could hear a *ponk* as he smashed his empty against a headstone in the graveyard. Bob would rent a surrey to take the
quarter-breed girls to a slow river where he catfished, or down
the road to the shanty of a squaw who told fortunes by burning hair. And I composed two pages of love letter with each
noon dinner, mailing the envelopes off to Miss Julia Johnson
with the address spelled in a careful hand of brown ink. The
snows came and we hunted quail and jackrabbit. Grat
chopped wood for a laundry in town and I was a regular at the
feed store pitch games, the only one of us three that the locals
accepted. Bob read the newspaper in the barber shop as well as
the weekly *Police Gazette*. He wrote an eight-page letter to
brother Bill in California and got one back of sixteen.

"Come west, young man," my brother Bill wrote. "The
women here are flaxen-haired; the fields are gold with am-
brosia. You can smell the eucalyptus trees and watch the sun
extinguish itself in the ocean."


Our quiet served to distract the citizens from the true Dalton
occupation; for we were stealing ponies piecemeal from the
Cherokees and mixed bloods, collecting another tidy remuda
that we'd already tagged for Kansas. We prowled at night in
the snow and had some twenty good horses by spring when
everything that was called Indian Territory—except for the
reservations of the Five Civilized Tribes—became Oklahoma
Territory.

That was in April of the year 1890. There were exploding
anvils and barbecues and prayer groups giving thanks for hard-
won civilization, and Bob and I visited a bordello run by our
second cousin Pearl Younger, daughter of Cole Younger and

Belle Starr, who took Bob upstairs for free because of the kin-
ship while I stayed in the sewing room with a prostitute of
fourteen who sat in my lap in a chintz rocking chair and listened to me talk about Julia Johnson. That is not me being
fanciful either.

"How does she wear her hair?" she asked. "Does she have
ivory barrettes? That's what I'm saving for. A man promised
me two but then he got the lumbago and it kilt him."

My brother stayed in bed with Pearl for most of the afternoon and he said afterwards he unfolded a newspaper on the
floor and scraped the mud off his boots with a coffee spoon and
his second cousin walked naked in the room with Bob's pistol
and holster slung low on her hips.

He asked her, "Suppose I put an outfit together like your
daddy Cole did. How would it be if I was the foreman?"

She stooped to look in a bureau mirror and brush wisps of
hair from her cheeks. "I don't know anything about it."

"Poor old Grat, he's dumb as a salt lick and knows it. He
can't even count to ten on his fingers. Emmett isn't but eighteen and he's always watching to see what I'll do next; he's not
all that independent. I think I have to be the top candidate,
and that's without boasting. I've got the brains and I don't get
rattled and I don't have hardly a vice except for stealing horses
and this. Down deep a man knows what he's best at."

Pearl unbuckled the holster and tied on a robe. She pulled
a brush through her hair. "Do you think I'm pretty, Bobby?"

He looked at her. "Sort of."

"I don't consider this sinful at all. This is what I was raised
up to do."


After that, Bob and I returned to Wagoner where Grat was
minding the stolen remuda. I wanted to bring the batch dis-
tinction before we sold it, so I convinced my brothers that we
should raid Bob Rogers's pastures for all his prime stock and
racers. We saddled up at midnight and drove our winter haul

of animals down a mud road in the rain. Young William Mc-
Elhanie and Bitter Creek Newcomb had hired out to us by
then and they kicked off with Bob and me to bring back what
we could with lariats, while Grat squatted in his slicker with
the twenty horses and made coffee for our return.

It was not a warm night. The rain hit our hats like pellets.
But Bob managed to set fire to a cigar, which was merely
occasional with him, and he sucked it down to a nub before we
got to the loam where horses were walking in that absent-
minded way they have, like they didn't notice the thunder-
showers. My brother and I herded them toward McElhanie
and Newcomb with dangling lariats that we slapped now and
then on their rumps.

The horses spraddled out and then they collected and
threw conniptions when McElhanie noosed them. But we got
them out of there somehow, separating the choicest from the
swaybacked and lame, and drove them with whoops and ki-yi's
back to our other remuda.

But rustling Bob Rogers's stock ruined us in the territories.
He was an Indian thin as a pick handle and a man to scrimp
and rage. He slept so little he never took off his clothes and
usually just closed his eyes for three or four hours in a straight-
back Shaker chair in the dirt-floor living room. That night he
woke up about three-thirty and stood in the kitchen doorway
mixing piss with rain and gazing at his mower and walking
plow and the horses that were standing asleep by the feed
trough. That they'd wandered down seemed odd to him, but
then he squinted hard and saw how many he was missing,
pulled up his right suspender strap, and got the loaded cap-and-
ball pistol from the pantry. He walked barefoot in high weeds
to the fence and took hold of the tail of the one sprinter Newcomb had left him by mistake. Then he started tracking us.


Newcomb collected twenty dollars from Bob and shoved it
into the bottom of his boot and galloped back to the Turkey
Track ranch for chores. McElhanie tried to stick around but

Grat kept glowering at him, so he rode to Annie Walker's tent camp to free-lance under the name of "The Narrow Gauge Kid."

We sold half the bunch in Columbus, Kansas, a dozen miles northwest of Baxter Springs, where we loitered like punks, whittling a café's chair legs or sitting in the saloon throwing peanuts at farmers or just straddling our horses and pointing unloaded guns at all the children.

He didn't need the bother of being a deputy marshal anymore, so Bob resigned from the Wichita court the next morning with a letter he wrote four drafts of, appending to it a list of grievances, of which most dealt with money. My heart sank when he gave the profession up since my job depended on his and I guess I'd always believed the rustling was just another form of prank that I could give up further on when paychecks became more regular.

So we were no longer peace officers when we urged our stolen remuda down the main street of Baxter Springs with bamboo fishing poles. We were grubby and unshaven horse thieves whose saddlery creaked from the rain. Grat was riding drag, Bob and I were middle and front, and we'd whipped the mustangs around a corner when we saw a posse of mixed bloods climbing out of their saddles. And carving his sprinter's hoof with a pocketknife was Bob Rogers in his oily shirt and chaps and his hair rolled under a red neckerchief. He no sooner saw us than he snatched up his rifle and tried to blow off our foreheads. But I had shouted "Look out!" and wheeled my horse, and Bob spun around stropping the stolen horses sharp and hard with his bamboo pole. They bolted and collided and pounded up on board sidewalks and Rogers's shots only smashed windows.

Bob and I bent for the wheel-rutted road out of town, lashing our horses with leather reins. The mud flew up like shoes. Before we were out of range, though, one of Rogers's vigilantes got off a shot and the bullet chipped off part of the right ear of my horse. The blood carried back like a streamer. We had no more than six miles' distance from the town when my horse played out and all I could think of was a rustler who'd been caught by some Indians and cut up by squaws to the size of trout fillets. Then out of the blue came a farmer with a team of hairy Morgans and a wagon and I lost no time in lifting my heavy six-shooter in both hands.

The granger was narrow and buttoned-up and he obeyed like a weakling pupil while Bob unhitched a Morgan and led it over to where I could cross over from my sagging horse. Then we put spurs to our horses and plodded heavily toward the trees and got away clean.

Grat was not so lucky. After Bob had stropped the horses with his bamboo pole, Grat took to a back alley at a gallop, kicking a garbage pail that rang and spilled behind him. He stopped his horse to hook a ladder that banged down and threw a pursuer's horse on its neck. Then Grat pushed his mount through yellow weeds tall as its belly until he was on the cinder siding of the railroad tracks where he tied a rope lead to the two stolen horses that had trailed him and continued down the bank to a crooked stream that was swelled brown with spring rain.

It was not difficult tracking in the soft earth, and within minutes the vigilantes were close enough to hear the splashing of horses that were led by a rope. They intercepted him at a beaver dam. He was still up in his stirrups and looking around like a tourist when the town sheriff yelled, "Reach for the sky, Dalton!"

My brother Grat shaded his eyes to look at the posse. He smiled and said, "I never been so embarrassed."

5 So Grat was arrested once again in territory under the purview of Hanging Judge Parker, his former boss, and my brother Bob and I went into hiding in the Ozarks near the Cookson hills. Reward posters were printed with faces not to our likeness but with the Dalton name bold enough, and newspapers carried slipshod accounts of Grat's

capture, characterizing us as "treacherous, renegade lawmen." What all the publicity meant, naturally, was that we had to disappear from the territories, and that we had no influence with the judicial branch anymore; if we wanted brother Grat released, we needed to collect a gang.

Newcomb was the first. George was his given name, but I rarely heard it spoken. His nickname came from the lines of a song that went, "I'm a lone wolf from Bitter Creek and to-night is my night to howl." He had an alias of "The Slaughter Kid," having assisted the popular ranger John Slaughter in Texas for a while. He was five-feet-two inches tall, the shortest cowboy I ever knew, and women thought him pretty. He had a sunburnt nose and a carrot-red mustache and goatee, and brown freckles everywhere. He usually kept a plug of tobacco big as a baseball in his cheek, and he'd broken his knuckles so often in fights he could hardly close his hands. Newcomb was unschooled but he could spell his name and he'd spend nights around the fire carving it into his belts and holster, little pig-tails of leather curling from his trench knife as he worked. Late in the evening he'd walk off into the wilderness where he'd close his eyes and stand with his hands behind his back, smelling the air. His best friend was the horse-racer Charlie Pierce, who was then dealing stock for Annie Walker but would sign on with us a little later and die with Newcomb on the Bee Dunn farm in 1895.

Also from the Turkey Track ranch was Blackface Charley Bryant, the victim of a freakish gunpowder burn that he ex-plained in a varied way every time the question came up. A third of his face was pale and handsome but the rest was a mottled patch, blue as a bad tattoo, with dark hair emerging from it so that he had to shave clean up to his left eyelid. It made him keep to the night and the darker corners of a room; it made him standoffish and resentful. He wore his coat collar up and his slouch hat down and he rested his blistered cheek on his fist whenever he sat down at the table. He was mean and stubborn and possibly insane. He once snapped the little fin-gers of a prostitute just for entertainment. Except for Bob and

Grat, I never met a man who wasn't afraid of Blackface Charley Bryant. He hardly spoke at all to me. Maybe he knew all I'd do was stammer. Bryant rode three days to get to the Ozarks, pulling a mule with beans and flour and baking powder and cured ham folded up in a tarpaulin, and, at a windmill where he'd stopped to water his animals, he was joined by William McElhanie.

McElhanie was a loudmouthed straw-haired boy, one year younger than I was, who'd been working from a saddle since he was six and therefore limped a little, both legs. He considered himself successful with the ladies and bragged that he'd raped two Choctaw squaws and a Mexican nun and a nine-year-old colored girl, but that is likely bandit talk he'd encountered in magazines. He wouldn't've had a chance of staying on with us except that he worshipped Bob Dalton and my brother was coaxed by the attention. Sometimes Bob was all McElhanie could talk about. He shifted his holster to duplicate Bob's; he watched how Bob cut up his meat; he traded a box of bullets for one of Bob's shirts and never took it off for a week. He once said to me, "You know what I just asked Bob? I asked him who was his most respected American—so I could read something about him? Bob said the American he respected most was Alexander Hamilton. That just illustrates how smart Bob is. I never even *heard* of Alexander Hamilton. *Nothing* gets by your brother."

McElhanie and Bryant rode into the Ozarks until they saw a fat woman with her hair pinned tight, slopping a pen of shoat pigs. She told them she'd seen two strangers yonder on higher ground, and that they had a string of ponies with them.

McElhanie winked at Bryant and they scrabbled up the mountain for an hour, arriving at our camp in a rain. Our tents were in a green clearing in a greener forest. There was moss on all the trees. Bitter Creek Newcomb had already come and was off somewhere with the horses; I was squatted down at a fire that was mostly blue smoke from the weather, an oil slicker draped over my head and an ancient Colt braced on my knee to point in their direction until I recognized them. Then I rose up and holstered my pistol and said, "You two are slow as the mail."

The two men covered their saddles with a tarp and slapped their animals into clover. McElhanie fired three shots into the air and I grudgingly put a can of water in the fire for coffee. Soon Newcomb clopped out of the woods on my stolen Morgan horse, a currycomb still in his hand. He was grinning and hallooing. He slid from his mount and shook their hands and the four of us joshed and heckled and carried on around the smoulderings. The rain fell thin and straight as fish line. Bob rode in after sundown, doubled on his horse with a half-reformed whore and spiritualist named Kate Bender who hugged him under his coat. He grinned at everybody and Bryant cooked a slab of ham that we ate with refried beans and pan bread.

Then we washed out our mouths with moonshine from a jug while the woman talked about how she communicated with Jesse James in the murky other world. She looked at our palms and felt the lumps on our heads and predicted ailments and satisfactions; and she dangled a witch's thimble over our hands to see if we'd become rich and if we'd get Grat out of jail.

Bryant wrapped a scarf around his face and came over to watch her work on Newcomb while my brother crouched close to peer at the thimble and thread. Bob said, "I bet I've met a hundred witches in my travels. Chickasaw woman I knew could throw her hair on a dead lake and largemouth bass would jump for it. Saw a gypsy down in Tulsa who could drop hailstones in her mouth at dawn and spit 'em out unmelted after noon. Walked into a tent at the Bailey circus in Joplin, Missouri, once and walked out with memories I never had: mumps in Rhode Island, white sailboats in Norfolk, Virginia; a fat Cree squaw nursing a striped coral snake at her breast. Returned me to Scripture, that did."

Bryant said, "It's the devil's work, sorcery is. I'm not surprised at anything."

Kate foretold that soon every brand of highwayman and tyro would be begging to join us but that we should keep the gang to a governable size. Then Bob sat on a three-legged milk stool while Kate read the fortune in his hand. She said, "You will be successful in whatever you undertake. You have been disappointed in love but a better woman will replace her. You are a born leader of men."

"Not very exceptional, is it."

The woman shrugged.

"How about Emmett?"

I was about as close to Bob as his clothes in those days; I sat cross-legged by his milk stool and shook my head, my fists behind my back. "I believe I'll forego the pleasure," I said. "I like a little mystery regarding the hereafter."

She said, "You're the kind that becomes prosperous."

Bob grinned. "This your full-time occupation, ma'am?"


Bob massaged her breasts by the fire, and during the night Bryant, then McElhanie, stole into the tent and used her under the blankets, and the five members of the Dalton gang argued into the small hours about where to go after we got my brother free from the Fort Smith jail. Options were New Orleans and California and Eureka Springs, Arkansas, where there were hot medicinal baths. But my brother Bob wooed us into deciding on the gambling town of Silver City, which was located in an unpopulated section of the country that would become New Mexico in 1912. There a former neighbor of ours named Ben Canty was now the city marshal. He lived on bribes and was mostly tolerant of rustlers.

That was May of 1890 and the five of us decamped and rode through the spectacular Ozarks to Fort Smith, staying in our saddles as McElhanie—who wouldn't be recognized as a criminal—walked bandy-legged into the office of the Fort

Smith *Elevator* and moseyed up to a man in visor and sleeves who was setting type. We could see the man talk and point directions; then McElhanie came out with the names of the jury and judge and prosecutor listed on a blank newspaper page.

Then we set about making fools of ourselves. We delivered to every prospective member of the jury a letter that had a crude skull and crossbones drawn over script that read: "There is no evidence implicating Grattan Dalton in the horse-stealing business. He is a respected former deputy marshal and a victim of circumstances."

Bitter Creek and Blackface Charley and I then visited Judge Isaac Parker, riding up so close to his house that the horses potholed his spaded flower garden.

His fat daughter came out, drying her hands on a tea towel and said her father wasn't home, what did we want?

I elbowed Newcomb and he said, "We're associates of a prisoner of your papa."

"The innocent Grattan Dalton," I said.

"Ah," said the girl. "You've come to intimidate us."

Bryant stood in his saddle, opening up his coat. Inside it a white hen ticked her head. Bryant yanked her out and wildly wrung her around, the chicken flapping and squawking until the neck broke off and the body flew up on the porch. The chicken walked around spurting blood while Bryant pitched her head on the roof. It rattled down on the shingles.

The Parker girl merely picked the chicken up by a white wing and walked into the house, locking the screen door behind her, and we walked our horses back to the street through the yard pansies.

I said, "That didn't work worth beans, did it."

Bryant said, "It stunk, is what it did."

And Bob rode his horse up the porch steps of the federal prosecutor's white house in the middle of town. He opened the screen and ducked low to ride in under the lintel. The

animal knocked over a porcelain candle stand and a lamp of
dangling prisms and then thudded over the woven rug to
the kitchen. A little girl turned in her chair like a spinster.
"What on earth!" she said. The attorney was getting out of his
chair, a napkin around his neck, when Bob ducked under the
doorway. They were having a supper of liver and onions.
The wife was gone. Two daughters were at the oak table
and the man was saying things like, "See here!" and "This is
an outrage!"

Bob slapped his pistol up from his boot holster, just like
he'd practiced. "My name is Robert Dalton. You have a warrant for my arrest and you have my brother Grat in jail."

The attorney sat back down, wiped his mouth with a napkin, and tossed it. "That's so."

"You can persuade a grand jury to no-bill him."

"That's exactly what I intend to do."

That stymied Bob. "You're letting him off? Just like that?"

The attorney had eaten of the liver. He was chewing.
"Aren't you going to thank me?"

The horse stepped from one shoe to the next. Its tail
swished flour on the counter. The girls were looking at that.
My brother said, "Excuse me but I'm just the least bit pixi-
lated by all this. Can you explain why you're letting him go
free?"

"The evidence inspires it. He was arrested on the suspicion
he stole Bob Rogers's horses, but none of those mustangs
carried the Rogers brand. Plus there's a problem with the ar-
resting officer abetting a vigilante group. And your brother's
defense attorney was going to call on Judge Isaac Parker as a
character witness. That might have been humiliating. It's a
complicated case. I've got plenty to do just pleading the easy
ones."

My brother hung onto those words like he could listen
forever. "Well, shucks," he said. "Now you got me sorry I
mussed up your house."

The older girl said, "Just don't tarry," and Bob walked his

horse down the back stairs and through the staked vegetable garden.


My brother Grat was released from jail the next morning and the *Elevator* for May 8th used our language, explaining that there was "no evidence implicating him in the horse-stealing business."

Grat walked out of town with his hands in his pockets. He could stand incarceration better than any man I've ever known. Parker had executed many rustlers in his past but Grat never suspected evil until he saw it plain, and all the time he was in jail he'd make gurgling, strangling noises whenever one of his keepers walked past, and he fashioned a hangman's noose out of torn strips of his bedding and wore it under his collar like a necktie. And it was closing his collar still when I clambered up from under the bridge with a horse and a mule on a leash.

He whispered, "You better skedaddle, Em. I bet the law is trackin' me."

"I already checked. There's a boy with field glasses in a cottonwood tree staring at us right now. Don't turn around." I gave my brother a big-bore Colt Dragoon wrapped in a gun belt and said, "You're supposed to ride north to a train depot and use the ticket to California I stuck in your saddlebag. Bob sent telegrams about you to Littleton and Bill, and here's fifty dollars expense money, but that's the bottom of our funds."

Grat legged up onto his saddle. "Where will you boys be?"

"We've expanded operations, Grat. We got ourselves a gang now. Newcomb, Bryant, McElhanie. We're traipsing off to Silver City, there to recover our lost kingdom."

Grat smiled with all his brown teeth. "Kiss me an octaroon whore if you can." Then he throttled horse and mule into a jog.

So Grat left the state unscathed and the Dalton gang rode the railroad tracks through Arkansas and the badlands to the

New Mexico Territory, stepping our horses off the roadbed and down into bramble to watch the big locomotive engines and the smoke-blackened cars pass by, waving our hats at the passengers in the windows.

The gang moped into Silver City hunkered over in our saddles, our slouch hats yellowish with the dust and brown about the sweatbands. We all wore big red neckerchiefs and hide chaps and slickers that used to be white. A boy who was pumping water in a horse trough ignored us and I knew it was my kind of town.

Some cowboys were slumped in chairs on the porch of a hotel and not doing anything else at all. Four hatless old men sat at a picnic table outside playing nine-point pitch, a nickel a game. A woman in a pale gingham dress and a sunbonnet crossed the street with a market basket. Bob kicked his horse up to a walk beside her but she said she didn't talk to strangers.

"Maybe I could find someone to introduce us," he said, but she hustled inside a dress shop.

Bob crossed over to a man in a bowler hat and a suit coat that was only buttoned at the lapels so that his checkered vest and watch chain showed. Bob told him he was looking for lodging in the town and a place to get a tub bath and a smith who could doctor the horses. They wanted new oats and new shoes, he said, and they were badly fistulowed.

The man directed Bob without taking his hands from his pockets and the five of us tied up at a boarding house where the widow had a sign up saying, NO COLOREDS. NO CHINESE. NO MEXICANS. NO IRISH. We heaved our saddles up her varnished stairs to a room of six single bunks and a dresser and a China washbowl and pitcher. There was a thundermug under each bed. We each paid a nickel and the widow fried up tomatoes and bread, put on a pot of coffee, and brushed down our coats and hats with a broom. We slept in our clothes until three in the afternoon and sat in iron tubs while a girl poured steaming water from a bucket. Then we sat in the widow's parlor in our wrinkled black suits, watching the brass pendulum clock until Bob descended from the bedroom with envelopes of spending money that he parceled out at the door. Thereupon we split up, each to his separate pleasure.

Blackface Charley Bryant knew the place and he left us without so much as a good-bye, and he walked the plank bridge across the arroyo with his head sunk down and the lapel collar up on his coat. He bought jars of green peppers and Chile Colorado from a Mexican and squatted down in the dirt to eat them. A dog came up to sniff and Bryant gave him a lick of a pepper he held by the stem. The dog grimaced as much as a dog can and Bryant got a big kick out of that. He ate the pepper and wiped his hands on his pants. The Mexican was staring at the ugly blister on Bryant's face.

"Do you sell peyote?" Bryant asked.

The Mexican frowned.

"How about tobacco? Do you have it?"

The Mexican sold him a pouch for a dime and they both sat in the dirt to roll it in papers and smoke. Bryant said, "What do you think of my scar?"

The Mexican squinted and smoked.

"I believe I'd rather be harelipped," Bryant said. "Came about when I planted a woman with child in San Antonio. She hunted me out when she got ripe and found me in a flophouse with a six-fingered whore. Tried to shoot me in the ear with a cap-and-ball pistol and burst the pillow I had my head on. Powder burnt my face like hot tar. The woman that deformed me lost every one of her teeth to the butt end of her pistol. I was careful not to miss one."

Bryant didn't move for a minute or two, then stood and brushed off his pants. "You have a sister or something?"

The Mexican showed Bryant to a one-room shanty with a blanket for a door. Inside there were two black girls and a Mexican woman of forty, smoking from a pipe. The black girls sat on their beds and watched him as the woman leaned back against a pillow and lifted the front of her dress.

Then Bryant walked to a Chinese laundry where he bought opium and a small metal pipe, and an ancient woman scraped at his cheek with a bone knife and pressed herb leaves to his face as he slept. Then he returned to the hotel room where each member of the gang discussed his own entertainments.

Bitter Creek Newcomb was calling himself "The Slaughter Kid" in Silver City so everyone would think him a Texan. He spent his afternoon whittling a reed flute and picked up body lice in his evenings with an obese Missouri farm girl. He treated himself with a hot bath and kerosene and from then on indulged in gambling at the green felt tables where a boy from Alabama called him a carping cheat and Newcomb thunked him in the Adam's apple with a quart bottle of Kentucky whiskey. The boy sat down hard on the floor and would have swallowed his tongue like a fresh trout had the bartender not gripped hold of it with a pliers.

Newcomb thought that was the end of the altercation and two hours later he was raking in a pot of fourteen dollars when the boy walked up behind him and knocked Newcomb to the floor with one of the tavern's beer pulls. Newcomb went for his gun but the boy stomped on his hand, splitting the thumbnail with his boot heel.

Newcomb sucked on it and asked, "Are you through now?"

"Yes," said the boy, "I believe I am." His mouth quivered and tears slid out of his eyes.

Newcomb just slumped there on the floor for a bit, staring at the bloody tail of the shirt he'd wrapped around his hand.

William McElhanie and I occupied ourselves at the bordellos, though it was only Bill who ever had his pants down. We crossed the arroyo to the cathouses after a twenty-five-cent breakfast of pancakes and four eggs and steak, and we hunched up on the stoops with weeds in our teeth, itchy and hot in our three-piece suits. We'd watch the chippies coming out of the four-holer in the back, or fetching water from the artesian well, or hanging their laundry out on the line. Those who were cursed in the month did the housework in the mornings. They did not dress to entice. Their hair was in strands and their long gray dresses were black about the armpits. They might've been farm wives coming back from the hen house with eggs. McElhanie would sit on the chintz parlor furniture at night and whisper to me whatever he'd heard about those available. "Word is, she's dry as pumice," he'd say. Or, "She stuffs sandwiches in her blouse." William McElhanie was sixteen years old in Silver City. I've always wondered how he turned out.

My brother Bob spent most of his first week in the city carrying on like a politician. He listened to excess, shook many hands, introduced himself to men of substance as a retired deputy marshal, and he bought shot glasses of good whiskey for the permanent residents though he was stern as a woman from the temperance movement when it came to the subject of liquor.

But he gathered information, he did not dispense it, so there were considerable moments of awkward silence whenever he lunched with strangers. Here I was of some use, for I could extemporize like a bicycle salesman. If a banker was discussing the Chicago Grain Exchange and had his thoughts peter out and got to staring at his fork, I'd get a nod from Bob and proceed to rattle on about Billy the Kid, whose true name was not William H. Bonney but Henry McCarty, of Brooklyn, New York, who'd headed west in a Pullman car and lived in Coffeyville at the age of twelve and became a criminal after escaping through the chimney of a Silver City jail, held there for stealing laundry. "It isn't gaudy," I said, "but it's fact." The banker would be amazed and Bob would sit back in his chair and consider the banker's face. I think my brother had a surprise in store for Silver City, but then he was introduced to Miss Eugenia Moore and got distracted from his plans.

It was Thursday evening of our third week there and I was speaking on subjects I knew nothing about to an audience of Bob and City Marshal Ben Canty, when the woman walked into the restaurant. Canty had a mouthful of boiled potatoes but put them out onto his spoon and stood with his napkin tucked into his shirt collar. "My, what a pleasant surprise," he said.

The woman walked over and smiled. She said, "Hello, Ben," and that sort of thing, shook the hands of the two Dalton boys, and spoke with me about Cass County, Missouri, where Bob and I were born and where she had her early raising, and where they say she's buried now. Bob let me talk, as was his custom. He sat back in his chair with a toothpick in his mouth.

Eugenia Moore was her alias; she was baptized Florence Quick. She was five-feet-nine inches tall and twenty-five years old and wore her blond hair in a bun. She was brown-eyed and pretty, if somewhat boyish, with teeth so white it looked like she'd never drunk tea. She had a sultry voice and a sturdy, broad-shouldered body and breasts that were not large; her hands were strong and branch-scratched and calloused; she chewed her fingernails down so close to the quick they looked like cuticle. When she wasn't in boots she was barefoot, but that evening she was wearing a white calico dress with ties on the sleeves and looked more like a lady than she was. She'd been to Holden College and she taught school for two years and there was a lot of that in her speech; when she didn't hear what was said completely, she'd say, "I beg your pardon?" She had blond bangs that she kept brushing with a finger as she talked. She said meeting us was a pleasure and glided away to sit at a smaller table by the burlap-curtained front windows. Her face was brown from the sun.

Bob leaned forward with his elbows on the arms of his chair, staring at her. He seemed about to speak and then thought better of it. He stood from the table, bumping it, and to Canty said, "Excuse me. There's something I wanted to ask her." Then he walked over and straddled the chair opposite her.

"Looks like somebody's in love," Canty said.

I said, "He's going to wind up in bed with her tonight. It always happens that way. You wait and see." I cut my steak up into forty pieces and then I added, "Dang it."

Bob asked her if he could join her and she nodded her head. He said, "You're really Florence Quick, am I right?"

She said, "You may be. Where did you hear it?"

"That's the least interesting thing I could say."

She said, "I hate the name Florence. It sounds like I crochet and gossip and succumb in the afternoon to hot flashes."

"Whereas I hear you've rustled saddle stock and cattle and you came to Silver City after a chase. Some prevaricator even told me you wear chaps of Angora goat hair and pretend you're a boy named Tom King. That's the most peculiar thing I ever heard."

The woman blushed a little and turned a page of the menu before her; my brother snatched up the second menu and glanced at it, rocking back in his chair. "Can I eat with you? I'm famished."

Miss Moore said, "Certainly."

Bob gazed at her. "Well, isn't that the most peculiar thing *you* ever heard?"

She smiled. "Lots of people are famished. Often two or three times a day."

Bob thumped forward on his chair. "I'm talking about the rustling and all the rest of it. They say you've busted out of every jail the marshals locked you in. They hint that you kneel for the deputies."

"And are you repelled?"

He crossed his legs. "I find it mysterious."

The woman cook lumbered out of the kitchen to the table and listened to each of them order with her red wet hands on her hips and her black hair all in spikes. When the cook was gone, my brother lifted up his water glass in toast. "I've just been recalling my past and I've got to say that you're the most beautiful and striking woman I've ever shared a table with."

She said thank you like she was bored.

He said, "I'm not a flatterer. If you were ordinary I'd just go out to some porch chair and snatch the wings off blue-bottle flies. When I say I'm a true admirer of yours I want it taken seriously."

"Serious is a little hard for me, given the circumstances. How would it be if I just winced now and then?"

Bob rocked back in the chair so that the front legs were off the ground. Then the chair thudded down and he sat forward close to the table and said, "You're an available woman in a city stacked high with cowboys who grab at themselves and miners who share sleeping bags and drummers who can't remember the time the chippy under them wasn't looking at the clock, and not one of those optimists won't slide you notes and say how like a rose you are when what he's really wondering is how he'll get his hands under your dress. I'll leave off all of that, thank you. I'm here to say I'm interested; that's all."

Miss Moore considered him with some amusement. "There's this suddenness about you."

He nodded. "Yes, there is."

The cook put their suppers down on the tablecloth like she was irked, slopping beef stew out of my brother's bowl, ham and split-pea soup out of Eugenia's, with a basket of hot buttered biscuits between them.

My brother stared and stared at Eugenia's soup. "Can I have that?"

"You're smitten by everything, aren't you."

"Can I trade? I suddenly got this craving for split peas

and ham. I don't think I could stomach beef stew. I think it'd just lump up in my cheeks."

There was such an appeal in my brother's eyes that she passed her bowl across to him and he grinned around his soup spoon.

She asked, "Do these cravings come over you often?"

"Yep. Usually get my way too."

I didn't overhear all of this, lest you think me a sneak. Some of it I got later from Bob and some from Miss Moore's letters to me at prison. Canty consumed two pieces of apple pie and I slumped across from him with my cheek on my fist. He scraped the plate with his spoon, glancing in their direction. He said, "They sparked right off, didn't they?"

"*I* can't figure it out."

"I've seen ladies stir for gamblers, pimps, every kind of sinner. Seems to me the best sort of woman likes to be tainted a bit."

Canty and I left the restaurant and I spent two hours in his office flipping through his brown photographs of outlaws hauled in dead by bounty hunters and leaned stiff as planks against jail-house walls.


My brother and Miss Moore remained in the restaurant until closing. Bob sat back in his chair with a toothpick and listened to her tell all she knew about the Daltons, which pleased him. Her information was substantial. Then the cook yanked shut her burlap curtains and Bob paid the bill and took off his boots and wool socks to walk barefoot with Eugenia on dirt streets as soft as talcum. They sat in deep bluegrass under mesquite trees beside the Mexican Catholic church, drinking rum from a hammered silver flask.

She said, "I was a schoolteacher and twenty-four years old and I washed my face with lilac soap and read novels by William Dean Howells. I spent my evenings grading papers on the porch or cooking in the kitchen, spooning melted wax into jars of apple jam. The only man I knew was landlord of what I rented. He was odorous and decrepit and he spoke ever so solemnly of the weather. He proposed marriage to me once and it took me a week to say no. Then I got my senses and knew I didn't want a wooden ice chest or Chippendale furniture or the crawl of a husband's issue in me each night in our four-poster bed. I didn't want to be one of those sullen wives who glare at the camera from the front of a plain sod house."

"I can understand that," he said.

"How old are you?"

"Twenty."

"How old is Emmett?"

"Eighteen."

She rolled her dress up over her knees for the cool night air. She said, "I saw your name on a wanted poster nailed to a telegraph pole in Dodge City, Kansas. The picture had not the neighbor of a resemblance to you but I subscribed to unsavory thoughts just the same. I thought of all the sweet favors I'd do this man Bob Dalton whom they'd given five hundred dollars for."

They talked until the town was quiet and then they walked to her narrow room above the grocery store. They took off their clothes and Bob washed himself in her porcelain bowl, looking into the round spotted mirror. His face and neck and hands were red, the rest of his skin was milk white. He saw her crouched up under a Navaho blanket staring at him with half a smile. He walked over to her with his hand disguising his manly condition. She was wearing a yellow flannel nightgown that she allowed him to push up over her breasts when he called upon her body.

The next morning she cooked coffee in the fireplace, spread biscuits with comb honey, sliced oranges from California, and they ate naked and cross-legged on top of the sheets, discussing their ambitions.

Bob said, "We were fifteen kids on a hardscrabble farm near Belton, and then again near Coffeyville. The barns leaned; snakes slithered under the porch; rats went into a frenzy every time I walked in the corn crib. In March the winds would strip off the roof, nine or ten shingles a day. My sisters used to have to walk four miles to town for sale merchandise marked down from three cents to two. My dad was not a good provider. He tended a saloon; he swapped horses for the Army; he worked as a carnival barker and played square-dance fiddle, a nickel a set. It brought in hardly nothing at all. One winter we got so poor I had to wear my mother's high-button shoes. And I can remember one time watching my dad talk with two livestock buyers at the gate. They wore black wool coats and round-topped gray cropper hats and when they leaned in their saddles their big irons showed. Years later, when the James-Younger gang got shot up on the Northfield, Minnesota, raid, my dad said at the dinner table, 'Well, I guess now I can say it. Those men you saw were Jesse James and Cole Younger.' He put his thumbs behind his suspenders and grinned like he was the richest man in the world. I think it was then that I decided I wanted to be somebody people remember, and not some no-account fool sawing a fiddle for nickels or wearing his mother's high-button shoes."

Bob got up from the bed and squatted by the fireplace to pour more coffee into his cup.

Eugenia said, "One morning I looked in the mirror and saw lines around my mouth. It didn't take any more than that."

6 The Dalton gang stayed in Silver City all of that summer and as long into the fall as our money held out, and Bob and the woman known as Eugenia Moore were together everywhere. They stood in front of the grocery store with the children and watched the circus parade and touched the nose of a camel. They sat on the blue lawn to the side of the moveable schoolhouse and heard a piano recital.

And they got the photograph taken that is still around today: of Bob looking teenaged and haircut and stern in a smallish pink-striped tan suit and wrinkled white collar; of Eugenia Moore posed standing, her left hand on his left shoulder, she with a nineteenth-century woman's hat and six yards of blue dress with a white frill of a blouse sleeve and collar showing; and neither of them facing the camera, both a little annoyed, as though the photograph was merely historical documentation and one of the obligations to their biographers they wanted done with soon.

And what of Julia? It worked out that I didn't see her for over a year, but we kept up a mail correspondence that kindled our affections far better than my clumsy courtship ever had. I have always been somewhat daunted by female emotions, and flat-out amazed at the way they spend love as if it wasn't something to save and purse away somewhere, so it was probably best that I was gone, for my sweetheart then was undergoing a romantic spell that soon would have exhausted me.

For instance, when the family still lived near Coffeyville, Julia would ride up to visit my mother and chat about me as they baked cherry cobbler. And she'd sit with my sisters on the white iron bed I'd slept in and, while Leonie swiveled in a dress she'd sewn, Julia would close her eyes and try to imagine me sleeping beside her there—the springs squashed down, my brown arm disposing of a pillow, my nose flattened against her thigh. She assumed my perspective and saw the kerosene smut on the ceiling, the plaster chip near the window sash, the crude pencil marks on the wallpaper that spelled, "I HATe coLLaRd GReeNs." She discovered shirts of mine in the closet and ironed them just for the chance to press them hot to her face.

She stayed with my brother Ben and his family for a week while his wife recovered from their fourth child, and Julia used her evenings to study Ben at the dining-room table as he tacked together a wren's house, and she'd find me in his eyebrows and jaw. She'd say, "You've got brown hairs on your wrists just like he does," and Ben would look bewildered. And when Charles or Henry stopped by for coffee, she'd bake butterscotch cookies just to hold my brothers there long enough to quiz them.

"You're asking the wrong fella about Emmett," said Henry. "All I remember about him was that he made believe he was Jesse James's son. This would've been when he was eleven years old. I mean he was *convinced*. You remember that, Ben? He had it all laid out how he was going to revenge his pa by killing Robert Ford. He was a character, even then. He couldn't talk about a walk to the privy without some embellishment."

"He was colorful all right," said Ben. "Plus he's got brown hair on his wrists just like I do."

Julia dug out the Dalton family Bible and memorized birthdays and deaths. Sometimes she'd wake up when her father did and like a good wife have a special breakfast of blueberry flapjacks and sausage patties waiting for him when he returned from his morning chores and kicked off his boots in the pantry. "What's this supposed to mean?" he'd say.

She'd brush her long black hair with my photograph in the lap of her flannel nightgown. She devoted hours to her diary, recording each night the fluctuating conditions of her heart and experimenting with her presumed name: "Julia Dalton," and "Mrs. Julia Dalton," and "Mr. and Mrs. Emmett Dalton," with the afterthought, "(and sons)." Her perfumed letters to me would end in sweet complaint: "Why aren't you here?" and "Will I never see you?" and "What can I promise to spur you homeward?"

It was nice to be revered and sought out but there was little in me to give back, and all I could muster in response to her was, "I sure do miss you. Love, Emmett."

When I saw her again, the spell had worn off.

The gang congregated for the first time in a long time on a Thursday night in October, clomping up the wooden stairs to Miss Moore's rented room. We were eager and loud and jovial and walked in like Christmas cheer, McElhanie carrying a brown bag of Congress Water and ginger pop and corked St. Louis Beer. Newcomb had some ears of sweet corn and he stoked the fireplace to roast them. Bryant sat down at the desk after his fashion, with his coat on and a brown wool scarf reaching up for his face. Newcomb opened the windows and the fire pulled the outside cool in and I played my mouth organ, announcing the songs before I commenced them. "Shenandoah," I said. "Oh, Susannah." "Shoo, Fly, Shoo."

Miss Moore had been drawing in charcoal pencil on heavy rag paper a picture of fruits on a plate. Bob bent over it and so did the others. "Eugenia did that freehand," he said. Bryant said, "I think you've captured it, Miss Moore."

Bob sat down on the floor next to his woman, tugged off his boots, and wadded his socks inside. Eugenia wore a white nightgown and her nipples showed dark underneath. Bob told McElhanie to blow out the coal-oil lantern, which he did, needless to say, and the only light in the room was orange and thrown across our faces by the fire. "Auld Lang Syne," I said.

Newcomb said, "You must have music in ya, Emmett, cuz I sure ain't heard any come out yet."

McElhanie snickered.

My brother draped his arm over the woman's shoulder and put his hand upon her breast. She whispered to him, "That's nice."

The six of us drank beer and ate hot corn on the cob; then Bob licked his fingers and saw Bryant across the room. "How much money you got in your pockets?"

Bryant snuffed and tossed his corn cob out the raised window.

"What kind of shape you in, Bitter Creek?"

"I can't even see the back of my neck."

Bob turned to Eugenia. "Shall I tell them?"

"If you want."

He said, "Miss Moore and I have been turning over in our heads a major money-making scheme."

Then he went on to explain that they'd decided to hold up a Mexican cantina located farther south between Silver City and Santa Rita in a town so small he forgot its name. The buildings there were only a half dozen or so and populated by mine laborers and immigrants and conquered people. But Eugenia had reconnoitered and counted more than three thousand dollars on the gambling tables on a typical Saturday night. "And here's the bonus: the house cheats. A gang can grab the cash in five minutes and have almost everybody on their side; all we'd have to worry about is the few scrub Mexicans who want their two dollar winnings back. The only law around is Canty and Eugenia's going to deal with him."

There was silence as the others chewed the idea; then McElhanie proposed, "How about a 'Hip hip hooray'?"

"Siddown," said Blackface Charley Bryant.


The gang rode out of Silver City on Saturday afternoon. Miss Moore was not with us. We did not ride at all hard for it was still blazing hot in the desert and we wanted our animals rested. And we tied up in the town at dusk and sat on straw mats in a Chinese restaurant. We could hear the cantina music as we ate. McElhanie said, "The band has a rousing tempo, don't it?" Nobody commented. Bob ordered five identical meals for the gang and none of us much complained, being somewhat fearful of Chinese cooking. It turned out to be clear celery soup with amber grease floating in it. Then we had something with bean sprouts and white roots and crumbly sheepshead fish still gritty from the river.

We drank green tea until eight and then crossed the wide street of the mining town, our irons big under our slickers. We opened two wooden doors with leaded stained-glass windows. Inside, the cantina was long as an alley and blue with tobacco smoke, with waxed board floors and a green tin fleur-de-lis ceiling and a loud Mexican orchestra playing on the stage at the very end. At the mahogany bar were miners in soot-black clothes and cowboys with great mustaches and big-roweled spurs and sunburns up to their eyes. They each had a boot up on the brass foot rail.

The left and rear of the house were mahogany gambling tables at which were seated every variety of gunslinger, most speaking the Spanish language, some rubbing a Mexican whore's behind through her brownish muslin dress. The whores did not use underwear.

Bryant sat down with Mexicans, paid a quarter for a pull of mescal, and lucked out, the bottle worm falling down into his swallow. He grinned happily as he chewed it and made himself no friends.

McElhanie bought one of the two white prostitutes hot beer and talked into her ear for most of a half hour. His tongue would reach out to lick her neck and she'd cringe. Then he made some kind of arrangement and followed her through a green velvet curtain and into a low-ceilinged crib not much wider than a bed and basin. He merely un-buttoned himself for her. And he was back before Bob and Bitter Creek Newcomb could find open chairs for faro.

Faro was the game in those days; you hardly see it any-more. Thirteen spade cards were lacquered onto the tabletop and bets placed on any number of them. The banker would turn over on his left the top card of the deck, which was called soda. On his right he'd reveal the next card, and any match-up between it and the board lost the bet. The next card he'd place on soda, and bets on the spade card like it would win. Idiots could play the game, which no doubt led to its extinction.

At the cantina, the auction for banker went to a profes-sional gambling man who called himself Fancy Jack. He had rings that glittered with glass on his thumbs and a red feather in a white hat. That was the only thing fancy about him. His fingernails were black-rimmed and his dark suit was white-stained with sweat. Bob and Newcomb sat down with him at last and he bothered them with questions as he dealt each pair of cards. "Did you vote in the last election?" he asked. "Ever ate fresh water clams?"

I sat with strangers at a corner table and got cleaned out in no time by a Mexican with teeth the colors of maize. He laughed out loud and slapped the dealing box every time he raked my money into his shirt. Whenever others lost he at least made sure to waggle a bit so that the silver coins would jangle.

I posted myself as lookout and stood at the bar feeling queasy at every glance toward the hundreds of guns in the place. Bob bought me a shot glass of whiskey and we jawed about the Remington Rolling-block .50 caliber rifle, also known as the Remington Buffalo Gun.

"Don't you think that sweetheart packs a wallop," I said. "I hear a miner in Creede, Colorado, got shot in the head with one while unscrewing a can of sardines and some of his hair floated as far as the assayer's office in Pueblo."

And Bob said, "These games are crooked. Nobody's going to risk anything for this place. I've got a premonition about it."

He left me with the shot glass he'd bought for himself and every fifteen minutes or so I'd take the meagerest sip.


Meanwhile Miss Eugenia Moore was having dinner with City Marshal Ben Canty back in Silver City. He wadded a slice of bread and wiped up the gravy on his plate. He used a small comb on his mustache as he chewed, and she told him the boys were gone to look for work in that unclaimed area of Texas, Kansas, and Colorado referred to as No Man's Land. She herself was heading north at the end of the week for Denver.

He stared at her. Finally he said, "I'm sorry to hear you and Bob are splitting up like that."

He walked her home and sat on her bed and bent over the drawings spread out on the quilt. "You've got quite a hand," he said.

She brought him coffee in a tin cup and they drank it facing each other.

"What kind of work would it be they're looking for?" he asked.

"Ranch work, I suppose."

"I thought they were free spirits these days. I thought they were doing without regular jobs."

Eugenia sat next to him and leaned back on a pillow, wrinkling a picture of flowers in a vase. "You're talking about rustling. I'm fairly certain they've given that up. But I can understand why life on the scout is so appealing. You take a job like yours. You are hampered and impeded every day by the very laws and regulations it is your duty to enforce."

He leaned back on his hand, destroying a drawing of tree-tops and a church steeple. "There's something you want me to delay, is that it? What do I get for the trouble?"

She said, "This is my last evening in Silver City. I'd like it to be really special."

Canty thought about that and swirled the coffee in the bottom of his cup before he lifted it and drank. He glanced at her face, then back at his boots. "Sometimes nothing important gets done. Sometimes the day just seems to drag by."


By ten o'clock the Dalton gang were leaning their elbows on the mahogany bar and muttering to strangers about how the professionals were misdealing the cards, so that it would seem we had an excuse for what we were about to do. Newcomb was the last to lose his stake, being swindled on what they call a cat hop at the last turn. He kicked the chair getting up and stood apart from the rest of us for his drink. He pulled his coat behind his gun butt. The bartender was rounded over, washing glasses in a tub. A señorita was talking to him. Newcomb shouted, "Who ya have to punch to get a drink around this place?"

The bartender said, "Are you talking to me, runt?"

Newcomb said, "Well, I don't guess I'm talking to the *spittoon.*"

The bartender reached for a beer pull and Newcomb slapped the pistol out of his holster and the gang brought our Colts up in every direction. We might have been farm machinery—we were that sudden and all-at-once.

Bob shouted, "Hands up! Everybody!"

"Bandidos!" one of the whores screamed.

The music stopped. The gambler Fancy Jack quickly rolled up his paper money and put it inside his cheek. The truly dangerous in the room just glared and slowly lifted their hands.

"You do not look much escared," I yelled, "but I think you ought to be. I have filed the sear down on this machine and have in my hands a hair trigger. So don't anybody move, understand? Or you're likely to find a gape in your face you could fit a beer bottle through."

Blackface Charley Bryant had two guns out—a purse pistol and a Peacemaker—and he kept turning around in the crowd. McElhanie and Newcomb scraped money off the tables and patted down the dealers for their wallets and money belts. My brother Bob was up on top of the bar, kicking hats off heads as he walked, smashing shot glasses and bottles into a shattering mirror. He pinched the folding money out from under the spring snaps in the register.

Little Newcomb took silver and gold from the dealer who'd bilked him, Fancy Jack, then as an afterthought cracked him hard across the mouth with his pistol. Blood and teeth spattered against the oil painting of a sundown on the wall.

The dealer knelt on the floor. I could see he was feeling a lot of pain. He spit out a roll of bloody money.

Each of us in the gang had two red wool socks connected with strong twine. We draped these over our necks and the weight of the coins held them in place. We did not bother with jewelry, watches, or gems, or anything the prostitutes might have hidden on their persons. Within four minutes we were backing toward the doors. Bryant's Texas spurs were the only noise. Bob said, "This will teach you hospitality to strangers."

We sprang onto our horses and blasted out the stained-glass windows. I danced my horse around, firing haphazardly until McElhanie got hold of the lead rein on the pack mule. Then the five of us in the gang galloped off, guns blazing. Shutters banged open in the few houses and men leaned out and only a dozen gamblers ran into the street with guns in their hands. Hardly any shot at us.

We ran our horses into bad shape, ran until we could barely make out the lights of the town; then we risked a walk and counted the loot in our socks and smoked cheroots that Bryant was handing out. Our horses quivered as they cooled. Newcomb threw all his pennies away.

We were relieving ourselves and watering our horses when dawn started outlining things. Bob climbed up into his saddle and scanned the open geography behind us and spied what he first mistook as a twister, then recognized as the dust of flying hooves. He turned in his saddle and saw me picking cockleburs off my pants leg. "Emmett, I think we have a posse contending for us." He said it not loudly at all, but like a man might say he believed his son had quit school and it was a terrible disappointment.

Newcomb heard him and clambered up onto his horse before he'd even tucked his shirt in. He stood in his stirrups and yelled for McElhanie and Bryant to saddle up and by then we could hear the thunder of running horses.

The gang of us spurred our horses to speed and rode down into a dry gulch that gave itself to a canyon littered with dead timbers that were washed up flat as railroad ties. Then the five of us turned our horses around and yanked our rifles out from scabbards underneath the saddle skirts. We backed up so close to the steep side of a cliff that the horses brushed their tails against it.

The cantina's posse was seven men, five of them wearing sombreros. They slowed a city block away and their horses nudged and bickered as the Mexicans reined back to argue the situation. They were so distant all I could see in the morning dark were animals and white shirts.

Bob said, "I think they've got us in a disadvantageous position. We might do better if we're shorter."

So we jumped down into silt as deep as our ankles. Bob stood inside the clumped roots of a tree. I crouched in a green pool of water the size of a tablecloth. The others were dispersed.

"I'm gettin' kind of sleepy," said Newcomb, but only McElhanie laughed.

Then there was Spanish shouting and the waving of pistols and they charged straight at us with what the dime novelists call bloodcurdling howls. The Mexicans lowered their pistols and their arms flew up as they fired and chunks of cliff exploded onto the hides of our horses, which skittered and walked, eyes bulging. McElhanie let go the first shot from the gang; then Bob and I and Newcomb and Bryant fired and the Mexicans' wrists jerked high as they answered and brought their horses up again and turned them this way and that.

Holes were being kicked out of the dirt cliff and one of the Mexican horses collapsed when Bryant's shot split its hoof apart. I aimed at the throat of a man with crossed bandoliers and pressed the trigger and struck him instead in the thigh. The skin burst out like a rosette and the man reached for it, wheeling his horse.

Then a stray bullet from the posse whanged off a skillet strapped to the pack mule and ripped into my right shoulder. The force of it knocked me off my knees and I sat down in the water looking at my pain. It felt like I'd been slammed in the arm with a crowbar. Blood was rolling through my fingers.

Bob asked if I was okay and when I nodded my brother shouted, "What'd'ya say we attack!" and he rushed at the men on foot, hurdling over the dead trees.

The Mexicans were emptying their cylinders and reloading as their horses jittered and bucked, and then the Dalton gang swung up onto their own horses and raked them hard with their spurs, screaming as they turned the posse into retreat and started up a chase. They fired now with their pistols, and one of Bob's .45 slugs plowed into the neck of a pony, bringing it down. The rider squirmed out from under it and limped as he fired his cylinder up. Three men ducked down behind the heads of their horses and rode east and the man shot down doubled up with a man in a black stetson and soon the cantina's halfhearted posse was gone, leaving faster than they came.

McElhanie whooped and howled; Newcomb swaggered on his boot heels yelling names in their direction; Bryant tethered the horses and put away the limping one he'd ruined. Bob wiped his pistol against his pants leg to smear the gunpowder off, then pressed it hot against my neck. "Feel that," he said. "It's on fire."

I said, "I take it we've scattered them."

"The wicked flee where none pursueth," said Bob.

I had my coat and shirt off and was pouring a canteen of water over my wound. The skin was so torn it was lacy. Blood was rushing down like a sleeve.

Bob crouched and worried over the hole, picking bits of shirt and thread out of it. "I'd say you earned your paycheck, Em."

I wiped at the hole with my shirt cuff. "I can read it with my fingers, Bob. The slug's as clear as a jawbreaker in your cheek. Hot fire and a sharp knife and whiskey's all I need."

"That's how I picture it."


Word got to City Marshal Canty when he was having breakfast. "Well, don't that beat all," he said. He ordered another cup of coffee, then set about getting reliable men for a posse. And he was so upset that it was almost noon before he'd even got a saddle on his horse. The day just seemed to drag by.

Miss Eugenia Moore left Silver City that Sunday afternoon in a buckboard and team she rented but would never return. Her valuables were in hatboxes. She stopped at an abandoned squatter's shack and put on a blue cavalry shirt and tan suede trousers and wore a headband without a hat. She clucked the team along a vacant road that went toward the Oklahoma Territory, and stopped for two men who were standing by their horses, rolling cigarettes with a bag of Bull Durham tobacco. One was Blackface Charley Bryant, the other Emmett Dalton. My arm was in a sling and I winced whenever I moved. I climbed up to the front with her while Bryant lay down in the back and smoked.

I said, "Bob and McElhanie have the pack mule and six hundred dollars. They're heading west by train to my brother Bill's place near Paso Robles, California. He said he'll send for you when he's established out there. I'd be with them except I got torn up by a greasy Mexican. Got me in the shoulder."

Eugenia frowned sympathetically. "Anyone else would be flat on his back right now."

I didn't say anything. I merely stared at the blank terrain as we jostled east toward Jim Riley's isolated ranch where the three of us would hole up that winter while Newcomb went back to his homestead claim near Guthrie.

I slunk down in my coat that night with my shoulder nagging me with a pain as sharp as the squeal of a saw blade finding a nail in the board. I couldn't catnap; I couldn't imagine the pale, naked women I'd seen on McElhanie's deck of playing cards; all I could do was remember the smell of the oiled gun stock against my cheek and the blue glint of my rifle barrel as I swung it at the rearing horse of the man with crossed bandoliers. And it only struck me then, in that complaining buckboard, what scary things these outlaw notions were. Besieged as we'd been it seemed the most natural, sensible idea in the world to aim a shot at the throat of a man I had no argument with minutes before, and my finger sought the trigger with no more heed than you'd give to an itch near your eye.

I looked at Bryant who was hunched next to me then, driving the team, slapping the reins on the rump of a horse while Miss Moore curled in sleep under a blanket pulled out of a hatbox. And for want of conversation I said, "Where the bullet went in you can see blue and red and a smatter of white which is bone. I think it's going to scar up real good."

7 Grattan Dalton had by then arrived at my brother Bill's wheat ranch but he did not stay long. His sister-in-law complained of him, as did brother Littleton's wife, so he packed a duffel bag and moved to the Grand Central Hotel in Fresno where the furniture was not so frail and he could poke three-dollar whores in his room and drink until his forehead struck the table.

His occupation was gambler in those days. He would sidle up to strangers in the bar, anyone with striped pants or checkered vest, and he'd be amiable for about an hour, grinning with brown teeth. Then Grat would haul the man to a gaming table where he cheated brazenly, like it was cards of a higher intellect he played. Those who argued with his calls he glowered at until they got up out of their chairs and departed. He bashed one man in the head with a cuspidor,

then dragged him outside where he slammed the man's mouth
against a wood curb. The man rolled bloody but the teeth
stayed there. Looked like someone had dropped a white brace-
let. The bartender, Patrick J. Conway, Grattan's sometime
friend, made sure the fearsome story got around and my
brother's winnings improved measurably. Grat paid Conway
ten percent.

But my brother began to notice a hotel resident who sat in
one of the Queen Anne chairs and smoked a long cigar down
to a stub each night, watching Grat at five-card stud. He was a
large man with a black mustache and a face made ugly with
brown cancers on his cheeks that were eating into the pink.
They were wet and he dabbed at them with a handkerchief.
He lived not much longer than Grat did.

One evening the man put a penny down and picked up the
Fresno paper and read it front to back, twelve pages. Then he
folded it and slapped it down to the floor and walked over to
Grat's empty table and sat down. Grat was shuffling cards.

"What game is it you're playing, Mr. Dalton?"

"I know 'em all. What's yer pleasure?"

The man smiled and leaned forward with his hands under
the table. Grat felt the barrel of a pistol punch him hard in the
crotch. He groaned and snatched for the gun but the hammer
clicked back.

The man said, "Woman once asked me what that felt like,
getting punched like that in the oysters. I said it was close to
having your eyeball poked with a spoon. Is that pretty ac-
curate?"

Grat pushed away from the table an inch.

The man said, "My name is William Smith, Chief of Special Detectives for the Southern Pacific Railroad. I am not
pleasant to look at and more unpleasant to deal with. That's
my word of caution. You are one of the Dalton boys. Railroad
circulars say you've had yourselves quite a time back east in
the territories, stealing and rustling and such. I hear you are
cousins to Cole Younger and that you used to be lawmen. I

gotta say that with a combination like that I trust you no farther than I can spit."

Grat said, "I wonder if you could withdraw your pistol? I'm gettin' a bit distracted."

Detective Smith sat back and said, "Mr. Leland Stanford's Southern Pacific Railroad and the Wells Fargo Express Company lost twelve thousand dollars to bandits in Pixley in 1889, and another twenty thousand this last year. I consider both them robberies blemishes more serious to me than this meal of a face. They are my very personal shame and I'll entertain no more. I want that understood. If I see you close to one of my trains I'll blow a hole through your head."

Grat smiled and leaned forward with his cheeks on his fists. "Now you may impress hobos and baggage clerks and little boys throwing dirt clods with that kind of slice-yer-pecker-off skit, but I have bit off earlobes and swallowed them, so you'll excuse me if the hot piss is not exactly running down my leg."

The SP's Mr. Smith got up from his chair and put the nickel-plated pistol in his belt holster. "I had already heard you were stupid."

Grat was not the only Dalton observed by Smith in California. He watched our brother Littleton, who was much older and harmless as coveralls, and after Bob and McElhanie arrived in November, he watched them in cousin Sam Oldham's house near Kingsburg. McElhanie he swore was Emmett Dalton using an alias. I guess we looked a little alike. Also, Smith watched my brother Bill Dalton, figuring him the most dangerous.

William Marion Dalton was six feet tall and twenty-eight years old in 1891, seven years older than Bob was, two years younger than Grat. He'd married, in 1883, a rich girl from Merced County named Jenny Blivens, daughter to a reaper. Bill was a happy man with a quick wink and a slap on the back and a memory for names, a man with blue eyes and great political ambitions and a chin beard like the martyred President Lincoln. He could talk like an editorial and he was as well-liked in Clovis and Paso Robles as the class clown in a boys' school. He considered railroads the enemy. They were the "they" in all his sentences. He'd been the campaign manager for Ed O'Neill when he won the job of sheriff for Fresno County on the anti-railroad ticket; and he was the boy-I-never-had to the respected criminal lawyer T. W. Breckinridge.

He had both those men and their wives over for a dinner of roast pork and rhubarb pie; then he kissed his children in their beds and sat in the front room with his friends and smoked green cigars while the women washed the dishes and sang hymns. The men discussed a try for the seat in the California Assembly. Bill could run as a Democrat or as a Populist, with the likely financial backing of Adolph Sutro, the railroad pamphleteer. My brother Bill rolled the cigar in his mouth and listened to himself being praised.

Then Mr. Smith of the Southern Pacific knocked warily at the door and stood there all shoulders and eyebrows when my brother Bill opened it. Bill grinned at him. "You a voter?"

Mr. Smith identified himself and Bill joked that he'd let him in anyway and the chief of security sat to the front of a pulled-out dining room chair with a handkerchief pressed to his face. Lawyer Breckinridge poured himself some bourbon and stood to the side, observing, and Sheriff O'Neill, whose face was so much nose he had the nickname of Mouse as a boy, kept a simple conversation going with Smith about police work. He asked how the Southern Pacific was doing in terms of profits. He asked if they'd determined who the perpetrators of the last two robberies were. Breckinridge brought over a drink for Bill and sat down. Both Bill and the lawyer were listening like they had nothing better to do. O'Neill asked if the railroad had taken any further precautionary measures to stop the looting of express cars.

Smith said, "We are keeping a close eye on suspects; that's the main thing."

"Ah," said Breckinridge. "Good."

Detective Smith turned toward my brother Bill and said, "There's a lot that's not being said here, so I'm going to get it over with. I predict a brilliant future for you, Dalton. You might even be president some day. Just stay clear of your brothers."

"Nothing wrong with them," said Bill. "They're just young."

"They're brash and they're heedless and they ain't gonna get much older," said Smith, who got up from his chair and left.

My brother Bob and Bill McElhanie had started out sleeping in my brother Littleton's fruit cellar. Littleton was in his middle thirties then but acting even older. He had a stern wife and a black beard that made him look Mormon, and he hardly talked at all and the couple went to bed each night at eight. Bob decided it felt like purgatory, so the two younger men kept mostly to cousin Sam Oldham's two-storey house near Kingsburg, playing rummy and nine-point pitch or walking alongside girls they didn't know, introducing themselves. They went to a Saturday night dance at the Brick Hotel and lounged against the women's side of the ballroom like tough customers, with pistols tucked under their belts and placed just-so to look like erections. My brother was interrupted in a dance by an oily city councilman and two others who let him know that gun-toters and thugs weren't welcome in their town, and Bob got into a fistfight later on with two teamsters and woke in the morning on a pillow crusty with blood.

The next day Bob and McElhanie gave up on Kingsburg and rode their horses up the gangplanks into a cattle car and then sat forward in the smoker as train Number 17, known as the Atlantic Express, made its regular run from San Francisco to Los Angeles. They stayed at a health resort two days, taking steam baths and drinking mineral water and bowling on a green lawn. Bob wrote a letter to Eugenia Moore that he mailed to Jim Riley's ranch. They ate oranges picked off a tree and rolled up the legs of their suit pants to wade into the Pacific. McElhanie walked into the ocean as far as his knees and turned to my brother, grinning. "I'd say this here is a major accomplishment for a simple Arkansas cowhand."

"William," said Bob, "you're going to have a long happy life."

When they returned to brother Bill's house, Bob gave his nieces dolls with heads of porcelain and mailed our mother two fifty-dollar bills with the face of Ulysses S. Grant on the front.

Sheriff O'Neill didn't show for Christmas dinner though he'd previously accepted, and lawyer Breckinridge stood in the doorway only long enough to see that Bob was there and leave his presents under the tree.

"What is it we've got that's catching?" asked Bob.

Bill said, "You're Satan's tools, that's all."

Coming back from the outhouse wearing just trousers one morning, Bob saw a man with purple cancer on his face sitting on a horse and staring at him, but the man rode off when Bob stared back. My brother walked through the kitchen buttoning on a shirt and saw that Bill was standing at the living room window with the lace curtains pulled aside. Bill said, "I think it's time you left us."

They did. They rode to a railroad siding in Tulare County where they made a camp among fruit trees and read borrowed books with pages so thin you could see your fingers through them. Bob would get bored after ten or twelve pages and search in his sack for another. Grat brought him a letter in red ink mailed six weeks earlier by Eugenia Moore who was signing her name Daisy Bryant. She said she was weary from playing house and mother-me-do with all the "cowboys with six hands" on Jim Riley's ranch.

She said it was sleeting against a window and she was writing by candlelight and she missed him terribly. Bob read the letter aloud to McElhanie; then he had my brother Bill read it to him. When they rode into Fresno for the weekend in February, Bob left behind a pair of cracked leather spurs by the fire. One of the star rowels was so rusted it wouldn't turn. The spurs became evidence.

Evidence because on February 6, 1891, the Southern Pacific's Atlantic Express was boarded by three masked bandits at the water stop of Alila. It was not us, but the Daltons were blamed. The best proof of our innocence was the flummoxed method of the bandits, which was never characteristic of any of our jobs. No money was lost because the engineer fired four shots at the robbers who got shook and leaped off the car into weeds and threw bullets hither and thither, like the guns were loose in their hands. The fireman was struck in the stomach before they escaped to their horses and he died the next afternoon spitting blood into a pan.

The Southern Pacific dedicated Special Agent W. E. Hickey to investigate the robbery attempt and murder, and Detective Will Smith was assigned as his special assistant. Smith hadn't even begun his investigation when he sat at a rolltop desk in the Fresno railroad yards composing a telegraph message to Hickey in San Francisco. After the words MAJOR SUSPECTS: he wrote: Grattan Dalton, William Marion Dalton, Robert Renick Dalton, Emmett Dalton, Jack Parker.

Parker was the brand name of the fountain pen he wrote with.

My brother Bob and McElhanie, the boy resembling me by a little, were then staying at the Grand Central Hotel in Fresno with Grat, gambling most of each day until the middle of March, and they were having breakfast at a linen-covered table when the bartender, Grat's friend, who also lived there, folded a piece of toast in his mouth and walked over. He talked to Grat about the Alila holdup and the manhunt for the murderers. He kept saying, "I wonder who it could be?" Before he started his ten-hour shift at two, bartender Conway ambled over to Sheriff Ed O'Neill's office where he read again the circular on the wall that offered "a reward of $5,000.00 for the arrest and convictions of all parties concerned in the attempted robbery."

Meanwhile, Smith's men sat on their horses in front of Bill's house, rolling cigarettes and smoking and writing into tablets. They followed Grat everywhere. Sheriff O'Neill arrested him on March 3rd, transporting Grat at Southern Pacific expense to the security offices in San Francisco. There, the San Francisco *Examiner* claimed, two other men were also interrogated: Cole Dalton and Jack Parker. This was make-believe.

Bill could only sit at his kitchen table with lawyer Breckinridge and fume as he read the local papers. He said, "Do you think we can pull this one out of the fire?"

"It's really too early to tell."

Bob, who'd always known when to leave, checked out of the Grand Central Hotel and lived for some weeks in the livery barn of a town where wines were made. McElhanie worked for a while tying grape vines up to wood posts.

Grat was released in San Francisco and picked up again in Fresno by William Smith, who thought the harassment would prompt the rest of the gang into revealing themselves. When that didn't happen and Smith tired of talking to my brother, he opened the jail door and Grat walked free to a whorehouse where he spent the night, and then to a shoe-shine stand and the hotel saloon. His erstwhile friend, bartender Conway, put on his white apron and gave Grat five free shots of whiskey. He said, "You did it, didn't ya. You can tell me. You boarded that train in Alila. The description matches you to a T."

Grat swallowed the last of his whiskey.

Conway lifted a pistol from under the bar. "Look what I have in my hand here."

"I think I've seen one of them things before," said Grat. "Some kind of noisemaker, ain't it?"

Conway's left hand slapped a card on the bar and he read from it. "I'm making a citizen's arrest of you, Grattan Dalton, for the attempted robbery of train 17 on the night of February 6th."

Grat shrugged and got off the bar stool and waited as Conway stripped off his apron and left the pistol beside the cash register and walked the accused man down the street.

That evening Detective Smith, acting on information supplied by Ed O'Neill, rode out to Clovis with two deputies and read an arrest warrant to Bill, who buttoned on a suit coat and kissed Jenny and his children and walked out smiling, with his hands way over his head. He said hello to one deputy, asked him how his hammer was hanging.

Smith took Bill's four-year-old son out to the back porch, unwrapped a peppermint for him, and asked the boy where his uncle Bob was. I never figured out where the boy got the notion but he answered, "Uncle Bob's gone to Seattle," and that seemed gospel truth to Smith. The manhunt never got close to Bob.

My brother Bill and his escorts got onto their horses and rode them in a walk to the county jail in Visalia. There Smith remanded Bill again for a newspaper reporter by reading aloud the arrest warrant under the yellow light of a gas lamp.

Bill said, "I sure wish I could read like you do, Smith. I bet you've got the women eating right out of your hand."


The evidence against Bill was a pair of cracked leather spurs said to belong to him and found in a Dalton hideout. He and Grat were indicted as accessories before the fact since each could be placed in the fifty-mile vicinity of Alila on the February night of the crime. Bob and his sidekick, the named principals, read of this in a March 26th railroad circular supplementing that of late February and reducing the amount of the reward to $3,600.00. They did not immediately fly, but fed their horses oats and corn and spent the afternoon leaning on sticks at a billiards table. They ate a large dinner at a restaurant and did not pay the bill and by eight o'clock were riding east out of California.

McElhanie and the lord of the Dalton gang were still riding through the Mojave desert toward Needles with their shirts off and red handkerchiefs on their heads, when my brothers Grat and Bill were led into a courtroom of dark oiled wood on April 6th. Presiding was Judge Wheaton A. Gray, a friend of Bill's and brother-in-law to the lawyer for the defense, T. W. Breckinridge. The attorney pleaded them not guilty and asked that Bill be released on his own recognizance.

"I admit some sympathy with your case," said Gray, "but I can't be any more partial with friends than I am with strangers. Bail is four thousand dollars."

Bill didn't have the money so he returned to jail with Grat. Trial was set for May 18th and then postponed to June. Meaningless evidence was accumulated and tagged as exhibits for the case. Two horses were produced that had been found roaming loose, and these were said to be those used for the getaway after the Alila raid.

"Oh, come now," Breckinridge said, but that was all. He assumed the trial would never occur, and he assigned the preparation of the case to one of his legal assistants.


Since our retreat from the New Mexico Territory, Bryant, Miss Moore, and myself had stayed at Jim Riley's place sixty miles southwest of Kingfisher, a white-painted, three-storey, ten-gabled house with scrolls and gingerbread for the porch trimmings. Riley was a huge, hearty, blustering man with a sudden laugh that was loud as a slamming door. He had a dark squaw wife who seemed to stand all day at a kettle in the kitchen and slipped through the house barefoot, holding her skirts up over her knees. Grattan had been Riley's go-between at selling cases of muddy whiskey to the Indians, and Riley made such a profit in the transaction that he felt beholden to every Dalton. So for a dollar a week he put each of us three up in what an eastern designer had intended as a music room: a long, sunny, yellow expanse of seven windows and oak planking in which Bryant hammered up clotheslines and Eugenia pinned up privacy blankets.

Bryant slept on a floor mattress striped like engineer coveralls and stained so bad I half expected it to sprout vegetables in the spring. I had an iron bunk and a tatter-crossed quilt and a rocking chair with a forest glade and piping nymphs carved into the headpiece. I could sit for hours in that chair and watch snow softly attach itself to the mullions of the window or listen to Eugenia's pen scratch at a letter to my brother Bob.

She kept mostly to herself that winter in that house. I'd nudge her privacy blanket up with my toe as I lay on my bunk, and see the blond hair on her ankles as she walked across the room to her drop-leaf table, see a green buttoned shoe pump up and down at her treadle sewing machine, see her step naked out of the pool of her fallen robe and hear her twist a sponge into her white ironstone basin as bathwater speckled the floor and balled up on a dropped magazine. On Saturdays she was allowed the claw-and-ball bathtub off the kitchen, and after supper she and I smoked black cheroots together while she read to me. Cowboys from the bunkhouse visited Miss Moore constantly, presenting her with boxes of candy and dates and dried fruit, conducting themselves as if they had an audience with the queen. It was enough for them to hear a lady's voice and kiss her hand when they left, but some would get drunk and incautious and I'd have to brain them with a bronze ashtray that bore the name of the Hotel Savoy.

My brothers in California sent letters and telegrams about the railroad frame-up, so Eugenia was not very much surprised in March when Deputy Marshal Ransom Payne stopped by to interrogate Riley as to the whereabouts of Newcomb and Bryant and McElhanie, who'd been seen once or twice on his spread. Eugenia was polishing silverware and had the sleeves of her dress rolled past her elbows and she brushed her yellow hair off her forehead as she pulled open the door for Payne, who mistook her for Daisy Bryant, Blackface Charley's sister, an identification he never swayed from unto the very last.

Payne was a tall, vain man born in Iowa and educated in Kentucky, a former real-estate agent who was forty years old and considered himself a rake. His pride was a waxed blond mustache that was wide as his ears, and when he sat in the parlor to make his inquiries, he was careful of the crease in his pants. Eugenia made tea and he talked of himself for two hours, mentioning his investigation of the Dalton gang for a California railroad. And he visited her again and again, giving her iris bulbs, a mezzotint of the new Eiffel Tower in Paris, a chocolate Easter egg that you could hold to your eye to view a handsome Jesus sitting among small children, and withal Eugenia got such complete information from Payne about the troubles in California that we were more enlightened one thousand miles away than any of the alleged conspirators.

In April I'd almost resolved to board a train for Fresno or San Francisco and turn myself in to Special Agent Hickey as the vaunted Emmett Dalton and thereby confuse the prosecution's case, but word came to Miss Moore via Ransom Payne that Bob Dalton had escaped the state, and I waited for his opinion, staring at the ceiling, flat on my back, listening to Bryant pare his toenails with a knife or mutter nonsense about a man named Esterhazy or take his pistol apart and assemble it, with a pocket watch near his knee; sixteen reconstructions in an hour was his best time.


By then I had resumed courting Julia Johnson and I didn't hanker to leave her again, for she was not so moon-eyed or convinced about Emmett Dalton after she heard I robbed the cantina. I'd ride a horse on slick roads to Bartlesville and shamble up to her porch steps in goat hair chaps that were snaggled with mud, and mud splattered on me like freckles and moles. And with an idiot's grin spreading over my face, I'd scratch my hat-matted hair and say, "I'm a regular tar baby, ain't I."

I'd wash in her kitchen and smear her dish towels drying my hands and I'd scatter cookie crumbs saying how pretty she was. A pharmacist from town would stop by in a spotless, pencil-striped suit to ask Julia to a church social, or an Army surveyor wearing dress blues and a sword would return from someone's party with a pint carton of melting ice cream, and he'd skewer me with one of those haughty first lieutenant looks before he galloped away. She was flattered and wooed by every unmarried man in the district and I was no woman's prize. I was a raw, scruffy, clumsy ranch hand, without education, without a cent, without even swarthy good looks, and with little more than my brothers' wanted posters to offer the girl I yearned for. I was infected by Julia's heartsickness. I worried so much over what we'd talk about that I'd outline conversations in advance and practice fancy ways of putting news about sorghum and down spouts and rim-fire cartridges. I'd work up an enlarged vocabulary with Eugenia, then insert the words cleverly in my spiel: "But I'm being verbose, aren't I?" I said. And yawning in my chair I'd say, "The cold weather months really bring on the ennui."

So it might have been out of desperation that I invited Julia down to the ranch where she could meet Bob's woman, Miss Eugenia Moore, whom I'd talked so much about. They were as different as oil and vinegar but I thought that would merely make them provocative and amusing to each other. That was not one of my champeen ideas. I did not win the nickel with that one. Riley had taken his squaw to a Dallas rodeo and Bryant was off experimenting with whores, so we had the house to ourselves. I hung around in the kitchen while Julia and Eugenia tried to cook an extravagant dinner, but they kept colliding with each other. Miss Johnson bumped Miss Moore's tin measuring cups of seasonings onto the floor; Miss Moore banged Miss Johnson's saucepan off a hot plate with a cauldron of water she wanted to boil. They each seemed to have designs on the same tablespoon, the same ladle, the same cannister of salt, and what started off with some good-natured titters turned frosty after an hour until Eugenia snapped, "Will you *please* get out of my *way*?"

We dined at a polished table that had a purple color to it. The wallpaper insisted that roses bloomed out of roses, and overhead there was a glass chandelier that was adrip with white candle wax. I played the jolly old king with ladies at right and left. They'd smile at me but rarely lifted their heads to see the provocative woman across the way, and when the table talk diminished to a five-minute lull of clinking knives and forks, Eugenia decided to fill it with confessions about her past.

She said, "I was expelled from Holden College in Missouri for moral turpitude. I was discovered *flagrante delicto*—"

"I don't know what those words mean," I said.

"Latin," she said. " 'While the crime is blazing.' The man was a bachelor geography teacher with a beard large as a neck bib. He took me down to a refectory table, and rucked my skirt up to my shoulders, and traced me with clammy hands. My chief regret about our brief encounter is that he heard footsteps and panicked before I could be defiled."

Somewhere in the midst of that I tried laughing, "Ho ho ho," but no one else seemed even tickled, and Julia's face was on fire.

Miss Moore continued, "I managed my fall from grace soon after that, then tried to restore my reputation by becoming a schoolteacher in Oklahoma, but found it ungratifying. Then I cohabited with an Indian gambler named Jesse White Wings who instructed me in horse thievery. And I learned how to walk out of jail scot-free simply by consenting to a turnkey's secret wish. Sometimes an abandoned pose was enough. None of it struck me as very distasteful."

"My! So many skills," Julia said. "I guess you'll never lack an occupation."

"Ho ho ho," I said.

Eugenia said, "I suppose I never considered virginity an enviable condition; and innocence seems no more blissful than admitting you can't read. I don't want to be one of those sweet, blank, coddled girls whose highest ambition is their impregnable chastity."

I made a deathbed appeal with my eyes but Miss Moore must have assumed it was the result of Julia's cooking because she went on, "I don't want to be one of those puling, simpering, sterile aunts who worry over the state of their souls if they let the dishes sit. The only approval I want is my own."

It had crossed my mind by this time that my special evening might very well be crumbling, and I sought to save it by exercising one of my learned words. "I'm sorry you've taken such umbrage, Eugenia," I said.

But then Julia rushed in. "I suppose you want excitement, don't you? You're one of those women who can't stand to be bored, who wish life could be more interesting. I'm frankly sick of things happening every second. Why does everyone have to be famous? Why do they want their names in the papers? What's so wonderful about being fascinating? I think I'd rather be sweet and blank and coddled and not fuss so much about recognition."

"Landsakes," I said. "Nothing I like more than a spirited discussion."

Eugenia ignored me and said, "Oh dear, I've disturbed you, haven't I? I've spoiled your appetite. Pity me for my bad manners. I believe I'd better excuse myself now and go tantalize the bunkhouse."

She smiled at me when she got up from the table and as she walked down the hall I could hear her exclaim like the most soulful tragedian, "Evil! I embrace you!"

"Well!" I said. "Lot of food for thought tonight, ay Julia?"

Julia was staring at her plate and making an effort not to cry.

I said, "I think if you made an inventory you'd find you two really have a lot in common. You've got different philosophies, is all."

"No," she said. "I think she just wishes Bob was here."

I reckoned that was true. My brother there would have been a relief to many people.

In late April, Bob and McElhanie made it to the Arizona border and slid their horses down the orange west banks of the Colorado River. They let them drink and crop at the weeds, then pulled them into the river and gripped the saddle horns and lost a mile with the currents as the horses lurched and coughed and swam scared across the red river, leaving California.

The boys uncinched the saddles and lay back in the river grass on their elbows while the horses rolled in the dust. McElhanie said, "My brain's too awkward for robbery, Bob. My hands are only happy with tools."

"What's that mean?"

"I'm tired of the chase, is what I'm saying. My stomach's all topsy-turvy."

"You want to split up," said Bob.

"That's it," said McElhanie. "You put the hammer square on the head of the nail."

So they sold their horses to a man in a shepherd's kraal and hopped a train for the Oklahoma Territory where the two split up. "The Narrow Gauge Kid" hiked to Arkansas where he would eventually work a small farm and die in his bed with a kitten under his hand and the radio on in the kitchen.

Bob would have gone to the family home in Kingfisher except he'd crouched in the top limbs of a sixty-foot cotton-wood tree all of one afternoon and saw that he was being trailed across the badlands by a railroad detective in a dark suit and gray businessman's stetson who would kneel by a track and look around and pack down his pipe with a match stick.

So instead Bob sequestered himself in a twenty-five-cent room in the ex-slave settlement of Dover, Oklahoma. Cowhands in flophats and raincoats would canter their horses down the main street, frowning and spitting and acting like nobility, but otherwise it was dark men in suspenders and rough wool shirts, dark women in bandanas, and children with their hair tied who'd throw things at Bob and run. My mother visited him once in the afternoon behind the Free Will Baptist church. They linked arms and strolled under blossoming trees and she smiled as he told her of Littleton and Bill and her grandchildren. Her only comment about money and work with him was that they were hiring in the coal mines.

Bob stopped shaving and took up snooker with some of the males and paid for a teenaged girl who smelled like a cellar floor and who had straightened her hair with a clothing iron.

He walked back from snooker one night and saw the curtains flying out the window of his upper room. He took the stairs three at a time, his pistol cocked high at his shoulder, and pushed the open door to see Eugenia Moore smoking a cigarette by the window, a kerosene lamp the only light. She turned and smiled and unbuttoned her blouse as she walked to him. "I hope you haven't used yourself up."

8 Afterwards they sat in the narrow bed with a bottle of red California wine Bob had wrapped in a gunnysack, and the two of them made plans. He said he was tired of being poor and he was tired of being pushed around and he wanted to make a strike of some kind instead of always reacting to whatever the railroads did. She said Bryant and Newcomb were hungry enough for anything, that it was Emmett who needed convincing, but she had an inkling I wanted to make a name for myself, make a haul that would guarantee lots of money so I could stop mewling about it.

The next morning they took the train to Wharton, Bob looking shaved and clean in the coach with a saddle under his boot and a horse in the cattle car, Eugenia in the smoking car dressed in Bob's photographed suit, her bleached hair slicked back to the color brown with pomade. She looked like a lady's man.

Bob sat on the bench in front of the depot in Wharton, reading the local newspaper, and the man he got off with went inside to talk to the local express agent. "Hello!" Miss Moore said loudly, but that was all Bob could hear. His horse was coaxed down the ramp from the slatted car. He watered it and wiped the sleep out of its eyes and threw on a blanket and saddle. And the man who was wearing his suit came out of the office and crossed to the water pump with a ladle. Bob walked over with a canteen. "What's happening in there?"

Eugenia said, "I told him I was a telegraph officer from New York; that the western air was medication for my lungs. He says there will be a shipment of currency on the Santa Fe–Texas Express, stopping in Wharton at ten-thirty on the ninth. Marshal Payne admitted the same thing; said he'll be riding with it as escort." She drank water and wiped her mouth crude as a man and smiled. "The agent looked a little scornful. I fear he thinks I'm effeminate."

Bob smiled and put the stopper on his canteen.

She said, "He doesn't know me like you do."


That was May 6th. On the 9th Bob and I and Newcomb and Bryant rode the hard dirt highway from Newcomb's shack near Guthrie to the stockyards south of Wharton, which was a cow town of five or six stores made of foot-wide unpainted planks. It is bigger now; named Perry. The four of us wore chambray shirts and chaps with the oil worn off and twisted red bandanas at our necks. We hung our spurs on the saddle horns and tied up our horses at the railroad cattle pens and walked to the tracks at ten o'clock, loading our revolvers in the darker side of buildings.

Bryant limped badly, swinging his leg with each step. He already had his mask up over his nose, which would've been a giveaway had anybody been up in the town. He noticed Bob staring at his infirmity and said, "I got the whore disease. My balls are swoll up like fists and my fly is caked green in the morning with pus. Brings tears to my eyes when I piss. They tell me you get suppurating sores and cankers like Bing cherries. I'd want my jaw blown off with a ten-gauge rather than worsen." He glanced at Bob. "Do you see what I'm saying?"

Bob said, "You tell me when you want it finished and we'll walk behind the barn together. But don't do anything stupid just so you can exit under fire."

Bryant didn't know what to do with his face so he smiled underneath his bandana.

"Don't kill anyone, understand? If you want to be shot dead, I'll do it. I don't need a murder charge tacked onto everything else."

He stared at Bryant until he turned. Bryant said, "Hell, I wouldn't want to offend anybody. Not for anything."

Bitter Creek and I had walked on to the depot. A male passenger with stains on his clothes was asleep on the varnished bench. A boy who was the night station attendant and telegraph operator, whose name has not survived, was buffing his Sunday shoes. Newcomb asked for the ladle Eugenia had used and walked out to the pump, scouting; I looked at the reward posters for three other men and then a yellowed one for the Daltons. I walked over to the counter and folded my arms and leaned against it. "Pretty quiet," I said.

The boy looked at the shoe his hand was wearing as he buffed it. "You got your ticket?"

I didn't answer. Newcomb walked back in, wiping water from his red mustache and goatee, and then the two of us left.

Newcomb said, "I think the lawmen must go to bed here at darn near eight o'clock. Walked all the way down the main street and never even heard a bed squeak."

I looked down at him and said, "How do you suppose he got to be a ticket agent and not even sixteen years old?"

"Maybe it's *easy*, Emmett. Maybe there was a 'Help Wanted' sign. Should I get you a job application?"

"Seems like a good life to me. He's got himself a blue suit of clothes at home I bet. Plus a railroad pension. I bet he's got a black lunch box he carries to work. I don't believe I'd mind that at all."

Bryant was north on the roadbed, squatting near the interlocking machine at the double-track junction, smoking a brown cigarette. Bob leaned against the mailbag post, his pocket watch open in his hand. I walked over next to him while Newcomb crossed the tracks and sat down in the soot-blackened grass, his back against a pile of taken-up ties.

My brother stared off down the tracks where the Santa Fe would come from. "I can remember the first time I rode a train. Farmers stopped their plows and wives came out of their houses, drying their hands on their aprons. Children stood in fields of yellow grass and waved until their arms got tired."

I said, "Won't that be something when the news gets back to California? Won't those railroad detectives be peeved? Grat will laugh so hard he'll cry."

I heard the rails hum and I saw Bryant throw down his cigarette up ahead, and then I saw the train, all smokestack and smoke and cowcatcher, the white steam flying out from its brakes. The engine boiler made its chattering noise while the wheels screamed on the rails, and the stoker was hanging onto the cab rail by one hand, the other hand swinging a lantern low and then holding it up to see Bryant. Newcomb ran out of the grass tugging his bandana up over his nose. Bob and I lifted our bandanas up and walked onto the vibrating cinder bed and stood facing the train like gunfighters. Bob raised his pistol high over his head and fired, wincing when gunpowder stung him.

Bryant yelled, "Brakes!" as the train clanked past him and he let go a shot at the firebox that rang off metal and banged into something else. Newcomb was plugging his ears at the screech of steel; then he ran alongside the locomotive and hopped up onto the footrest as it slowed. He struggled up the two-step ladder and shoved his pistol straight at the engineer's head, striking him hard enough behind the ear to start a trickle of blood and knock him onto his right leg. Then Bob was in the cab with his red mask up and his broad hat pulled low. He slammed the stoker against the boiler and slapped him with the flat of his pistol. The stoker groaned and sat down on the floor with his cheek in his hand. Bob glared at the engineer and took him by the striped coat and swung him off the stopped locomotive. He hit the cinders stiff as a chair. I kicked the engineer off his hands and knees and pushed a boot heel down on his throat and clicked the hammer back on my pistol. I was too scared of myself to talk. The pistol quaked in my hand.

The stoker in the cab had tears in his eyes. The newspapers said he was fifty-two years old. His left cheek was as swollen as a balled-up woolen sock; his left eye was drooped and closing. He said, "What do you want us to *do*? Say something."

"Get down from here," said a masked man.

The stoker cautiously climbed down a ladder step and jumped.

Bryant was walking backwards past the passenger cars, limping like a man with a six-inch wooden shoe. He held his pistol straight out with both hands, lifting it from one window to the next. Faces ducked out of view.

After he heard Bryant's gunshot, the Wharton ticket agent rushed out from behind the counter and suffocated the lamps. The train conductor took off his cap and sat down on his step stool, frozen. The mail car attendant, called in those days the messenger, jammed the bolt up into its seat at the top of the door and threw the double latch bolts above the handle. Then he removed the money of large denominations from the safe and stuffed the bills into a Franklin stove, where we missed them.

A tall deputy marshal in a dark, three-piece suit and waxed mustache walked down the aisle in the second class car, peering out at Bryant. He'd been reading some federal arrest warrants and he left these in his seat.

When the conductor saw the marshal's badge he said, "My heart is about to erupt."

"My name is Ransom Payne." He leaned out the window and said, "It's me they want, not the money." He opened the door on the left side of the car and hung his large white hat on the handle and walked slow as a bridegroom into the sunflower stalks where he crouched down with his gun in his hand.

My brother and Newcomb had by then climbed the iron stairs to the green mail car, and Newcomb swung a fire axe into the door. It middled open on the second blow and Newcomb reached in to pull the bolts free.

The messenger cowered down in a far corner by a coat tree. There were varnished boxes along the right wall as they faced it, and stacked canvas bags and steamer trunks on the floor. In the center of the car was the small Franklin stove, used in the winter for heating. It was empty now except for the big money the messenger had just stuffed inside. Neither Bob nor Newcomb ever thought to look there and the messenger was later to receive a gold watch for his genius.

Bob glared at him and tapped the barrel of his pistol on the safe. "Open it," he said.

"I can't help you there," the employee said. "I don't know the combination."

Bob kept tapping the safe to annoyance.

"The vaults are closed in Kansas City and the combinations wired down to Gainesville. I never hear a number."

Eugenia had been told otherwise, so Bob splintered the coat tree with a bullet. A wood chip flew into the messenger's eye. The eye turned red immediately.

"He thinks you're fibbing," Newcomb said.

The man reached for a chair back and pulled himself up and held a handkerchief at his eye socket. Newcomb unbuttoned his shirt front and unfolded a burlap sack he'd stuffed under his belt and he stood to the left of the messenger as the man moved the safe's dial numbers around. The mechanisms dropped and the man pulled the handle down and offered Bob a large wrapped package which my brother took to be the big money but was actually waybills and canceled telegrams and newspapers torn to pieces. We would not discover the ruse until morning.

My brother pitched the bundle into the burlap sack, as he did the smaller package which was the one and two-dollar bills we eventually divvied up. Newcomb kept the heavy bag wrapped around his hand, letting the bulk of it hang by his knee.

Outside, Bryant kept the stoker and the engineer shoved down into the cinders while I tended to the getaway horses. "Pretend you're snails," he said. He fired his pistol randomly anywhere it wanted to go. He said, "Your passengers are fouling themselves by now."

I was low ranny on the job so I had to sprint down the street to the stockyard where I unwrapped the reins from the fence and pulled the horses long-necked and into a trot. Bob and tiny Newcomb were banging down the mail car stairs when I neared, Newcomb holding the filled sack aloft and grinning under his mask. The two of them swung up onto their mounts at a run, not even using the stirrups. They pushed their horses up a short cliff and over onto a road that they pounded down.

I stayed behind on my horse with my scabbard rifle shouldered, scanning the area as Bryant released the stoker and engineer and limped on over toward me.

"Go on," he yelled. "I'll stand the cowards off."

"You sure?"

Bryant spit tobacco. The scar on his face looked purple.

I kicked my horse up to the road and caught up with my brother and Newcomb in a dark farmyard among apple trees. "What's taking Bryant so long?" Bob asked.

I shrugged. "When Charley's definite about something I don't like to interfere."

Bob frowned at me. "Where'd you learn words like that?"

The horses shifted and stamped and rubbed their chins on the stirrups as the three of us counted nickels and dimes and quarters from the canvas currency bag.

Bryant stood spraddle-legged on the rockbed siding, looking down the quiet train of railroad cars, a rifle in the crook of his arm. He unbuttoned his pants and pinched himself open but could only shudder a minute. He wiped his eyes with his gloved hand and lifted his left boot into the stirrup. He shoved his pistol into his holster and cradled his rifle in his arms and watched the stoker and engineer spider under a coupling to the left side of the train. People were walking inside the cars. He nudged his horse with his knees and walked it slowly past the depot, talking to himself.

The male passenger in the depot walked outside thinking the gang had disappeared. The Wharton ticket agent lit a kerosene lantern and hung it by the calendar over the telegraph key and opened up his Morse book.

Bryant saw the boy begin his signals; then he lifted his rifle some with his elbow and smashed window glass with a cartridge that slammed the boy in the ribs. His body didn't know he was dead until he'd spun and walked backwards over a castered chair and pulled the wooden ticket slots down. The boy looked flabbergasted.

Bryant nudged his horse into a trot and never said a word about the killing so that we didn't discover it until several days later. And then we didn't know what to do about it. Bob made no diary entry.

After it had stayed quiet in Wharton for a minute or two, Ransom Payne got up out of the weeds and solemnly boarded the train. He was already writing reports in his head. He said, "That was the Dalton gang."

The conductor stared at him.


The Dalton gang abused their horses for twenty miles; then we slowed to a walking string of four on the road south and east to Orlando, a saloon town with nineteen worn-out whores. Bryant hung his head down and tried to sleep; I played "Just a Closer Walk with Thee" on my Harpoon; Bob packed some of Newcomb's Mail Pouch tobacco under his lower lip. It looked like his tongue sitting there. The horses were wheezing and they nodded their heads with each step and sometimes just stood in their tracks to jerk the leaves off low trees.

Newcomb shouted over his shoulder, "You're gonna like it at the place we're headed, Bob. Ol Yountis, the owner, he's got an ugly sister who eats snuff and one of the dogs barks 'arf arf arf,' like he's read it in some cartoon."

We reached the Yountis homestead at four in the morning. Two dogs that were brown with mud in the belly and legs rushed out from under the porch to tell us what the property lines were. The horses just ignored them. Bryant knocked the dog that arfed in the head with the butt of his rifle and the two canines backed up to bark and settle deep in the grass and pant.

Yountis came out with a shotgun and no clothes on at all. He had unwashed, leafy hair and hands that looked blue and teeth that were so crooked in his mouth he seemed to snarl. He peed off the edge of the porch while we pulled the saddles from our horses. Ol Yountis cupped his hand in the dogs' water dish and wiped his eyes and face. "How much ya get?" he asked.

The gang walked inside his shack and emptied the burlap sack on the table. Ol's sister came out of her room in a gray dress, parting her black hair with her fingers, wiping black snuff from her lip. She simpered some at Newcomb, who dealt with her when he was hard up, and she started fixing breakfast as Bob tore open the big package and saw the worthless paper and threw it against a wall where it slapped apart and the pieces fluttered down.

Newcomb couldn't believe we'd been tricked and chased down every waybill and canceled check to see that it wasn't money. Bob ripped open the other package and saw the one and two-dollar bills and I began stacking them in piles of fifty. Yountis came out of his room in awful bib overalls and he walked out of the house in disgust when he heard the whole take was barely five hundred dollars. He made only twenty dollars of that for the rental of his pasture and our board.

Esther Yountis cooked a meal of beans and suet and pancakes and sat down on a bedroom chair as we silently ate it, smiling whenever we looked in her direction. I leaned back in my chair and said what good food it was. I believed in putting the best face on things.

She responded, "It's not. Not really. But thank you anyway."

Bob turned around in his chair to tell her that he and I used to be peace officers in the territory; we knew the geography like it was our backyard.

She said, "I keep asking Ol to chop down some of these trees. I don't think we've got a pretty yard at all."

Bob turned back to his food and that was the end of conversation except for him saying over his coffee that it didn't matter how much money we got because we were practiced now for the next time.

Esther stacked dishes, then walked the four of us down a narrow weedy cow path. There were too many trees too close together, like mourners around a grave, and there was green moss on everything. Below the trees were green grasses, green creepers, green ivy. The dogs were bounding deep in it and hardly showed their tails. Sun slanted in like rain. The place where we camped was a small clearing caused by two slabs of sleek rock and a trickle of clear water that talked as it fell into Beaver Creek. Esther walked back with Newcomb beside her and about halfway to the shack they sat down in plants that milked when they broke, and after some persuading she removed her dress so he could do it to her.

The men were asleep under blankets when Eugenia Moore stepped her horse through the briars at noon. She was dressed as a man in buckskin pants and a wool shirt that she stripped off at the creek to wash the horse smell from her with lavender soap. Then she walked naked to Bob and slid in under the blanket and woke him up by unbuckling his belt. He smiled and they kissed without speaking. She unbuttoned his shirt and he kicked out of his pants; she unbuttoned his underwear and she let his fingers find her.

Bryant was on his side five yards away, staring. He watched them for a long time, then rolled to his other side.

Ol Yountis came down at two o'clock lugging a bushel basket against his right leg. He smiled at the man and woman under the blanket and lifted her discarded clothes out of the basket. "I believe these might be your'n."

She stood up naked and made no secret of herself as she buttoned on just her shirt and walked down to her horse for a long skirt.

Yountis grinned. "Not a bit bashful, is she."

My brother lifted his .45 and clicked the hammer back. "I don't want you weaseling around down here. I don't want you to expect her or covet her or even dream about her. I catch you in Miss Moore's vicinity and I'll attach an animal to ya."

Yountis got up out of his frog squat. "I like my whores just fine," he said. "There's two that got real educations about men." He carried the bushel basket to where Bitter Creek and I were sleeping. He kicked us awake and set out a supper of corn bread and hog jowls and kidney beans with capped jars of grainy coffee. Then he walked up to his shack.

By which time Ransom Payne was riding drag and shouting headlines about himself to a posse of Cherokee policemen. Ahead of him were five Oklahoma marshals and an ex-sheriff from Kansas, Ed Short, a robust man who could not have suspected that he had only three months to live before he'd be gunned down in a railroad baggage car by Blackface Charley Bryant.

The posse was misled so often by informers that they soon

gave up the hunt. They never got within twenty miles of the gang: the Daltons had that many friends; the railroads were hated that much.

We stayed on the sad farm of Ol and Esther Yountis three days. Whenever Yountis walked out to plow with his middle-buster, Newcomb called upon his sister. Bryant and Newcomb and I played cards and dominoes on a horse blanket spread over bluegrass and wild onion. Bob and his woman walked down to the creek where they knelt and washed each other in running water so shallow they could hear the stones click under it.

Eugenia washed Bob's chest with a sponge and said, "Do women get weak when they see you?"

"Nope. Mostly they just look bored."

She said, "That's because they're defeated. They probably think you're out of reach."

"Aren't you a comfort," he said.

She said, "I let only one man visit my body while you were gone the winter. He was heavy and an informant and I didn't stir until he left me. I spent my afternoons with the pleasure of you, feeling you there and wishing whenever I saw my bed I would see Bob Dalton in it with his gun on the blankets and the sparkle in his eyes and all the bones showing in his chest. I'm not a good woman at all. I'm fickle and strange and common as a hotel, but I do love you Bob Dalton; you're my permanent resident."

His answer was to kiss her and to pull her down to him.

She left that afternoon for Hennessey to arrange a purchase of land.

One hundred and twenty-five dollars apiece wasn't hardly enough for the gang, so that night, after drinking potato whiskey, Newcomb and I left the camp at midnight to laugh like kids and thrash through the bramble and grabbers until we came to a horse pasture owned by George and William T. Starmer. We peed against a fence post and took off our boots and hats and slunk through the wet grass until we saw a dozen horses and foals asleep on their legs or reaching for short clover. I used comforting talk on the animals until I could pet the velvet of a horse's nose; then I fed it sugar lumps and pulled it away to Newcomb with a rope thrown over its ears. A few got peeved and tossed away but many just nickered and sleepwalked behind us and in this way we got ten horses by three in the morning and rode them back in a trotting string made noisy by the two Yountis dogs. We picketed the herd with wooden stakes in the ivy and planned to leave with them in the morning after alteration of the brands.

George Starmer discovered the missing broncs when he carried out the milk pails. By six-thirty he'd collected his brother and William Thompson and four immigrant farmers they'd sponsored out of Sweden. And the first place they checked was the Yountis property because he was slovenly and disliked in the county.

The dogs announced themselves to skittish horses and Ol emerged from the shack in his bib overalls and he kept on rubbing his eyes as the farmers shouted. He turned his back and slammed the screen door behind him without ever answering them, so they rode around to the back of the yard and saw the puzzle of hoofprints and the broken weed stalks, the grass beaten down, and the farmers went after us in a rush, ducking low as the flanks of their horses to escape the maul of the trees. But Bryant had been sleepless with his pain and heard them soon after the dogs barked. And the gang was gone and somewhere in the trees when the farmers dropped from their horses.

William Starmer had been a military man in the War Between the States, and he directed a sweep through the forest, but it did the men no good because the four of us took off our boots and clothes and smeared ourselves with black mud and hunkered down under broad leaves while Bryant towed the horses south to the road. Then we crashed loudly through the weeds or we yodeled or pitched stones, drawing the farmers where we willed.

The farmers were unequal to it. They hunted like a parish men's club out for a rabbit shoot. They fired at screams and shadows and flashes of a runner in the trees. Seven men used up four boxes of cartridges by noon. At which time they discovered themselves exactly where Bob had wanted them, in canebrake one mile from Beaver Creek, slapping gnats from their eyes, biting nettles from their wrists, feeling the sting of sweat in thorn scratches. Bob and I and Bitter Creek crouched behind a havoc of lightning-struck timber in the dark of standing trees, looking down at the brush-stopped farmers from topography known as Twin Mounds.

Bryant was with us, sitting with his trousers at his ankles and his sick parts exposed on a flat rock that was hot from the sun. Then he loaded the two chambers of a ten-gauge shotgun he'd bought from Yountis for thirty dollars. He buckled his trousers and limped over next to me. He said, "What do we have for targets?"

The immigrants were yelling in Swedish to each other and firing at the unseen but the four of us didn't answer until we saw the front rank of men struggling in the weeds below us. Then Bob whispered, "Now," and we lifted our rifles overhead and fired down into the bracken without raising to see if we'd even got close to any mankind.

Somebody struck William Thompson at once and he slumped against a tree. When a friend lifted him to standing, the whole front of his shirt was sagging heavy with blood. The gang of us fired again but sporadically, cautious about the few unspent cartridges still in our pistols, the six cartridges grating together in our hands.

Two farmers pulled Thompson by the collar of his coat into a shaded clearing of wet leaves. "What a bellyache," he said. "Merciful Jesus, it hurts." He rolled to his side and vomited food and blood. He heaved until he was empty and it was coming out of his nose. A friend wiped Thompson's face with his sleeve. "Feels like acid and razor blades."

Word carried back to William Starmer who became so crazy with rage that he lurched straight at the two breasts of land where we were hidden, firing at us until he'd shattered much of the bark off the timber, until he'd used up all his shells. Weeds snatched at his legs like heavy dogs and he was clutched and slow and scratched in the face, only ripping his coat sleeve free of thorns, when Bryant wandered out into the sunlight with his ten-gauge and blew the jaw off Starmer's head.

Bitter Creek Newcomb left Twin Mounds at a slow lope. He had one hundred fifteen dollars in his bedroll and one of Starmer's brown horses jolting behind him on a rope and the brim of his hat slapped up in the front like a cavalryman's. He stopped in a small town that afternoon, ate chili in a tavern, and drank warm beer with an egg yolk in it. He found the town prostitute doing laundry outside in a washtub and they leaned against a trellis that was strung with green beans. She was four inches taller than he was. Her wet sleeves were cold to his skin.

He had a squatter's farm of sixteen acres near Guthrie that he arrived at on a Sunday. He swapped Starmer's horse for a mule and some farm implements, and he gave over the next three days to cursing his animal and driving a two-blade plow, and his summer was spent walking the plant rows under the hot sun with a soaked bandana tied to his head, sloshing water from a bucket.

In June he had somebody who was educated, possibly Rose Dunn, a pretty girl he'd begun courting, print a letter to my brother that said, "I think you should consider expanding the gang to include Bill Doolin, Bill Powers, and Dick Broadwell, who are exceptional men with real sand in the craw who do not wither under gunfire. The railroads are getting nervous. We'll want the extra security."

Since I was closer to Guthrie than he was, Bob sent me to chat with Newcomb about the proposal and Bitter Creek agreed to make the necessary connections. And I sat up in bed that night to smoke a cigarette and saw Newcomb in a rocking chair on a hill of Russian thistles and blond grass in the middle of his property, feeling the gun in his lap like a blind man, clicking the cylinder around. A summer wind filled his shirt. He stared at the stars until his neck hurt.

After the gang dispersed at Twin Mounds, Bob gave me control of the horses and was bold enough himself to ride into Kingfisher where he paid for a bath and a haircut and had supper that night with Mom and our sister Nannie Mae and her husband J. K. Whipple. Whipple owned a meat market in Kingfisher and he later spied on us for Marshal William Grimes, the top lawman in the territory and later a Republican governor. Whipple gave Bob a six-cent cigar.

Then my brother splashed his horse along the river and hurried it up a silt bank where I was growing a smokeless fire. The stolen horses all had their heads down in the sweet grass, their tails flinging and shoulders twitching flies away, stomping whenever they walked. I was scraping dried green saliva from a clove bit so I didn't take hold of the newspaper section on farm sales when Bob unfolded it for me.

"Which one?"

He said, "The circled one, doorknob. Hundred fifty acres, spring-fed."

I read about a farm sale from someone recently deceased. The bereaved were coming down from Wichita on Thursday to hold the auction. That meant we could hide the remuda at the farm for a day or two. "Is there hay in the barn there?" I asked.

Bob nodded and poured an inch of coffee into a cup.

"Dropped by to check this afternoon. Wasn't nobody home. Best keep the horses in stalls until Annie Walker sends her buyer."

I hung the bridles on a branch and then the two of us squatted by the fire and I stared as it burned down to nothing. He said, "I didn't sleep at all last night. I just hunched next to a tree and stirred the dirt with a stick and tried to decide if I had any remorse for those men that got shot. I couldn't find anything. Sometimes I wonder if I'm human."

I said, "It's the railroad's fault, appears to me. They grab up land and cheat the farmers and make these tremendous profits. It ain't right. They got all the money in this country locked up and pay almost no taxes at all. They're the working man's enemy, is what they are, same here as in California. And if somebody sides with them and gets killed in the bargain, welp, that's too bad and it makes me miserable but it's like that in every battle. This is civil war."

Bob got a cigar out and pushed it against a coal and when it was drawing he stood. "I don't feel guilty; I just feel sad. I guess that will disappear too."

"You leaving tonight?"

"Yep."

"What do I do? Mail your half to the Hennessey post office?"

"Care of Daisy Bryant," said Bob, and got up on his horse and hauled its head around. I doused the fire with what was left of the coffee and it whispered for a while.


I stared at the face of my pocket watch and told myself to wake up at three. I opened my eyes at 3:10, and dunked my head in the river and buttoned on a wool shirt and strung together eleven horses with quarter-inch rope I looped through the bit rings. And even with them kicking and jostling and making indignant noises, I had them stabled in the vacant barn by nine. I forked silage into the feeders and carried a bucket of oats from stall to stall and pushed their noses away. Once they cooled they gave off a smell like apples that've gone brown.

I locked the barn and walked through a hairy yard of rusty machines and tools and implements waiting for auction: three hog pens on limb skids, a bee house, a pile of harness and leather yokes, a roll of barbwire deep in weeds, and two un-painted wagons with extra wheel spokes in their flatbeds. I smashed out the window to the kitchen door with a dry mop and walked through a shut-up house with all the valuables crowded on the dining-room table or tagged on the living-room floor. Drapes lifted at me when I opened a bedroom door and I saw that Bob had climbed through the window and left the sash halfway up. On the lavender bedspread were the printed tags for what he'd stolen: "1848 New York crystal." "A valuable silver set made by Paul Revere." "A fine authentic oil painting depicting Venus and the four seasons."

I opened a closet door and found a laundry bag hanging by its drawstring. I dropped the laundry itself on four pairs of polished high-top shoes and I walked out of the bedroom with a teakwood letter opener, a bottle of perfume still in its velvet box, and a pair of eight-inch Army binoculars in a black case skinned brown at the edges.

I cooked three eggs and I sliced potatoes and bacon to-gether in a skillet and sat at a kitchen table with coffee and the binoculars up to my eyes, counting blackbirds and grackles in a hornbeam tree a half a mile away. Then I washed off my plates and sat in a green wingback chair and stayed the binocu-lars on the north road where a man and a horse were walking the rightward wheel rut. He rocked deep in a Mexican work-ing saddle and sucked a toothpick between his front teeth and his nose looked like it was pressed against a window.

Annie Walker's buyer. Charlie Pierce. A jockey-sized man nearly forty years old with deep vertical lines on his face. New-comb's bosom buddy.

I ran to the barn and tugged two horses that walked into the afternoon sunshine as if each leg weighed ninety pounds.

Charlie Pierce sat in his saddle next to a birdhouse, then threw his reins and his horse clopped up into the yard.

"I seen you a mile away," I said.

He sneezed into a folded white handkerchief. His nose was flat as a thumb. "So?"

"I think that's pretty amazing."

Pierce got off his horse and nodded toward the binoculars. "You own them things or invent 'em?" He walked up to a filly I'd pulled out and he ran both hands along her. He lifted a shoed hoof and dropped it. "Look at them bent-over nails. That's a scandal." He pried open the horse's mouth and wiped his fingers on his pants as he squinted at the teeth; then he walked right past me into the barn. His boots were collapsed at his ankles like ice skates on a child. He stood in front of the stalls watching the horses and came back out drying the inner headband of his hat with the elbow of his shirt. His hair was oily and creased where the J. B. Stetson had been.

"Emmett, you got one Roman-nosed bay mare looks pretty funneled to me; another one's so hard in the mouth a cowboy'd have to steer her by the ears. If I was a horse trader like your dad was I'd say three of those broncs are going to be cheaters. Plus, you got a roan back there with four white socks and a white face. That's about a two-dollar animal and you know it. You'd do as good if you took him out back and shot him."

I patted the neck of a yearling next to me. "Cast an eye this direction, though, Charlie. This one's got superior conformation, don't it?"

He talked to the horse and walked around it with his hand. "Good shoulder angle, spring of the rib; cannon turns out some but that's all right. Nice hind leg if he didn't pass so close at the hocks." He straddled a rear hoof and dug at it with an open pocketknife. "Soft as a biscuit," he said. "If I had the money for carrots and sweetfeed I might groom this one myself." He scraped the varnish around the shoe, then stood away, folding up his knife.

"I'm gonna have to cut off these brands and eat 'em," he

said. He took out a piece of paper and wrote on it with a stub of a pencil. Then he said, "You outlaws are beginning to worry our first territorial governor, the Honorable George W. Steele. He says you're retarding Oklahoma's progress toward statehood." He handed me the paper. All it said was: $300.00.

I nodded and opened the barn doors wide. I said, "I saw a paragraph in the newspaper said Grimes is after us with something like fifty other lawmen."

"There's mucho consternation, I'll say that." He unbuckled a saddlebag and counted fifteen twenty-dollar bills out of a limp white envelope with fingerprints on it in brown. He tied the horses bridle to tail and when he had them in train he got up on his saddle and rubbed his white handkerchief under his thumb of a nose. "I only do chores for Annie Walker. She wouldn't fuss if I left for more satisfying endeavors."

"I'll mention you to Bob," I said.

He smiled. "I'll write your name in my Bible."


Blackface Charley Bryant spent half of June in the Rock Island Hotel in Hennessey, about twenty miles north of Kingfisher. The hotel was named for the railroad spur that served it and was run by a pretty lady named Jean Thorne and her brother, who had known Bryant as a cowhand. For a dollar a day, Bryant got a spring bed and a bureau and a cotton-stuffed chair with doily protectors on which he'd pinned a new reward poster for the murder of a Wharton ticket agent. Miss Thorne brought up his food on a tray and she put a poultice on his thighs and stomach where they were streaked red with infection and she scrubbed his sweating face with a washrag. But he got tired of the mothering and limped downstairs and skinned a yard-tree branch for a cane and rode over to Buffalo Springs one Tuesday at nightfall. There was a cow camp there of five hundred cattle and some cowboys in Confederate Army tents. He'd pay a nickel for his chow and sleep on his bedroll under an Army cot and some afternoons he'd ride forty miles for doctoring from Jim Riley's squaw. The cowhands all swore by her. She could cure baldness and croup and rheumatism and she could urinate on your hands and heal warts. I don't know what she did to Bryant, only that she used a glass chemist's pipe.

My brother heard of Bryant's treatments and to needle him snipped out a newspaper advertisement that he mailed care of Jean Thorne. The clipping read: "Weak men! Vitality weak. Made so by too close application to business or study; severe mental strain or grief; sexual excesses in middle life or from the effects of youthful follies. All yield readily to our new treatment for loss of vital power. Drs. Searles & Searles."

Below that Bob wrote, "Or else you might consider the Ripans Tabules. They regulate the stomach, liver, and bowels. The perfect remedy for biliousness, Bright's disease, catarrh, colic, hives, nausea, salt rheum, scrofula, torpid liver, water brash, and blotches on the face."

My brother Bob had twenty pounds more nerve than I did. I would have feared assassination from Bryant over something like that, but as far as I know he just tossed the letter into a fire.

That summer I stayed fifteen miles from Riley's main house where I rode the south fence of his ranch for two dollars a week and otherwise worked with spade and axe on a dugout I'd paced off as eighteen feet square and marked off with railroad spikes. Bryant would stop by and lean on his ash tree cane and spit tobacco while I chopped at the red clay in my bare feet and no shirt on my back. I dug it four feet deep and raftered it with tree limbs and when I was done I had a house for six men in the cedar brakes next to the South Canadian River. The roof was sod kept green with a watering can and inside I'd lashed together bunk beds and cut portholes into the clay walls for rifles and ventilation. Bryant hung a Navaho horse blanket in the doorway and he stole a smokestack from somewhere and bricked up a four-burner stove. After Pierce sold the Starmer remuda for Annie Walker, he joined us too and spent three days swinging a machete in the willow brush until he'd made a bramble corral that was tall as his neck and big enough for thirty ponies. At a hundred yards you could barely see that hideout; at a quarter mile it wasn't there.

I'd curry the horses after supper and dip the scum out of their water, then take my binoculars and wade miles through yellow buffalo grass that was high enough to seed the pockets of my shirt. I'd squat on a hilltop and see five miles to a farmhouse where a woman was washing her hair in a trough with her gray dress stripped off to her waist. Or I'd see a nodding man on a slack horse take the wagon road up the Gloss Mountains or I'd just admire my handicraft from afar. Toward the end of summer Bill Powers would lift the horse blanket and stand outside with a calabash pipe, or Dick Broadwell would slide down the ravine to the river and later climb back up buttoning his trousers, tucking in his red shirt. It was a good summer place and when the word got out every kind of Oklahoma badman would ride by to visit and report and to sleep for a night in its cool. It got quite a reputation. When I married Julia and moved to California after those years in the Kansas prison and working as a policeman in Tulsa, one of the first things I did was tell a man I'd dig him a basement for fifty dollars. That was 1918. I've been a building contractor going on twenty years now.

Bryant kept himself at the cow camp in Buffalo Springs and Pierce was busy with rodeos and horse racing all that summer, and Broadwell, Doolin, and Powers didn't arrive until almost July, so about the only man besides myself who was constant at the dugout was a black cowpuncher named Amos Burton, forty-four years old and raised by whites and one of Bob's good friends. He'd drive a buckboard to the nester settlement of Taloga and come back with flour and beans and baking soda, or he'd load a shotgun and hike along the river stuffing a grain sack with rabbit, squirrel, grouse, and wild turkey. Afternoons I'd lay in my bunk in a small square of porthole light and read the Sears Roebuck catalogue, pointing at things I wanted, and Amos would just hum to himself and carve duck decoys out of beechnut.

I rode up to Bartlesville on a Sunday in June to visit Julia Johnson, who'd managed to convince both herself and her parents that the railroad and Wells Fargo claims against me were preposterous; and yet she seemed remote and subdued despite my strenuous attempts at humor, and I feared that she was lost to me forever. We walked under fruit trees and I rolled my jeans to my knees and waded out to watch the Caney River move over my toes. I ate ham hocks and navy beans at a supper table of women in bad-smelling dresses and hired men in suspenders and white shirts with brown stains under their arms. I smoked a cigarette on the porch with Texas Johnson and listened to him chastise President Benjamin Harrison and the Republicans. He had already decided that he'd vote for Grover Cleveland in 1892, that is, if Sockless Jerry Simpson didn't run.

He said, "What we need is a man to take on the national banks and twist them around to the farmer again. Then he'd have to roll up his sleeves and take on the railroads. You know it costs three times as much to freight wheat east to Chicago than the longer distance from Chicago to New York? Corn was selling for ten cents a bushel in Kansas—ten cents!—and the shipping rate on it was nine. A man had to harvest a bushel for his kids and another for the railroad. That don't seem right to me. I go along with Mary Lease: I think we oughta raise less corn and more hell. The railroads forgot the little man a long time back. They favor large shipments over small, cities over country towns; they own every dang legislature west of the Susquehanna—the railroads miff you too?"

"They could use some enlightenment," I said.

"You said plenty." He tamped a pipe and struck a match

on the chair bottom. "You gonna tenant farm or cowpunch?"

I told him I was a hired hand and I lived in a bunkhouse at Riley's but I had half a mind to enlist as a U. S. deputy marshal soon as Grat and Bill were acquitted in California.

"I think the dishes are done," he said, and got up out of his rocker.

Julia and I strolled down to the pond where Hereford cattle chewed the sweet grass and stared, and green duckweed encroached on the water. I said, "Your dad and I hit it off real good. We see eye to eye on a lot of things. We're just like hammer and tongs."

She walked barefoot through the grass with her head down and I galumphed in my boots to catch up. I slung my arm around her and she said, "When my sister's gone I lock the bedroom door and cry into my pillow, or sometimes I take my clothes off and swim in the pond so my tears don't show. If I owned a house it would have a special room with dark blue walls and a leather fainting couch and a drawer full of hankies."

I said, "What do you have to be sad about?"

Her eyes stayed on me for a second and then she turned to walk to the house where she sat in a swing with her cheek against one of the ropes while I leaned against the hemlock tree playing soft on my Harpoon. At nine she walked me to my horse and I gave her the stolen teakwood letter opener and the bottle of perfume still in its velvet box that I picked up at the auctioned house.

I wanted to tell her then that I loved her; that I'd get a steady job and marry her, or some real loot and sweep her away; but she touched her finger to my lips and handed me a page of diary paper folded up four times. "Don't read it here. Read it later."

I could see her at the screen door as I rode away; then the screen door closed and I stopped my horse in the center of a road under a white moon. I tore open the paper and held it close as my nose until I could make out her writing. It was

Scripture: " 'But we urge you, brethren, to excel still more and to make it your ambition to lead a quiet life and attend to your own business and work with your hands, just as we commanded you; so that you may behave properly toward outsiders and not be in any need.' Paul to the Thessalonians, chapter 4, verses 10 to 13."

That just about sunk it.


Newcomb busied himself and made connections, and three saddle hands I'd roped with on Oscar Halsell's Bar X Bar ranch, the same three Bob stole me away from in his peace officer days because he considered them bad company—Dick Broadwell, Bill Doolin, Bill Powers—stopped by in late June and stayed on.

Dick Broadwell was a wild and comical man, the second son to a prosperous family in Hutchinson, Kansas. He'd married a green-haired woman who'd run away with his belongings after a mere two weeks in Fort Worth, Texas, and he moped back up to the territory with the alias of Texas Jack Moore. He was thin and pale and book-smart and suspicious. He wore canvas goggles with glass lenses to keep the blowing dust from his eyes and he was bald to halfway back on his head where he kept his dark hair eight or nine inches long. It would lift in the wind like pages and scatter over his eyes. He'd do anything on a dare: leap off the roof of a boxcar, swallow a live cigarette, throw a jackknife between his toes. He came to the sod hut with a black kitten he called Turtle that he fed sardines from a tin. He had warts on his fingers that looked like cauliflower.

I spied Bill Powers three miles off from the dugout walking his horse through grass high as the wooden stirrups, solemnly staring at the cedars and the light snapping off of the river. I recall he had a red bandana over his nose for the chaff, his shirt collar buttoned, a rifle crossed over an apple-horn saddle, and a violin case in his left hand. He was using the name Tim

Evans in those days. I never discovered why. He was a tall and clean and handsome gentleman with a big mustache and no sideburns, as quiet and unemotional as a good butler walking upstairs. He spoke fluent Spanish; he could make a pipe draw two hours; he had chipped fingernails that were pale as piano keys. He used to sit on a bottom bunk with a meerschaum and an oil can and an alarm clock with its hundreds of gears and pins and washers on the blanket, wiping each down with a handkerchief, fitting each with its mate, until he could lie back with the ticking next to his ear. He'd eat lunch in the sun with his eyes shut and he'd walk the Canadian with my binoculars and Mr. Audubon's book, identifying birds. Broadwell would call out, "You see any of those double-breasted mattress-thrashers, you be sure to call me, okay?" Powers would smile and strike a match to his pipe bowl.

Last of all was Bill Doolin who rode in from Eureka Springs, Arkansas, where he took the medicinal baths for his rheumatism and courted a preacher's daughter by the name of Edith Ellsworth. Doolin later had a gang of his own that included my brother Bill, but in those days he was merely a lanky, red-headed, hat-rack of a cowboy with gander blue eyes and a woebegone look and a mustache long as his lower lip. Tied to the tail of his saddle horse was a pack mule with a tarpaulin cover over his skillets and cake pans and jars of spices: cayenne red pepper, arrowroot and chives, mace and dill seed and cloves, rosemary, ginger, basil, and thyme. He was a good cook and took Old Lady more than his share and he would have lasted with us longer than he did if he wasn't so sure to his bones that he was tougher than two men and smarter than Bob and the natural bona fide president of any company he kept. He'd smirk and ignore and argue whenever my brother talked. He was contrary as a teenager sometimes. Deputy Marshal Heck Thomas organized a party that used a shotgun on him in a cornfield in 1895, and they took a photograph of Bill Doolin dead in a chair with his shirt off and his blue eyes open, staring at the ceiling. The shotgun holes looked like pennies on his chest.

My brother left me with the stolen horses in late May and I didn't see him again until July. He rented a wagon and drove it west of Hennessey twenty-three miles, to a big farmhouse being hammered and scraped and painted white by three black men hired out of Dover. Bob walked to the back porch with a net bag of oranges and a man on a ladder took off his felt hat.

"The lady of the house around?"

"Mrs. Jones, she in there with the othuh gemmun."

The gentleman was Blackface Charley Bryant who'd stopped by to visit on the way to the Rock Island Hotel. He'd left his run-over boots by the butter churn in the back and was slouching on a red divan, his feet on a coffee table, while Miss Moore stood on a footstool and hung white draperies. She heard Bob's footsteps on the kitchen tiles and let the draperies fall. Bob stood there in black corduroy trousers and a blue shirt with mother-of-pearl buttons, his hair combed with kitchen water.

"Pleased to meet you, Mrs. Jones."

She said, "It's been nearly a week."

"I know that." He walked into the front room and nodded like a country boy at Bryant. "Hey Charley. How're things?"

Bryant crossed his legs. "Pretty quiet."

Bob smiled at Eugenia and hugged her off the footstool and lifted up the net bag. "I brought you oranges."

She kissed him and said, "I think we should go upstairs."

So they went upstairs to a bedroom of six tall windows with a bed of carved walnut where they stayed the afternoon. They could hear putty knives grate and sing on the wood. A two-section ladder banged all around the house. And I guess Bryant was still on the divan eating orange meat from the peel when Bob and Eugenia came back downstairs for a dinner of

chili and corn bread. Bryant scraped out the bread pan with
his knife and rolled the crumbs into a cornball. And Eugenia
said, "I tried on stitched aprons in a Hennessey dry goods store
and asked the ladies their opinions while letting it slip that I'd
just divorced a brute of a man named Harry Jones in the
Dakota Territory and that the settlement was substantial
enough to buy and repair this homestead. You've never seen
such pity."

Bryant grinned. "Ain't she the cleverest woman, Bob?"

My brother banged his spoon down and said, "When I'm
gone this house is off limits, Charley. I don't want you anywhere near her. Soon as you're gone I'll probably throw your
plates in the compost heap."

Bryant merely smiled.

Bob poured coffee from the pot at the stove and lifted the
apron hanging there. "What are these supposed to be on the
pockets, Easter lilies?"

She looked and turned back to the table. "Yes."

He let the apron drop. "Don't wear it. It gives me the
shivers."

After Bryant left that night, Bob hauled inside what he'd
piled on the wagon: a spindle rocker and two pink-flowered
lamps, a wedding-ring quilt, a trivet, a peach crate stuffed with
wadded newspaper and 1848 New York crystal. Also two books
of poetry, one by Tennyson, one by Longfellow; a fountain
pen and an inkwell; a valuable silver set made by Paul Revere,
a drop-leaf cherry wood table, and a fine authentic oil painting
depicting Venus and the four seasons.

He said, "This is better than money can buy, Miss. You
don't see finery around these parts like this. Do you? The
answer is no. This is San Francisco quality; every blessed
piece."

And they sat naked on top of the sheets upstairs with warm
champagne and a white candle burning orange on a chair seat.
She asked, "Do you enjoy having people afraid of you?"

"Yes."

"Did you like your father better than your mother?"

"Yes."

"Is Emmett your favorite brother?"

"Yes."

"Umm. If you had a choice would you rather live in the city or the country?"

He poured champagne into his crystal glass and put the bottle down on the floor. He drank the champagne looking at her. "City. New Orleans maybe. Next to the ocean."

"Do you dream about me?"

"Sometimes."

"Am I naked?"

"Yes."

She smiled and kissed him on the shoulder. She got off the bed and poured the rest of the bottle into her glass and blew out the candle on the chair seat. "When you're inside me what does it feel like?"

He looked down into his glass and finished off what was there. "Ask me another question."

Eugenia stared out the tall windows. The wind was teasing the curtains. She rolled the glass against her cheek. "Okay. Spend some time on this. Don't give just a short answer. What do you think about when you're alone?"

He rocked forward with a pillow mashed in his face, worrying it and muttering. Then he drank from her champagne glass and shut his eyes. "How famous I'm going to be. How it's just around the corner." He opened his eyes as if that were enough.

"Amplify," she said.

He shouted, *"How famous I'm going to be. How—"*

"Idiot," she said.

He kissed her hand and put his head on her thigh and brushed the blond bangs from her forehead. "My name's going to be in all the New York and Chicago and Denver papers; boys who only saw me once will say we worked a hay baler together, and Easterners who never stepped in a cow pie will make up adventures about me for Beadle's Half-Dime Library. I'll be as important as Jesse James and soon as I'm dead they'll steal my clothes and auction off my pistols and strangers will visit my grave. I'm looking forward to it."

She sat there in the dark.

He said, "Do you want me to ask you questions now?"

He never told me what they were.

9 They honeymooned all that summer. They'd sleep until ten and swim naked in Canton Lake and sit on a yellow porch-glider at dusk. They didn't even farm. But they put tables in the front yard for a cookout in July and the whole of the Dalton gang was there: Bob, Eugenia, Julia, myself; and Doolin, Broadwell, Powers; Bitter Creek Newcomb and his buddy Charlie Pierce; Blackface Charley Bryant came with Miss Jean Thorne, and the black cowpuncher Amos Burton brought three prostitutes from Dover who ate their suppers on the back porch and later walked into the crab apple tree shade with the cowhands.

That was diamondback rattlesnake country. Newcomb and Broadwell stuffed their pants in their boots and hunted dry coulees and burnt ground and the stone rubble of hills with forked sticks and gunnysacks and they came back at two o'clock with a dozen live snakes that Broadwell dangled over the chopping block so they could strike and flutter their tongues before he lopped off their heads with a hatchet. Powers skinned them and Doolin fried them up and we ate them with scrambled eggs and strawberries on biscuits until the sun was glinting in the leaves of the trees and our black shadows were long in the grass. Eugenia stood at the head of the table and lifted a glass of warm tea. "Here's to robbery," she said.

Newcomb and Pierce went out back to the shed where they practiced leaping from the tin roof onto their saddles. Doolin and Broadwell arm-wrestled, the loser having his fist slammed into a plate of butter, Broadwell red-faced and grunting, Doolin laughing in that odd way of his, "Hayuk hayuk *hayuk*." And Julia sat across from gentleman Bill Powers as he resined up his bow. He said, "My tomatoes burned up in the sun this year. Cornstalks went brown and shredded apart before they'd reached my knee. I chopped the heads off thirteen rattlers out by the privy. Walked everywhere with a hoe and was glad I never married. It's too dry in the West for gardens."

Julia looked especially genteel in that rough company. She had a parasol she stayed under for most of the hot afternoon and she gingerly lifted the hem of her white dress whenever she walked through the grass. My brother and I sat at the table playing checkers and she sat very quietly next to me while Eugenia sketched her with a copy of *The Woman's Home Companion* that she was using to fan herself. I'd jump a checker and king myself and Bob would lean to gaze at Miss Moore's drawing pad. "That's very accomplished," he said.

Eugenia wiped charcoal off her fingers with her shirttail. "Julia's easy to draw. She sits still so long. Most people shift around all the time."

I said, "She got rid of all that when she was younger."

And Bob said, "You know, that's really something to comment on, Julia. How'd you get grown-up so fast?"

"Are you teasing?"

"No! I swear you've got ten years on me."

"You're *very* mature," said Miss Moore.

She turned to me. "They're making fun of me, aren't they."

"Nope. I think that's genuine."

She smiled shyly at Miss Moore. "I can be awfully holy sometimes."

Then it was dark and everything broke up and Charlie Pierce drove Julia home in a surrey he'd sold to someone in Kansas.

Blackface Charley had hired a buckboard to escort Miss Jean Thorne there and that was how I came to visit the Rock

Island Hotel in Hennessey. I sat on the hard boards of the wagon-back, swinging my legs while Bryant hunched forward on the bench seat with his shirt collar pushed up where his scar was. He'd blotted ladies' facial powder on it and it gave him a chalky look. He had a mean-looking canker sore pulling his lip awry.

It was ten at night by the time we hitched the team in Hennessey. There were paper balloons in the shape of donkeys tied to the hitching racks. Railroad flares were spitting and spewing in the street and some salesmen who were meeting at the Rock Island Hotel were pitching them back and forth at each other. The railroad men stood watching with their hands in their overalls.

Bryant took Miss Thorne to sit with him on a bench at the depot and I sat on the chintz furniture in the hotel parlor reading the newspapers.

A big blond man in chalk-striped pants and vest came out of his room and locked the door. He had the sleeves rolled up on his white shirt and a cowlick he'd tried to wet down. He must've weighed two hundred pounds. He asked the proprietor for the night register and wrote down all the names in a pocket notebook. He pointed to me. "Who's that?"

Mr. Thorne told him he didn't know.

The marshal stood on the parlor rug with both hands in his pockets. "What's your name?"

I was reading about a farm boy named McLaughlin in Tulsa who knew how to make a baseball sink when he pitched it. "Charlie McLaughlin," I said. "How's your day been?"

He ignored that. "Where you from?"

"You ever heard of Liberal, Kansas?"

"I was city marshal of Woodsdale when they were battling Hugoton over the Stevens County seat."

"Well, it's near there all right."

He read from his pocket notebook. "How come you aren't registered?"

"I just come here to read the papers." I folded it up and walked out.

I saw Bryant sitting on a pile of railroad ties alone while brakemen walked along the tops of boxcars, turning the brake-release wheels. I didn't ask why Miss Thorne had left him. I just told him that Deputy Marshal Ed Short was in town and he'd better stay somewhere else. So he rode east to Mulhall where his brother Jim had a homestead, but there the same man kept walking his horse by the house day in and day out and Bryant figured him for a detective, so he took off again and stayed until late July in the cow camp at Buffalo Springs.

Mr. Short was a hired gun who got federal money from Chief Marshal William Grimes for policing the second judicial district. Short had put on spectacles and read through the files of outlaws that a deputy marshal named Christian Madsen kept in the Guthrie courthouse, and Short matched the cowboy from Texas called Blackface Charley Bryant with the train robber at Wharton described by the fireman and engineer of the Santa Fe–Texas Express. So he'd rented an office in Hennessey and lived at the Rock Island Hotel where a drifter had told him Bryant had a sweetheart, and Short rode west on a regular basis to sit on his horse with binoculars and see an acre away the white-painted two-storey house that he'd been informed now belonged to the wanted man's sister, Daisy. I guess Short never saw my brother. Bob was savvy that way.

By August the four or five or six of us at the dugout had wild vegetables and stray calf to eat and Doolin and I would sit by the river at night fishing for bullhead with bamboo poles while the others squatted around a bonfire and passed a brown jug, playing spoons on their knees while Powers played fiddle. I visited Julia just once, for a Saturday evening of doing nothing, which is what I could afford. She wore a yellow dress with a lace collar and we threw yarn balls at the cameos on the piano. I stuck a knife in a tree from ten feet away and I sat in the dirt while she sat in the swing and she wet my hair down and middle-parted it. She asked me questions about Miss Moore but she was still in a snit about her. Julia thought I was being corrupted. I was nineteen years old; she was eighteen.

By August, Bryant looked awful. There was green in his eyes and his skin was yellow and he couldn't hold a supper down. Whenever I saw him he had a washrag over his face and his hands at his crotch, rocking from side to side on his bedroll. The disease had infected his brain too, and he'd sulk under a tree and contort his mouth as if he were yelling at hecklers in his own private saloon. Then he'd explode to his feet and dash out into the sun and punch his fists very rapidly, then walk back to his seat and repeat the brawl over and over until Pierce or Powers shook him.

He left for Mulhall and his brother's doctor on August 1st, a pint of whiskey that was hot as Tabasco beneath his shirt, his legs tied to the saddle. But he fainted and almost choked on his vomit before he spurred his horse up onto the wooden porch of the hotel in Hennessey and yelled for the hostess to fetch him.

He was carried to an upstairs room and Miss Thorne gave him a pan bath. Then, while a local physician attended him, she walked across the street to what was once a lawyer's office. Ed Short had a checkered dinner napkin spread on his desk and his revolver disassembled under the light of a kerosene lantern. He raised his eyes to the woman in the doorway.

"He's here," said Miss Jean Thorne.

The next morning she walked into Bryant's room with a tray of breakfast under a white hand towel. He was flat on his back in bed with his Winchester against his leg on the blankets. All he moved was his eyes.

"I don't think I can eat," he said.

She left the door open and set the tray down on a bureau and then United States Deputy Marshal Ed Short appeared in the doorway in a black suit, his gray hat held over a pistol.

"We're going to Wichita, Charley."

Short took Bryant's rifle and put his six-shooter in his suit-coat pocket. He let him use the bedpan and wash himself in the basin, then handcuffed him and pushed the limping man into the hallway where the pregnant girl who cleaned rooms was wiping lamp smoke off the ceiling. Short and Bryant stayed in the deputy marshal's office that night, eating chicken gizzards, playing cribbage. And on the afternoon of August 3rd, a crowd followed the two men to the Hennessey depot and stood behind them as they sat on the bench awaiting the northbound train. A tall man with a stationary face told Short he'd heard the Daltons were going to stage a desperate rescue. Short said, "Let 'em try." Then the train came chuffing in and they boarded with two coach tickets.

The train stopped again at Enid and Bryant asked to have a cigarette, so they both walked forward to sit in the smoking car. Short rolled one for Bryant and one for himself and then he looked around at the smokers on the parlor furniture: men with handlebar mustaches and dark suits and derbies, reading newspapers or the Bible. One opened a pocket watch and snapped it shut. The cars banged forward into a roll and the tobacco smoke grew toward the opened tops of the windows where it was sheared off by the breeze. The men were staring at Bryant, who had to raise up both manacled hands to take the cigarette out of his mouth.

"They're gawking at my face," said Bryant. He turned his shirt collar up.

"They never seen a murderer before."

"That's just the excuse. It's my scar they're staring at."

He said that so loud the men turned their heads away.

When they'd smoked their cigarettes down, Short stubbed them both out on the floor and told Bryant to stand. They lurched down through two swaying, vestibuled Pullmans until they got to a baggage car that he hammered with his fist. "You won't be so uncomfortable here," said Short.

A slot opened and closed and then the baggage door slid and Short pushed Bryant inside. A bald man in suspendered trousers and a yellowed union suit that was stained with food near the buttons sat down on a chair next to a trunk. He had an inch-long beard along his jaw.

Short handed across his own revolver. "I left his rifle in the coach. Can you watch him while I get it?"

"Wasn't doin' much anyways, Ed."

The man put Short's revolver in a mail sorter over his head. Bryant sat down on a box with his hands between his knees. He rocked calmly with the train. With his mind focused he wasn't crazy at all. He said, "This scar come from when I was a four-year-old child. Slept too near the stove and my mother tripped over me one morning."

The baggage man looked. "Ain't hardly noticeable at all." He cut a chunk of barbwire with a tinsnips and stapled the wire to a board.

"That a hobby, is it?"

"My barbwire collection."

"I bet you get plenty of examples, travelin' as much as you do."

The baggage man faced a board of twelve strands towards Bryant. "You an old cowhand?"

Bryant squinted. "That top one's a Kelly with a staple barb."

"Patented 1868. What's this one?"

Bryant got up from the box and walked over. "Hell, that's just a Glidden barb on two wires."

"When was it patented?"

"How am I supposed to know that?"

"*I* do: 1874. I've made a regular study of this," the baggage man said.

"That last one I can't get at all."

The baggage man looked down. "This one? This is what they call an A. Ellwood spread."

Bryant kicked the board away and snatched Short's pistol out of the pigeonhole. He snapped the hammer back and slumped down on top of the trunk. He was panting with just that little movement. "Don't you stir now. You just continue with what you were doing. I don't have no reason at all to hurt you yet."

"Well, it'd serve me right for being so stupid."

Bryant gasped for air and wiped his face inside his sleeve. The baggage man said, "I wouldn't've suspected you was so sick."

"I'm as bad off as a man can be and not have maggots in his nose. Each morning when I wake up alive, I'm surprised. That's why I needed the gun. I can't stand the suspense anymore."

"This your last roundup, is it?" the baggage man said.

Short bumped back through the cars with Bryant's Winchester at carry. A black porter stood on the platform between the Pullman and the baggage car holding a step stool against his knee. Short took his hat off and leaned out into the air. His blond hair blew flat on his head.

"What's the next stop?"

"Waukomis. About two minute away."

Blackface Charley Bryant heard Short's voice, shoved the baggage door open, lifted the deputy marshal's revolver up. "You should *see* the surprise on your face, Mr. Short."

Short glared at him, then swung Bryant's rifle up to his hip and fired it just as Bryant pulled the trigger of Short's revolver. It sounded like two doors slamming, and all the air was blue. Bryant was flung back against the steel of the car; Short staggered back a step with a dark hole in his vest that he brushed at like it was food crumbs. Bryant grimaced and started to sag down and the deputy marshal shot him again and Bryant sat down hard.

Bryant saw his legs twitching and the urine making a stain on his pants but his back was broken and the nerves were dead: his pain was small as heartburn. He closed his eyes and lowered the pistol and Short took him for dead. Short leaned against the railing with blood oozing through his vest and saw the depot a quarter-mile ahead with women in bustles on the dock. He pushed away to drag his prisoner out of the doorway and spare the women's eyes, but he hadn't walked a half a yard before Bryant lifted his pistol again and fired five explosions, even clicking the trigger through three empty cartridges before he let the pistol drop to his lap.

Short slammed back against the Pullman door with the blasts and took bullets in his lung, his liver, his kidney, his spleen. Smoke rolled between the cars and sucked out as the brakes screeched on the rails. The porter and the conductor were crouched at the end of the Pullman and passengers knelt on the floor. The baggage man shoved the baggage door wide and wrenched the pistol from Bryant's hand and dragged him back by the collar of his shirt and kicked his head until it was soft, shouting, "You bastard!" over and over again.

Short heaved forward from the Pullman car and walked across the platform and into the baggage car. (I've never heard of a stronger man.) The front of his suit was blood. "Let's lay him up on this trunk," he said.

The baggage man stared at him, disbelieving. Short bent for Blackface Charley Bryant's trouser cuffs and the baggage man took his shoulders and they lifted the body up that way. The dead man's eyes were closed and blood slid out of his mouth like saliva.

Short said, "I'm pretty woozy," and sat himself down on the board floor. Then he leaned on his elbow and sagged against the trunk. He shut his eyes. "Have you ever rode a horse hard for two days without sleep and laid yourself down on a feather bed?"

When the train stopped in Waukomis he was dead.

**10** That summer Grattan Dalton spent in a California jail. Railroad detective Will Smith came by his cell in middle May with an Oklahoma paper. He put on spectacles and read aloud the accounts of the Wharton train robbery. The coward Ransom Payne was one of the quoted witnesses. Smith folded his spectacles up and said,

"I've been puzzling it in my mind but I can't figure out why your brothers would do such a thing when you got a jury trial coming up. Seems to me that might prejudice the court just a little."

Grat lay on his mattress with his hands behind his head. He said, "Maybe there wasn't nothing better to do. Maybe choir practice was canceled."

Smith walked six cells down to where Bill Dalton was reading a law book, his finger moving under the words. Smith inquired about Bill's family and his upcoming trial but my brother started reciting aloud from the text until the detective left.

Bill had so many friends in the county it seemed unlikely to the prosecution that they'd convict him for anything, so they let him out after the arraignment. It was not so with Grat. His trial for "assault to commit robbery" at Alila was held in the Tulare County courthouse in Visalia on June 18, 1891. His attorney, Breckinridge, walked into the courtroom reading his law clerk's brief for the first time. He shook hands with the prosecution and several Southern Pacific executives in the gallery, whispering something and laughing longer than they did. He sat down next to Grat, smelling of witch hazel. Grat's hair was shaved off because of lice in the jail pillows. His ears stuck out; his face was pale. He wore a white shirt that was too big for him and a tie he'd already unknotted.

"Are you nervous at all?" Breckinridge asked.

"I learned the tiniest bit about the law from being a marshal in the Oklahoma Territory and I know for a fact you can't convict an accessory unless you've got one of the supposed principals arrested. I don't see how this trial can last longer than afternoon."

"Stranger things have happened," said Breckinridge, and he unfastened the clasps on his briefcase.

The trial lasted three weeks and defense lawyer Breckinridge arose from his chair in objection no more than a dozen.

times. He did not cross-examine Smith or the óther detectives. He accepted Bob's worn spurs as exhibits, also the plug horses said to have been used for the getaway, even the locomotive engineer's identification that Grat must've been the robber because he was "similar in size."

In July, Breckinridge came in from a lunch recess blowing off his mustache comb. "I just had the best chicken and dumplings I've ever tasted."

"Good," said Grat. "Appears to me you needed the energy."

Breckinridge glared at him. "The way to handle this case is to simply ride it out. Let the prosecution make all the mistakes. We'll get a mistrial on the rules of evidence alone."

"Maybe I'm just the least little bit cranky because a lawyer named John Ahern told me I was being jobbed. He said the Southern Pacific Railroad made you a wealthy man."

"That's nonsense."

My brother scratched the itch in his hands. His knuckles were big as steelies. "Them are my sentiments too, Mr. Breckinridge. You shoulda heard me defend your honorable self from them lies. I was danged vociferous."

On July 7th, the jury found Grattan Dalton guilty as charged. Breckinridge stood at once to say he'd appeal the verdict to the Supreme Court of California. He packed his briefcase and Southern Pacific Detective Will Smith stepped over the oak fence toward Grat with a handkerchief at his cheek. "I told you I'd land you," he said.

Sentencing was July 29th, then postponed until September 21st so the court reporters could type transcripts for the appeal.

So Grat was kept that summer in a sweltering jail cell with a slat bed and gray wool blanket and chamber pot and water pitcher. He'd read the Visalia *Weekly Delta* until his eyes hurt (not long), and then he'd just sleep on top of his bed and feel the sweat roll down his ribs; or he'd stand at the jail bars at night and spit chewing tobacco as some of the other prisoners made women of each other.

After Bryant's death, Bob and Eugenia both left the Hennessey house to travel east, Miss Moore attending the funeral at Mulhall for the gang, then proceeding to the Oklahoma town of Wagoner thirty-five miles southeast of Tulsa. There she posed as a female reporter for *Harper's Weekly*, sent there to gather articles about the territory and the end of the frontier and the last of the Old West gangs. She'd step timidly into a bank and sit on the edge of the chair in the bank president's office, taking notes like a college girl. She had lunch with a railroad official who got tomato soup in his beard, and a senior man with the express company escorted her to a Sunday Chautauqua lecture on the lessons of ancient Greece. She sat in the shade with a parasol and he bought her lemonade. "I find you beautiful," he said.

She hired a one-horse cab to drive her four miles north to a railroad depot at Leliaetta where she sat at the one bench with a heavily mustached telegraph operator who kept brushing flies from his face. His eyebrows were black as electrician's tape.

He showed her the water tower and track switch and coal yard and the telegraph lines with the porcelain insulators. He leaned against a tall semaphore blackened with coal dust. "Leliaetta's just a flag stop. If there's danger of any kind or mail to be picked up or passengers, well this here blade with the red glass lens is swung in front of the hanging lantern and the train stops."

She wrote that down like her brain was a little lame. "So red means stop," she said.

"That's right." He tapped the blade with the green lens. "Otherwise I throw the green and the train just has to hesitate some till it clears the city limits."

"Green means go."

He sighed. "But this is where it gets complicated. Since the
Dalton gang's been boarding trains and causing such a ruckus
we switched everything around." He stuck his hands in his
pockets and gazed down the rails. "The engineer blows a
whistle before he rounds that bend. I take a look around the
place and if I put up the *green* blade, then the *red*, that means
I haven't seen any outlaws and he can brake for the mail." He
stared at her. "This must be confusing as heck to a woman."

"But you explain it very well."


Bob rode across the range with Pierce and Newcomb and
they came to the dugout in a September rain that fell so hard
it dented hats. Doolin, Powers, Broadwell, and I stood under a
cottonwood tree with slickers on and water on our faces or
wool blankets draped over our heads. Broadwell had his cat
Turtle inside his shirt. He blew cigarette smoke in its face.
Amos Burton had gone to Dover the week before to dally with
some colored ladies and we never saw him again until 1892.

Bob had on the white slicker he wore when he rustled
horses in winter. His hat was so heavy with rain the brim was
sunk down past his ears and nose and he had to tilt his head
back to see us. He smiled. "How about robbing another
train?"

We made a canopy with four tree limbs and a blanket and
cooked a pot of Doolin's herbal tea over a smoking fire. As was
the habit with sod huts, mine was dissolving in the rain. Water
dripped through the grass and earth of the roof and plunked
on the bunks and stove like coffee and coffee grounds. So we
squatted outside in the rain and discussed the Missouri, Kansas, and Texas Railroad, also known as the MK&T and the
Katy. The summer cotton crops were being sold and the
money carried to banks in Fort Worth and Dallas. A gang of
men could take it, he said. Eugenia had already collected the
particulars and would report the next afternoon. Doolin listened for a while, then got out kettles to collect rainwater

since the river tasted of gypsum and spoilt his cakes and bread loaves.

The rain wore itself out by the next morning and we spent the afternoon inside a dugout that was crossed with a clothes-line of drying socks and shirts and long underwear. Newcomb peeled sweet corn and shook the garden dirt from his onions, green peppers, and lettuce, and spread them out on a table for the feast commemorating our return to the train-stopping business.

I squatted naked on the bank of the Canadian River with a razor and leather strop and a spotted piece of mirror while Bob and Doolin and Powers dunked themselves in the brown water and scrubbed pretty hard with soap. Powers was white as ala-baster except for his face and hands; Bob was brown all over from swimming naked with Miss Moore. Dick Broadwell slid naked down the bank, his good clothes folded over his arm, a brush and mug in his right hand. He said, "Lookit Doolin out there staring at his pecker." He shouted, "What'd'ya doin', Bill, trolling?"

Doolin smiled. "I can always hope for a nibble."

Broadwell waited until my razor was next to my lathered cheek; then he slapped me on the thigh. "Emmett, my boy! Good to see ya!"

I said, "You can get sort of wearisome, Dick."

My brother stood ankle deep and grinned at Dick as he dried himself. "We're gonna have ourselves a wild fandango, aren't we?"

"Can I dance cheek-to-cheek with her, Bob?"

Powers swam out into the river and floated on his back to the bullrushes.

At dusk I sat on the sod roof with the binoculars to my eyes while the others squatted outside with cigarettes, passing a mirror and comb around. My brother said, "I don't want any rough talk or lewd suggestions or taking the Lord's name in vain. Remember how you were taught to act around ladies."

Then Miss Moore arrived and seven beaming men stood

with their hats in their hands and white shirts and neckties on and their hair slicked down with rose oil.

Bob picked her up and swirled her around and they kissed for two or three minutes while the gang whistled and made noises. I ducked inside to stoke the stove and I could hear Bob making introductions again in case she'd forgotten names. After that she came inside and gave me a hug and a sisterly kiss. I think she wanted to tousle my hair but I had too much size for it.

I fried plank steaks of deer meat and Doolin cooked the rest of the meal with underwear tied on his head like a chef's hat. Then we sat outside in the cool breeze and Miss Moore discussed Leliaetta and the farmhouse she'd just rented in Woodward for the winter. Bob dealt out cards to indicate who would do what on the job and Powers got out his fiddle and bow. Bob clapped his hands and did the calling for "Turkey in the Straw" and some Virginia reels and Broadwell and Pierce danced with each other, interweaving with Newcomb and Eugenia.

Then Bob and his woman retired to spend the night indoors with two bunks pushed together while six men slept on bedrolls under the white moon. It was near autumn but what we heard were summer noises: frogs at the river and crickets in the grass and cicadas rattling out of shells that looked like brown blisters on the trees. Night birds dived and swooped.

Newcomb said, "Bob's a lucky devil, ain't he."

Powers rolled away to his side.

"This is a hell of a life," said Pierce.

I watched the lightning bugs turn green-gold in part of the night and then green-gold someplace else. I remembered what Julia had said about her crying into a pillow, and I wanted to be rich very soon.

For an hour on the evening of September 15, 1891, seven men in black raincoats sat with their horses under cottonwood trees across from the depot in Leliaetta. Three of them smoked cigarettes; Broadwell sat on a tree stump cleaning the glass lenses of his dust goggles with the blue bandana he'd wear. I hunched up on my saddle cantle with my ankles crossed over the horn, tapping tobacco into paper. The horses shook their reins and pulled what green weeds they could; then they just stood there with the dumb-animal stares, sliding their jaws, tails whisking from side to side. Powers leaned forward with his calabash pipe to squint down the railroad tracks; then he and Bob chucked their horses and skidded them down to the siding where a black man and woman were walking on the cinders with a pail.

They both wore shawls on their heads and the woman's right eye was milky with a cataract. The old man stayed two feet behind the woman, touching her coat with his hand.

Bob kept under his coat collar; Powers tipped his hat to the lady. "Lookin' for something?"

She gripped the pail with both hands. The old man slowly looked up. He wore glasses but one of the lenses was gone. She said, "This old man and me, we tryin' to find a little stray coal to warm the shanty up. We be camped over yonder by the sidin' and the hawk been talkin' awful bad. Get measly cold in the night."

The old man asked, "You gentlemen be wantin' a man for a job of woik?"

"Nothing you could handle," said Powers. "But you go on up the track to the gantlet and see if you don't find some coal after the express goes through."

After they'd gone, Bob said, "You did good, Bill."

"Thankee."

I licked a cigarette paper and twisted it tight and struck a match off my stirrup. The old woman stared at the red of my cigarette in the dark as they walked along the tracks. Broadwell lifted his saddletree to ventilate his horse, then tightened the cinch again. Newcomb climbed off his horse, complaining. "What's he doin', talkin' to niggers?" He spread a big raincoat that was long as his heels and unbuttoned his pants and leaned his hand against a box elder. Our saddle leather creaked. Somewhere in the dark town a dog barked. Doolin said, "My back hurts." My brother and Powers stayed down at the siding. The cinders crunched as the horses picked their shoes up and put them down again. I watched the depot where a man had been bent over a desk all night, turning the pages of a book and penciling in all the closed letters, every a, e, g, o, b, d, q, and p.

Bob stabbed his spurs and his horse clambered over the tracks and trotted along the siding to the semaphore with Powers skirting beside him with a forked branch he'd stripped and whittled on our ride over.

The station attendant glanced at the pendulum clock behind him, then walked from his desk, opened the door, and stood on the loading platform, scanning, three wide boards between his boots. Two mail sacks sat on the trolley. Bob and Powers had their gloved hands clamped over their horses' noses not fifty yards away but the attendant's eyes didn't get used to the dark before he heard the smokestack of the train and started to close the depot door behind him. Then he stopped and saw the five of us in the trees across from the loading platform and he gave us one of the most comical faces of shock I've ever seen before he slammed the door and bolted it.

I saw him sidestep around his desk and then he was out of sight. Pierce twittered like a bobolink and Powers shoved up the green blade of the semaphore with his branch and held it there until the train got to the tall white whistle signpost and the steam whistle cord was pulled. Then he let the blade drop and the depot's air pressure semaphore swung up and the danger blade glowed ruby in front of the lantern. But the engineer had already seen the green and the locomotive started braking.

My brother put my binoculars down and the solemn man beside him said, "You got yourself a good woman."

"You bet."

The five of us still in the dark of the trees coaxed our horses down the incline. Mine had tugged the leaves off an elm tree but it didn't think much of the taste.

Doolin said, "Bryant's dead now. Let's have no wanton murder."

My brother urged his horse and it knocked up onto the wooden stairs and across the loading platform to the door. The kerosene lantern inside the depot had been snuffed. My brother got off his horse and stood next to the door, his pistol next to his cheek. "Hey? Hey, I'd like you to live through this." He heard a desk drawer slide open and closed. He heard the desk chair squeal.

Meanwhile Newcomb and I took positions on the east side of the tracks, Broadwell and Pierce on the west. There we lifted blue bandanas over our noses and backed our horses up as the bell clanged and the whistle went off again and I got the scares like you do when you're next to monster machines. The locomotive was black and hot and big as a shoe store. The cowcatcher had tumbleweed in it and the front lamp was grimy and spattered with insects. Smoke rolled brown out of the tall stack and tore apart gray in the trees and white steam climbed out of pipes and jets and nozzles everywhere. My horse jerked its head from the steam as from a bad smell. I held my ears at the noise and watched the steel rails squash down on the ties and then lift up spikes and squash down under the wheels again. The tender and express car and baggage car creaked by and the train jolted to a stop with me facing the single Pullman. There wasn't a dining car or smoking parlor, just three more coach cars and a caboose. I saw a woman standing next to a Pullman window lifting a blue-veined breast with the back of her hand. Her baby lost the long maroon nipple and jerked around until he found it again.

Doolin had crouched down next to the blackened switch with his pistol between his legs. Then he ran gawkily some forty feet until he could snag a boot on the cab ladder and bang on up the steps. Bob just stood on the platform like a passenger, his pistol hanging from his left hand, and stepped out onto a fender, lifting up his mask. The stoker had been about to carry coal to the boiler. He banged his shovel down when he saw Bob's gun.

I observed that and I saw Newcomb masked and on his horse with the sleeves rolled up on his raincoat, his rifle barrel propped on the open platform between the express and baggage cars. I walked my horse along mostly dark passenger cars and to the empty caboose. In order to demonstrate to God and man what a young tough I was, I broke the glass tail lamp with the butt of my pistol and flame tore away from the wick. When I bent I could see the legs of Pierce's and Broadwell's horses. I saw a man walk out on a center coach platform lighting a cigarette. I raised my rifle high over my head and nodded at Newcomb and both of us fired warning shots, as did Broadwell and Pierce, so that it sounded like iron doors banging shut in a house of many rooms. The cigarette dropped off the man's lip as he jumped back inside the coach. There were yells and screams about holdups and the train being robbed. The lights went out in all the cars. Faces disappeared from the windows. Steam leaked out from under the wheels.

Powers walked out of the darkness like a railroad inspector and he used the handrail as he climbed to the fenced platform of the express car. He tried the handle, then kicked the front door four times with the heel of his boot. "This is a robbery! Open up!"

The messenger said, "Not gonna and you can't make me. Every door here is padlocked."

Powers fired three shots through the porch roof overhead. Strips of tar roof flapped up on top of the car.

The messenger said, "You can shoot till doomsday and I ain't gonna open this door."

"Well, I've got some encouragement here in the form of dynamite. Says on the label it'll blow you into the middle of next week."

Bob and Doolin had pushed the engineer and stoker back to the express car by then. Both of the crewmen wore bib overalls and striped caps but the stoker was shirtless and he smelled worse than sparrows burned dead in a chimney. Doolin had the hammer of his pistol cocked and poked down the front of the engineer's overalls and he spoke into his ear like a lover. "Tell your money escort to please, *please* do what we say or I'll blow your sex life to smithereens."

The engineer shouted something convincing and after a minute of dead silence the broad side door rumbled open on its rollers and the messenger backed to his desk. Broadwell trotted his horse up with his rifle back on his shoulder; Bob threw a leg up and climbed in the car and saw canvas sacks and a stove and a wall-long mail sorter and a lunch bucket open on the desk. He lifted the iron plates on the stove and saw it was empty, then threw the latch on the south door. Powers walked in and saw the messenger and punched him in the throat. The man fell to his right knee and almost swallowed his tongue but I guess he came out of it okay.

In the passenger cars the men were throwing up windows and leaning out to see what was going on. Two had pistols in their hands but I could see they were reluctant to risk anything so I didn't pay them no mind and they heavily sat again on their pillowed coach seats. But five or six of the bolder travelers were standing on a platform between coach and Pullman, talking to each other. A man in a bowler hat leaned out on the opened exit door and yelled to me, "What's the name of your gang?"

My horse was prancing and nodding its head and lifting off of its front legs. I could hear Pierce yelling at passengers on his side to get back up the stairs.

The man in the bowler asked, "Is it the Dalton gang?"

A man with a drooping red mustache said, "Oh! How could it be, Manion? That boy's not fifteen years old!"

"Well, the Daltons aren't old as you might think."

"Older than *fifteen*."

"I'm nineteen," I said.

"See there?"

"Don't talk to them," said Newcomb.

Doolin was on his horse when the messenger staggered forward dragging a heavy meal sack between his legs. It was filled to half with silver dollars and it scraped the varnish off the floor. Pierce was at the platform of a rear passenger car yanking a mouthy boy off the stair by his coat collar. Two men leapt from the platform onto the cinders and grabbed for Pierce's raincoat sleeve or his horse's bridle. Pierce looked a little shamefaced at Broadwell and Bob as the men tussled over him, and Broadwell yelled, "You get back inside there this *instant!* Do I have to take a strap to you?"

Then a fat man in a checkered vest pulled a small caliber pistol out of a shoulder holster and stalked toward the masked desperadoes at the express car, and Doolin groaned. "Fools like that just make me tired." He pulled his pistol out of his holster and hauled his horse around. "Watch me make the hair stand up on his neck."

Bob said, "You stick where you're ordered."

But Doolin broke away and whooped and hollered and flourished his pistol and fired it. He galloped his horse straight at the frozen passengers, his raincoat sailing, the front of his hat flopped back. The men scurried out of his way. At the caboose he pulled his reins left and turned his horse around and charged down the train again, jousting. The fat man in the checkered vest sat down in the cinders and covered his face with his elbows, and Doolin kicked off the man's hat with a stirrup. Then he stopped his horse next to Powers, grinning and breathing hard. "Scattered like hens, didn't they."

Powers had the heavy money sack on his shoulder. When he tied it to Doolin's saddle horn, the saddle canted to the side. "Bob's a trifle displeased with you. He said you should carry this."

"Does he think that's the dunce cap or something? Carrying away all the swag?"

"I don't know," said Powers. "I didn't think to ask."

Coming from the rear my horse stalled and stepped across the tracks like a sissy, so I was late getting in front of the locomotive. But I managed to raise my rifle up as Bob hustled the engine crew up to the cab. Broadwell heaved the sliding express door closed and Pierce brought Powers's horse up by the reins.

Bob said to the engineer, "I calculate the MK&T lost about five minutes so you'd better hurry out of here if you want to hit Dallas on time." He stepped off the train onto the depot's loading platform. "Oh, and when you get to the gantlet, slow up and have your firemen shovel off some coal. And don't be too stingy about it or I might introduce you to serious trouble."

Steam hushed and I saw the wheel eccentrics drop and then the five-foot drive wheels started to spin, the couplings gripped in a succession of clanks, and the coaches howled into sway.

Newcomb climbed onto the depot roof from his saddle and jinked along the peak until he found the porcelain insulators and the depot telegraph lines. Don't know why he bothered about them. Maybe it was just meanness. The wires sprang away from his snippers and Newcomb hung by a gutter and dropped back onto his saddle; then he and Bob spurred their horses down the wooden stairs and along the creosote-painted ties behind the rolling train. The fat man in the checkered vest was shaking his fist from the last coach; the old black woman was stooped over at the siding dropping coal into a pail. It was as sweet a picture as you'd ever want to see and it did us no harm at all in that country to rob from the rich and give to the poor. That shovel of coal kept many on our side unto the very end.

The seven of us slept under yellow leaves that night. At five in the morning I sat up smelling coffee and I saw Bob walk up to each man and drop a jangling canvas sack into the leaves near his head. "You look like Santa Claus," I said.

He smiled. "I'll divvy up with you later."

I've said elsewhere the take was nineteen thousand dollars. I reckon it was closer to ten. Divided seven ways it would've come to almost fifteen hundred apiece, but Bob gave the five men of the gang not kin to him wages instead of shares: four hundred dollars for a night's work.

Newcomb walked over to the fire and poured a tin cup of coffee and squatted to count the silver coins and paper money into his hat. "I can't believe this, Bob!"

"Believe what?"

Doolin kept his head on his saddle pillow and stacked the money on the leaves. He glared at Bob. "Where's the rest of it, Dalton?"

"That's the arithmetic," said Bob.

"But I carried that sack," said Doolin. "There must've been three thousand dollars just in silver!"

"There was," said Bob. "And there's also the sod house to supply and Bryant's funeral expenses and implements and tools and payoffs to the local police, plus Jim Riley gets a little something for allowing us his property. You don't give a thought to that."

"Meaning you and Emmett split fifteen thousand dollars," said Pierce.

"I don't know where you're coming up with your numbers. Four hundred dollars times eight—"

"Eight?" asked Doolin.

"Miss Moore," I said.

"Is three thousand two hundred dollars. I counted the spondulix three times and only arrived at three thousand eight hundred and forty-five bucks. The rest was nonnegotiable securities and I fed them to the fire."

"Ah, so that's what you did," said Doolin. "Well then, my mind's completely at rest."

"Heck, when we robbed the Santa Fe at Wharton we

hardly got a hundred twenty-five cutting it just four ways. Ask Bitter Creek if you don't believe me."

Newcomb threw a stick into the fire. "That's right. Didn't last me the summer."

"It's not that profitable an occupation," said Bob. He picked his saddle up by the horn and jammed his hat down and smiled. "It's just that it beats moving longhorns on the prairie and eating sowbelly and beans."


I stuck by my brother, of course, but the others murmured amongst themselves most of the day. The gang slouched in their saddles and rode single file through snatching weeds along the Arkansas, Cimarron, and Canadian rivers until we got to the sod house. I had to break a morning skin of ice to wash in the river; then I shaved in my spotted mirror piece while Doolin cooked a big kettle of whatever food we had left. Bob rolled all his property into his bedroll and tied it to his horse and rode over to the six of us as we squatted with bowls by the fire.

"Adios," my brother said.

"Where the hell you goin'?" Doolin demanded.

"What's it matter?"

"Well, how we gonna get the next job arranged?"

"No such thing as a next job, Bill. Emmett and I are through."

Broadwell swallowed. "Through! Are you loco, Bob? Why, I haven't hardly started yet!"

"You're full of surprises today," said Pierce.

So another argument went on for most of an hour but I didn't say a word and Powers just listened with his eyes closed. I washed out my bowl in the river and put on my cleanest dirty shirt and rolled everything else in my raincoat. I heard Doolin say how the express companies were tying money up in pink and blue baby ribbons and that the gang ought to step up and say thanks for it. I pulled a pack mule from the corral and strapped my tools and boots and whatall onto the carry rack.

When I got on my horse, Bob was saying he didn't give a dang about all the deputies that were crowding on our heels; he wasn't talking about lack of nerve when he said he wanted quit of the gang. He said it was plain horse sense though that you can't keep robbery up for long and get away with it.

Something like that. I wasn't listening very close.

He said, "I'm twenty-one years old and I know my mind. You boys and I have always understood each other and there's no misunderstanding now. This is where Emmett and I call a halt—and you can tie to that."

I said good-bye with some real sadness, and I printed addresses and said we should get together for Thanksgiving. Then Bob and I rode northwest for the Fort Supply reservation and the town of Woodward where Miss Moore had rented a house. I saw the five of them sulking and brooding and loitering near the fire like men in a railroad yard; then Newcomb jerked the Indian blanket from the doorway and Broadwell came out of the sod house with his cat Turtle under his red flannel shirt and Powers crouched through the pole gate of Pierce's corral and saddled up his horse.

By late afternoon it was very cold for September. The sky was cobbled and the river was purple and red leaves floated on it. The wind ruffed the weather hair of cattle bunched at a fence. Mud hoofprints froze hard by nightfall and the knuckles turned red on my hands. I buttoned up a sheepskin and rode ten yards behind my brother until he stopped at Canton Lake.

"Look yonder," he said.

I saw a four-horse team and a wagon far across the water. The white canvas had U.S. GOVT. painted on it and I could see lawmen leaning on rifles and jolting in the box.

"The manhunt," he said. "Remember you and I doing that? Seems like a long time ago."

The wagon was gone in the trees.

"You know what I wish, Bob? I wish I could get a wet rag and scrub the year 1891 clean off the slate. It's been nothing but trouble and misery for nine months now."

"That'll stop," he said. My brother borrowed my tobacco pouch and papers and constructed a cigarette. "Did you get taken in by all I said back there?"

"I'm not exactly sure."

He smiled. "There's three thousand five hundred dollars in each of my saddlebags. Seven thousand dollars, Emmett. How's that for a yearly income?"

I suppose I should've said something about it not being right to short-pot and steal from your friends, of doing unto others, but the words failed me just then.

He said, "I can see you're disappointed in your brother."

I asked, "What'd you do it for, Bob?"

He smirked and nudged his horse ahead and without facing me he shouted, "*Greed*, Emmett darlin'! One of the seven deadly sins!"

11     Grat was still in jail in California. With my brother Bill's considerable help, he'd written several narratives about the abuse and indignities he'd suffered during his incarceration which the San Francisco *Examiner* had published. And he was reading the back pages of that newspaper when he noticed two brief articles reporting the September 15th robbery of a train in Leliaetta in the Oklahoma Territory, and a September 16th robbery of another at Ceres, California, two hundred miles from Visalia.

The Ceres holdup, of course, wasn't ours. A Southern Pacific employee named John Sontag had been hurt pretty badly at work but the railroad wouldn't pay him compensation, so he joined with Chris Evans and pulled some smallish jobs all over the state. My hunch is the Alila train robbery which Grat and Bill were framed with was the Sontag-Evans gang's too. I know that Ceres was. But the Dalton name was famous then and we somehow took the blame for most everything lawless in the forty-four United States.

Grat folded the newspaper to the ads for ten-dollar suits, "made from an honest piece of cassimere." A prison trustee leaned on his mop handle to push a sloshing bucket on rollers down the aisle between the jail cells. He was a huge, slow, black man made forever back-sore from chopping cotton in Sarepta, Louisiana. He stopped at Grat's cell door. "You know the law just hauled in your brothuh Bill again? Wants to ax him some questions about those train holdups."

My brother licked a thumb and turned a page of the newspaper; then he noticed a hacksaw blade under the trustee's foot. Grattan slipped it into an inseam of his trousers while the black man straightened the tongue on his high button shoes.

He said, "You don't have to thank me. I been paid." He dragged his mop behind him, streaking the floor wet; then he was gone.

The jails were not very difficult in those days. My brother sawed the bars at night and covered the damage with lampblack and soap. And after supper on the Sunday evening of September 18th, three days before his prison sentencing, Grat Dalton popped four bars of his window into the gravel outside. They made a *pong* sound when they hit. He stood on his bed and climbed out; then two other prisoners walked from their cells and dropped into the dirt behind him.

From a Baptist church hitching rack, the three of them stole a light buggy and a team of gray horses that were powerful enough to pull a beer truck. At Goshen the two jumped a freight train north while Grat drove ten miles farther to the ranch of a gambler he knew named Middleton. This Middleton was a toothless man who constantly wore the same white shirt that he laundered once a week. He gave Grat his mattress for the night and hitched the buggy and horses back in Tulare to throw the detectives off; then he loaned Grat an

Appaloosa horse and a canvas tent and half his closet of clothes. He sketched a map of the Sierra foothills above the town of Sanger. "I'll be up in about a week with tobacco and fresh meat," said Middleton. "A convict named Riley Dean may be around there already. You have any money for the grub?"

"There's sposed to be a check waiting for me in Visalia."

"Okay. You stay pitched in this vicinity—"

"Where the X is," said Grat.

"So I'll know where to find you."

Grat folded the map inside a blue flannel shirt that had the bacon grease smell of the rancher, pulled down a high round-topped gray hat, and slapped the Appaloosa ahead with the reins.

After he was gone, Middleton rode down to Visalia to read the wanted posters and collect a fifty-dollar check intended for Grat and mailed care of general delivery by Eugenia Moore. He spent it on a desk of twelve drawers and three secret compartments. Then he rapped on the glass of the Tulare County Sheriff's Office and a deputy turned in his chair. Middleton opened the door. "I wonder if you and me could jaw for a bit."

But Grattan was more canny than people gave him credit for. Horse and rider climbed a winding bridle path into thin air, Grat ducking under tall sequoia pine trees, hooking on a mackinaw, cradling a single-action rifle. Then he tore up the map and let it flutter away and swung right instead of left. He said, "What's that fool done to your lungs, horse? You sound just like a freight train."

Afternoons, Grat slept on black earth and blue pine needles, or he fished for trout in a tossed mountain stream that was so cold it made his sinuses ache when he drank it. He whittled forks and spoons out of green wood and hardened them in a fire. In a brand new baking soda can he kept rocks that seemed like animals to him: lion, magpie, buffalo head. At night he lay inside the tent with his hands behind his head, watching cigarette smoke ascend to the canvas and flatten out, or he'd open his trousers up and imagine pasty women and his semen spill would dry crusty on his stomach.

He fried squirrel for breakfast one morning and saw a greyhound that was just ribs and tail slink out from the trees. Grat threw a squirrel strip in the dirt and the dog snatched it down; she broke a hard biscuit in two and coughed on it and Grat poured water into his hat. Then the escapee named Riley Dean walked out of the trees in torn shirt and trousers, a big stick in his hand. "I see you've introduced yourselves," he said. "Do you have food? I've been eating cave bats and that's it. They sit in my stomach like glass paperweights."

My brother hid with Riley Dean until the California winter rains came, which was snow at that altitude. A posse used information supplied by Middleton and risked the weather and crags and cliffs to climb Mill Creek Canyon in search of the two dangerous men. They caught Dean as he waded through drifts in his shirt and trousers.

Grat was with the greyhound hunting a small pocket mirror he'd dropped, when the dog lifted her head and whined. Grat stood and brushed the snow from his knees and heard the creak of a wagon and the cough and rasp of too many horses; and he backed up to the tent as the dog glanced over her shoulder, then back to whatever was down there. Hair stood up on her back as she growled. Grat tied his clothes inside a shirt and shoved what food he had in the pockets and sleeves of the mackinaw, and the dog was barking loudly as he grabbed his canteen and rifle and hurdled over scrub brush and snowcapped tree stumps into a drifted gulley. He heard the greyhound say everything over again to the horses, and he lay on his belly in snow that had yellow grass poking through it. Aspens rattled in the wind; a bird folded its wings and sailed out of the blue sky into the green of the pines. My brother saw the veined legs of roan quarter horses, then heard the springs of a wagon and more horses scrabbling up the stones of the hill.

The dog was talking to them from the white ashes of the fire. Riley Dean was bound and gagged in the wagon. Soon a deputy sheriff and six other men in derby hats stood around the tent with shotguns and rifles carried in two hands like they were abnormally heavy. The sheriff yelled, "We've got you covered, Dalton. Come out of there with your hands up."

Grat sat deep in the snow, roofed by a spread oak, and saw the possemen in their dark suits and fur coats and trousers tucked into Wellington boots. A mustached boy with a long muffler let his shotgun blast the canvas flap and then another gun went off and then all of them were firing. The tent pegs broke and the pelted canvas flapped and gunsmoke reached into the trees. It was loud and then it was quiet and Grat slid down the mountain shale dragging his stuff through the snow. The dog chased after Grat, and a deputy in a string tie stood on the brink of a cliff firing down at the dog and the snatches of mackinaw coat that he saw. Grat crashed through snow-heavy bramble and dodged between trees and after he sloshed across a flashing stream he sat against the mud bank and looked up. Aspen leaves were curling with the smoke and the posse was shooting every which way. Then they must've lost heart because the shooting stopped and Grat never saw the posse again.

The dog limped to the other side of the stream. Her front right paw had been destroyed by a bullet. Blood had splashed up on the dog's face.

"You stay there, you hear? Don't follow me. Stay."

The dog sat down in the snow and licked at her blood. Grat made slings for the rifle and the canteen and walked eighteen miles in cold, squelching boots, through flannelbush and larkspur and vertical shafts of sunlight, until he got to a flatlands farm in Harmon's Valley where a man with a neck beard named Judd Elwood was squatted against a fence post peeling the brown skin off an apple and into a paper sack. He had a two-horse team harnessed to traces and a heavy logging chain that was wrapped around an axe-trimmed sequoia. He

turned when he heard Grat walk out of the forest and he
looked on a mountain man, all coat and stubble and broad
hat pulled down on his head, his rifle at slant on his arm.

"Did a posse stop by here the other night?" Grat asked.

The farmer squatted in snow and looked at the axe still
stuck in the tree. "I suppose it was you they was cross with."

Grat said, "Unhook your team and strip the harness off
that near horse."

The farmer grumbled and slammed his apple into the
paper sack and did as he was told. My brother then stole a
frozen gunnysack from the farmer's shed and jars of preserves
from the farmhouse cellar, dust puffing out from the sack when
he tossed the plunder in.

So he could find out about himself, Grat rode the farmer's
horse from Merced to Tulare on the dirt road that is now
concrete and Highway 99 and traveled by black Chevrolet
coupes at 35 miles per hour. He had a skunk smell to him, his
scalp hair was knotted, and his bristle beard had yellow seeds
in it, so he could clomp down the board sidewalks of Tulare,
raincoat over his mackinaw, and not be recognized by anyone
but kin. Sheriffs stepped out of his way.

That afternoon a boy ran up to him with a note telling
him to situate himself in the rear of a blue hotel that night.
There he discovered an Indian pony with saddlebags crammed
with hard biscuits and beef jerky and three canteens on the
saddle horn. He gazed up to a second-storey window and
nodded to my brother Bill who sat by a kerosene lamp.

Grat hammered thick plate shoes on his horse at Bakers-
field, the cowboy capital, and he took the Tehachapi trail for
Barstow and the Mojave desert, thence to Needles and across
Arizona, New Mexico, and Texas, sleeping afternoons in caves
or in the tangled shade of mesquite or Joshua trees, feeding on
fence lizards, salamanders, greasy peccary and drinking sulphur water. The land was bare as worn carpet except for the
balls of tumbleweed and the animal carcasses and the purple
mountains in the distance. He'd see strands of smoke from

Hopi and Navaho fires fifteen miles away, but by the time he got there the cooking stones would be cool, the wickiups would be empty, and vicious travois dogs would bark and lunge at his horse. Sheep would stare as he slumped by at night; rattlesnakes would stab at his stirrups and flop down to squirm under sagebrush; small tarantulas crawled over his face to drink water from his eyes as he slept.

He lost thirty-two pounds, pried out an aching tooth with his dinner fork, blistered both heels so far down to the bone that he could pour blood when he took off his boots. I suppose Grat's brain cracked just a bit with aloneness because he invented a cowboy named Dangerous Dan who supposedly rode an albino mule and caught turtledoves in his hands and talked to Grat about railroads and how they were going to get even. "Old Dan, he was good company," said Grat. His journey from California to Oklahoma took one hundred and seven days.

**12** My brother Bill was in the Oklahoma Territory by then. Soon after Grat escaped, the railroad detectives uncovered evidence that seemed to put the blame for the Ceres train robbery on the Sontag-Evans gang and might even have implicated them in the three previous holdups. Given those circumstances, the Tulare County district attorney thought a second conviction of a Dalton might be difficult and he ordered my brother Bill, twenty-eight years old, released on his own recognizance.

Bill returned to his farm near Paso Robles for the harvest, then took a hotel room in Tulare and sat on its blue porch in a spindle-back chair, whittling dolls' heads and gaining an audience with talk: "Making these for my girls," he said. "Not like when I was a boy. When I grew up we were so poor we couldn't pay attention." Nervous laughter. "I said, 'Momma, I don't have nothin' to play with,' so she chopped the bottoms off my pockets." They chuckled. "Told my dad I wanted a watch for Christmas—so he let me." Somebody giggled; other men hooted. "Not that I learned anything. I was so dumb back then I thought girls were just bumpy boys." And so on.

I personally find talk like that tiresome, but the Tulare menfolk laughed and laughed and Bill would grin along with them. He'd have the porch chairs filled and men sitting on the hitches, and then he'd spice his ramble with sermons about politics and the railroad and at sundown stand up and stretch. "Oh me, but I'm tired. I feel like I've been rode hard and put away wet." Like as not a man would then buy him supper and whatever liquor he wanted in a saloon. And down the block there'd be a man in a gray vested suit and brown shoes with a pistol in a sweat-black shoulder holster and a Southern Pacific badge in his pocket, watching for clues and information that might lead them to the apprehension of Grattan Dalton.

My brother Bill was aware of that and of the detectives on horses in the Russian olive tree shade back on his Paso Robles farm. Yet there he kept, in plain view, until the winter rains came and he saw an oily, wild-looking man with a beard and a skunk smell to him clomp along the board sidewalk on the other side of the street. Then Bill sent a boy with a note and he paid out a hundred dollars and tied an Indian pony up behind the hotel and sat at the screened window that night, watching as brother Grat, in all his coats, rode off for Oklahoma.

Bill packed a suitcase and carried his best serge suit down the street on a hanger and left it with an actor friend named Lonnie, I believe, who thereupon shaved his jaw beard until it duplicated Bill's chin brush. He proved a good impostor.

The railroad detectives lost Bill in Tulare but the men staked out at my brother's farm said they'd picked him up there. And for two weeks they sent reports to San Francisco saying Bill was puttering in his toolshed or picnicking at Pismo Beach on Sunday or driving his wife to town in a buggy, wearing his blue serge suit.

It was only then, two weeks after Bill took a night train to the Oklahoma Territory, that the detectives learned they'd been duped.

And it was about that time that Chief Marshal William Grimes and authorities of the Southern Pacific decided to combine their manpower and intelligence to bring in the infamous Daltons; and dispatched to San Francisco was a new U.S. deputy marshall from El Reno named Christian Madsen.

Chris Madsen was our undoing.

He was a wide and blue-eyed and sober man, built from the belly up like he should've been six-foot-six, but he walked on runty legs that sawed him down to five-foot-five. His sideburns were cut off at the top of his ear; he had a brown mustache that was six inches across his face; he was losing his wispy blond hair. He was foreign-born, forty-one years old, a Dane; slow to anger, methodical, organized; a retired Army supply sergeant from Fort Reno who'd bought sides of beef in the past from Nannie's husband, J. K. Whipple, and who knew my brothers and me and Eugenia Moore—whom he called "a hard-bitten bitch"—ever since my brother Frank was shot dead and promoted to Glory.

He had a three-ring notebook of wanted posters and a mahogany file cabinet with information about every criminal who'd spent any time whatsoever in the territories. When he boarded the train for San Francisco, he had a twine-wrapped bunch of manilla envelopes and printed on each was a name: R. Dalton, E. Dalton, George Newcomb, and so on. When the train made a water stop at Kingfisher, he looked up from his notes to see my brother Bill with a goon face on, his nose smashed up against the window so that he resembled Charlie Pierce. Bill backed away, grinning, rubbing his nose, and shouted through the glass, "*Hello,* Chris!"

"How'd you get back here?"

Bill cupped a hand to his ear. "What say?"

Madsen glowered at him.

Bill said, "Maybe we can chat a little longer next time you're passing through." He strolled down the platform into the station house and then the train banged into motion.

Deputy Madsen stopped first at Visalia to talk with Sheriff Kay and see the green London-made safe with three thousand dollars stowed inside, the reward for Grattan Dalton, dead or alive. Then Madsen interviewed a trustee in the Tulare jail, Sheriff Ed O'Neill, the railroad's chief detective Will Smith, and lastly attorney Breckinridge who would die shortly thereafter with a glass of port wine in his hand, five thousand dollars richer, it's said, for his perfunctory defense. Then Deputy Marshal Chris Madsen, with more material for his files and three new photographs, took the train back to Guthrie, the territorial capital.

Not thirty miles west of Guthrie was the Kingfisher farm my mother Adeline was working with two of the girls. Bill would shovel silage or nail tar paper down on the roof or lard his arm to shove it up a cow to feel that her unborn calf had turned breech. Soon there weren't many heavy chores left to do, so he borrowed a stable mare and took it to Woodward where Eugenia Moore had rented a small bungalow that was completely darkened by sagging evergreens.


Bob and I had stayed cooped up there since Leliaetta in September and now it was late November and I was growly when Bill rode up into the yard. It was seven o'clock in the morning and I was sitting in the two-seater porch swing using my fingers to rub brown paste polish into my boots. I heard his horse nicker and cocked a pistol that was folded into my coat; then Bill lifted a pine branch aside from the lintel and green needles cascaded down. He said, "Excuse me but I'm looking for Pecos Pete."

I grinned and said, "You got the next best thing."

Bob heard Bill's voice and hopped barefoot in his bedroom, hurrying into bib overalls, then banged out through the screen door to clap Bill's back and hug him in welcome and call for Eugenia to meet his older brother.

Her blond hair was unpinned onto shoulders of a white robe that she was tying as she came out. She shook his hand and stayed shy and tilted her head for her comb. I don't think she liked Bill much.

My brother Bill put on an apron and cooked a Spanish omelet and fried potatoes and the four of us sat down for a long breakfast during which Bill announced his plans. He wanted a fresh start, to get into Oklahoma real estate, move his wife Jenny and the kids back, study law. He'd settle scores with the railroads, talk with the common people, run for the state legislature. He'd be governor when he was forty. He'd be the good Dalton, the front. He'd invest whatever money we stole and mail what we needed down to the Argentine. And he could spy for us, take the heat off, coddle the lawmen and maybe wangle a pardon for us some day. "It'll work, Bob. By God, it will!"

"I take it you're asking Bob to stake you," said Eugenia, blunt as a ball-peen hammer.

"I'm asking, Miss Moore, for a loan; that's all." He winked in my direction. "I'd borrow from the Katy but I heard the railroad already gave all its money away."

Bob rocked back in his chair, amused. He folded his arms and looked at his woman, awaiting her response.

I said, "I couldn't come up with a more bodacious idea if I tried."

Eugenia turned her coffee cup. "Have you had experience in the real estate business, Bill?"

Bill rolled his eyes at my brother. "I confess, Miss Moore, that I haven't traded in land, not in this neighborhood, but I guarantee that during the last thirty-nine years I've been out of the nest I haven't exactly had my thumb up my keester and my mind off in Arkansas!"

Bob said, "I get asked for loans all the time, Bill. I'm try-ing to clamp down. How much was it you needed?"

Bill purchased a farmhouse in Bartlesville, which was oil coun-try then, about five miles from Julia Johnson's place, about thirty from our hometown of Coffeyville. Soon after he arrived he took the train up to Coffeyville and stayed two days in the Eldridge House where he had businessmen up to his room to taste his Jack Daniel's Green Label whiskey. He had his hair cut by Carey Seaman, bought buckle overshoes from Charles Brown's shop, and reintroduced himself to the bankers, C. T. Carpenter at the Condon bank, Thomas J. Scurr, Jr., president of the First National. They were suspicious at first because the Dalton exploits were well publicized thereabouts, but you didn't dislike Bill for long and by afternoon of the second day, he had them convinced that Bob and Grat and Emmett were merely bad seed.

Then he went around buying. A farmer would die and his widow would ache to go back East. Bill would handle the sale. Homesteaders from the East who rushed out to the territories to grab the cheap land would discover farm work was hard and the weather mean, and they'd give up the caboodle—barn and plows and ox yoke, dirt-floor house and artesian well—for barely five or ten dollars. Bill would pick up the title and split the resale profits with the railroad land bureaus that solicited settlers for the West. And he staked claims for us along the South Canadian River far ahead of the federal government's approval for public sale: we were "Sooners."

Whenever I visited Bartlesville, I'd sit in Bill's rocking chair with one of his law books in my lap while Julia stitched a sampler next to me, and I'd see Bill at the dining room table with the kerosene lamp turned up, scratching out ten or twelve pages to his wife, long essays about the economy, the Farmers' Alliance, the Royal Neighbors of America, the wolves of Wall Street, and the railroads: the Southern Pacific, the Atchison & Topeka, the MK&T, the Rock Island, the Santa Fe. Julia would put an ironstone kettle on the fireplace logs and lift it off with a kitchen towel. She'd ask, "Would you like some tea, Mr. Dalton?"

Bill would look up with glazed eyes. "I'm sorry, I've forgotten your name."

"Julia," I said.

"That's right, that's right." He touched her cheek as if she were his eldest daughter. "No, Julia, I'm very busy now. I have to put some thoughts down before they're lost forever."

Julia would bring me tea and a half-dozen macaroon cookies and whisper in my ear, "He's kidding, isn't he?"

I'd sip from the cup and stare.

Jenny answered her husband's letters with daily notes mailed general delivery to whatever remote post office Bill considered safe that week: Cleo Springs, Anadarko, Bushyhead, Sapulpa. Whenever legal fees were required on deeds, he paid the court officer something extra. Wherever he went he made friends with the sheriff and attended the local trials, taking notes on procedural matters on the backs of his wife's envelopes. He flattered and joked and gave horehounds to children; he had a private table in Guthrie's Silver Dollar Saloon where he weighted his stack of greenbacks with a shotglass and poured "toddies" out to strangers and talked like a newspaper about monopolies and jurisprudence. He got people to believe the Daltons were on their side, near saints, that in stealing from the railroads we were doing them a good turn.

Bill talked and strutted and Bob and I laid low. I'd stay in the bunkhouse on Jim Riley's ranch and ride fence for a couple of weeks or I'd sojourn in Dover to chat with my mother and bobber fish on the Cimarron, or I'd spend a month in my brother's farmhouse in Bartlesville reading the middle sections of Bill's thick ancient books in a rollaway bed, listening to the squeal of a pumping oil derrick, visiting Julia Johnson at her papa's big boarding house, which wasn't far away.

I'd devour a peach and throw its stone at her window and

she'd hunker down with me in the weeds beside the Little Caney River, a quilt thrown over our shoulders and her black hair against my cheek.

I asked, "Do you need any money?"

She shook her head.

"Because I've got it. I've got plenty. More than I can spend."

"You're very nice but no thank you."

"Late at night I stroll the road in front of Bill's house smoking a cigarette and stargazing and somehow I see you sleeping naked under a sheet and I want to be next to you and kiss you under the ear and have you turned to me in the dark.

"I want you in whichever house I'm at, I want to hear you singing in the next room when I look up from work at my desk, and I want you to bring me pump water when it's hot and I'm chopping weeds in the sun. I'd be willing to pay a lot for that. I'd give you the best I could afford. I've got more money than I know what to do with."

"But it's ill-gotten, isn't it." She gazed at me. "Isn't it. That makes it impossible. That makes your romance just a storybook dream, doesn't it."

"About whether it's ill-gotten or not, well, you can't look at it that way. Indians ate the heart of Father Marquette and farmers stole land from the Cherokee; in Mississippi they raped and sold brown women slaves and the Union Army looted Savannah; railroads pushed Chinamen into tunnels with explosives tied to their backs and now train robbers stuff money into grain sacks. The world rocks a little off balance and then it adjusts itself. There's misery in every human enterprise and whether the outcome is good or evil depends pretty much on who you're talking to at the time."

Julia looked at me with one of those "do tell" expressions. "And who have you been talking to?"

"Bill," I confessed.

She put her head back where it had been. "Bill. That's what I thought. At least Bob doesn't make believe."

"Nope," I said. "That's his real attribute. Bob neither shirks nor confuses."

**13** Miss Moore took a stagecoach from her bungalow to my mother's Kingfisher farm where she helped with the canning and made applesauce and left a cigar box with two hundred dollars in it hidden behind the apricot preserves. At the standard Sunday meal with the family, she said she was moving to Guthrie to hunt work as a seamstress. Ben and Littleton ate like machines but my brother Bill let his fork clink on the plate and looked at her as he drank a glass of milk.

My sister Nannie Mae's husband J. K. Whipple leaned over his mashed potatoes, his tie sliding in gravy, to see Eugenia at the end of the table. "What about Bob? Where's he hiding these days?"

"I honestly can't tell you," said Eugenia. "Bob and I have split up. For all eternity."

"Well, that's a bolt out of the blue," said Ben.

My frail mother folded her napkin. "Just the same, you're welcome here irregardless, dear. You don't have to be relatives to visit."

Whipple whispered into his wife's ear and giggled. Nannie Mae frowned. "Oh shush."

The next morning Eugenia sat in a shawl and coat beside Whipple in his decorated sulky. The woodrows were furred with white frost that was turning to sweat in the sun. She could see the horse exhale as he walked; steam curled off his back.

"I take it that's true what you said about you and Bob going your separate ways. It isn't just a smoke screen?"

"I don't understand."

"I could see how you'd profit if you threw certain people off the track."

Miss Moore crawled down in her coat. "Everything became

unbelievably complicated. This seemed the simplest thing."
She saw Whipple smiling stupidly at the harness and reins, a
scour of barn dust high on his neck, blackheads sprayed over
his nose: the face of a chimney sweep. She said, "I'll miss Bob
very much but I doubt that I'll ever see him again. I'm telling
you this because you're family. He's retired the gang and resigned from train robbing. He's leaving for Tampa, Florida,
soon."

"You're a fountain of news, young lady." He grinned self-
consciously, like they should be pals.

The barbed wire fence to her right was tufted with brown
cattle hair. A bunch of white eyelashed Herefords stood in
hoarfrost, staring at her. Steers climbed up on each other.

He said, "I'm a meat market proprietor, Miss Moore, and I
have an associate in Guthrie I'm trying to swing a deal with.
Name is Mundy. Mr. Mundy. Never been married. Lived with
his sister for thirty-two years until she passed on to her final
reward. He's looking for a housekeeper and being as you're
looking for work I figure we might just satisfy a whole slew of
situations. Now Mundy ain't young and he ain't handsome
and exciting like Bob, but he's stable and honest and owns his
own house and butcher shop, and I reckon you'd be the most
special woman he'd ever laid eyes on. Heh. He'd be beholden
to me for many a year if I connected you two up."

The woman in the shawl smiled. "Introduce us at lunch."


Whipple talked business in the restaurant and wiped his plate
with slices of white bread until it gleamed, while Mr. Mundy
smiled at Miss Moore. He wore a gray wool sweater over a
blood-stained butcher's apron. He had a nose like a shoe and
pouches under his eyes and a thin mustache that made him
look Belgian. He paid for lunch and hung his apron on a nail
in his shop and walked Eugenia to a scroll-porched white
house with a white picket fence and a yard that he cut with a
heavy iron push mower. He showed her the dark green sitting
room and the kitchen with pots and kettles and skillets hang-

ing over the stove, and the dining room with his cup and
saucer and tableware already set out for his supper. They
walked up quiet carpeted stairs to the bedrooms. "You'll have
my sister's. The dresser drawers are cleaned out. There may be
some dresses in the closet you'll want." He walked to a walnut
door and opened it to a bedroom that smelled of pipe tobacco.
His hands shook at his sides. "And this is where I sleep."

Eugenia brushed past him and sat on his quilted bed.
Three scratched brown window shades were pulled down and
the sun was on them like yellow hairs. His combs and brushes
and shaving mug and razors were neatly arranged on his mir-
rored dresser. She looked at the books on his vanity. "Oh, you
have the Montgomery Ward catalogue!"

"You may need some household goods. I don't know about
those things. If you want anything just put the order in."

Eugenia lay back on the bed with her hand behind her
head and her dress curled off her ankles. He walked over to the
bed and stood there. The black dye he used on his hair leaked
from his scalp with sweat. Her left hand dangled against his
pants leg. "Can I visit you in the night?" she asked.

His left hand was in his pocket; his right hand reached out
to stroke her hair. She kissed it on the palm and gazed into his
eyes as she slid his hand over her cheek and down her neck and
onto the laced bodice of her blouse. He took a breath and
quavered.

"You can touch me here—"

"Oh God."

She moved his hand lower. "—and here."

He dropped to his knees and crushed her dress to his eyes.
"I don't. I don't believe it. I've waited so long. I've been without *companionship*—she treated me like a child!"

She put her hand in his hair. "We'll tell everyone that
we're married," she said. "My name will be Mrs. Mundy."


She cooked pork sausage and four eggs for him every morning
and washed the breakfast dishes. Then she window-shopped in

a bustled dress and veiled blue hat and drank tea across the dirt street from the office where Deputy Marshal Chris Madsen worked at a rolltop desk with his files and newspaper clippings —he'd lost Bob and he'd lost Daisy Bryant; there was a rumor they'd left for Tampa. Tall Heck Thomas, who had a harelip scar from a pistol shot by the outlaw Sam Bass, was Madsen's closest buddy and he'd carry in jars of banana peppers or chili; Deputy Marshal Ransom Payne would stop by to chat and rock back in a chair with his white sombrero on his boot toe; or dignified Bill Tilghman, later Oklahoma City police chief, would pull a miscreant handcuffed to him across the street planks to the office so Chris could copy a statement about us: we were planning a bank job in Carthage, Missouri; we'd stolen twenty-six cases of dynamite from the Army; Bob and one of the gang had fought and Bob's eye was poked out with a spoon. Chris Madsen checked out every lie. And Mrs. Mundy would note all that and, wearing chaps and sheepskin and a ten-gallon hat, Bob's red woolen scarf over her nose, she'd meet my brother Bill at cold feed stores in Stillwater, Vinco, or Agra.

Sometimes Doolin was with my brother, smoking his corncob pipe in a ladder-back chair and turning away when they talked about Bob. In Stillwater, in a snowstorm, she sat with my brother Bill and Powers and Broadwell in a wagonbed with a potbelly stove bolted to it. They roasted corn and drank to the holidays with grain alcohol and made coffee from snow in a frying pan. Then they decided to visit Bitter Creek Newcomb at the close-by ranch of Bee and Rose Dunn. She was Rose of the Cimarron; pretty and dark-haired and convent-schooled, for several years the sweetheart of both Bitter Creek Newcomb and Bill Doolin, but eventually the wife of a prosperous man whose name I won't divulge. Her brother Bee Dunn was a badman himself so he made every kind of rapscallious outlaw welcome on his place; he even constructed the famous Rock Fort on Deer Creek, as lodging for men on the scout.

My brother Bill took Eugenia on a tour of the property.

Their horses broke through snowdrifts and the two riders ducked their heads from the sleet; then Bill, in his fur-collared greatcoat and three-piece suit and galoshes, jumped from his saddle and waded through snow and tore away some stacked tree branches until he'd revealed a dirt cave. Eugenia nudged her horse to the entrance.

Bill stood inside grinning, his hands on his hips, tarps thrown off frozen kegs of water, cases of food, a wooden box of shotguns and rifles. His voice had an echo to it. "What'd'ya think? Pretty fancy? You give me time, Miss Moore, and I'll have hideouts in every county. We'll have the best escape and intelligence network the West has ever seen. I'll have every sheriff paid off, every circuit judge bribed, every banjo-assed politician running scared for his job. They might even make me director of a railroad."

Eugenia touched a handkerchief to her nose and lifted the woolen scarf up again. "Maybe you ought to go slow on this, Bill. Bob and I really do want to quit for Argentina."

Bill blew on his hands. "My little brother isn't the only train robber in the world. I've been talking a few things over with Bill Doolin. We may just reach agreement one of these days."

Snowflakes were dissolving on her face. She brushed them away from her lashes. "Shall we go back?"

"We could wait out the snowstorm in here. I've got a stash of food, mattresses, blankets."

"I don't think so."

Bill pulled the tarps back over his provisions and propped the dead trees again. He lifted an overshoe into a stirrup and swung on and slapped the snow from his pants legs. He reined his horse southeast towards Ingalls. "We'll have a toddy at Old Man Murray's saloon." He turned in his saddle. "Or doesn't that meet with your satisfaction?"

She spurred her horse past him. "Sounds fine."

He followed and for three miles never lifted his eyes from her deep tracks in the snow. When they tethered the horses at

Ingalls, he said, "I'm not really such a bad guy, Mrs. Mundy. I'm liked by most who know me."

She slouched in a saloon chair drinking whiskey with Doolin, Newcomb, Broadwell, and Powers. Bill hung his greatcoat on the hall tree and walked from table to table in his chalk-striped suit, the buckles jangling on his overshoes, shaking hands and finding anything in the world to laugh about and paying for drinks with bills he snapped from a silver dollar money clip. Eugenia wore greased wing chaps and a nappy coat and her tall hat was canted down to her nose so that she looked like a male hired hand. She said, "That's Bob's money Bill's throwing around."

Doolin looked over his shoulder at my parading brother and back again at Eugenia. His voice was sweet with sarcasm. "Now how could that be? Bob didn't get but a measly few hundred bucks from the Katy holdup in Leliaetta, same as the rest of us. And mine's already gone. What about you, Bitter Creek?"

"Swiped cash is fast cash, just like they say. I ain't seen a smidge of my take in six weeks."

Doolin settled in his chair and his eyes blazed at the woman. "See there? You must be mistaken."

Down the block was Madame Mary Pierce's whorehouse-hotel, so her chippies walked in, shaking snow from their coats, and stood at the bar reading catalogues and taking sweet gum out of their mouths. Bill sidled up to a girl with green eyes and henna-dyed hair who looked just about sixteen.

"Do you know who Tom King is?"

"Does he come here?" she asked.

"Tonight he did. He's a gunslinger from away back. Put many a mean desperado under flowers. That's him at the rear table."

The girl looked and saw what she thought was a man in wing chaps with one leg over the arm of a chair, a red woolen scarf lumped up on his face, turning an empty shot glass.

"The feller with the scarf?"

"He's fairly swooned over you since you walked in."

"You mean he wants me?"

Bill stripped a two-dollar bill from his clip. "Asked me to give you this."

The chippy dragged her wool purse off the bar top and swung it as she walked over to Miss Moore. There were words and then the woman in the greased chaps glared at Bill and out of spite squealed a chair away with her boot and hauled herself up on the girl's arm.

Doolin scowled and turned away in his chair. Newcomb and Broadwell folded over with their sniggering. My brother shouted, "You two love birds snuggle up in this cold, y'hear?"

They slogged through snow and Eugenia heeled off her boots on the newspaper that was spread on the carpet; then they climbed the stairs to an upper room.

Later, Eugenia sat top-naked on the bed pulling boots back on over her wool socks and jeans and the girl lay flat on her back with the sheet drawn up to her neck, staring at the yellow gas lamp next to the door. "Some of the others, they said I'd get around to this someday. They said it would be a relief."

When Eugenia returned to Guthrie the next night, Mr. Mundy was in the dark at the dining-room table with knife and fork in his hands. She was wearing a collared white cotton dress over which she tied on a yellow flowered apron. She carried a candlestick out from the kitchen cupboard.

"It gets dark so early these days. Don't you want light in here? Your supper smells delicious. You get along without me very well."

Mr. Mundy carefully cut up two lamb chops, crossed his silverware on his plate, and sat very still with his fists on the tablecloth. He could hear Mrs. Mundy pumping water into a percolator and lifting the black lids on the stove. She called, "Do you want your coffee now?"

He didn't answer. The candlelight fluttered.

She pushed open the dining room swinging door. "I could bring applesauce up from the cellar. Have you had applesauce with lamb chops? That's one of my favorite combinations."

His voice was croaky. "May I ask where you've been?"

She looked at his white shirt, his narrow, hunched shoulders, the black dye stain on his neck. "Certainly."

He waited. "Where?"

"A cousin in Ingalls was sick with the stomach flu. I had to stay up with her all night. Mercy, I hope you don't catch it. I seem to be immune."

She walked outside and lifted the broad cellar door, letting it *whump* in the snow. She got a jar of red applesauce from the board shelves and screwed off the lid and smelled it. She leaned her forehead against the earth wall.

**14** My brother Bob left Woodward soon after Bill came up with his proposition and he stayed in a sod house until late December with an Osage Indian on Bluestem Lake near Pawhuska. They fished from a rowboat for smallmouth bass and crappie and fried them with bread. They'd sit in the weather in rickety chairs and smoke shredded weed in clay pipes they'd made. All of this is contained in his copious diaries of that period—the temperature varied only thirteen degrees in his entries; there was a skin of ice on the lake every morning; a fish froze near the surface and birds walked around it on the ice, cocking their heads and pecking. Sometimes it would be three hours before the Indian and Bob said anything to each other. The Indian believed that he could fly around the chimney at night; he would walk into the house as Bob made breakfast and say, "I have been flapping my arms."

I guess Bob was bored stiff with that because he saddled a mare and spent a weekend with me in Big Jim Riley's bunkhouse, pitching pennies, cooking brass for a bullet mold, and stringing Glidden barbwire with me in the cold. I'd nail the wire snug and look up to see Bob shivering with his hat pulled down, his coat collar up, his hands pushed deep in his pockets. "We're going south, darn it. I didn't rustle and rob trains to end up with sniffles and fingers about to freeze off."

By that time, Eugenia had put the first and last month's rent money down on a small, peeling house in vacant Greer County, which was then Texas land, a hundred miles southwest of Oklahoma City and twenty-five from the nearest settlement. The furniture and kitchenware came from the Montgomery Ward mail-order house in Fort Worth, charged to her husband's account.

Bob took a rag-leather suitcase with him and stayed there through the winter, making ten-hole wren houses. Eugenia would visit Mr. Mundy in Guthrie just long enough to soften him and stuff an envelope with his money and pick up any newspaper that had Bob Dalton's name in it. Then she'd be back with Bob in the creaking bed at Greer with stories about the jasper and about incidents I would have been inclined to keep secret. For example, Eugenia's night in Madame Mary Pierce's house at Ingalls, with the girl of the henna-dyed hair. Bob said he'd heard already, from brother Bill.

"Does it upset you?"

"I find it mysterious, that's all. Maybe I shucked it from my brain."

He walked outside and shivered in the night air as he stood naked on the soft board floor of the outhouse. He smelled ammonia and lye. He imagined a naked woman kneeling to a woman on a bed. He walked back to the bedroom rubbing the gooseflesh from his arms and he stood behind her as she unpinned her hair in the tall dresser mirror. She said, "I wanted to find out what it was like with a woman. It was curiosity mostly. Afterward I was afraid that you'd feel spurned. You shouldn't be, you know."

He could see his clavicle, the jut of his hip, how each sinew was tied onto a bone; he saw the sway of her breasts under a collared white nightgown of flannel, and the hidden green veins of her hands. He picked yellow hair away from her brown eyes. He said, "I love you; I don't own you."

The money was gone, except what Bill had invested, which he claimed was turning profits like a small manufacturing business. We weren't living that high, as the foregoing should've made amply clear, but we had to make payoffs and gifts to every tickbird and sheriff and nose-wipe of a farmhand who could identify us from the REA Express photographs. Bob paid for a four-hundred-dollar pinewood stable for a rancher who'd hinted he needed one pretty badly. Because we kept rustled horses in one farmer's stalls and his wife wanted their daughter to know the joys of music, Bob had an eight-hundred-dollar piano hauled out on a wagon that flattened on its springs. Then we had supper of ham hocks and chick-peas and listened to the girl hunt the keys until "Lead Kindly Light" was over. A case of whiskey was dispatched every month to two craving deputies in Kingfisher. And in my study I can see displayed an 1873 Hopkins & Allen handgun given to a Dr. Steaman by my brother "for professional services." Don't know what those services could've been, but then I wasn't privy to every blessed thing about Bob.

It cost plenty but we needed the protection because we were hounded as badly then as the more vicious and profitable James gang had been twenty years earlier. A train was robbed in St. Charles, Missouri, on the same night that another was held up in El Paso, Texas, a thousand miles away, and yet we were blamed for both though responsible for neither. A rancher's steer would turn up lost and he'd claim we chopped it up for flank steaks. A house broken into in Fayetteville; school desks overturned and ink bottles smashed on the blackboards in Durant; a jeweler burglarized in his Pullman coach at a nightstop in Amarillo: all bore, the newspapers said, the unmistakable traces of the Daltons.

And with that came detectives: Chris Madsen, Heck Thomas, Bill Tilghman; then more. Book salesmen without sample cases walked door-to-door in Guthrie, looking the closets and living rooms over as they delivered a canned speech about encyclopedias; Pinkerton men sat on the cracker barrels in those general stores and post offices where Bill had received his steamed-open letters from his wife. The Southern Pacific sent Will Smith east to Kingfisher to interrogate my mother. He sat on the stuffed purple sofa with a burlap bag clutched to his stomach and his handkerchief pressed to his cheek, waiting for Adeline to return from the kitchen, while my sister sat leaning on a Shaker chair and touched her ankles together and stared. My brother Littleton stood in the kitchen doorway, drying his hands and frowning. Water spotted the front of his work shirt dark blue. "I'm given to understand you're a distributor of sample garden seeds."

My sister turned. "He's waiting for Momma to finish cooking the ketchup."

Detective Smith shoved the burlap bag aside and stood. "You're Littleton, aren't you?"

"We're not informers, Mr. Smith. We've had about enough of your kind."

"I know exactly how you feel. I must've lost all respect for myself to try this penny-waste disguise." He picked up the burlap bag and walked over to the front door. He saw a robin in the yellow grass of the yard. "Looks like an early spring, doesn't it?"

When he left he slammed the door so hard a piece of window caulking broke off. Then he turned the knob and leaned in. "I pray every night that your brother Grat is not being picked apart by vultures. Out in the desert. Where I can't see it."

All these intervening years of meditation and repentance have not leached away my contempt for that man.

After his record-making one-hundred-and-seven-day journey over two thousand treacherous miles, my brother Grat rode

into Oklahoma and the pole corral that Charlie Pierce had
constructed in the cedar brakes near my dugout. A tickbird
supplied the directions to it. Nobody was there of course,
which surprised Grat; he didn't know Bob had dissolved the
gang. He found tins of deviled ham, sardines, and apricots I'd
cached away in the damp earth next to the stove. He flopped
back on a bunk mattress and jabbed open the cans with a
pocketknife and spooned the food out with his fingers. Then
he slept until the next day, washed with a brick of laundry
soap in the South Canadian, and sat naked on the warm stones,
letting the spring sun bake him dry, waiting to be discovered.

The same tickbird who'd got him there told us where he'd
be and was rewarded with ten dollars, half what he demanded.
I rode down to the sod house to see a bearded, gaunt, and
pitiful-looking man, all eye sockets, cheekbones, and ribs. The
first thing he said to me was how his pal Dangerous Dan could
balance a bowie knife on his tongue.

I rode with Grat to a hotel in Dover and he told me about
a woman from the East he may or may not have met on his
trip. "I told her I'd read all I wanted to about New York. I
said, 'You got trolleys and art museums and foreigners selling
hot pretzels. You got Wall Street and sneak thieves and dan-
dies who wear spats and chew chocolate-covered cherries.' I
said, 'I'm glad you decided to venture west and discover
human beings.' "

"You get anywhere with her?" I asked like a bumpkin.

He said, "I've been so long without, Emmett, I've lost the
inclination. And I don't like the way women smell."


The family made a whoop-de-do over my brother's return. Bob
hired out a Dover restaurant and the entire clan, including
Eugenia, excluding my inamorata, partook of a Sunday meal
served by shy black girls wearing bandanas over their hair,
bossed to the kitchen and back by the black cowpuncher,
Amos Burton. The women were happy, the men ate with rifles

crossed in their laps, the girls sang "A Frog Went A-courtin'"
and "Shoo, Fly, Shoo," and I stood guard, leaning against the
doorjamb with a shotgun in my arms, looking out over puddles
of rainwater in the street, worrying about when the massed
lawmen would attack and wipe us out. They could've had us
easy then.

My mother kept a hand on Grattan's wrist and just gazed
from one to the other of us most of the way through supper.
She weighed about ninety pounds then and her weak right eye
drooped pretty badly. She smiled and said, "Have all my boys
come home at last?"

After supper, Bob walked outside with Eugenia for an
hour, discussing a railroad depot in Red Rock she'd visited.
Then he stood at the doorway and nodded at Grat and me. I
gathered up my saddlebags and my mother followed me. "Are
you boys going—so soon?"

Bob sagged against the door frame and said something
sonly to her.

She gave him a pinched look and said, "Well, keep your
courage, and leave this wild country before you hurt anyone.
Seems it's too late now to do anything else." She put a hand on
my wrist and Grat's. Grat seemed hypnotized by a lantern
hanging over the door. "Promise me you boys will always stick
together."

Then we pushed out through the door and unhitched our
horses. Bob said, "I hate that kind of stuff, don't you?"

I was almost in my saddle when Eugenia remembered my
harmonica for me. She held my horse by the bridle and when I
returned to the table for my Harpoon, my mother asked me to
pray with her. I took my hat off and bowed my head, sliding
my eyes at my younger kin who were snickering at me in the
restaurant. She said, "May the Lord bless you and keep you
and may His light shine upon you, in this world and the
next."

I hung there.

"Say 'Amen.'"

"Amen," I said, and soon as I got out the door I hopped on my horse and galloped away as fast as I could.


I don't recall the dates for any of that. I only know that it was in May that my brother Bill, sweet-talking and convincing, in brown jodhpurs and tie, rode with Bill Doolin to Ingalls and Stillwater and to a cattle lot in Texas, collecting Charlie Pierce and Bitter Creek Newcomb and Bill Powers and Dick Broadwell. And it was on June 1, 1892, that the Dalton gang, minus my brother Bill as always, but including Grat at long last, rode to the railroad station at Red Rock on the Otoe reservation.

It was a dinky town and still is: a depot and a section house and a cluttered store with all it sold lettered on its outdoor wall advertisement. Red Rock sat about twelve miles north of Wharton on the Atchison, Topeka, & Santa Fe lines that connected Wichita, Kansas, with Guthrie and Oklahoma City.

We broke from trot to canter at the limits of the town and our horses threw their nozzles up, clicking the bit with their tongues. Grat was so excited about our intentions that he couldn't bring himself to slow, so he galloped ahead and backed his horse up to the store and waited, his flop hat wadded in his hand. There wasn't any cover near there, because it was wheat and grass and bicycle country, but we wore what we had at Leliaetta—black raincoats, black hats, blue bandanas—so we were unseen as we stood our horses stock-still on the main street of town about fifty yards from the trestle: eight strong and violent and unafraid men, the largest bunch we ever were. Doolin and Pierce shared a pouch of Bull Durham tobacco and used the same match on their pipes. Newcomb rolled the long sleeves of his raincoat up. Twenty miles west I could see rain hanging from thunderheads. Lightning was crooked out of the purple clouds; then it flashed in threes, each split like divining rods, and all I could hear was the slightest grumble of noise, as if an old boarder were reading aloud in his room.

At that time in Kingfisher, my brother Bill strolled into a hotel lobby with his hands in his pockets, a green cigar in his mouth. That afternoon a grand jury from the fifth judicial district had questioned sixteen local men regarding the whereabouts of Bob and Emmett Dalton and asked each to confirm or deny the rumor that Grat was back in the territories. The jury got nary a word from those storekeepers and farmers. Bill had a list of every name and he wasn't shy about knocking on doors and reminding folks of gifts and favors and of how surly and cross we could get. And he'd grin at the witnesses as he was grinning when he plumped himself down on the gold satin couch across from Chris Madsen and the federal judge and the federal prosecutor. He rolled his cigar to a cheek and folded his arms and smiled largely at each man. "Well. It's nine o'clock and we've got nothing to do. Why don't we play charades?"

At Red Rock, Bob dismounted and gave me the bridle reins, worked the lock on the depot door, and walked around to the side porch. He leaned into the window glass, cupping his eyes, then walked to the rear of the depot and looked hard through that window. He saw an uneven table with a kerosene lamp and four yellowing newspapers, also an oak fence and gate and the telegraph key, another cold lamp, a grilled ticket counter, and the edge of an oak desk. He had a feeling the depot wasn't vacant, that a station attendant was crouched down behind the grill or in the cubbyhole of the desk. He pressed his ear to the glass and closed his eyes and walked down the road to me and his horse. He forked his saddle and gingered his horse into backing up to the dark of a cottonwood tree. "Let's be a little secret why don't we, and not get illuminated."

I looked over my shoulder and danced my mare back; the others did the same; and Grat jogged back from his walk along the railroad tracks, scratching the knuckles of his hand. "I think I heard the train."

Bob smiled. "That right? Then it's early."

Pierce said, "I think you're speculatin', Grat."

I asked, "Nobody home, Bob?"

"I haven't figured out just what the peculiarity is. Maybe the attendant is having supper."

Bitter Creek took out a tin of tobacco and pinched some under his lip, while left of him Grat took every bullet out of his pistol chamber and pressed them back in again.

Bob said, "Don't be too disappointed if we let this opportunity go by."

Broadwell questioned Powers in whispers about that, but Powers didn't react. Doolin bit his pipe and leaned over his saddle horn to glower at Bob but he didn't say a word. Grat let some brown soup of tobacco cud drop out of his cheek to the dirt. It sounded like marbles hitting the road.

In Kingfisher, the federal judge had already retired in disgust to his room. The fifth district's prosecutor swirled Madeira in a snifter and listened to my brother Bill entertain. (Whenever I tune the radio to NBC and hear Jack Haley joke on the Maxwell House Show Boat, I think of Bill and smile. He had real zest with people.) After some stories for Madsen and the lawyer, Bill began rather loudly noticing women: "Wow, what about the galloons on that one!" or "I bet her legs go all the way up to her playground. How about it, prosecutor?"

The attorney banged his snifter down on the coffee table and pulled himself up from the sofa. "Marshal, it's nine-thirty." He bowed toward Madsen, glanced some disdain at my brother, and walked across the green carpet of the lobby.

"He's free to disagree," said Bill. "He didn't have to go off and pout."

Madsen sat in a corner of the sofa, squinting at Bill, a full snifter clutched in his lap. "Maybe he was tired."

The prosecutor climbed the hotel stairs, his right hand dragging along the bannister. Bill could hear the slow crump of his shoes in the carpet. My brother smirked at Madsen and shouted, "How can you fellas sleep at night with those Daltons running around loose?"

In the coach of the Santa Fe train, men with rifles sat next to a boy curled up in the wooden seat, a woman resting her brow on three fingers, and a man rattling a newspaper open and reading through bifocals under the light. A white conductor in a blue suit walked down the aisle touching all the seat backs. "Red Rock, the next stop. Red Rock." Then the men stood up and sidled out to the aisle and followed each other to the smoker. The front man knocked just once and the smoker door wrenched open. It was black as a movie theater inside.

A railroad detective slammed the door shut behind them. "How's it look?"

"Normal," the first man said.

"There's empty places in front."

They ducked low and scuttled forward past windows where men with shotguns were scrunched down, picking shotgun shells out of boxes or squashing cigarettes out.

The railroad detective went out the front door onto the grated platform and hopped onto the green express car's carriage. He thumped the door with his elbow as he held onto the ladder.

When the back door was opened a slide of light bent to the cinder roadbed and the weeds. He stepped in and the door was kicked shut behind him. Three men in suits sat on chairs with shotguns held like pole lamps; a man in a gray fedora sat on an empty safe idly kicking it with his shoe heels. A man in suspenders and arm bands was loading a rifle next to the wooden mail slots; the messenger was braced against the side door, a pistol hanging from his hand. The man on the safe took his fedora off and tossed it onto some mail sacks. "How'd you know about this?"

The railroad detective said, "One of our operatives. Madsen put him to work in the area."

(Eugenia Moore had gone to the Red Rock railroad station in a pink flounced dress and talked to a boy who wrote shorthand whenever the telegraph signaled. When he next worked the graveyard shift, she had allowed him to take her into a broom closet and she showed him how the French kiss and she asked him questions about trains and money shipments, and when he answered she pushed his hand under her blouse.

Two or three minutes after she left, a man in a black suit and bowler walked in throwing his badged wallet down on the boy's desk. "I hope it was pretty good.")

Then the Dalton gang saw the train, grimy lantern and smokestack and roiling black smoke, a dead robin splayed in its cow catcher. And noisy enough to make you deaf, all steam brakes and bells and steel versus steel as it slacked speed near the station. Over all that, I said, "Something's wrong when a smoking car's dark. Lookit that dang thing."

"I only just noticed," Bob said.

Grat nudged his horse forward but Newcomb grabbed its mane hair and jerked it to a stop. "The practice is to wait on Bob. He's the one with the caution."

Broadwell pulled out of line and nuzzled his horse in next to my brother. "Something's inappropriate, Bob."

"That's been a subject of discussion."

I could make out the coach windows: a sleeping man, a baby's hand flat against the glass, a man turning a newspaper page, a gas jet turned down to dim. But that smoking car was black, not even the glow of a cigarette ash, not even a gas jet lit, and the shades up on every window.

Grat had his Winchester unstrapped and standing barrel up on his thigh. He slapped Bob in the right shoulder with the back of his hand. "Come on, Bob! Fool! You're acting like an old woman."

"It's a deadhead, Grat. A setup."

Powers sagged and crossed his arms on his saddle horn and moved a toothpick over his teeth. "Surely does have that appearance. Looks like a little ambuscade."

The front door of the depot opened and the ticket agent stood on the threshold with a rifle in his hands, looking right and left, somehow missing us. He walked out to the siding with his eyes as big as they could be, and he banged twice on the express car's wall before he returned to the depot brushing sawdust from his knees, his rifle in the crook of his arm.

As the train pulled out, the conductor peered out the window but couldn't see us for our black slickers. He broke open his shotgun and extracted the shells. "Wharton, next stop!" he said.

The men in the smoker got up off the floor, slapping the dirt from their seats, releasing the hammers on their pistols. One said, "That was a real disappointment."

The men in the express car were breaking open their guns, rocking with the train. The man with the fedora was still alternating his shoe heels against the safe door. His hands were under his knees. "Do you know what's going to happen next? They're going to stop the second section, hold up the regular train. My goodness, we're sharp as tacks, aren't we."

Powers got off his horse and ventilated his saddle. Grat said, "I need a plug of tobacco. Who's got a plug of chew they can lend me?"

Doolin got down and yanked hard on his cinch, making his horse look askance. "I think we've been buffaloed," he said.

His raincoat squealed when he moved. He mumbled, "Skimpity dinners, heels off my boots; damn scurvy hat makes my hair itch." He said aloud, "Coulda been there wasn't no smokers on that train. You ever consider that? They mighta been Latter-Day Saints."

"Maybe we oughta be quiet," said Broadwell.

"May I ask why?" said Doolin. "May I ask why we're sittin' here? Seems to me the engineer pulled the throttle a couple of minutes ago."

Soon as he said that we heard the second train and Bob smiled broadly at each of us. *"Wheoo!"*

"Ain't that somethin'?" I said.

A kerosene lamp was turned up inside the depot and the train came on with gas jets burning in all of the coaches and some of the window shades were pulled down and even Doolin was grinning. "Well, la dee da," he said. "La dee da."

When the train stopped we spurred our horses and Grat banked up to the engine cab alone and knocked the two-man crew into their handles and pull-rods and switches.

Broadwell climbed onto the caboose and opened the door. It was dark inside but he could see bunk beds. "Is anybody in here?"

A man got up on his elbow. "Who is it?"

Broadwell sat on the guard rail and balanced his rifle on his knee. "The next time you're in this situation and somebody asks you that, you oughta just play dead."

The rest of us sat on horses alongside the train. We didn't whoop or shout or fire guns at all, and some of the people who slept in the coaches didn't know the train had been stopped by us until the newspapers said so the next day.

Two Wells Fargo employees have since sworn they engaged in a shoot-out with us but I recall no such thing. I recall that Bob and Doolin and Newcomb rolled the door back while I pranced my horse this way and that on the siding, pointing my weapon everywhere.

Bob told the money attendant to open the safe door but

the man said he didn't know the combination. Bob had been through all that once before at Wharton and he found it more than a little boring. He pulled his blue bandana down and unfastened the hooks of his raincoat for the cool. The halves of his raincoat swished and dropped to the floor as he sat down on the spindle-backed chair as if just that much drama had exhausted him. Newcomb took over and threatened the messenger with every manner of penalty and discomfort; then Doolin brandished a sledgehammer he'd unearthed.

"Hey now," said Bob. "That'll work."

Doolin made a horrible face and swung the weight up and posed with the sledgehammer high as the ceiling and only a sudden fall away from dashing the messenger's head down into his rib cage.

Bob sucked with horror. "No no! I meant on the safe."

"Oh, I *know*, Bob! Damn it! I was just trying to get a laugh."

Doolin tapped the safe mechanism with the sledgehammer head, testing. Then he laid into the latch once and the door indented; with the second blow it cracked. Newcomb pried it free with a crowbar and pitched the money into a mail sack while Bob yawned and Doolin looted the mail for boxes of merchandise.

Bob hopped down to the cinders, took hold of the bridles of Newcomb's and Doolin's horses, and pulled them to the express car.

Grat bounded down from the engine ladder and I took his horse to him; the others trotted along the siding.

In Kingfisher, my brother Bill opened a pocket watch and said, "Golly, ten o'clock. If I don't get to bed pretty soon I'm going to turn into a pumpkin."

Chris Madsen brushed his mustache with a thumb, put his untouched snifter of Madeira down on the coffee table. "What was the reason for all this tonight?"

"Can you keep a secret?"

Madsen pulled his vest down over his belt and looked at Bill without emotion.

Bill said, "I was going to be in a real jam if I couldn't prove I wasn't at Red Rock tonight. I needed an ironclad alibi."

"What happened at Red Rock?"

"Oops! There I go again. Kiss and tell, that's me. Well, you're going to have to learn the rest by yourself. I'm not going to be the one to spill the beans, not even if you tickle."

"Did your brothers stop a train?"

"You're the detective, Chris. I just dabble in real estate."

Madsen said, "It is only a matter of time, Bill." He lifted his snifter, then put it down again. "It is now June of 1892. We'll have them stopped before the year's out."

At Red Rock, Doolin walked off the express car platform onto his mount, strapped his rifle into its saddle boot, and snatched two lunch boxes off the express car floor. The guard and messenger were hog-tied with baling wire next to the broken safe. Their faces were red as apples. Doolin gave the lunch box with the liverwurst to Grat, and Broadwell came up from the caboose and then we all crashed through sunflowers and vamoosed west into the blue hang of rain.

**15** Then began the great manhunt. Conductor Harry Wilcox got off the train and sent a telegram to the Santa Fe dispatcher in Arkansas City, Kansas, then unwound the wire from the wrists and ankles of the men in the express car. The station agent tapped out a message of the robbery to depots along the line and it was intercepted in Wharton by a spectacled widow who'd replaced the boy murdered a year previous by Blackface

Charley Bryant. The railroad detective there showed her long-hand transcription to the Wells Fargo man in the gray suit, then commenced organizing the others. The man in the fedora whistled a tune from his chair and then read the woman's note when the others were done with it. "You have nice hand-writing."

The woman said, "Yes. I do."

Deputy Marshal Heck Thomas pounded doors that night until he'd collected a reliable five-man posse, and he hurried north from Guthrie to Red Rock. About an hour behind him was Deputy Marshal John Swayne and the Santa Fe special officers from Purcell, Oklahoma. Logan County Sheriff John W. Hixon had breakfast with a newspaperman, then stood in front of twenty-five brand new deputies so they could be photographed with their shotguns and dirks and bandoliers, pistols at each pocket. He said, "We'll press on until the trail ends or until the robbers are overtaken."

Deputies Frank Kress and George Orin Severns and thirteen other lawmen chose to hunt us in the Cimarron Hills, which is country mean as a brickyard. Ransom Payne and sixteen men thundered westward for Greer County whence rumors had come regarding a married woman suspected of being Daisy Bryant. Cherokee police, some of them Bob's deputies in a happier year, sat on the Red Rock depot floor, chewing on straw, and they rode out with whatever party they felt wouldn't botch things. And some businessmen from Caldwell, Kansas, rented horses and strapped on three too many guns and went full tilt after the villains, horsewhips clenched in their teeth.

And nothing came of it. We were ex-lawmen and cowhands and horse thieves and we'd studied Oklahoma geography from a saddle. We likely knew as much as any marshal or Indian after us, plus we had my brother Bill's expensive grapevine in our favor and the fact that we had considerably more to gain by getting away than any of those fifty or one hundred did in catching hold of us.

Whenever we saw cattle that June night, we rode among
them until our hoofprints were lost. We lassoed whatever
ponies we could and pulled them along for confusion, then let
them stray wherever they would while the eight of us split up
into fours, then twos, and the rain soaked our hats down to our
ears. Dick Broadwell and I sat under hackberry trees by a
creek bed until four in the morning, anticipating the divvy,
watching mud collapse into the brown water rush, listening to
the pattering in the green-leafed summer trees.

I have maintained for over forty years that our take from
that train was eleven thousand dollars. The Wells Fargo Express Company's accounting was sixteen hundred dollars lost
and that's closer to the truth, which was actually about four
thousand.

Bob divided it honestly this time, in the presence of the
gang at a surveyor's monument forty miles west of Red Rock,
and we each got about five hundred dollars. And though five
hundred dollars or thereabouts went farther then than it does
in 1937, I had trouble seeing it last out the year, let alone get
me and Julia out of the country to South America. But I was
not hangdog. I recall I was weary and saddle-sore and my eyes
hurt from staying awake that whole night, and yet I got out
my harmonica and played without finish the tune about sweet
Betsy from Pike who crossed the wide prairie with her husband Ike, and my brother Bob ambled ahead of Grat and me
to the ranch of Lee Moore on the North Canadian, fifteen
miles away.


I don't know where Newcomb or Pierce or Broadwell went
after the distribution. It could have been Cowboy Flat or the
Rock Fort, where Bitter Creek could romance Rose Dunn. I
know that Powers and Doolin made their getaway to a ranch
on the North Canadian near the Texas panhandle, owned by a
beefy man for whom Powers, then using the alias Tim Evans,
had once been a hired regulator.

The rancher inspected their slavered horses, skating his hands along the withers and croup and cannon, wiping the sweat on his pants, and traded them for a piebald and a red he had stabled.

Doolin walked backwards to the barn. "How bad are we gettin' twisted on this deal?"

The rancher smiled, his hands in his pockets. "The marshals are thick as fleas around here. I'm gonna have to lie pretty good."

They gave the new horses a nose-bag of oats and then the two Bills stripped their shirts off and dunked their heads in the trough and saddled their mounts, dripping water. They cantered between two rows of fruit trees to a creek and saw three deputies slowly riding a gulley, looking at the ground.

Doolin said, "I could have myself three notches right this instant. They'd topple like boxes of cornmeal."

Powers carved out a pipe bowl with his pocketknife. "You'll recollect our early agreement was no unnecessary violence to marshals. Bob's been insistent about that."

Doolin had a cloud of gnats around his head. He brushed at them and turned his horse. "Bob this, Bob that," he said.


Doolin and Powers located the three Dalton brothers at Lee Moore's ranch and we voted for discretion. And the five of us took off that afternoon for the Cimarron Hills, that difficult country of crags and corners and hiding places. It was reckoned we could get lost there for a good two or three weeks. However, no sooner had we made our approach than we ran spang into deputies Kress and Severns and their crowd, standing in their stirrups, shading their eyes to make us out.

The five of us reared around and spurred our horses down a yielding slope into a coulee. We galloped along it, sinking deep where the rainwater wasn't baked up yet. The posse split up along the breaks and almost got lucky a time or two.

A deputy would stop to wipe the band of his hat with a

shirttail and see the Dalton gang in slow trot on the badlands a quarter mile away, one horse spavined and limping, white saliva dangling from the others' bits, a black raincoat flopping loose from its roll behind the cantle. But before he could get his rifle up he'd see one of us point and one of us clamp his hat down and we'd kick around into chokers of runt trees or scrabble over orange pileups of rock and drop out of sight for an hour. They fired some shots that spent themselves with distance, that reverberated over the hardpan with the yarp of a twisted saw. Once Kress gazed up from a shaded canyon to see Bob hallooing from its roof. I went for a skillet of water one morning and saw a deputy in his long underwear fling a rattler up by the tail and hack off its snapping head with a machete. Then he saw me, a far-off boy in long underwear and boots, and lacking a gun to shoot me with, he grinned and held his trophy up high, blood dripping from the snake's neck and onto his armpit and knee.

After two days of chase, the horses were dying. You could hear it in their lungs. Blackflies bunched at the eyes and ears of the horses and one keeled over from sunstroke. I can still feel the shock in the road. It was like the front of a building collapsing. Two others lost their shoes and Grat's animal bloated with sulphur water and we might have been done for except that Bob and I were able to swipe five healthy Cherokee ponies, and we abandoned the others at an old squatter's shack.

Severns found our spent horses and the hoofprints of our fresh mounts and the poor lawman's heart almost broke with frustration. Soon thereafter they larruped those animals left behind up into a slatted stock car and took a solemn train ride back to Guthrie. Kress limped to the smoking parlor of the train and fell exhausted into a seat across from Severns. And at the next stop the two deputies were joined there by Deputy Marshal John Swayne. "You lose 'em too?" Swayne asked.

Severns lit a cigarette and sat back and looked out the window at the badlands. "Sons a bitches," he said.

On June 17, the Stillwater *Gazette* announced: "All the pursuing party have now returned and the chase of the bandits has been entirely abandoned."

Sometime in June, the house in Greer County was broken into by Ransom Payne and sixteen men. He walked up onto the kitchen porch in his stocking feet, his black suit white-ringed with sweat, and he busted out the storm window with his pearl-handled pistol butt. He opened the glass doors of the pantry and lifted up new china plates. Another deputy hunched to poke into a brown wooden ice chest next to the sink. They heard the drumming of men walking above them in the bedroom, shifting stuck drawers out of the chest, ringing hangered dresses to the other side of the closet. The woman they wanted was gone.

She'd returned to Guthrie to spy. In her absence, Mundy walked into her room, sunk the springs of her bed, and touched the pedal sewing machine he'd given her to make dresses. He stood in her closet and pressed her clothes to his face. He sat down on a divan and unfolded spectacles and read a letter addressed to her that he'd found pressed in the book *Italian Journeys* by William Dean Howells. The letter said:

"I have since loaned my share to B. as he was mighty strapped for cash what with the impending arrival of his family from California. So you will need to secure one thousand dollars somehow! The house I have in mind resides in Argentina near Buenos Aires and is spoken of in glowing terms by the engineer who used it. His acquaintances will handle the transaction. It is white stucco with a red tile roof and three bedrooms, so maybe E. and J. could join us. The one thousand dollars is essential and if you cannot come up with it, I will have to seek elsewhere and I am hesitant to do so. Otherwise we are all well here. We have had some close encounters but are a jump ahead of them every time. Sincerely yours, Bob." Undated.

I was with him in the sod house when Bob wrote that. The words "impending," "transaction," and "hesitant" were mine. Mundy couldn't make heads or tails of the letter and folded it back in the book. At night he got up from his bed and put his ear against her door. He tapped on it with a finger. "Can I come in?"

"Of course," she said.

She closed the book *Italian Journeys* and slid it under the vanity. He stood next to her bed in his striped pajamas, his fingers twitching by his legs. "Can I climb under the covers with you?"

She smiled and pulled the quilt aside. He curled down with his cheek on her breast and his eyes pooled. "I don't know what comes over me sometimes. I get so suspicious and angry. I resent everything you do. Then I contradict myself. I want to give you the world, fulfill your every heart's desire. But I'm not a rich man; I'm a butcher. I've already spent everything I had. You're a beautiful lady in a country of rude, evil men." He kissed her breast, her nipple, the hand that lay on his head. "All I can offer you is myself. And I get so scared that I won't be enough."

Mrs. Mundy was quiet; then she said, "I've been misleading you. I don't have sick cousins anywhere. I've been gone because I've been consulting a variety of doctors about a serious illness I've contracted. None of their medications seem to work. My last hope is a rest cure in Silver City in the New Mexico Territory, but they say it will cost in excess of a thousand dollars. You've been so generous with me already that I couldn't possibly mention the malady or their prescription for fear you'd want to care for me and we *aren't* married, I'm not your responsibility, anything you did would be just too much, too much, and I don't deserve it. I've treated you very badly."

"A thousand dollars?" he asked.

"I'm afraid so."

He crawled up to her and whispered, "Who's B? Who's E and J? Who's *Bob?*"

They were motionless for a long time; then Mundy slid out of the bed and walked in his old man's slump to the door where he leaned a hand on the wall. "I don't want to know about him," he said. "I want you out of this house."

By then Bill's wife Jenny and two of their six children had arrived in the Oklahoma Territory. He'd mailed her a post office money order of a hundred thirty dollars to pay off a bank note in Visalia but she'd used it to buy three railroad tickets and some twenty-five-cent basket lunches and she made the long trip east by train with three rope-tied suitcases and a hatbox.

Bill left his little boy and girl with Littleton in Kingfisher and took his wife up to Coffeyville for a second honeymoon. They stayed in the pink suite of the Eldridge House and saw Gilbert and Sullivan's *Trial by Jury* at the Opera House across the street. He introduced her to Charles Ball of the C. M. Condon and Company bank and they asked for a loan on a two-storey house in Havana, Kansas, that would be big enough for a family of eight. His collateral was the wheat farm in California that his father-in-law was now managing. But there was a financial panic in Wall Street and Washington in 1892 that was nearly equivalent to the Depression we're just climbing out of, and it was a bad time to need money. Ball gave them an application to complete, a procedure not common then, and Bill tore it up and littered it as he stomped out of the cashier's office. He crossed the bricked plaza to the smaller First National Bank, which looked like a hardware store, and parlayed for a while with Tom Ayres, the chief cashier. Again he was denied. Ayres said, "I'm not trying to crawfish out of it, Bill, but it's something I simply can't do. This bank can't be dealing with Daltons. Your brothers've gummed it up for you."

So Bill remained with his wife and kids in Bartlesville for a week and then he snuck down to the sod house, bringing two angel food cakes and his fiddle, and we had a jamboree that night: the Dalton gang and three stout whores who sashayed in corsets and garters, plus two scrofulous job applicants about three years younger than I was whom Bob invited to stay for chow but then to mosey on.

Visitations like that were becoming common as we gained in notoriety. Plowboys and scudders and gandy dancers, sneak thieves and Mennonite farmers, would stand next to their horses in the rolling grass a mile or two away and then wade in to the sod house with their coats buttoned up in the heat, grinning from two hundred yards out so as to illustrate confraternity and good will. All they wanted was to see us up close and clamp handshakes on an outlaw and say that when the subject was Daltons, they read every word the newspapers had to say, disagreeing the while with the slant most publishers took. They said we were great lions of the plains, living legends, saints, that we'd already bested the James gang and our names would be enshrined and writ large in the annals of history. At nightfall once a girl of thirteen hiked her dress up for Bob and pleaded, "I want to have your baby." My brother merely said he was in the middle of the *Farmer's Almanac* and he wanted to see how it ended. It did not surprise me that Deputy Marshal Chris Madsen had us under surveillance there, nor that a photograph of the sod house was in a swelling file kept closed with three rubber bands.

The day when my brother Bill came down with two angel food cakes, he asked me if I wanted to go to the river and squeeze cornballs on hooks and maybe snag some channel catfish. I didn't mind, so Bill and I lazed in sticker grass with trotlines set out and fishing line tied to our toes, like a calendar painting of a better American past.

Bill said, "I've got another job planned."

I spit the shells of sunflower seeds.

He said, "It's in our old stomping grounds: Pryor Creek. Train runs from Kansas City, Missouri, to Denison, Texas. Should be perfect for us."

I said, "It's too soon to bushwack a train again, Bill."

"Says Bob."

I licked the last seeds out of my palm and slapped the dust from my hands. "Welp, he's the executive."

"You're his favorite; you suggest it. You tell your pampered hero to hold up that Pryor Creek train and he'll have travel fare to Buenos Aires or Vancouver or Hartford, Connecticut. Then he can couple with that blond bitch in Woodward and raise himself a whole board of directors."

A raccoon trundled along the bank and stopped to smell a fish head. I untied my line and reeled it in on my fist. I said, "You must need the money pretty bad."

"I've got four kids who barely remember me sleeping on the front porch of my father-in-law's farmhouse. I've got a crippled girl with a leg brace that pounds and squeaks when she walks. I've got mice in the sofa and toads in the well and right now my financial affairs are a thousand percent more dismal than Dad's ever were. I've spent all my loans and borrowed still more and if my mule dies I'll be bankrupt. So yes, I need money. I need money bad. Emmett, I'm on my ass."

I stood up and walked to the sod house where the three braying prostitutes were squirming out of their dresses. "When, Bill?" I asked.

"July."


Miss Moore had repaired to the Woodward bungalow and Bob rode up there to quench himself. He sat on the porch swing at evening with her, shelling green peas into a tarnished pan, his boots hooked like ears on the back of a spindle chair. The pea vines laced an arched trellis that gated the backyard where he'd tied his horse to a picket ring stamped in the earth. Baked rhubarb pie was cooling beneath a white dish towel that flies were crawling over. The split pods were dropped to a newspaper that was soaking gray at its folds.

"Bleh," she said, and dropped her paring knife into the pan. "I feel so middle-aged."

Bob smiled. "Can't allow that," he said. "Let's play a quick game of kick the can. Let's have a spelling bee."

She plucked the brown hairs of his arm. "Do you think we could brazenly stroll down the street, like normal people, like lovers?"

"I reckon."

They took their socks off and walked in lank blue grass to the Woodward depot, then teetered on rails still warm from the sun. They clutched each other and swayed down a road and Eugenia giggled when Bob whispered. An old man with his shirt off snapped hedge clippers at a forsythia bush while his wife watched them, screened by the door, her hands in the deep pockets of her apron.

Eugenia asked, "So when is Pryor Creek."

"Don't know exactly but it's been passed down from higher-ups that it might be July 15th."

She flipped her loose hair back away from her ear. She felt his biceps flex when they turned to the house. She smelled the soap in his shirt. She said, "I'm going to Silver City on the premise that I'll be cured of a malady there. Scarcely will I have arrived before Eugenia Moore succumbs to a hideous death. I think I can get Ben Canty to fudge on the certificates and whatnot. Then this winter Bob Dalton can drown in an undertow in the Gulf of Mexico whilst casting for albacore. We'll have a South American resurrection."

"That would be dandy," said Bob.

Eugenia worked in the kitchen while Bob ate rhubarb pie and sugar. Then Eugenia sat with him and wrote a last letter in blue ink. She'd stare out the window, thinking of words, and then her pen would scratch. He licked the crumbs from his plate.

She screwed the cap on her fountain pen and flapped the letter dry. Bob rocked back with folded arms. She read: "Dearest Bob, My affliction has overtaken me despite my return to the health-giving climate of New Mexico; indeed, I now write you from this, my final bed, with the fervent hope that you are well and that I shall be at least a little remembered after my death by the one who meant so much to me in life. How curious it is that my malady of the heart cannot be healed even by the surfeit of love for you that is the cure for my pain, the consolation for my loneliness, and the only condolence I require as I now yield up my soul. I fear I shall draw my fatal breath soon, and soon begin that voyage toward our heavenly Father that is everyone's last grand adventure. I pray, my love, that I shall forever imprint your heart just as you have mine. Yours, Eugenia Moore.''

Bob leaned across the table and kissed her. "That was nice, Honey. It really was. *Dang*. Every time I turn around you're doing something else to impress me.''

Within two weeks she was stepping off a train in Silver City. She waited in the steam that hissed from under the wheels, lifting up the black veil of her hat, brushing her velvet-trimmed black dress. Then City Marshal Ben Canty walked up and took her elbow and strolled with her to the end of the depot, nodding as she talked.

Within three weeks, Whipple hurried to Guthrie and visited Mundy's butcher shop to tell him what he'd just heard from a marshal, that Eugenia Moore was dead. Mundy kept chopping away at a rib roast while Whipple talked; then he sat down at his butcher block table with his forehead in his hand.

**16** Forty-two days after the Red Rock heist, we tied our horses in a copse of trees and camped overnight beside the Neosho River, there to wait on Bill's perfect train, and on the first holdup Miss Moore hadn't planned. It was unsurprising geography, since most of the Dalton boys grew up in the town of Vinita not too far north. The Cherokee capital of Tahlequah, where Grat had been a peace officer, was about forty miles southeast, and closer than that was Claremore where Bob accidentally shot Alex Cochran's son and shortly thereafter resigned from the Wichita court. I could hardly remember being on the right side of the law. It seemed like I'd been a criminal all my life.

Broadwell had his cat Turtle along and it slept on his belly in the sun or it pawed at millers and mosquitoes, or it dropped from branch to branch hunting sparrows in the trees. Doolin was full of Arkansas voodoo and superstitions and his eyes would glass as we squatted around the firestones at night and listened to Bob story about the headless horseman or the premature burial. For my part, all I did was sweat and itch and cuss at anybody absurd enough to try to cheer me up. I was weary, weary of my occupation; and Julia wasn't having much to do with me of late. Her father had put me off-limits.

On the morning of July 15th, we crouched around a blanket mottled with sunlight while Grat dealt out playing cards that would indicate our jobs. But then I looked up and saw a teenaged boy in plow boots and a wide straw hat battering through Devil's Walking Stick and blowing his nose because of the weed dander. He wadded the hankie inside his sleeve and saw the eight of us grouped at the blanket and the boy just stood there in the heat and dust looking pop-eyed and brainless, with ears as big as butterflies. He had a smile so wide his molars showed. "Campin'?" he said.

Grat would have snatched up a rifle and plugged him but Bob had pressed his toe on the muzzle.

"Just passin' through," said Broadwell.

The boy didn't walk out of the weeds. He had stickers of every sort on his shirt and nettle bumps all over his hands. He said, "Say, just for shits and grins: I'm lookin' for some shoats strayed out of the pigsty after sloppin' time this mornin'. I can't find hide nor hair of them."

None of us said anything and the silence was so overpowering that the boy got the message and walked back through jabbing, pocket-high weeds until he got to the Katy railroad tracks. I met that boy once again in 1907 and he told me he then stomped clumsily along the ties, scratching his hands and panting, until he got to the Pryor Creek depot. He jumped three steps onto the platform and leaned against the door. Inside a man in a fedora was drinking water from a ladle.

The boy flopped down on a bench. "It's the Daltons all right." He held up eight fingers. "Eight men. Camped up on the Neosho."

The man looked at the telegrapher. "Wire that to Kinney in Muskogee." He carried the water ladle to the boy who grabbed off his straw hat and emptied the ladle on his head.

"How do you like being an operative, Loren?"

Loren kicked off his plow boots. "Oh, boy. It's really tiring."

They'd known about the Pryor Creek raid since the 13th, when the two snipes who'd come by looking for jobs and stayed on to eat angel food cake were caught by federal marshals while bootlegging whiskey at the Watonga reservation. They said they could swap some information if the lawmen would go easy, so they were shoved down into chairs in Madsen's office in Guthrie.

One of them was quiet and glanced under his eyebrows at everything and he kept squeezing pimples and wiping his thumb on his shirt. The other was a smirker, as doughy and slack-jawed as Billy the Kid. He slumped in the chair and rolled his boots on their heels and told Madsen how my brother had repulsed him because the gang was already too large. But he said he'd stuck around long enough to pleasure one of the whores there and he overheard some talk about the MK&T and Pryor Creek, set for sometime in mid-July.

"I hear tips like that all the time," said Madsen.

"That don't mean this ain't true."

So Captain J. J. Kinney, chief of detectives for the Missouri, Kansas, & Texas Railroad, was notified in Muskogee on July 13th, and when suspicions about us were confirmed by the boy at Pryor Creek two days later, Kinney called for Dep-

uty Marshal Sid Johnson of the Wichita court, and Cherokee
Police Chief Charles LeFlore, the cleanest Indian I've ever
seen, always wearing an excessively white shirt, with his black
hair oiled and cut and exactly parted.

Then fifty special deputies, of which thirteen were railway
officers, bunched up on the Muskogee platform in muley hats
and derbies, leaning on barrel-down rifles, spitting tobacco
onto the railroad ties, speaking venom about us in ninety-four
degree heat, while women blanched and squeezed their children's hands and men in celluloid collars stood aloof and
talked quietly to each other about the big surprise the Daltons
had in store for themselves.

Passenger train Number 2 chuffed in and the volunteers
boarded a spanking new smoking parlor car with cushioned
green seats and gas jets lit and glass chandeliers on the ceiling.
Then the train was rocking north toward Pryor Creek and the
volunteers were bragging or hooting at jokes and it was as loud
and hale as a men's club excursion to see a baseball game.
Three tubs of warm, bottled beer were carried in, "compli-
ments of the Katy." The conductor walked down the aisle, idly
chatting with the men, showing them a derringer stuffed in his
white cotton socks. Johnson, LeFlore, and Kinney sat in facing
seats at the front and shouted over the noise about how they'd
known the Daltons in the past—first Frank, then Grattan, then
Bob and me. Sid Johnson still considered Bob one of his five or
six best friends, and one of the profoundest marksmen in the
West; he said he'd once seen my brother turn the pages of
Amos and Obadiah in King James with a bent-sight .22.

In the Pacific Express Company car, the money attendant
fastened a padlock the size of his fist onto the sliding side door.
He sat in a chair in the dark with his hands on his knees.
Slumped among mailbags in the dark was a boasted badman
from Texas recently commissioned by the railroad to escort
the safes for seven dollars a day. He never talked to the messenger. The messenger would turn and see the red ash of a
cigarette or he'd turn and see nothing at all.

At Pryor Creek, a railway guard knelt at the back of the depot tying his laces over the hooks of ankle-high shoes. On the platform, a man in a derby leaned out and dropped cottony spit onto bed rocks that were blackened by soot. A man sat in a chair with a ten-gauge shotgun in his lap, breathing moisture onto each lens of his eyeglasses. Inside, the cash drawer was gone and the ticket window was closed and two men sat on the varnished bench while a man in white spats walked from window to window. There was a clock on the wall with Roman numerals that said it was 9:05. He said, "I bet they've seen us and called it off. I bet that's what they did. They're not stupid, you know."

By that time the men in the smoker had begun their preparations. They snapped shotguns closed or pulled up their socks or stood on the platform between the cars urinating onto the couplings. Then the conductor opened the connecting door and said, "Pryor Creek, the next stop," and they sat like quiet schoolgirls. "Sweet Jesus, the Daltons," a man said.

But the Dalton gang wasn't at Pryor Creek. Kinney stood on the iron walkway between the smoker and baggage car and squinted into darkness and cinder smoke, his tie flying wild in the wind. Then his tie settled on his shoulder as they slowed and he saw three railway detectives with legs spread wide on the platform, rifles relaxed in their arms. He saw the fireman swing down and talk with a man in white spats. They waited three minutes and all they heard were crickets and the slow pant of engine steam.


The bandits were at that time striding the main street of Adair, the next stop north, in every variety of wide, scurvy hat and striped collarless shirts and famous black raincoats, blue bandanas loose at their throats. The horses were tied to the town water tower where Pierce sat on a springboard wagon peeling the sunburn off his thumb of a nose. Three-pound pistols in grimy brown holsters sagged from our trouser belts near our front pockets. Doolin had a Winchester crossed over both shoulders; Newcomb, Powers, and Grat had their rifles hugged close, as you'd carry a long loaf of bread.

The night train was a summer event in small towns and Adair wasn't sleeping at all. Lace curtains curled out under a window sash and I could see a girl with her short legs stuck out straight on an overwhelming stuffed chair while her father picked at a banjo and the oil lamp flame grew and lessened in its glass chimney. There was a girl skipping rope with petticoats flouncing and a bent woman weeding marigolds who straightened when we passed. A boy was riding a bicycle in circles with a small squealing boy on his handlebars. Two doctors were in the drugstore reading the label on a brown remedy box. A woman sat on an upstairs windowsill for the breeze, looking on like we were railroad crew and that we must be especially hot in our coats.

I hunched at a back depot window, smelling window putty, and I saw the unsuspecting Katy ticket agent chewing the hairs of his mustache, turning the pages of a Prudential life insurance brochure. Then my brother Bob banged the back door open and the man's head jerked up and seven giants stalked in, spurs clanking and black raincoats shrieking and boot heels pounding the slivery floorboards like we were stallions in heavy lead shoes: a bad nightmare of meanness, the stuff of night chills and story books, the scariest bunch of desperadoes that ticket agent ever saw.

A coat tree wobbled and little Newcomb kicked it over, a branch snapping off into a dance on the floor. Bob clicked a hammer back on a .45 caliber pistol and stuck it straight out to touch the nose of the agent who was standing up from his desk. "You keep those hands up and don't say a blessed word," said Bob. "Don't even think about talking. Back up flat to the wall and sink down until you're on your butt. If I look over and see your hands at all moved, I'll lean over this counter and blow a hole the size of a bucket in your crotch."

I stood there being ferocious while Doolin pushed a castered chair aside and slammed desk drawers over onto the desk top, picking up from the paper ruckus quarters and matches and a white box of Smith Brothers cough drops. Powers sat with his ankles crossed on a quiet hickory rocking chair at the front of the depot, a rifle standing in his lap. Newcomb was in the back room clawing boxes open with a garden sickle. Broadwell unlocked the money drawer and handed some limp paper bills through the grill to Bob. Broadwell pushed the drawer shut with his stomach and I saw the agent staring at the legs of Broadwell's jeans, which were stickered with cockleburs and foxtail and had yellow seeds in the cuffs.

I wasn't doing anything. I was the lookout, I guess. There was a calendar on the wall with a long arrow drawn through a week of dates and "Harold Higgins on vacation" printed over it. A glass ashtray cradled a crusty black pipe.

My brother Grat slouched around, smelling like green cheese and fish heads, making noise with a bleached axe handle he'd picked up, striking a bench seat, a sill, a waste can, a clock, like a circus bear with a tin drum. He bashed some mahogany wall pigeonholes and a stack of MK&T tickets slewed out. He stood in front of the ticket agent and before I could yell out Grat's name, he whapped the axe handle bingo into the man's nose, the sound like a snap of your fingers. The man cried out in pain and blood gushed over his chin and shirt and he fell down to his elbow with his nose skewed over like it was hinged. He kicked out at my brother's shins and said, "You bastard, what'd you do that for?"

Bob stood on his toes to see the man's bloody shirt. He asked, "Was that really necessary, Grat?"

Grat smirked and walked out the front door, and I collected Newcomb and the package loot, and then the whole Dalton gang was gone from the waiting room, there for barely three minutes, leaving behind us chaos and silence and the very first robbery of a depot in American history as far as I know. We stood on the board sidewalks or sat on benches and talked brief sentences to each other. The boy on the bike rattled up to the depot; then he turned his bike around. Mosquitoes whined in the air. I walked the railroad ties and saw a woman shooing her children into the house, her hand latched onto a boy's wrist, while a crowd of elders stood under an elm tree, talking and gesticulating, and a man in slippers climbed down his porch steps loading a double-barreled shotgun. Don't know what ever happened to him. I hooked my steamy raincoat over my pistol butt and walked back to the depot, theatrical as they come. I was sweating like sweat was my full-time job. Powers said, "Looks like we're going to have an audience."

Doolin said, "They won't be around long."

The station agent stopped his nose bleed with twisted railroad stationery and sat obediently with Broadwell on the front bench. Bob wavered a lit match over the schedule board until he found what he wanted and blew out the flame. "Comes at 9:22," he said.


Passenger train Number 2 was then about three miles away and men who'd boasted after Pryor Creek about having repelled the Daltons and made us turn tail now sat stony on their cushioned green seats, swaying with the coach, sweating and smoking and letting the scares crawl all over them. A man vomited into his hat. Reports indicate that at least three of that crew walked out to piss and flung their rifles away, and the cowards crashed through coach doors to the rear of the train where they slid down into safer passenger seats with their badges in their pockets.

The engineer pulled the whistle cord twice and saw the Adair way signal flash red and he threw up the long throttle valve lever and turned the valve cutoffs that let air pressure escape from the drive cylinders. Steam rolled out white and unribboned in the air and the boiler gauge arrow swung left and fell while the air pressure gauge arrow climbed and they were coasting with the bell ringing loud and the engineer hanging an elbow out the cab window while the fireman drank the last of his vacuum bottle of coffee, what trainmen call crank, and fastened a sweaty suspender strap on his overalls. The engineer pushed the valve levers for the drive cylinder brakes and the steel tires screeched on the rails. The fireman said, "There's two men in black raincoats at the depot. That would be the railroad guards, I suppose."

"Oughta be more than *two*."

The fireman leaned out to see and got swacked in the neck with Grat's bleached axe handle. Then the ladder clanged under Grat's boots and I was hooked on the left ladder with a dangling leg and my pistol was cocked in my hand, the grip seated on the board floor next to the ash-pan damper handles so the gun was pointed mostly at a tallow can they used for oiling cylinders.

There was a purple mouse under the stoker's hand at his neck. The engineer asked his buddy if he was all right. "Neck's just a little scratchy," he replied.

I was still making an effort to climb into the cab. I shouted at the two crewmen, "Hey! Look down in this direction!"

The engineer looked down at me, at a burly boy with steel-colored eyes and a blue mask over his nose, while the fireman touched the welt on his neck and backed away from Grat who was then large in that hot square of space. Grat poked the engineer against the furnace with his handle and heaved against the air-brake lever and momentum jerked us a little off our boots. The engineer leered at my brother's exposed pistol, which waggled in a holster near his watch pocket. Grat noticed and said, "How would you like your nose broke? I just discovered a talent for it."

The engineer smiled. "Could I still drink whiskey?"

While the train was still rolling, Kinney had lifted a window shade in the club car and seen the depot platform and Bob and Broadwell solemn at the elbows of the ticket agent. Sid Johnson, a man with prominent cheekbones and squint wrinkles around his eyes, peeked under the shade on the left side of the train and saw Doolin pass below him, stroking his red mustache and staring toward the caboose. Johnson raised his pistol and whispered, "Bang."

LeFlore stood at the front connecting door waiting for Kinney's go-ahead. All the other volunteers were sunk down in their seats with their hats off, revolvers cold in their hands, fear of us recruiting them man by man. Kinney said, "Okay, this is it," and stood in the aisle like a boss politician. "Well, boys, shall we go out and fight them?"

I guess his boys didn't answer.

Johnson, LeFlore, and Kinney braced on the seesawing iron platform, hearing the slow click of the wheels and some words in the engine cab and the abrupt extra whine of brakes when Grat muscled the air-brake lever. Then Kinney leaped from the stairs into a sprawl of soot-black ivy that was taking over a coal shed to the left of the train. LeFlore and Johnson hung waiting a second for the train to stop, then scurried inside the coal shed's open door. That's when I saw them, when they ran from the club car like children playing let's pretend. I thought they were frightened passengers and didn't pay them proper attention.

Kinney maneuvered into the shed and the three of them stood there in silence for several minutes, smelling coal dust. A black cat skipped across some crate tops and dropped to the earth and rubbed against Kinney's pants leg. They quietly listened to the cinder crunch of Dalton boots on the roadbed and heard Bob shout for Grat to bring the stoker and a coal pick back to the express car. Sweat blotted through their shirts. LeFlore had his pistol cocked and next to his ear and his eye kept sliding toward J. J. Kinney. Finally, Sid Johnson said, "Should we get them now or wait for the suspense to build?"

I looked down the siding and saw Newcomb and Doolin standing in weeds like signboards, and Powers, Broadwell, and Bob pounding the wooden door of the express car, and suddenly the three lawmen in the coal shed cut loose and a bullet hit the ladder *kapang* and then a dozen shots struck off the boiler, triangulating inside that steel cab so that not one of us should've been spared; deflected slugs that were flattened like mushrooms whizzed close to Grat and me and the crewmen but not even a raincoat was nicked and all we heard was *clang* and *peeyow* as the hot lead swiped at our faces. Grat and I were quick with our guns and returned two shots for each we received, letting all fly at the coal bin since the firebox had blinded us to night-seeing and we couldn't pick out the three bushwackers to draw a bead on them. The engineer and the fireman bellied down to the floor; ricochets sparked off the drive wheel eccentrics, and a wild shot skidded a coal shovel off the tender and it landed *bawong* in the grass. (If I sound excited, I am; I was.) I rammed six cartridges into my smoking chamber and waited for a pistol flash intended to rip my face off, and I fired everything I had straight at it. I must've done that several times. A man traveling from St. Louis later claimed that over two hundred shots were exchanged before the firing lessened. He must've been an accountant.

Then Bob drew his pistol and crouched under a baggage car to see how many were the shooters, and he saw men he recognized: LeFlore sitting down on an abandoned shuttle car that was poked through with weeds, cupping his left elbow, blood bulging out of his coat sleeve. Kinney had been downed by us too. His white shirt was twisted out of his trousers and his pale belly showed, so that he resembled a workingman napping in the grass at lunch hour. Sid Johnson knelt in a coal pile, his right arm out stiff and the pistol smoking out of its muzzle and chamber. The pistol kicked up when he pulled the trigger and then he let his arm stiffen again.

My brother Bob waddled underneath the carriage until he wasn't twenty feet from the shed. And he said, "Sid Johnson! You old scalawag!" And the deputy marshal swiveled and then one of his five or six best friends, the one who could turn the pages of a Bible with a bent-sight .22, put a .45 caliber slug into Johnson's shoulder and knocked him onto his seat in the coal. There were black circles on his trouser knees. (I heard when the doctors pulled off Sid's shirt, his shoulder flapped loose like a stocking cap. "Boy oh boy," said Johnson. "Bob'll *never* let me live this down.")

Two or three special deputies were firing from the smoking parlor car, a foot-long blaze with each report, but they didn't have much for targets. About six volunteers braced themselves at the rail of the smoker trying to muster up courage with their guns in their belts and their brains as slow as cattle and sheep and mud hens. They saw my brother Bob stand from under the baggage car and two of them had the wherewithal to yank pistols from their holsters at least, but Bob potted just one gas lamp over their heads and they withdrew back into the dark of the car like slugs.

With the shooting from the coal shed stopped, Grat and I clambered out of the engine cab with the hoghead and the stoker, who carried a coal pick over his shoulder. Dick Broadwell grabbed it from him and chopped the pick into the sliding door, wood barking and yelping and flying away in splinters. We heard a key and the padlock clicked open and the door rumbled as it rolled wide. Oven air rushed on us and the messenger trembled there with his hands high and his blue shirt black with perspiration, sweat trickling down off his nose.

Bob couldn't figure out why the attendant had opened a door that was secured, so he stood back and asked, "Is it just you in there? Are you alone?"

The messenger swallowed and shook his head from side to side.

I could hear the Texas badman sit down hard on the mailbags. "*Shee-oot,* Williams! Real flaming smart!"

Broadwell and Grat jumped up inside the express car and covered the hired man in the corner. Grat hurled the man's rifle out into the night and I saw it glint once, twice in the moonlight as it wheeled. Broadwell said, "You wanted that reward money pretty bad, didn't you. Would've been Christmas in July, wouldn't it."

The hired gun ignored him. He glared at my brother Bob. "We ain't gonna give you squat."

But of course they did. They offered the worn-out argument about not knowing the combination and Bob tantalized Williams with a pistol shot that was so close to his brainpan it singed his hair and repeated itself in the messenger's ear for most of the following week. The safe was opened and we carried money out in a mail sack and threw it down into the clattery springboard wagon that Pierce had driven down from the water tower.

My ox of a brother, Grat, pushed the ticket agent and fireman and engineer back to the front of the train where he told them to hurry it out of town. Then Grat hopped down from the ladder and bumped the ticket agent onto his seat just for meanness.

Doolin and Newcomb backed along the train with their rifles on the faces of the distraught volunteers; then Newcomb and Broadwell started laughing about something and instead of coming up with Bob and me, they jumped in the wagon with Pierce, and Pierce slapped the long leather traces against the horse team and they barreled down the siding past the coach cars, howling and ki-yiing, shooting their pistols through windows. Broadwell stood on the wagonbox, glamorous as Custer, and shot a man of fifty-five in the shoulder, then plowed a bullet into the vest pocket timepiece of a passenger named Frimbo. Afterward, Frimbo laid the watch out on a sheet of paper and demonstrated for Chris Madsen's men that it was in so many pieces it could be gathered up and sifted through his fingers.

Broadwell, Pierce, and little Newcomb ringed the train twice, taunting the volunteers, daring them to shoot; then the train clanked and squealed and strained in its hard pull forward.

Newcomb said, "Why don't we board her and run through

the coaches assassinatin' the villains? Wouldn't that be havoc?"

But they saw Bob fussing and me waving them back and they turtled the wagon over the moon-gleaming tracks.

I inquired of my brother, "Wasn't that Sid Johnson shooting at us?"

Bob had on his surprised and mirthful and enchanted-with-life expression. "And Charlie LeFlore!" he exclaimed. "Can you beat that! You've got to help me think of a way to really rub it in next time I see those coots. Something really humiliating."

I saw the brakeman's lantern on a second-class coach as it rolled past. I said, "I bet they're so danged embarrassed already they'll shoot ya soon as you walk into town."

"Naw! Do you think so? Naw. They know the conditions. It's like a prizefight, Emmett. You don't go slamming the other guy around after he's out of the ring."

"I forget: we're gentlemen."

He looked at me like I was simple.

Johnson, Kinney, and LeFlore had struggled up the stairs of the smoking parlor car and sat down bleeding onto newspapers in the aisle. The ticket agent had ducked inside the depot and bolted shut the doors and was probably at that moment signaling yet another posse. And the Dalton gang backed down the main street of the quiet town of Adair, taking some last shots from the caboose without reply.

I was sick of trains and the mulish routine of robbing them and I was frankly a little scared of being shot at, scared enough to make my stomach hurt. Pierce drove the wagon ahead to where the horses were hitched and we walked through town as we had entered it, seven slimy men in noisy raincoats, striding out of Adair under elm trees, except now we were alone in the town, every lamp was extinguished, the doors were shut, and children were crouched down in closets like we were boogeymen. I was as hot as I've ever been, and I had to keep slapping at mosquitoes that swarmed at my face and hands. I took the boardwalk in front of the drugstore and saw a shattered window with the two doctors flat on their backs in shards of glass.

My brother Bob and I stood there, struck mute and motionless by what we saw, which was Dr. W. L. Goff, who'd suffered the freakish accident of a wild pistol shot that exploded his left eye. Blood covered all of one half of his face and slid away from his head with the slope of the floor. He'd die within the hour. The other doctor, was named Youngblood (according to the newspaper clippings), had been struck in the throat with a ricochet. His fingers curled and uncurled. He saw me staring and turned his head and blood and food surged out of his mouth like he'd spilled a soup pan onto a table. "Help me," he said. "Please help me." And I ran away as fast as I could while my brother Bob looked on, fascinated, his hands deep in his raincoat pockets.

**17** The Dalton gang rode northwest toward Kansas and into the Dog Creek hills, while three posses of over a hundred city boys, each a clanking arsenal, strove after us in several wrong directions. At four in the morning, the spoils of Adair were apportioned, Bob doing the mathematics as always, at which he was baffling, fast as a gambler with cards.

Bitter Creek Newcomb stole twenty eggs from a farm chicken coop and fried them with wild onion in a skillet, talking as he did so about the engagement ring he was going to buy for his fiancée, Rose Dunn. The other men loitered next to the fire or washed their faces in the creek and I napped with last year's rusty leaves while a daddy longlegs walked over my neck and ear.

If I slept at all it was with a nightmare about that Adair holdup. That was the first time we'd really been shot at during a robbery, the first time I'd ever been scared of dying. I could hear Newcomb sizzle onions at the camp fire but with that I heard railroad detectives shouting and the noise of guns going off and the whiz of slugs crossing the air near my head. I could open my eyes and see Powers tamping tobacco into his meerschaum or tinkering with his alarm clock, but if I shut them I saw running men and muzzle flashes and pistol chamber sparks near a coal shed, or the drugstore and the shattered plate glass window and the exploded left eye of Dr. W. L. Goff. It doesn't seem exactly real to me now; it seems like cap pistols and chicken blood and dead men who'll rise up and dust themselves off and eat cafeteria food at the RKO film studio. But that morning in the Dog Creek hills I was pretty shaken and whenever I thought about Dr. Youngblood, I saw Bob lying there. My brother would see me staring and turn his head and blood would brim out of his mouth. "Help me," he'd say. "Please help me." And I'd run.

I wanted to quit but my brother Bob didn't; he wasn't haunted at all. He handled Adair like all the other jobs and after distributing the shares he delivered Bill's percentage to Bartlesville in a shoebox and stayed for a lunch of fried tomatoes on toast with the child Grace in his lap, her steel and leather leg brace hanging from the back of the chair.

I combed out horse manes with a stolen lady's brush; then Bob rode in at sundown, breaking through river cane, green circles under his eyes and dust and chaff in every wrinkle of his clothes. He told us to saddle up, so we did. And we walked our horses up to Coffeyville, Kansas, arriving at two in the morning.

Bob hammered the door to the Farmers' Home on Eighth Street, a hostel no bigger than a camera store. I could see the owner sleeping with his wife in a brass bed in the dining room, saw him scrape a match and feed it to an oil lantern and spread the window curtains apart. What he saw was a hulking young man with a dark, brooding look and my black pistol cocked and pointed at his eye.

He opened the door to Bob Dalton, who pushed in followed by Powers and the rest of us, stamping our boots on the rug, opening cabinet doors, letting a water glass roll off the table and crash loudly to the floor.

The owner's wife was sitting up in bed, drawing a sheet up over her nightgown. I'd only seen her before with her hair braided and circled on each side of her head like earphones. Now it frayed long over her shoulders. Bob sat on the bed and bounced it, squeaking the springs. He smiled at her. "Am I a figment of your imagination?"

The woman cooked supper and the cleaner four of us used the bathwater in a single wooden tub, and then we slept on iron bunks in the rear of the place, an hour of nightwatch assigned each man.

I woke up at noon to see Bob on the striped mattress beside me, the very same on which I would lie dying in something short of three months. He had a tin cup of coffee and the Coffeyville *Journal*, the Stillwater *Gazette*, and the Kansas City *Star*, each spread open to the story of the daring train robbery at Adair. I got up on an elbow and he handed me a small, handwritten, railroad poster that was torn where the tack holes had been. Dated yesterday night and rushed out to every depot in three states, it said the Missouri, Kansas, & Texas Railway Company would pay five thousand dollars for the arrest and conviction of each of the masked men engaged in the robbery, to an amount not exceeding forty thousand dollars. (I have that poster on file.)

Bob grinned at me as I read it. He said, "Forty thousand dollars. That's the largest reward ever put on the heads of an outlaw gang, bar none. And that's not mentioning the offerings attached to us still from California and Wharton, Leliaetta, and Red Rock. I am impressed as hell with myself."

I groused, "Well I'm plain, flat-out tired of trains. I don't want to hear one word about them. What would make me darn impressed with myself right now is if I was to interview and land a two-dollar job digging sump-holes, or filing nails to a point, or stacking canned figs in a grocery store. I've had a bellyful of excitement." I plunked the newspapers onto his mattress.

He said, "I guess most folks would shoot a little higher for the stars, Emmett, but each to his own vista I always say." He slumped back on the bed. "But let me tell you about our next job. I've been thinking that banks are where the money is."

"I've got wax in my ears," I said.

"My! You're already churned and clabbered on the issue, aren't you?"

"Yep. You're talking to yellow headcheese. You ain't gonna get me theoretical about banks, Bob. I'm just gonna sit here and stink."

"Dear me, I went and did it, didn't I? I got you in a snit. I better hide before you start chucking pillows." He got off the bed and walked barefoot to the front room where he bummed a cigarette from the owner he'd tied to a chair.


We stayed in Coffeyville two nights, which was stupid, because somehow word got out that the Dalton gang was headed south from there and a posse of thirty men piled out of wagons for an ambush at the Caney River crossing. They dunked handkerchiefs in kerosene and wiped their skin to keep mosquitoes and chiggers away; then they squatted in high weeds and sweated and itched in their coats, or they sloshed through the river in high rubber boots to sit under the bridge, waving their hats at gnat swarms, staring up at the rotting, moss-green, overhead boards.

They would've had us for sure except they'd tried to recruit Julia's older brother Garrett and he talked about the ambush at supper that night. She excused herself from the table and dressed in Garrett's overalls and a blue denim jacket. She rolled up the cuffs and snuck out of the house to saddle a gray mustang that she galloped along the hard, moonlit road in the direction of her intuition. I recall that we heard hoofbeats like the wooden block noise they use in radio plays, and the gang trotted our horses into the dark of blackjack trees and sat there with hands on our holstered pistols.

I recognized Texas Johnson's mustang, then Julia, and she

cut from gallop to stop when she saw me ride out of the trees. "Emmett, thank goodness I found you," she said. Her horse nodded with his exertions and pranced around in a circle and I grabbed ahold of his bridle and walked my horse alongside as she warned me about the posse at the Caney ford.

I saw Bob and the others sitting on their horses in the trees. Newcomb lit a cigarette. I said, "It was brave of you to interfere."

"Why? Because you're wanted men? Because this makes me an accomplice?" I couldn't see her eyes well enough to know if they carried tears but there was a pitch of anger in her voice, and she chose her words with care. She said, "I still care about you, Emmett. I know that doesn't matter much to you but it's more than enough for me."

"You know what I heard about you? I heard you'd taken up with a farmer who honks when he laughs, and with a cowhand forty-five years old who calls you Daughter all the time."

"They just live at the house. They're boarders."

I stared at the road and watched my horse twitch his right ear free of flies. I said, "What's that mean when you say you care about me?"

She said, "I suppose it means I'm going to be steadfast. I'm going to be the girl you send pictures to and visit when you're in the neighborhood, the girl who pines away at night and will probably soon be bereaved."

My brother Bob rode over and she pulled her high-headed mustang around and galloped home in her brother's clothes. He called hello to her but she didn't answer; then he signaled the gang out of the trees. "You get everything squared away?"

"Everything is just grand, Bob. Thanks for asking."

The gang sashayed across the Caney River about a mile away from the posse and we got into no trouble at all. Then we split up. Grat and Doolin went southwest to summer at Cowboy Flat; Pierce and Newcomb returned to Bee Dunn's Rock Fort at Ingalls. Bob walked his horse off to Hennessey, where Eugenia had set up housekeeping again after her return from Silver City, New Mexico. Broadwell and Powers and I headed south for a bunkhouse at Skiatook, near Tulsa, where we could cover as hired hands and I could salt my money away for my South American fantasy.

I had the alias of Charlie McLaughlin when I worked on that Skiatook ranch; Broadwell was Texas Jack Moore again, and Powers was calling himself Tom Hedde, after a local badman he had a resemblance to. It was unbelievably dull work. I'd be in a saddle under an unpleasant sun sometimes seventeen hours a day, sore in the crotch, perspiring, walking my horse among hundreds of Hereford cattle. Their hides were glossy with sweat and their white eyelashes opened and closed on bluebottle flies, and incapable steers would keep climbing up on heifers until I kicked them off, raking my spurs on their pink nostrils if I could. I'd look across a panorama of heat wave and dust and dry yellow grass and see Broadwell in his dust goggles and his red bandana over his nose, dragging a wide-looped lariat, and Powers would have a brown-stained sombrero off and canteen water dripping from his hair, and the cattle would ruminate and stare as if I were the least challenging example of God's creative imagination, and I couldn't hardly believe that I'd ever robbed a train or scared any of the brave, stout hearts of the West. I forgot my fears and my arguments with Bob that quick. And I canceled out everything Julia had said. I wanted to be a dangerous man again.

Bob stayed quiet in the two-storey house near Hennessey. There he and Eugenia had a milk cow and three chickens and zucchini, green peppers, and corn in a garden marked with string. He walked the plant rows in the hot sun, sloshing water from a bucket, a soaked bandana tied to his head, while Eugenia sat in the shade of an elm tree with a wooden butter churn.

Then my brother Bill rode out to visit, bringing along a newspaper he'd picked up at a barber shop. He drank whiskey and water on the front porch swing while Bob read an account of an outlaw gang that had walked into the town of El Reno and robbed a bank in broad daylight. It had been ten in the morning and the streets were crowded with wagons and surreys, and women walked from window to window in their bustles and parasols, but the bandits strode right in and the wife of the bank president fainted and the gang remounted their horses with ten thousand dollars in a satchel.

When the article stated the outlaws were presumed to be Daltons, Bob slapped the newspaper down. Then he and Bill walked with their heads down and threw apples against the barn wall and made plans that they discussed with Eugenia as they washed and dried the supper dishes.

Then there must've been an argument about limiting participation, whittling down the gang. Newcomb was too interested in marriage these days and with him went Pierce. That was fine. But my brother Bill couldn't fathom why Bob would want to cut out Bill Doolin in favor of Grat. "Doolin's tough and smart and dominating, and Grat, well, he's my brother and I love him dearly but the poor guy is dumb as a turnip."

They weren't convinced and I guess Bill left in a huff that night; then Bob and Eugenia collaborated on a letter to Broadwell, Powers, and me at the Skiatook bunkhouse. They faced each other at the kitchen table, reciting sentences and composing. Eugenia poured tea and Bob leaned on his fist and passed an index finger through the lick of a candle flame, formulating tortuous paragraphs that Miss Moore copied down in her perfect schoolteacher's hand.

The gist of the letter was that they wanted a gang of five men to attempt a bank robbery in either Van Buren, Arkansas, or Coffeyville, Kansas. Van Buren, because the Clinton County Bank's president was Chief Marshal Jacob L. Yoes, who'd been Grat's boss two years ago and chided him on several occasions. Coffeyville, because we knew the town and the banks seemed easy and the Condon and the First National had both had the gall to deny brother Bill a loan.

Eugenia walked with a teacup reading the letter aloud to Bob. " 'But our plan is more provocative than it appears, for we choose not just to rob a certain bank in a town, but to rob *two banks at the same time!* an amazing exploit no other gang will dare duplicate, and awesome enough to overshadow the most famous raids of the James gang and the Youngers and others of that ilk.' "

My brother grinned. "Laid it on a little heavy there, didn't I."

She shrugged. "You need to evangelize sometimes."

I received the letter a week later and showed it to Broadwell and Powers in the bunkhouse. They'd signed it, "Yours affectionately," but just above that scribbled in, "Your comments are solicited." I didn't have many, nor did Bill and Dick, and I didn't hear another word about banks from my brother, so I figured it was just something he'd worked out on paper because he was peeved.

I remained a cowboy through August and most of September, and Bob and Eugenia vacationed on their stolen money. They watched the sun go down from the porch swing with their coffee cups and saucers in their hands. They lay on top of clean linen sheets and saw the morning sun whenever a breeze pushed the bedroom shade. He told her again about the thousand longhorn cattle they'd have on the ranch in Bolivia or Argentina where pasture grass grows so high it tickles your chin. She told him about the white plaster walls and the red tiles on the floor and the orange flowers in vases of crystal. She told him she'd wear a sun hat and carry an easel down to the beach where she'd paint pictures of the surf and sea gulls and South American fishing trawlers.

They picked green apples from the trees behind the farmhouse and they made love in the cool of the morning and night. And he smoked a pipe of Danish tobacco on the sofa while she read him poetry by Alfred Lord Tennyson.

" 'Though much is taken, much abides; and though we are not now that strength which in old days moved earth and heaven, that which we are, we are—one equal temper of heroic hearts, made weak by time and fate, but strong in will to strive, to seek, to find, and not to yield.' "

Eugenia closed the book. Bob blew pipe smoke and sat there.


**18** I think the informer was Bill. I think he rode down to Cowboy Flat, fifteen miles southeast of Guthrie, and talked with Doolin on the stoop of the Fitzgerald bunkhouse with tin cups of whiskey in their hands. It would have been night and the wind would have smelled like cattle and they'd talk about partnering in an outlaw gang, the Doolin-Dalton gang. My brother Bob's plans for Coffeyville, Kansas, would be somewhere inside of that. Doolin would glance at my brother and act like he didn't hear what was said about the two-bank job and he'd stand up to piss into pigweed, but before the month of September was half out, some cowboy with green scales on his teeth and a smell strong as turpentine would tell Marshall Jacob Yoes some of Doolin's gossip about how it was with the Daltons and banks.

Yoes took it kind of personal that his bank was being considered and he printed the man's words on yellow tablet paper and mailed a letter to Chris Madsen in Guthrie. "What do you make of this?" he wrote. Three cases of government issue rifles were shipped to the Isham Brothers and Mansur hardware store in Coffeyville, and a dozen men wasted the last of September and October 3rd and 4th clicking magnets together, picking through plumbing supplies, expanding and closing monkey wrenches, while they stared across a brick plaza at the Condon and Company bank.

When Bill Dalton was reached at his Bartlesville farm on October 5th, he had the sleeves of his white shirt rolled up and was chopping with a hoe in his garden. A newspaper reporter stood at the gateposts with his skimmer under his arm. "Am I the first to inform you?" he asked. My brother paused and leaned on his hoe. "Oh God."

I think it was Bill.

In middle September, Bob and Eugenia closed up the Hennessey house and sold the animals and Eugenia left to stay a week at the stockman's ranch of Dan Quick, her father. She said, "I'm going to South America. I've come here to say good-bye."

He stood at the stove stirring a cauldron of chili. After a while he said, "I thought you said good-bye many moons ago, Florence."

"I did. It needed repeating."

Powers, Broadwell, and I bid the Skiatook ranch good riddance when Amos Burton rode out from Dover and said Bob required us. It wasn't that I thought yea or nay about banks; Bob assumed I'd be there, so I went. The four of us stayed a week in the dugout, playing Monte next to a bonfire at night or relaxing in the sun smoking cigarettes with the broad leaves of Paradise trees on our heads. And when Bob came in from the west at last, my brother Grat was with him, two crockery jugs of cornmash in his lap.

Bob uncinched his saddle and unfolded the horse blanket on grass where the sun was while the men sat in the shade of the dugout overhang, rolling tobacco in papers and passing the jug. Bob slapped his hat off on his pants and found a currycomb in his saddlebags and squinted at me over the rump of his horse. "You make your proposal to Julia yet?"

"Nope."

"That's something we'll have to do then."

I said, "She won't marry me. I mean, it's not like she's some mail-order bride. She's like Miss Moore; she can have her pick. I'm gonna ask but she won't elope, not Julia. I think I'd be kind of disappointed in any girl who'd want to settle for me, anyway. That's true, I would. How smart could she be? Julia's going to say NO in capital letters. And I don't blame her, not one bit."

My brother seemed to think all that was funny. He said, "I believe your sales talk could use a little work, boy." Dust floated from the horsehide whenever he raked the comb. The mare's coat was polished with sweat where the blanket had been.

I said, "I reckon you and Eugenia had yourselves a good time on her farm."

"You bet," said Bob. "It was romantic as hell."

I stood there with thumbs hooked in my chaps and a cigarette between my fingers. I said, "Women can fix it, can't they."


The gang made Kansas by dusk of the next day and Coffeyville at midnight. This was practice, a trial run, Powers's and Broadwell's first real acquaintance with the town. We broke our horses out of a trot when we entered the Coffeyville city limits and walked Eighth Street past the Farmers' Home into the downtown business district. The street lamps were lit at the corner of each block and Ozark breakdown fiddle music was coming from the Masonic Hall at Maple and Ninth Street, but it was quiet and black otherwise and Bob had some trouble making out structures. Out of a sock in his saddlebag he got some reading spectacles I'd never seen him wear before and he hooked them on an ear at a time. "I can see clear to Nebraska with these."

He stopped his horse in front of the Opera House and said, "We'll wrap the reins over this hitching rail. That puts us in striking distance." Then we followed Bob in a walk around the west side of the Opera House past a short alley that no longer exists, that's now filled by the Chamber of Commerce office, the side limit of that alley being the rear of the two-storey Luther Perkins building which was narrower in front than back because of the angled convergence of the side streets of Walnut and Union, the resulting trapezoid considered as baffling an architectural wonder in the Sunflower State as the Flatiron Building was to New York. It was an 1890 construction, the pride of the town, as fussy and gimcracked as wedding cake, and occupying its front windows and first floor was the C. M. Condon and Company bank.

I sat down on the porch under its tin awning while the other four in the gang walked across Union Street, Bob whispering names and instructions in a voice so low I couldn't hear him three feet away. I read that the façade of the bank was designed by Mesker Brothers of St. Louis in 1887. The red bricks between my boots were manufactured by the Coffeyville Vitrified Brick and Tile Company, no date. Left across Union Street and hardly a spit away from the Condon's southeast door was the plate glass window of its rival bank, the smaller First National, which Bob and I would take.

It would happen this way: The Dalton gang would ride in on Eighth Street, park in front of the Opera House, split up to pilfer the banks. We'd return to the animals and cover the exit of whoever was last out and fire some shots to stall a commotion. We'd haul east on Eighth for our getaway, horseshoes sparking on the bricks, and turn south on Patterson Boulevard, behind the stores, galloping next to the Santa Fe tracks to Elmwood Cemetery where Eugenia would pick us up. Then we'd meet black Amos Burton in a schooner wagon of cotton bales, hiding under them until we got to the Missouri River where we'd board a riverboat south and then a transatlantic steamer.

The two banks did not seem difficult at the time.

I kept a lookout in that midnight town while Broadwell and Powers hunched over to peer at the walnut counters of the First National, while Bob delivered lessons. I saw Grat sag against the doorjamb and stare across the plaza to the Lang & Lape Furniture Dealers and Undertakers parlor which was next to Slosson's drugstore. Slosson sold medicinal liquor.

That must've given my boozy brother the notion. I saw him spit tobacco juice between his teeth and amble south along the boardwalk past the Isham Brothers and Mansur hardware store next door to the bank, then past McDermott's millinery, Smith's barbershop, Boothby's drugstore, and Barndollar's Dry Goods and Sundries store, where he turned the corner and I lost him.

I learned secondhand that Grat stepped over the white picket fence to the yard of a house owned by Mr. Benson of the Slosson store. Grat kicked at the storm door panel until Benson opened up, and the man was so terror-struck at seeing a Dalton that he later claimed Grat was Bob, and it's been handed down that way ever since. He even invented two pearl-handled revolvers and swore the ruffian demanded a bottle of Austin Nichols Wild Turkey, a probability. Benson alibied pretty good, however, saying Slosson's store hadn't traded in whiskey since the Populists were elected, so Grat stayed thirsty, and he was fuming by the horses when four of the dangerous-looking Dalton gang finally returned to the Opera House.

Our horses were standing asleep at the hitching rail and Grat was watching a jet of tobacco juice squirm down the Opera House window glass. Grat said, "By morning this whole town's gonna know we been here. So don't count on no big surprise."

Bob unwrapped his reins from the rail. "How will they know?"

Grat decided not to answer. He slipped his stirrup over his boot and jerked his horse around so hard getting on that the whites showed in its eyes.

Bob asked, "How?" again, and his thirty-one-year-old brother slumped in his saddle, smiling with brown teeth. Grat said, "I peed my name against a door."


That morning Marshal Jacob Yoes and Deputy Marshal Chris Madsen were sent telegrams about us from City Marshal

Charles T. Connelly. And the five of us slept on the autumn-cold earth beside the Caney River. I woke up with a backache and I did nothing all day but watch a woman and two small children dressed in brown walk slowly through the afternoon, shucking corn from the husks. The woman had water in a goatskin. She shaded her eyes once and she must've seen us, but she just picked up her bushel basket and lugged it toward the barn.

I danced around in the muck of a smarting-cold river, washing with laundry soap; then shaved and dressed in a black wool suit and practiced my speech with Bob. Then he and I stood on the porch of the Texas Johnson farmhouse with the sun going down red in his cherry trees. I had rose oil in my hair and a borrowed white hat in my hand and my brother had brushed down my clothes with a straw broom. Julia pushed open the screen and she flustered with the surprise of our visit and poured tea and sugar into two glasses. Bob carried his out to the backyard garden where he sat with a frightened Mrs. Johnson on a peach tree seat and was as pleasant as a seminarian.

Julia and I sat across from each other in the front room, drinking tea and eating gingersnaps. She'd changed into a blue gingham dress with puffs and bows and her long black hair was coiled and twisted with ribbons. She'd rouged her cheeks with the stain of artificial geraniums and she'd powdered her dark skin with cornstarch.

I stared at the labels of canned goods and coffee packages they'd tacked up on the walls as decorative art—the practice in those days. On the front of a package of clothing starch was a pinafored girl on a swing. I told Julia she looked pretty as that.

She blushed at her shoes, then put her glass down on a doily and asked, "Would you like me to play some music?"

I said I would and she moved to the piano bench and I listened with my finger at my temple as she played "Amazing

Grace," "Washed in the Blood of the Lamb," and "Jesus, Help Me to Remember."

I said, "What's that one they call 'Here Comes the Bride'?"

She kept her back to me and turned the page of a music sheet. "That's not the name of it."

I said, "Why don't you play that?"

She got up from the bench, smiling ever so gaily at her guest. "My fingers are getting tired."

She had a white kitten that she put pendant earrings on. It clawed at my pants leg and nipped my knuckles and the jewelry waggled from its ears and we spent more time than necessary being amused. Then the kitten got bored with the taste of my fingers and pawed at something under the piano and I said, "I'm supposed to ask you to go with Amos Burton in a schooner and meet Bob and Eugenia and me, thence to Joplin and a boat south, posing as immigrants."

I think she listened twice to every word. Her face was pained and touched and worried and in love, all at once.

I said, "I'm supposed to ask you to elope."

She shook her head. "But you're not going to ask me that, are you. You won't want to hear me say no to you so you won't even venture the question."

I don't know what I did then. Maybe I was nervous with my hands. I said, "No. I reckon I'll be too flummoxed and shy."

We walked outside and she sat in the swing and we were quiet together for a long time, watching clouds devour and relinquish the moon. I said, "I never wanted it to happen this way. I wanted to stop it a long time ago. I guess one thing just led to another. It's like I fell into a river." I threw a stick. "That sounds stupid, doesn't it."

She leaned on the ropes of the swing. "No. I suppose that's exactly what it *is* like."

"I'm twenty years old, Julia. I got everything still in front of me. There's a little something I have to do yet, but then I'm going to say good-bye to the past and start my life all over again. And it would truly choke me up if you'd consent to be my company. You don't have to say anything now. You can just send one word to the telegraph office in Joplin: Yes or No; that's it."

We strolled around to the backyard where one of the boarders sat with Mrs. Johnson and Bob was smelling the sweet William while they talked about the water on the moon. I shook hands with Julia's mother but I was sour-faced over my smile, and the man who called her Daughter glowered with suspicion as Julia linked her arm with mine and walked me slowly to my horse. I kissed her cheek and she hugged me and cried into my coat, "I don't want you to leave."

I didn't say anything more. I just petted her hair until my brother came up, and then I rode off with him, pushing the animals pretty hard. Then we let them tarry on the road but I still didn't say diddily-poop to my brother Bob who always got what he wanted. He knew what there was to be quiet about but he said at last, "How was it?"

"She fixed it all right," I said.

He crossed his arms on his saddle pommel and we heard the mutter of a rainstorm somewhere in the distance. He said, "Emmett, you've got no *idea* how your life is going to improve. Pretty soon you're going to have any woman you want. You'll come back to your hotel room at night and they'll be standing at your door. They'll steal handkerchiefs from your pockets and buttons off your coats and they'll write you letters pleading for locks of your hair. Wait a month and you'll see. You just can't conceive of what it's like to be famous. That's how special it is."

And he was right. I couldn't conceive of it.

Miss Moore had the gumption to steal six horses from her hated father, and the five of us stole our clothes. Bob used the keys the general store owners in Gray Horse had given him when he was the Osage police chief and he opened the front doors one night and the Dalton gang bumped into each other in the dark, hardwood aisles, pulling starched white shirts out of blue boxes mailed from Chicago, wadding and throwing out odorous long underwear, slinging striped pants and checked pants and corduroys on our shoulders. We skimmed our sweat-browned hats to the floor to try on white round-tops, black slouch hats, and bowlers, derbies, muleys, silk top hats, and tan stetsons with indented crowns. Powers buttoned a cable-knit sweater over a vest and blue flannel shirt; Broadwell wore an ankle-long gentleman's coat over a sheepherder's tweed; Grat stood his stiffened jeans against a corner.

From another store we got saddles: not just Texas working saddles with the leather soiling black and the lead wearing through the horn and the ties forever breaking off like shoe-strings, but Mexican saddles, five of them, with stirrups of plated silver, all sturdy as pews and deep as trousers, with roses and tulips hand-tooled at tree and hindbow and side bars, and this leather so soft it was slow to recover from the prod of a finger. They creaked with the newness like boats and hinges and snow at ten below zero. I never felt so regal.

Then we went south in buffalo grass that was high as our flashing spurs, seeing six horses in the sod house corral, seeing Eugenia Moore hang clothes on a line, snapping them out of a bushel basket. Next to the sod house was a schooner with the white tarp off its ribs and a black man caking grease on the front axle and sliding on a spoked wheel. Amos Burton said something over his shoulder about the approaching riders and Eugenia turned and waved.

My brother Bob yawed his horse to meet her; Grat and I stayed in a walk with Broadwell and Powers as they talked animatedly about hopping a freight train to New York after-wards so they could eat prime ribs at Delmonico's and attend the Wintergarden Theater with consorts. I said, "Maybe I'll just join you boys instead of traipsing off to South America. I've always hankered to be a city slicker and I think you ought

to travel to somewheres really eye-opening when you come
into a ton of money."

"Yep," said Grat, who hadn't a single plan beyond per-
petual drunkenness. "Kind of gives you ants in your pants,
don't it?"


I don't remember much about that last week in the sod house,
only the blankets strung up between the bunks and the whisper of a man and woman behind them and Broadwell walking
around like a circus clown, lifting off his tall hat to show his
cat Turtle underneath it on his head. I spent mornings in the
sun combing out a brood mare's tail and I watched the white
clouds castle in the blue and I lay by a cooking fire at night
with an oil can and cotton rags and a handkerchief spread on
the red dirt, disassembling a nickel-plated pistol while that
shipment of government issue rifles arrived in Coffeyville,
Kansas. They were stored in the Isham Brothers and Mansur
store which commanded a view of the plaza, and for two days
in October too many men spent time at the bins and crates
and nail kegs, waiting on us, so that by the 5th there wasn't
much worry anymore and City Marshal Connelly would leave
his gun in the middle drawer of his desk as he took his morning walk.


Then Amos Burton hitched a team of four horses to the wagon
and left. Grocery boxes squeaked against each other; bottles
clinked on the bumps. Broadwell and Powers watered and
shoed Dan Quick's horses while Grat and Bob and I took turns
sitting under the freckled shade of a poplar with a bed sheet
under our chins and a soap mug, black strop, and razor in our
laps. Eugenia rolled up her dress sleeves to give us haircuts
with scissors and comb. She brushed the snippings into paper
bags she'd lettered with our names and she and Bob sat at a

three-legged table out of the sun, gluing hair onto linen for imitation mustaches and beards.

Bob said, "We'll have a hacienda with paddle fans on all the ceilings and hired women to iron the sheets and important men in white suits and Panama hats will wait on the verandah with teacups and secretaries while you and I sleep in the afternoon."

She smiled. "You should see your eyes sparkle." She pressed a goatee to his chin, then took it off and trimmed it. "I want you to look like Sir Walter Raleigh."


**19** Soon as it was dark enough, we saddled our horses and took a road to Kansas that was baked hard as adobe. The sumac leaves were bright red, the maple trees turning orange, and the farmers were burning firebreaks and weeds and scrub timber so a blue haze clung to the earth. I could smell leaf smoke in my shirt. I rode quite a ways with my arm up to my nose, intoxicated by the scent.

We made the P. L. Davis farm on Onion Creek by middle afternoon of October 4th. Broadwell cut the barbwire fence with nippers and then tied the horses under box elder trees while Powers and I snuck through Mrs. J. F. Savage's corn patch stuffing husking ears in our shirts.

The gang ate supper on saddle blankets, not saying a peep to each other, and we were still awake at eleven when Bob knelt by a small corncob fire to draw the city streets again for Broadwell and Powers and Miss Moore. Then my brother emptied his pockets and dropped into the fire a bill of sale, a solunar table, and a business card with a calendar on the back. Broadwell had letters from his Hutchinson, Kansas, home in his saddlebag and these he burned one by one so he couldn't be traced back to them. I used a penknife to pry a locket photograph of Julia from my watch fob and I saw it curl black on the embers. It seemed a solemn occasion until Eugenia performed, amidst guffaws, the dolorous farewell letter she'd sent to Bob via Silver City, which she then tore up and let flutter away from the fire on the wind so it could be found and puzzled together.

Then my brother and his fiancée retired to a blanket by the river. She lay between his legs and scratched her name into his stomach with the fingernails she'd grown for him. And Bob sat up on his elbows in the autumn leaves and said, "You know, when you think about the kind of prig I was as a kid, it seems peculiar I ever got into stealing. I wanted to be a saint back then. I wanted to be as great a lawman as Pat Garrett, as noble as King Arthur's knights. I don't know where those notions went but I think they've vanished forever. Thievery isn't my vice anymore; it's my habit."

Eugenia smiled and drew a valentine heart where his heart was, her chin on her other fist. She said, "Same here. I can't look at a hundred-dollar horse without thinking it's mine by default. As a girl I used to see handsome men I wanted and I'd wonder how they could possibly consider themselves married to anyone else. Whenever I walk through a store, I see thousands of exquisite things that I'm sure really ought to belong to me, and it's as if I owned them already."

They were quiet in the dark. The river moved. She said, "Chris Madsen once arrested me and asked how an educated lady could ever involve herself with rustling. I didn't really have an answer."

My brother said, "You should've told him the temptation was very strong."

I don't think they slept a wink that night because the two of them were walking in the trees when Broadwell shook me awake for the dogwatch at four. I cooked some coffee and hunkered down in the chill under the sickle moon and I shivered there with my rifle against my cheek until I could hear the roosters crow on the farms.

I walked among the men in the bedrolls, kicking them in

the feet. Powers jerked up with a gun in his hand and looked around at the morning. I cooked bacon in an iron pan and made another pot of black coffee and observed Eugenia kneeling in front of Bob sticking a brown mustache and fancy goatee to his face, and holding a mirror up. "I look Shakespearean," he said.

"At least you don't look twenty-two."

My brother Grat kept scowling and chewing his bacon as she worked on him and he merely glanced at the mirror and scratched his face when he saw the dark mustache and side-whiskers they call muttonchops, which, Colonel Elliott later claimed, "gave him the look of an ancient pirate."

Powers knelt near the fire and shoved a pipe cleaner down his pipe stem. Broadwell lifted back his long top hair and looked at his baldness in the mirror. "Do you think if I cut my hair it would thicken? It does that for grass you know. Only thing I'm afraid of is that I'd be short and sparse at the same time."

Powers blew air through his pipe stem and screwed it onto the bowl. He said, "The trouble is you're too brainy, Dick. Your brains cut off the blood supply to your scalp."

Because I was a mere twenty years old, Eugenia gave me maturity with a dark beard that blew in the wind and showed the linen underneath. The mucilage stuck so hard it burned my skin later when John Kloehr bent over and ripped the mustache off.

She said, "Do you know where I was five years ago, Em? I was in a dinky Missouri town putting makeup on school-children for a play about Captain John Smith and Pocahontas. I was Eugenia Moore, the schoolmarm, and I was convinced the rest of my life would be no more exciting than a Sunday piano recital."

I said, "This is kind of a change of speed for you then, isn't it. You'll knock on the pearly gates a dang contented woman."

She finished with my disguise and I stirred the fire out with a stick and poured coffee onto the hissing coals. Last night's eggshells were scattered on the ground. Bob stood at his sad-dlebags and put an oil can and a pair of gentleman's gloves into the pockets of his black suit coat. He wore a six-button vest and a blue wool lumberjack shirt and a tall, bell-crowned hat that was duplicated by William S. Hart in his movies. I could've been my brother's twin that day because I dressed exactly as he did except for a white shirt with a celluloid collar and a fantastic wide tie that resembled blue-veined marble. Grat had the stain of chewing tobacco on his chin as he sur-veyed me. "You gonna curtsy to the queen?"

My horse was a fifteen-hand roan-colored stallion with orange mane and tail, called Red Buck. He nickered when I walked over and fed him a ration of oats in a canvas sack with leather ties sewed into it. Then I slapped the feed sack clean and folded it up under my vest and Broadwell asked, "Are we ready?" and I climbed up into the saddle.

Bob sat on his dapple-gray gelding with a toothbrush in his hand, rinsing baking soda out of his mouth with night-cold canteen water. In his black holster he had a .45 caliber pearl-handled Colt with floral engravings on a blue metal frame. Snug under his vest in a left shoulder sling was a small .38 caliber Brisley Bulldog. They're now in museum display.

Eugenia rode out of red and yellow trees in buckskin britches and a sheepskin coat and a dark brown stetson with her blond hair pinned underneath it. She looked like a boy of sixteen. Bob smiled at her. "You're great."

Then the Dalton gang jogged along Onion Creek at 8:15, thudding and clanking like cavalry. Broadwell put on his dust goggles. Powers was so quiet you'd forget he was there. Grat gouged out some earwax with a toothpick and said, "When I was crossing the desert rattlesnakes struck at my stirrups and spiders drank from my eyes as I slept. I pried a tooth out with a dinner fork. I don't think I can be scared anymore."

"That happens," said Bob. "I saw a soldier who was scalped and left for dead by the Sioux. Nothing else could ever touch him after that. He walked around like he was asleep."

I unbuckled my saddlebag and handed my binoculars in their leather case across to my brother Bob. He hung them over his neck and they were later claimed by the undertaker W. H. Lape. Black crows picked their steps in the yellow corn stubble, and freshly shocked corn stood shredding brown in the fields. I heard the hound's groan of a windmill.

Just then James Brown's ten-year-old daughter was riding a barebacked mare to the schoolhouse in Coffeyville, and she saw six horses and riders ladder up the bank under a rickety bridge of curled boards. She followed close after us with her books strapped in a belt but turned east when we missed the shortcut.

In Coffeyville, Charles Brown, a shoemaker of fifty-nine, rehung the big wooden boot on the signpost in front of his shop. Next to the sidewalk was a bare, twisted oak tree enclosed in a square picket fence that he swept around with a twig broom. The mechanic George Cubine, thirty-six years old, Brown's partner, stood with his shoulder against the doorjamb, a coffee cup curling steam in his hands. He smiled. "See any evildoers?"

"Nope," said Brown. "And ain't that a cryin' shame?"

Young T. C. Babb peered in the window of Mitchell's restaurant and saw Charles M. Ball push an unfinished bowl of oatmeal away and put a dime on the table. Babb was crew-cut and twenty years old and worked only part-time at the Condon bank. Ball was the cashier. They walked across Walnut Street to the bank and Ball opened the southwest front door with two keys. "What was it again you had to get done?"

"Oh, those government checks to the Indians. What a pain."

Ball kept the shades drawn and walked to the vault room and stood there watching the hands on his pocket watch until the safe's time lock clicked off at 8:30. Babb slammed record books down on the counter. "That time lock's quite an invention," Ball said. He snapped his pocket watch closed.

A stout man with a handlebar mustache, Henry Isham, crossed the Santa Fe tracks at Tenth Street. He could see his clerks Louis A. Dietz and Arthur Reynolds standing with lunch boxes on the loading dock of the hardware store owned by himself and his brother and son-in-law. Dietz had a rusty monkey wrench he'd discovered by the tracks. He rubbed it on his pants and dropped it into his shirt pocket when Isham walked up the stairs to the dock. Isham shook out his keys. "Sun feels good, doesn't it."

At the country road two miles from town, we turned east on what is now Highway 166. The horses were skittish and surly and showed their long teeth over the mouth bits like they'd been gagged. Their tails swung at flies; their shoes skidded on pebbles. I could make out the scaling red paint on a barn a quarter mile to the right. In the shaded backyard of the house a woman was hanging bed sheets on a clothesline. They billowed suddenly white in the sun. To the left of the road I could only see a boy turned around on the seat of a mule-powered high-sided wagon while two farmers in straw hats and rolled shirtsleeves, one of them William Gilbert, quickly shucked husks of corn and tossed them against the bangboard.

Bob had his horse in a swinging trot and his woman was riding next to him, with wisps of long hair squiggling out over her eyes in the breeze. I rode up beside her but she didn't look in my direction. I said, "Autumn is my favorite season; because the colors are so radiant and the air smells like apples and you can reap the bounty of the hot weather's toils. If there was a country where it was autumn all the time, I believe that's where I'd go."

Eugenia said, "It's autumn every day in Argentina. That's why so many Germans inhabit the place."

I said, "I don't like Germans and they don't like me."

My brother complained, "Why don't you two go over what we're about to do instead of prattling about foreign countries? Do you know what your jobs are, and where and when they have to be done? Ask yourselves those questions."

Eugenia smiled at me. "Do you feel chastened?"

The gang passed a dairy barn of mortar and stone and the cheese factory where a boy was shrugged under the weight of two sloshing milk cans. Soon thereafter I could see white church spires over trees piled with colored leaves and rattling under them was a maroon carriage with fancy gold trim containing Mr. and Mrs. R. H. Hollingsworth, who later swore that we were six, not five, that our appearance was peculiar, and that we were heavily armed. Grat and Broadwell swept off their hats for the missus and bowed low on their steeds. Two brothers, J. M. and J. L. Seldomridge, approached in a weathered gray wagon with crates of white hominy and onion they were trucking to Sedan. J. M. was blowing his nose in a brown handkerchief and did not recognize me because of my beard. He stuffed the handkerchief in his pocket and knelt on the box seat to stare backwards at us. He shouted, "Hey, which posse you with?"

Powers turned in his saddle and glared and J. M. sat down in his seat facing front.

They too claimed there were six.

It was only when we got to what was known as the Hickman property on Eighth Street that Eugenia kissed Bob on the cheek and wished us good luck and skirted her horse south through yellow bars of light in the trees. The sixth man has ever since been a mystery, becoming at various times Bill Doolin, whose horse at the last minute came up lame, or a Coffeyville hoodlum named Alley Ogee, or a gabby liar named Buckskin Ike, or Caleb Padgett, who made that confession from his deathbed in 1934. The sixth man was a woman named Eugenia Moore, who stood her horse at my brother Frank's grave in the Elmwood Cemetery and walked down the rows reading headstones with her hands in the pockets of a man's sheepskin coat.

**20** The Dalton gang loped our horses along Eighth Street with our gear slapping and clanking and the road loud as wood under the horseshoes. There were houses to the right and left of us with women in aprons at the screen doors, shading their eyes, and a man in suspenders in a backyard with a wheelbarrow and a shovel, and a small boy in short pants and a lunch box, kicking a tomato can down the sidewalk. We were still two and three in formation, with Bob and me to the front, as we crossed the street where the limestone Episcopal church was. A girl sat on the board sidewalk in a yellow dress, staring at us as she yanked up her stockings. Our coats skirted up off our holsters and the Dalton gang was riding hard to Walnut Street when Bob pulled his horse to such a stop it almost sat down. The four of us stopped with him or circled our horses around until they quit and road dust drifted over us.

Three black workmen were prying loose the bricks of the plaza where they'd buckled up in front of the Opera House and the Eldridge House, and the hitching rack was torn down in a mess of disrepair.

"Ain't this a pisser," said Grat.

One of the black men leaned on his pick. I said, "I guess we call it a day and go home, huh Bob?" But my brother was already wheeling around and he kicked his horse back to Maple Street and swung south and our horses jostled to follow him. Left on Maple was the office of the Long-Bell Lumber Company and the Davis blacksmith shop where a man was banging iron on an anvil. He did not look up as we jogged our horses past. We turned left into a wide alley of cinder and dirt that ran east and west between Maple and Walnut streets, with the Long-Bell lumberyard along it quite a ways. An oil tank wagon with a dark brown workhorse team belonging to the

Consolidated Company, later Standard Oil, was parked up ahead in the alley and near the city jail halfway up there was a stonecutter who was tilting a rock curb up, examining it, and cracking it back down. Otherwise the alley was empty and it was 9:30 on an autumn Wednesday morning in 1892. The sun was yellow and warm, and leaves were burning not far away.

Bob tied his horse to the pipe that was the top railing of the hitching rack at the rear of Police Judge Munn's lot, which was brown with cornstalks and braced tomato plants that had burnt up in the sun. The rest of us got down too and the horses cropped grass as we strode east in the alley, not speaking; Grat, Dick Broadwell, and Bill Powers in front, Bob and me after, five Winchester rifles loose in our arms and the gang dressed in black hats and silk-trimmed black coats and trousers as fine as you wear with tuxedos.

Aleck McKenna was in a denim apron smoking a cigarette under the rolled-down awning of the McKenna and Adamson store to our left. He looked at us as we walked into Walnut Street and he later claimed he recognized Grat by his slouched walk, but he just stood there then, holding his elbow. Dray wagons were slanted up to the hitching racks of Union Street and a woman in a white bonnet walked down that board sidewalk from Barndollar's store at the corner to Brown and Cubine's shoe shop where a bell rang when she opened the door. Cyrus Lee chopped an ice block in the back of his wagon and shouted small talk to a man in Slosson's drugstore to my right. Lee ceased stabbing his ice pick and frowned at my artificial beard.

We crossed the plaza and our boots rasped on the brick and I could see the three plate glass windows of the C. M. Condon and Company bank and the porch-shaded glass of the smaller First National on Union Street between Rammel Brothers drugs and the Isham hardware store which sat just opposite the alley. The bank looked green and the wood was dark. Bob said, "I made a mistake, Em. It should be the other way around. You and I should take the Condon."

But by then Grat had his hands down in his coat pockets and his rifle tilted down and Powers glanced from window to window in all the second-storey rooms, and when I turned and walked backwards I saw that Aleck McKenna was talking to Cyrus Lee about us and they were shading their eyes to stare. I almost lifted my gun.

Grat bent to spit a half-yard of tobacco juice; then he stomped up onto the porch of the Condon bank and jerked the closest of two pairs of doors as Bob and I ran across the bricks that were Union Street and ducked unnecessarily under the awning of the First National Bank. I held the screen door open and looked around. My brother turned the porcelain knob on the lettered door.

Charley Gump sat on the tailgate of his wagon with a toothpick and he soaked up what he'd seen—five men, five rifles, two banks—and when he noticed Broadwell and Powers lift blue bandanas over their noses inside the Condon bank, he limped down the sidewalk leaning big-eyed into the open stores, shouting, "By God, it's true! It's the Daltons! The Daltons are robbing the bank!"

The cry carried and women in bustles ran from the streets and dogs took up barking. McKenna walked up to his store and Cyrus Lee hustled down into Slosson's to borrow a rifle and soon men were crouched behind windows staring out at us. I saw the beginnings of a commotion but I didn't say anything. I slammed the door of the bank behind me, rattling the glass, and pulled down the shiny green curtains.

Three customers were already there: Deputy Sheriff Abe W. Knott, J. B. Brewster, the contractor, and C. L. Hollingsworth. They were big men in dark suits and Brewster had his hat off as he did arithmetic. He'd combed about six strands of black hair from one side of his head to the other. Knott had just cashed a four-dollar check.

The cashier's cage was seven feet high with walnut up to the writing counter, then grillwork and frosted glass. It had a marble base and one barred teller's window at which stood

Thomas G. Ayres, the cashier. He had sleeve garters on. The teller was W. H. Sheppard who was Bob's age and polite as you please and always unaccountably happy. He was slouched in the chair of the rolltop desk, his bifocals off and crossed on a page, when tall Emmett Dalton, the one with the fake dark beard of his summer hair, slammed the door and disturbed whatever was going on.

Sun streaked off Bob's rifle when he swung it up from his hip. He yelled, "Hands up! Everybody! You men stay right where you are!"

The cashier flinched and the customers frowned like we were spoiling their morning.

I levered the hammer back on my rifle and shouted, "You pay attention to this machine, cuz I can put a chunk of lead in your chin that'll rip your face off like it was only a washrag with eyebrows."

Ayres said, "Oh, come now, Emmett."

I ignored him.

Deputy Sheriff Knott kept trying to lower his hand to his vest and I was scared he might have a purse pistol there until I saw he had his four dollars wrapped on his fingers and wanted the money in his wallet. I said, "I don't want your chicken feed, Abe."

Knott said, "I think—"

"Shut up."

I tossed my brother the canvas feed sack I'd pulled out from under my vest and he wadded it and pushed it through the grill and the cashier slowly shoved ones and twos and fives and tens inside, then gathered coins from the tray in both hands and started heaving them in.

Bob said, "Keep that silver out. It's too heavy." He tapped the counter's marble base with the toe of his boot and smiled at Brewster next to him. "Was it a deposit or a withdrawal?"

Brewster said, "I was checking on a mortgage."

"We leave the papers whenever we can."

Brewster nodded. "That's considerate of you. It can be a real inconvenience."

Bob kicked the swinging door and walked back to the private office where Tom's son, Bert Ayres, was standing at a bookkeeper's desk. He'd pissed his pants with fear and his shirttail was out to hide it.

My brother said, "You go up front and help out your dad. Just your paper money."

Bert obeyed and Bob unlatched the spring lock to the iron-grated back door and, with his pistol up next to his cheek, leaned out into the back alley. It was sunlit and vacant. Red maple leaves skittered and stuck to the screen. A black dog was leashed to a delivery door and was chewing at itself. A dozen other dogs in the town were barking the same news over and over again.

I had my rifle at my shoulder and I squinted from Sheppard to Hollingsworth to Knott. The gun turned them all into women. I heard the clomp of boots on the sidewalk and turned to see J. E. S. Boothby crouched at the plate glass peering in while the boy Jack Long watched the Condon bank with his elbows on a railing in front of Rammel's drugstore.

I yanked the door. "You son of a gun, Jim! Get in here!"

Boothby was hardly fifteen then. He flung up his hands and his face drained white and he tottered when he walked in. I banged the window with my rifle stock and young Jack Long dashed next door into Rammel's.

Boothby said, "I sure don't know what I could've been thinking."

Then Bob walked out of the back office and took the feed sack and Mr. Ayres with him into the vault room where there was a safe not much bigger than an oven, manufactured by the Mosler Safe Company. Bob slouched against the office door frame and glared over his shoulder at all the Kansans in the front room while Ayres knelt to turn the combination and toss out some currency rolled in rubber bands. He sat back on his heels and closed the vault door.

Bob frowned. "Is that *all?*"

"You don't want the gold, do ya Bob?"

"Heck yes, Tom. Every cent."

Ayres opened the strongbox again and carried out gold coins in his shirt. They jangled when he walked and some got loose and rang across the floor when he poured them into the feed sack.

"Is that everything?" Bob asked.

I called from the front, "Let's go, Bob!"

Bob displayed his rifle to Ayres. "I want to know if that's everything."

Ayres said, "You bet."

Bob slammed him against the frosted glass. I could see the white imprint of Tom's shirt, then shadow again, and I heard Bob bang open the strongbox. Ayres stood by the swinging door of the counter and shrugged at Sheppard as if it had been a noble effort. Sheppard smiled back. Hollingsworth had his eyes shut. Knott was frowning at me, his hands still high.

"How do your arms feel, Abe?"

"I'd have to say they're pretty sore."

"It won't be long now," I said.

I could see south on Union Street where one of the teamsters was teaching his horses to back up. He got a flatbed wagon and a lumber truck into the middle of the street, barricading it; then he snuck back into Isham's hardware. Bob came out of the office with two packs of bank notes worth five thousand dollars apiece. "What's this, Tom? Huh? Why'd you lie to me?"

It was 9:40.

Bob stood at the depository and angrily dumped a bag of silver coins on the floor. He lifted a box of gold watches but Sheppard told him it was merely fiduciary papers and I told my brother we'd better leave, so Bob left the box and he wrestled Bert Ayres back through the swinging door to stand next to Sheppard, and told the two of them to stay put. Meanwhile, Tom Ayres, Boothby, and the three customers stood at the front door with their hands raised while I took up the feed sack of money. It was heavy as a milk can and my fingers went white with the strain. Bob turned the porcelain knob and pushed open the screen and the five men walked on out like schoolchildren.

The mechanic George Cubine was hunkered down with a Winchester in the doorway of Rammel's with the boy Jack Long and Mr. C. S. Cox, who had a Dance Brothers percussion revolver. Soon as Bob took a step out onto the bank porch there was a *whang* and the door casing splintered. Bob sprang back inside and grinned sheepishly at me. "Who was that, Cubine?" He peered through a gap in the shade to see the three bank customers crawling away on the bricks. "*He's* a shabby marksman, isn't he. Spose he could hit me with a banjo?"

I set the sack down and regripped it and picked it up again. "Can we get out the back?"

"I think so."

But instead he cocked his rifle and walked out onto the sidewalk as calmly as a man looking for a newspaper and a chair. Neither Cubine nor Cox showed themselves but Bob swiveled to see Charley Gump next to the horse collar that hung on Isham's awning post. Gump was bringing back the hammer on a ten-gauge when all at once there was a blast from Bob's rifle and Charley's hand tore apart and the wood stock splintered off at the shotgun's pinion and Charley cried out with pain that stung clear to his teeth. Then Bob was inside the bank again, shoving past me for the rear. I yanked Sheppard out of his chair as hostage, leaving Bert Ayres behind, and Bob held the iron-grated door for me and then the three of us left the cool of the bank for the heat and dust of the alley.

As I said, Grat slung his rifle on his arm and spit his tobacco and walked inside the C. M. Condon and Company bank and the yellow shade slapped the window glass when he closed the door. Bill Powers leaned on an outside awning post while Dick Broadwell walked the board porch and then the two of them opened the two pairs of doors, Bill at the southwest, Dick the southeast. Sunlight sprawled across the floor and the bankers wrote in their ledgers and there was the clack of typewriter keys in the office. The bank counter was larger and more ornate than that at the First National. It had pegs instead of nails, the wood was carved walnut made dark with linseed oil, and it cost more than a small farm. Over the teller's grill was a sign that read: PROTECTED BY NORTH BRITISH AND MERCANTILE INSURANCE CO. OF LONDON AND EDINBURGH, ESTABLISHED 1890.

T. C. Babb stood at a desk on the east side of the front room, writing out government checks, when he saw Broadwell on the board porch lift up the blue bandana on his face. He picked out Grat as soon as my brother shut the door and Babb snuck into a back room where he hid behind a ceiling-high rack of ledgers and journals. Vice-president Charles T. Carpenter wore a cardboard collar and a striped blue tie and he had a counter drawer open and the spring clasps up, counting twenties and tens when the three robbers entered.

My brother Grat walked forward like he was five men, like he weighed nine hundred pounds. Carpenter backed away from the counter. Grat yelled, "We got you now, God damn it! Hold up your hands!"

Charles M. Ball sat in his yellow office at the rear, unwrapping a throat lozenge as he read half a letter to the Wells Fargo Company that was rolled into his typewriter. He had the side door onto Walnut Street open for the breeze. He heard noise in the front of the bank and pushed himself up from his chair and walked out into the front room where Powers quickly shouldered his rifle. "You can just get your hands in the air."

"Is this a robbery?"

Powers said, "Yes sir, it is."

Grat got behind the counter through Carpenter's office on

the right. He jerked open all the counter drawers and saw Ball standing there and pitched him a seamless two-bushel grain sack. "You hold this while your boss fills it."

Carpenter pushed packets of bills still wrapped in paper tapes into the bottom of the grain sack and Grat sat up on the counter, swinging his legs. In Carpenter's office was a wall clock with three vials of mercury in the pendulum. The clock read 9:36.

Carpenter lifted the money to Ball, the bills flapping together. "Look how my hands are shaking."

Mr. Ball held the sack out and stared at my brother until he was sure the burly man under the muttonchop whiskers was the oldest of the notorious Dalton boys. He remembered what speed Grat's brain was.

Grat asked Carpenter where he kept the gold and didn't like the answer. So he pushed both bankers toward the vault room in the back, then saw T. C. Babb crouched down next to the purple bound ledgers. He swore and grabbed the book-keeper by the shirtfront and swung him into a chair. Powers poked his rifle through the teller's grill at Babb. "Now I want you obedient, boy."

The Condon had a black, walk-in, two-door vault with gold leaf trim and a time lock on the safe that had clicked free at 8:30 that morning when Ball had opened up. The safe and its combination lock were guaranteed burglarproof by the Hall Company, the manufacturers.

Carpenter dropped three canvas bags of silver coins, three thousand dollars total, into the grain sack. He was swallowing back his breakfast. "I'm sorry but I have to sit down."

Grat pressed his rifle sight into the man's cheek. "I want your safe opened."

Carpenter sagged. "Ask Mr. Ball. I never handle those things."

Grat pulled his rifle away. There was a red mark on Carpenter's cheek. Grat glared at Ball, a sickly, disciplined man who couldn't climb stairs without rests on the landings, who couldn't take food much rougher than soup. Grat demanded that Ball open it.

"Don't I wish I could," said Ball. "It's automatic, ya see. Operates off its own clock."

Grat tried to read the cashier's face but I guess he missed the lie. "What time does it open?"

"9:45."

Carpenter looked dumbfounded at Ball and then he looked down at his shoes.

My brother asked, "What time is it now?"

Ball opened up a steel pocket watch in his hand and snapped it shut. "9:38."

Carpenter lightly tested the safe handle. It rattled but didn't budge. "See there? It's closed up tight as a drum."

Grat squatted down opposite Carpenter. "We can wait seven minutes."

Dick Broadwell knelt at the varnished southeast doors and sat back on his heels and stared through the plate glass at the hitching rack in front of Barndollar's store. A man in long johns and suspendered trousers heaved against the breast chains and traces until his horse team warily backed up and his flatbed wagon blocked Union Street. Then he yanked hard on the harnesses of another team and a lumber truck got in the way. The horses' iron shoes grated on the bricks. The man ducked to run inside Isham's where men with crowbars were wrenching open wooden crates. Broadwell took six rifle cartridges out of his left coat pocket and laid them down between his knees. He saw two boys at the front of the First National Bank: a boy at the railing who was squinting at Dick, kicking the bricks with his toe, and another crouched to peer under the green shades on the door. Dick saw me yank open the front door and yell for Boothby to come inside, and he saw the boy Jack Long dash into Rammel's next door where a mustached man in a blue shirt and a leather apron revealed himself and a Winchester rifle for a second and then went back to hugging the door frame. Dick cocked his rifle to shoot the assassin but a porch post was in the way. He threw his hat down by the brass coat tree and wiped back his long thinning hair.

Meanwhile both heavy doors to the Isham Brothers and Mansur hardware store were opened and a dozen men who'd been on the street went in and crowded at the windows. Henry Isham used a claw hammer to break open the lid to a case of rifles shipped by Marshal Yoes. Isham's clerks Louis A. Dietz and T. Arthur Reynolds loaded them and Read's hardware store clerk Lucius Baldwin carried them front. Lucius slipped under his shirt the small Smith and Wesson revolver kept on a nail beneath the cash register.

At George Boswell's store across the street the German John Joseph Kloehr, who was then thirty-four, sat on a keg of nails with a penknife, cutting an X into the lead of his cartridges so they'd split apart on impact. M. N. Anderson, the carpenter, lifted up Kloehr's rifle. The silver housing was engraved with pictures of quail and turkey and turtledoves.

Kloehr said, "With that one I win the Kansas State Trapshoot Championship. You never seen anything like it."

In Slosson's drugstore, two doors north, stood Aleck McKenna and Cyrus Lee and the assistant pharmacist Frank Benson. They knelt at the lettered windows with rifles, scrutinizing the banks. John B. Tackett, a young amateur photographer then, walked in through the back with a tripod and a small wooden box that was a primitive Edison movie camera. McKenna frowned.

Tackett said, "I'm going to get it on film."

"What are you talking about?"

Tackett said, "Stay out of my way. That's all I ask. Just don't get in front of the lens."

The barber Carey Seaman had just driven a buckboard back from the Indian Territory where he'd shot three quail and ten rabbits. They were his only meat for the month. He slid the stable door and pulled his horses in and leaned his shotgun against an old piano covered with blankets. He was a block and a half away.

City Marshal Charles T. Connelly was having morning

coffee with Dr. W. H. Wells in the Masonic Hall on Ninth Street. Connelly was a thin, quiet man with a mustache and long chin beard, a professor of rhetoric and classical languages then on sabbatical. The city job was only temporary. The same yellow-haired boy whose head is in some of Tackett's pictures of the dead ran up on the back porch of the hall and told Connelly about us through the screen door. Connelly set his coffee cup down and looked at the doctor. "Do you have a gun?"

Wells shook his head. "I'm sorry."

Connelly crossed through the backyard toward some houses.

At the cemetery, Eugenia Moore got a pencil and paper out of her saddlebags and knelt in front of Frank's monument copying down my mother's sentiment: "Thou art gone to the grave but we shall not deplore thee. Whose God was thy ransom, thy guardian and guide, He gave thee; He took thee; and He will restore thee. And death has no sting for the Savior has died."

She folded the paper into her coat pocket and stood up. She could hear dogs barking in the town.


Grat was stomping his boots on the floor. Ball sagged against the rolltop desk and swallowed two pills without water.

Grat said, "You used to faint in church all the time."

"I'm no better now."

"You oughta try New Mexico. They say the climate there's pretty special. What time you got now?"

Ball opened his watch and snapped it shut. "9:41."

Grat said, "I believe you're lyin', Mr. Ball. I've a mind to put a bullet through your eye." Grat thought hard. Vice-president Carpenter wiped his mouth with a handkerchief. Ball unbuttoned his collar and peeled it off. Grat asked, "How much cash did your books show last night?"

"Four thousand dollars. One thousand dollars currency and three thousand dollars in silver. It's all in your sack. Nothing in the safe except some nickels and pennies and deeds to squatter's farms. There's money on order from the Denver mint but the express office hasn't delivered it yet."

Bill Powers listened to that, then pulled his rifle from the cashier's cage and sidled to the southwest casement when he heard boots on the Walnut Street sidewalk. It was John D. Levan, the moneylender, and D. E. James, a dry goods salesman, come to warn the bank about the Daltons. I guess that sounds comical now but it was dang brave under the circumstances. I truly admire those men. Levan opened and shut the door and still had a hand on the inside doorknob when Powers clutched his coat sleeve and kicked him in the ankle so hard the old man fell to the floor like boxes. He split open his lip somehow. Blood spattered on his white shirt. The dry goods clerk sat down with his hands high and a bowler hat cocked on his head and he looked across at a wild-looking bank robber with a blue bandana over his nose.

Broadwell grinned. "Did you wake up this morning thinking this was your lucky day?"

The sound of a rifle climbed over a pistol shot and Broadwell looked over to the First National Bank where a string of pale businessmen stood on the bricks with their hands up while Cox and Cubine cowered in the drugstore and gun smoke rolled under the porch roof where a door casing had been splintered. Broadwell saw Bob walk out and fix north, then swing around and fast as that break apart Gump's shotgun and his hand. Then Bob was in the green dark of the bank again and the hostages scurried away.

There was a dead silence for about a minute; then with the suddenness of rain, gunfire cracked off the Condon porch posts and bricks and metal roof, and a front window near Powers that was lettered BANK in gold paint crashed into pieces big as a carpenter's square.

The men in the front room flattened themselves and Powers scooched to the brick wall where he slapped broken glass from the casement and put his gloved hand down on the windowsill for a rifle prop. He fired his Winchester six times, moving from left to right, then swiveled away from the window to load and hear the rifles from Isham's chop at the wood sash and boardwalk.

Broadwell knelt by the southeast bank doors and saw Parker L. Williams stooped low on the porch roof of Barndollar's two hundred yards away. The man was in his white stocking feet loading a Colt .44. Broadwell shot a half-dollar hole through the plate glass but the bullet strayed wild of the man on the roof and shattered some queensware stored on the shelves in Barndollar's clothing department. Broadwell's second shot broke a shingle in half; then Williams lowered his Colt in both hands and the revolver bucked up and the shot ripped through Broadwell's right arm as if it was a long pipe. He tore his sleeve with his teeth and looked at blood and a tatter of shirt and the flat blue slug that split the bone. His shoulder screamed when his fingers moved. "I'm shot, darn it. I can't use my arm."

Powers looked across the room. Broadwell's eyes were scared and his right hand dripped blood from the fingers. "It's no use, Bill. I can't shoot anymore."

Powers had nothing to say.

My brother Grat hunched at the teller's window but couldn't see much for the gun smoke. Powers would fire up whole magazines, then sit with his legs crossed and load while bullets smacked the window shades. Broadwell was slumped against the brick wall with his eyes closed and his mask pulled down and his arm bloody and loose in his lap.

Grat went into the back room where Carpenter and Ball now sat on the floor out of harm's way, flinching whenever a bullet peeled the wallpaper or punched a hole in the floor. Ball's shirt was so soaked with sweat you could see through it. The skin of his chest looked yellow.

Grat asked, "Is there a back door to Eighth Street?"

Ball answered no.

There was.

Grat asked, "That time clock about to go off, is it?"

"Nope," said Ball. "You've got a couple of minutes yet."

My brother couldn't manage it. He dropped to his knees and his hands squeaked on the rifle as they slid. Each shot from the street was loud as planks slapping together and his brain wasn't giving him anything. He pushed the two-bushel sack between Carpenter and Ball. "You two grab that and carry it to the door."

The two men bent with the weight of it and Grat walked behind them to the front. The room was blue with gun smoke and lead was flying every which way. Powers slumped by the southwest doors where the glass wasn't busted out yet, loading a rifle that hung in the crook of his arm. Broadwell hefted up his single-action pistol and it picked up when he fired it south. His right sleeve was slick with blood and he could hear the bones grate in his arm when he used it. He shot T. Arthur Reynolds in the right foot. The doctors removed a toe.

A shot knocked a chair off one of its legs; a shot hit a fountain pen and blue ink spidered the walls.

The bankers lugged the sack and then dropped it. Powers said it looked too cumbersome, so Grat had Mr. Ball cut the twine with a penknife and haul all the silver out. The coins clinked and rolled on the floor. Ball refolded the paper money and pushed it deep and twisted the neck of the sack. Broadwell stared at the cashier's work and rubbed the blood from his hands with a white handkerchief. "How much is there?"

"A thousand dollars," said Ball.

"I think you've been honkered, Grat."

My brother didn't say anything. He squinted through the blue haze in the plaza where the citizens were firing still, then took the grain sack from Ball and shoved it down in his pants and grinned. "I can't wait to see their faces when we get away with the loot, can you?"

Broadwell let his right arm hang with a pistol and lifted his bandana up on his nose. Powers stood with his hand on the doorknob and nothing at all in his face. "Ready?"

Tackett got it all on film that is now orange and disintegrating.


When Bob and I left the First National Bank, guns were going off everywhere and Lucius Baldwin, who'd played baseball with Bob, was standing in the rear doorway of Isham's facing us soberly like we were the sheriff's men. I pushed W. H. Sheppard and he sprinted free across the railroad tracks, but Lucius stepped off the threshold and walked up the alley, no doubt to warn us about the Daltons. A lady's pistol hung in his right hand.

I yelled, "Whoa, partner," but Baldwin was nearsighted and pretty confused and he continued walking with that pistol by his side.

"What's he *doing?*" said Bob. He shouted, "Better hold up there, Lucius."

Baldwin didn't hear. He wore a clerk's apron and he was working at the tie string as he walked. Again Bob warned him to stop but to no avail, and then he shot Baldwin in the chest and staggered him. By then Baldwin was so close that gunpowder sparks burned his apron. Baldwin sagged against the brick wall, slid down, and coughed blood into his fist and wiped it on his pants leg. It took him twenty minutes to die.

My brother took off and I ran after him to Eighth Street where the sun was yellow and hot and men in dark suits stood in shops with folded arms, talking. They slammed the doors when they saw us. A grocer in a white apron stood across the street on the sidewalk with his hands cupped at his mouth, shouting, "You are killing innocent people!"

I lifted my rifle and he walked back into his store.

Bob stopped when he got to the pried-up bricks of Union Street. The plate glass of the Condon bank had shattered like hardware and Broadwell placed his rifle against the door window and shot out a half-dollar hole and gun after gun was going off south of the plaza. Horse teams skittered at their tie-ups and some saddle horses ran wild and dogs were still barking at the noise. A little girl knelt at an upstairs window holding her ears.

Bob sprinted across Union Street to the brick pile at the front of the Opera House where the horses should've been hitched. He stood in the shade of an overhang with his back pressed against the wall while I clutched the heavy mail sack under my coat and ran in boots heavy as twenty pounds.

George Cubine stood on the board sidewalk in front of Rammel's and next to him was the cobbler Charles T. Brown, unarmed. I could see the black shoe polish on his hands. Bob and I walked into the street and Bob shot Cubine twice: left ankle, left thigh. He started to keel when Bob shot him again. The slug stopped his heart and tore off his left shoulder blade. His face smacked so hard on the pavement his dead eyes blinked and blood came out of his nose.

Brown couldn't believe we'd kill as heedlessly as that. He didn't know whether to bluster or cry. "Why, you *bastards!*" he shouted. "You sons a *bitches!* We made *boots* for you boys!"

Brown got off the sidewalk one leg at a time and picked up Cubine's rifle and my brother aimed at the old man's shirt pocket. A pencil broke in half when Bob fired and Brown sprawled backwards clutching his heart like an actor. The boy Jack Long stood transfixed on the porch and Bob fired close to him in warning. The boy ducked inside Rammel's again.

I started to clomp away in my heavy boots but Bob stayed where he was in the street, his rifle still lifted up. I looked down the sidewalk a hundred yards and saw Tom Ayres, the First National Bank's cashier, jamming cartridges into a government rifle at Isham's. He had his sleeve garters off. Bob's shot smashed the bone under the cashier's eye and broke out through the back of his skull. It ruined half his face but Tom lived for years afterwards and when he died I sent a sympathy card to his widow. She graciously replied.

A dozen hotel residents were crouched in a coal pile behind a board fence, and housewives hustled their children down into the cellars where the rifles sounded like the popping of corn in a skillet; a scared deputy sheriff crawled under the plows at Read's hardware store and when a bullet screamed off one of the blades, shouted, "Pile on more plows!"

I switched the sack of money to my right hand and ran across Walnut Street, ducking low, and then I was off the bricks and I stopped on the dirt of Eighth Street where I bent to take the pain from my sides. I couldn't find enough air. The black workmen who'd torn up the street had crawled under a porch floor and they stared at me from the dark, their chins on their fists. Bob jogged across Walnut with his rifle in both hands. He stood beside me and looked along Eighth Street. Each window was like a snapshot of a face.

"You okay?"

"Just winded," I said.

Bob grinned like he was having the time of his life. He'd torn off his worthless goatee disguise and now he peeled the dark beard off my face, leaving on the mustache. "Take it easy, Emmett. Go slow. I can whip the whole dang town."

Miss Moore had sunk to the grass of the cemetery, her forehead against my brother Frank's cold headstone, when the scary street battle began. And now she could hear too many guns making too much noise in the plaza, as loud in the cemetery as a thunderstorm with shutters banging at every window and shingles tearing off the roof and empty jars at the windowsills crashing to the floor. She sat in the grass rocking back and forth, her knees in the hug of her arms, and tears brimmed out of her eyes.

Grat bulled out through the bank doors and squared himself on the porch. The money sack bulked under his coat and his rifle was crossed in front of him and a vein stood out on his forehead. His face was a fist and he was as red as a man who'd heard his wife insulted, like he'd just run down a long flight of stairs and crashed into the parlor and was about to break off the neck of a bottle. He hulked on the porch and the shooting stopped just long enough for Powers and Broadwell to dash out into the street in their black clothes and their black hats and the blue neckerchief up on Broadwell's nose.

Then Grat took off in a crouch and the three bank robbers rushed west across the pavement and guns started going off again. Broadwell and Powers got into the alley and Grat walked backwards firing across into Isham's store and a man kneeling by the door shot back and knocked Grat down to the bricks with a bullet that blew part of his stomach into the back of his coat. Grat sat up and another shot struck him so hard in the chest it kicked him back to his elbows. He rolled to his knees and the money sack slipped from his vest and belt but he wasn't thinking one thousand dollars at all. He saw the horses down the alley at the pipe tie-up and staggered for them. His shirt flopped heavy with blood.

Bill Powers got hit with a shot meant for Grat. It ripped through his left coat sleeve and stopped inside his bicep somewhere next to the bone. He slumped against the wall of the McKenna and Adamson store and skidded down a little before he leaned a shoulder against the wall of the building and stumbled to a back door and rattled the latch, wanting in. He pounded the door with his fist and then his rifle stock; then he quit to hug the white door frame close so he couldn't be seen. He crushed his hat in his armpit to slow the bleeding and waited with a revolver in his hand. His coat smeared red on the wood.

Dick Broadwell made it as far as the oil tanker parked next to the icehouse. The horse team backed up from him and stamped their shoes and their hitch chains clanked when they tossed their heads. There was black oil on everything. Broadwell saw the Long-Bell lumberyard down the alley and scurried to it, cradling his arm. But the defenders were walking out into the street now and a man in a collarless shirt and a bowler hat more than eighty yards away stood still and aimed a buffalo gun and the bullet slammed into Broadwell's lower back like something five inches wide. He was kicked forward but he kept rockily on his legs. He squeezed the pain in his belly and his boots crossed over each other as he lurched into the lumberyard. He collapsed against a stack of warped two-by-twelves and bunched a handkerchief inside the back of his shirt. He could smell pinesap and sawdust and the urine of children. He closed his eyes. "Get me through this, okay? Just let me ride out of this town."

My brother Grat was spilling blood from his mouth when he pitched inside a small dark barn the size of a two-car garage. He propped himself on the wood studs of a wall that held shovels and rakes and hayforks. There were packets of seeds on the workbench. The barn doors were open so he could shoot into Walnut Street but Slosson's outside stairway to the second floor of his drugstore was deflecting whatever was thrown at Grat. He fired southwest at the Masonic Hall and some men standing there dived to the grass. He unbuttoned his shirt and saw how his blood bubbled pink from his chest when he took air. But the pain in his stomach was displacing everything else. He walked over to the workbench where a potato was rooting white in a clear water jar. He picked out the cutting and drank the water, staring west through a four-pane window to the horse tie-ups where Bob and I stood loading our rifles with cartridges from our saddlebags. Grat smiled.


Bob and I had trotted down the middle of Eighth Street until we reached Wells Brothers' store where the south-running alley was. We walked down that way looking for snipers in the buildings. I rubbed gunpowder off my face with my sleeve. We'd guessed Grat and the other two were out of the bank and shooting from their saddles by then but it was not yet so; Ball was still shoving currency into the sack and raking the cumbersome coins away.

Bob stooped at the Wells loading dock and was as careful as an assassin with his shots. One struck a butter churn directly in front of Henry Isham; another just missed two cases of dynamite next to the stoves. A shot fired at Louis Dietz struck the monkey wrench in his pocket and veered off into a roll of Isham's brown wrapping paper. The shock of the blow knocked Dietz out but he was only sore in the chest for a while. Bob had as good an eye as there was in the West. Whenever he missed he meant to.

Then Grat was on the porch of the bank and Broadwell and Powers rushed out to the plaza bricks like outlaws in the dime novels. The sun flashed off their rifles and Grat backed across the street shooting everywhere. I fired nine times, quick as I could, at the wagons and window and rooftops. I saw Grat stagger back but then I lost him because of the buildings. Bob pushed away from the loading dock and pulled his Brisley Bulldog out of his shoulder holster and took off for the alley. I heeled after him and ran for the horses and fired whatever I had into the plaza while Bob loaded and walked straight into the guns.

I tied the money sack to the saddle horn and laid my rifle on the bedroll to fire east over the considerable distance to Isham's hardware store where they had us good, had the notorious Dalton gang walking in front of their guns in an alley as open as a main street in early morning.

Bob was by then crouched against the barn where Grat was, jamming cartridges into his rifle. He pushed his hat down on his head and ran down to the Consolidated oil wagon where he leaned on the bench seat and fired into a plaza that was screened blue with smoke. There were sparks red as cigarette ash whenever they fired back at him.

I saw Carey Seaman standing with the German, John J. Kloehr, on the corner of Ninth and Walnut. Seaman broke open a twin-hammered twelve-gauge, shoved in two shotgun shells, and snapped it closed. I could see this because of Munn's vacant lot which was to my right and overgrown with

Russian thistles. But then Kloehr nudged the barber and they walked west on Ninth Street and it was too late when I saw them again.

City Marshal Connelly was walking up the sidewalk of a house to borrow a weapon when he saw Kloehr and Seaman stalking us. He opened the gate and crossed the street. "I left home this morning without a pistol."

Kloehr pointed to Swisher Brothers' machine shop. "You ask Swisher, professor. I think maybe he keeps there a gun."

Seaman trotted toward the lumberyard; Kloehr unlatched the door to his livery barn and walked inside. A sick horse slept on its side in a stall. Kloehr opened the bottom half of a Dutch door and ducked out into a paddock where two horses he rented out leaned for a bale of brown hay. He could hear the gunfire from Isham's but couldn't see anything but our horses tied to the pipe. That was enough for him. He waited.

Connelly came out of Swisher's with a carbine and loaded it as he walked back towards the city jail and the alley as if we'd tremble and throw down our guns once we saw him. He shook out a key and used it and the jail door's Scandinavian pig lock clicked open.

Grat was slumped against the barn wall with his eyes closed. He hung onto a nail and spit a mouthful of blood at his boots and then opened his eyes to see Marshal Connelly step out into the alley like a man at a railroad siding who has a ticket for the train. Connelly saw me loading and steered in my direction, neglecting to look in the barn not ten yards away. Grat tried to raise his rifle but couldn't. He pushed away from the barn wall, saw Connelly's back, and let the hammer snap from his thumb.

I saw the marshal coming at me; I saw his vest button fly; I saw him stumble and pitch forward with Grat's bullet. Connelly groaned and tried to swallow and rolled over to his back. He'd lift his knee and drop it down every so often; dirt caked on his vest where the blood was.

I don't know why but the defenders were stunned by that

murder and the shooting stopped just long enough for Bill Powers to lurch out of McKenna's doorway and it was so quiet I heard his boots as he ran for the horses, holding his arm. It seemed for that brief half-minute that we could make it out of there alive; then the shooting was worse than it had been before and my brother Bob defiantly sat back on his boot heels in the middle of the alley and used up his magazine while bricks and wood and clay chipped up all around him and bullets zipped in the air. I saw him wince so they must've come close, but my brother had magic then.

Grat backed out of the barn with his coat buttoned up and his rifle clutched under his arm. Except for smears of blood around his mouth, his face was as white as a bed sheet.

"You okay?"

"I'm a little sick to my stomach," he said.

A wayward shot damaged one of the horses hitched to the Consolidated oil wagon and the team went crazy. They broke loose from the icehouse tie-up and stampeded down the alley with the wagon swinging and skidding and banging off the outbuildings. Grat brought up his pistol and put a shot into the white star on the face of the injured horse. It stumbled dead and the other horse tripped to its knees. It tried to get back on its legs again but a shank bone was broken and jagged under its hide. The horse fell down and got up on two legs and quivered.

I think Bob had ducked next to the icehouse when the horses panicked. I couldn't see him. Grat backed to our horses, shooting east, and Bill Powers stood next to me with his boots spread wide and his pistol lifted up, his left arm useless beside him. He fired everything in the revolver and shoved it in his coat pocket and yanked another revolver out of his shoulder holster. He told me not to wait too long on Bob and then took off for the horses.

Carey Seaman unroped the gate of the Long-Bell lumberyard and walked under sycamore trees through high wet grass with his shotgun in two hands. There were stacks of joists and planks and tongue-and-groove and two-bys. A board shrieked off a pile next to the alley and he saw a man's shadow stutter over a pallet in the grass. Then the man he knew as Texas Jack Moore was cramped over in the alley, untying his horse's reins from the pipe. Broadwell grasped the saddle horn and fitted a stirrup over his boot with considerable pain and pulled up onto the saddle with his horse already running. Seaman fired a shot that sprayed gravel; Broadwell kicked his horse hard three times and was yanking it north onto Maple Street when Seaman fired again. Broadwell was slammed forward into the pommel like he'd been hit in the back with a hay rake. He jounced almost off the saddle while getting away and he clung there losing blood until the horse threw him a half mile west on Eighth Street, just out of the city limits. Broadwell dropped from the saddle and broke his ankle in the stirrup and dragged and bounced twenty feet before he'd tangled his horse enough to stop it. His skin was scraped and his coat and shirt were bunched up next to his throat when a posse found him dead.

John Kloehr had heard Seaman fire toward the horses and saw Broadwell pull himself onto the saddle. Kloehr had fired a bullet then but missed him. He saw Seaman raise up his shotgun again and jolt with it and he saw the sudden stain on Broadwell's coat as he tilted off the saddle. He saw Seaman break the gun open and pry the shells out and grope in his pocket for two others; then Kloehr saw a solemn, mustached man jerk his horse reins loose and slide his rifle into a fleece-lined scabbard. Kloehr pressed his rifle stock to his cheek while Powers danced his horse around on the ground, yanking it down to four legs when it reared. Bill was just climbing into the saddle when Kloehr fired a slug he'd split with a penknife into his back. It hurled him over the saddle and his arms and head dangled down and the horse stood off of its front legs and Powers slid off the horse in a heap. The hole in his chest looked like blood worms.

Bob squatted against the back wall of Slosson's drugstore with his holster unbuckled and clenched in his teeth. He pushed all the cartridges out of the webs and loaded his rifle and shook the others deep into his coat pocket. He glanced left and saw the pharmacist Frank Benson bend under the rear window sash, climbing out with a gun in his hand. Bob picked up his Colt and a foot-long flame shot out. The window glass shattered and Frank Benson disappeared.

Bob buckled on his holster staring at McKenna's roof and walked out into the middle of the alley staring up at all the other roofs. He backed up like a boy hunting pigeons. Henry Isham stood on the porch of his store and slowly raised his rifle. The rifle jerked back and Bob heard a thud and it seemed as if he'd been punched near his lungs with a fist. He sat down hard on the rock curbs piled near the jail, his right hand holding his side. There was a hole the size of a quarter in him and a rib poking out like chicken bone and he must have felt a lot of pain because he just sat there biting his lip.

I was back with the horses. The legs of Bill Powers jiggled with death and his pants stained black with his water. Grat sagged against a barn wall and pushed away and stumbled out into the alley.

Kloehr saw Grat stop next to the dying city marshal and drop a hand with a pistol close to Connelly's head like he was going to put him out of his misery. Kloehr shouted, "You there!" and my brother turned and Kloehr shot him in the throat. Grat's hands went up like he'd swallowed a fishbone. He keeled backwards over the marshal and his head bounced when he slammed to the ground. His mouth and eyes were open when he died.

Men in white shirts and suspendered black trousers stood in the plaza and in the north alley by the Wells Brothers' store. Kloehr couldn't find me. Carey Seaman used up two shotgun shells on the heads of two of our standing horses to prevent a getaway. Blood splattered Red Buck, my horse, and he screamed and plunged and I had to grab him by the bit ring to unfasten his reins from the tie-up.

I saw my brother Bob sag back on the rock curbs and stare

at his rifle and grope at the rocks to stand up. I saw his face when the pain climbed. Bob saw the sun flash silver off Kloehr's fancy trigger housing but he couldn't convince his arms to raise his own rifle up and his shot at the liveryman only ripped weeds. He staggered forward and slid against the north wall of the jail, a kite's tail of blood on the stone, until he stumbled into the adjoining ramshackle barn and collided with its west wall. Kloehr had a pirate's eye to his rifle sight. Bob fired but the slug only split a rotting board of the stables. Bob fired again and the grass made a spitting noise.

Kloehr saw a twenty-two-year-old desperado with sweat on his face and his shirttail out, sagged against a barn wall. The gunpowder was black on his hands and neck. Kloehr fired a cut bullet into the middle of Bob's dark vest at the sternum. It exploded his chest and hurled him back against a pile of farm implements. Sunlight came through the barn roof and striped him. My brother opened his eyes and lay there and got up on one elbow. He heaved strings and clots of blood onto the straw and he puked again until he was empty and he wiped his mouth on his sleeve. He saw men talking to each other on Eighth Street but they weren't coming any closer.

I was the last. I had a boot in the stirrup and my left hand on the money sack and the saddle horn when someone drew a bead on me and a slug hit my right arm and shattered the bone not two inches from the scar I had collected south of that cantina in New Mexico. It hurt terribly bad. I let my arm hang in its sleeve and swung up into the saddle and the horse skittered around lifting a hoof with every gunshot. Then I got hit again pretty hard with a second rifle bullet. It smashed through the back of my hip like a railroad spike and tore out through my groin and my right pocket. Hot blood streamed down inside my boots but I couldn't feel my right leg at all so the ache was worse than the hurt.

I was almost deaf from the gunfire. It was coming from everywhere, snapping branches, knocking things down, singing off anything hard. My horse was cantering and champing at the bit and he was so scared the whites of his eyes showed, but I pulled him back with my one good arm. I wasn't thinking that a coward would do this, a brave man some other thing; I merely saw that Maple Street was vacant and that I could gallop out like I'd seen Dick Broadwell do and maybe get away, but when I skirted the horse around I could see men in sleeve garters and suit coats and aprons running across the bricks and men were at the back door of every place I looked at, loading rifles or lifting them up, and my brother Bob, whom I'd loved and been next to for twenty years, was sunk down and dying and there wasn't any question, no, I went after him. I jerked my horse around and he balked at the smoke and I kicked him at the stifle with my good leg. I sat tall as I could, lifting out of the bouncing jog with my stirrups, my Winchester rifle crossed in my lap with smoke still twisting from it, and I frowned for all the good citizens like thirty years of badman and desperado. I leaned for Bob without stopping my horse, bent as far as I could with blood dripping off my fingers and my shattered arm hanging down to help him lift to the back of my saddle. Bob was near dead; I could see that. He had his hat off and his hair stuck out and his neck and face looked blackened with coal dust except where the sweat streaked it white. He saw me and said, "Don't mind me, Emmett. I'm done for. But don't you surrender, boy. Die game!"

Carey Seaman stood in the alley not twenty feet behind me with both hammers cocked on his shotgun and a bead on my back where he figured my heart was. The shotgun kicked and I was blasted into my horse. His mane straggled across my face. It was hot from the sun. I was sliding from the saddle and I saw Julia in a white dress and it was only a second later when the shotgun kicked again and I took all the double-ought shot in my shoulder blade and shoulder and when I dropped to the ground it was like slamming into a board of eighteen nails, for I had eighteen black shot two inches under my skin, ruining muscle and bone.

I stared at my brother Bob but he was slunk down and his

cheek was in his vomit and his eyes were rolled back in his skull and a fly crawled into his open mouth.

**21** I couldn't hear anything. Nothing at all. Then the dogs barked, maybe fifty dogs all over town, and there were boots rasping in the alley and Kloehr was yelling, "They are all down!"

He nudged Bob with his boot and squatted by me stern as Melchizedek, his hot rifle against my temple. "Put your hands up, you no-good-for-nothing!"

I was stupid with shock and awfully woozy but I lifted my left hand as well as I could, then dropped it down. He grabbed the money sack. "What's your name?"

"Charlie McLaughlin."

"I got something to tell you: you're dying. I bet you never believe it is possible."

I turned my head. About twenty men were already in the alley and others were running through the side lots with their rifles clenched, hollering the news. Only twelve minutes had elapsed from Cubine's first shot to Seaman's last. Henry Isham turned around in the middle of the alley and saw four dead horses, four dead men, and me. He said, "We got 'em, by God, didn't we? We put 'em *all* down!"

They tenderly lifted City Marshal Connelly but his head flopped back and his soul departed before Dr. Wells could see to him.

Carpenter stood at the Condon bank's southwest doors, his fists on his hips. Ball had the discarded silver in a tin box. He sat with it in a chair. Carpenter said, "I guess we'd better board up these windows."

"Yes," said Ball. "That should be the first thing."

Teller W. H. Sheppard of the First National Bank had ambled through Kloehr's barn and paddock to collect the money sack, and he tilted back to the bank counter with it, escorted by three men. Women carried blankets out of Boswell's store and spread them over Lucius Baldwin, George Cubine, Charles Brown. Children ran everywhere, dogs hopping up at them and nipping at their ankles. Some boys stood in the front of the Condon bank counting over three hundred bullet holes in the plate glass windows.

Aleck McKenna knelt by Grat and peeled the whiskers off his face. He stood and slapped his hands clean. "That's Grat Dalton all right."

Grat's .38–.56 caliber Winchester was taken by Dr. W. C. Hall as a souvenir.

Carey Seaman had wiped his shotgun down with a handkerchief and bragged about himself to all the men. He straddled me and stuffed the handkerchief in his shirt pocket. "I thought I'd introduce myself. Name's Carey Seaman. I'm the one who shot ya."

I said, "You're going to be famous, Mr. Seaman."

"Yes. I believe I am."

An ugly man in a derby hat had carried a rope out of a barn and he squatted near me tying a noose and spitting through his teeth in my direction. I could hear a lot of talk about lynching. It didn't faze me one way or the other. Colonel David Stewart Elliott, editor of the Coffeyville *Journal,* walked up the alley with Tom Callahan, sheriff of Montgomery County, who was to take custody of the outlaws. Some men lifted Grat's body to a sit and Colonel Elliott agreed about who it was. Callahan recognized Powers as Tim Evans but most of the newspapers put down Tom Hedde and spelled my brother's name Grot. Elliott strolled over to where the men were bunched and heard the talk about hanging me off a rope and he declaimed it like a stage actor. "We won't disgrace our community by lynching a dying man!"

A boy sat cross-legged near my head, fanning me with the *Police Gazette;* then Elliott stood tall over me in his long cloak. "Emmett Dalton," he said sadly. "How many years has it been, and who would have thought it would come to this?"

"Take my guns from me, Colonel."

He took the pearl-handled pistol out of my shoulder holster and then the pistol shoved in my pants, and they bulked in the right pocket of his cloak when he turned to someone responsible and shouted, "How long must this boy remain here without proper medical attention? I want him removed and cared for at once."

Women and children walked through the alley now and men were yanking the boots off Grat and Bob and some teen-aged girls walked from outlaw to outlaw cutting snips of hair with a scissors. Squire Davis got Bob's hat; Peter Sprague got the oil can from his pocket; T. C. Babb unbuckled his cartridge belt and gave it to C. M. Ball; Perry Landers removed the pair of gentleman's gloves from Bob's black suit coat; Hiram Smith got his five-point spurs. His trouser pockets were turned wrong side out and when the gawkers came his spent brass cartridges sold for a dollar apiece. A woman crouched with pinking shears and cut a swatch from his bloody left trouser leg. Don't know what she did with it.

There must've been two dozen people bunched around me by then, spitting, kicking cinders at me, saying how puny I looked. I couldn't see but two or three pieces of blue sky. Then my bedroll was unstrapped from my saddle and they hefted me onto it and over to an upstairs room and a long bare table in Slosson's until Dr. W. H. Wells could come over from the alley behind the First National Bank where Lucius Baldwin was dying. They spared me nothing in the carrying. It took the bite of my jaw not to scream. A sheriff's deputy stood on the second floor landing of the outside wooden stairway and four sheriff's men sat on chairs inside the upstairs room with rifles on their knees. I said, "I used to be an assistant deputy marshal. I bet you didn't know that."

The men just stared at me. One of them tore off a strip of loose wallpaper and chewed it, looking at me. "I heard that a long time ago. You ought to be ashamed of yourself."

I guess Miss Moore rode out of the cemetery. I guess she wasn't seen. I don't know where she went.

I was sinking into sleep and staring out the rear window at

over a hundred men and women inching past blood spots in that narrow alley like people at a backyard furniture sale.

I was too near dying then to hurt much for my brothers. I wanted Bob alive and standing next to me and whispering instructions, but that was as close to grief as I got, and I didn't flinch at all when I saw the sheriff's men handcuff Bob and Grat and stand the bodies together on their stocking feet so Tackett could take a picture. Cyrus Lee lifted one of Grat's arms up and blood gushed out the hole in his throat, spraying Lee on the shirt front. Somebody whooped with laughter and it became sport that morning for boys to jerk Grat's arm up and dodge the blood that came squirting out like tobacco spit.

I woke up to the whispering of doctors and saw my bloody, sopped shirtsleeve being cut up the seam with silver medical scissors. Blood from my wounds traveled twenty-five feet across the floor. Wells had called in doctors G. J. Tallman and W. J. Ryan to assist him in what looked like four hours of surgery, prying out buckshot and tying my lower guts together, and amputating my arm. They had buckets of water under the table to splash their instruments in, and Dr. Ryan walked up the stairs with a bone saw he was wiping with alcohol.

I said, "I'm gonna keep my arm. This arm is gonna stay."

Dr. Wells said, "It's badly smashed. You won't even be able to pick up a pencil with it. And the chance of infection is enormous. The poison will shoot straight up to your brain."

"If I'm gonna cash in, I want to go to the grave in one piece."

The doctor named Tallman continued snipping my shirt away at the collar. "Let him keep the dang thing. Let the arm rot off. It's better than seeing it pickled in a jar at county fairs for the next twenty-five years."

I kept sliding in and out of wakefulness, but mean, thumping pains, like your fingers slammed in a car door, were with me constantly for a week. I remember hearing the clink of instruments and Dr. Wells's voice on the wooden stairs as he argued with a shoving crowd that wanted to lynch me. He convinced them that I was already dead and he was just filling out coroner papers, and suddenly it was late afternoon in the room and a cool sheet covered me to my chin and I saw vomit on my shoulder and felt a puddle of it next to my ear on the table, heard it dripping to the floor, and one of the deputies was frowning, a rifle crossed in his lap. He said, "You're making a mess of yourself."

I could see the alley still but now there were two thousand gawkers walking the scene like it was a crowded museum, all of them brought in from Kansas, Missouri, and Oklahoma on special half-fare railroad excursions. Bob and Grat and Broadwell and Powers were piled on the dirt floor of the city jail with stiff erections and fouled clothes and hundreds of blowflies walking all over them, so visitors could hunch at the barred windows and poke the bodies with sticks and John Tackett was already developing the pictures that would become three kinds of post cards.

When I woke up again it was morning and I was on the mattress in the Farmers' Home that Bob had slept on after the Adair train robbery. If I lifted my eyes I could make out strange faces at the mullioned windows behind me and children squealing that they wanted to see. And next to me was Julia Johnson in a black lace dress, a white handkerchief clutched in her hand, and she was like a woman with an appointment; she'd marshaled herself into something as crisp as the snap of a closed pocketbook.

I said, "*You're* a sight for sore eyes."

She glanced across the room to where Sheriff Tom Callahan sat in a split-bottom chair reading a stack of newspapers Colonel Elliott had brought in.

I noticed the headlines and said, "I went and done it, didn't I."

She whispered, "Emmett, please don't make me cry."

"I do love you," I said. "I mean that. I think you were what I wanted all along."

She stared at me without emotion for a minute. She said, "A newspaper reporter stopped me before I came in here and asked if I was your sweetheart, and I realized that I was nineteen years old and your sweetheart is all I would really ever be; that's as important as I'd become."

Sheriff Callahan pulled up from his chair with the newspapers under his arm. "I think I'll stand outside for a while."

She waited until he was gone and said, "I guess what I'm saying is that I'll stay with you as long as I can and I'll wait for you, no matter what happens, because that's what sweethearts do. I love you too but I'm property and I'm not used to that feeling yet."

I couldn't think of an answer. I said, "I don't have anything more comforting to say, Julia. My brain's empty."

"You're very tired," she said.

I closed my eyes and she petted back my hair and I woke with her gone and strangers in plow coats and yarn shawls and bonnets filing past the window, buttons scraping on wood.

I asked the sheriff, "Can you turn this bed around?"

He saw the people staring down at me and thought it over for a minute." I don't see why the hell not," he said.

Not only that, he put the bedposts on bricks so I would be raised up a bit, and after that you just had to stand two-by-two in the dining room to walk by, and railroad men would sneer, "You're not so tough now, are ya?" and glum women would freeze me with scowls and pray that God have pity on my soul, and a man leaned on his fists at the foot of the bed to tell me, "This is the Lord's way of saying, 'Thus far shalt thou go and no further.'"

Meanwhile there was talk about forty Dalton sympathizers riding into Coffeyville some night to free me and burn the town down. Someone in Arkansas City, Kansas, wrote a letter that was mailed to John Kloehr and said: "Dear Sir: I take the time to tell you and the citizens of Coffeyville that all the gang ain't dead yet and don't you forget it. I would have given all I ever made to have been there the 5th. There are five of the gang left and we shall come to see you some day. That day, Oct. 5, we were down in the Chickasaw Nation, and we did not know it was coming off so soon." And so on. Some cowhands got a little drunk and condemned the murder of the bank robbers and they were jailed. Some boys from Guthrie called themselves "The Dalton Avengers" and barged through town pushing tourists off sidewalks, shouting cusswords at the defenders, and they made such a nuisance of themselves that they got beat up in a side alley and one boy went home via stagecoach with thirty stitches in his head.

But Emmett Dalton was still the big show in that town and I hear the line of mourners and curious waiting to gaze at me snaked west on Eighth Street, then down Maple to Death Alley, which it is even now called, and down past the bent-pipe hitching rack to the jail, like I was a Hollywood premiere or Jesse James on his white satin funeral bier, and I wished my brother Bob were alive instead of me because I knew that he'd love that; how he'd love that. It would have been a discipline for him not to smile.


That night Eugenia Moore sank the springs of my bed when there was only a kerosene lamp in the room and the sheriff was gone somewhere. She still wore her greased wing chaps and a sheepskin coat that smelled of leaf smoke and horses. Her face was streaked with dirt and her hair strayed over her eyes as she reached to remove a cool washrag she must have pressed to my forehead.

"How'd you get in here?" I asked.

She smiled briefly. "I snuck in. I thought I wanted to talk to you but I guess there's really nothing to say." She folded the washrag and dropped it into a white ironstone basin and when she looked up there were tears in her eyes. "Are you all right?"

"Yes."

"I just wanted to know that you were all right," she said, and then she got up from the bed and walked out of the room, spurs clanking.

A man named Alfred Kime who never did anything in his life worth retelling, is here remembered by me for digging a common grave in the potter's field of the Elmwood Cemetery. The stiff bodies of Broadwell and Powers and my two brothers were dragged like heavy mahogany doors from the jail to a dining room table in the parlor of Lang and Lape's furniture store where Bob and I carried the corpse of Charley Montgomery that December night in 1888. Little boys would rush up and slap Bob on the sleeve and a crowd followed with handkerchiefs cupped to their noses. There was a toe hole in Bob's left wool sock and his mouth was open so that his teeth looked bucked and he was no longer the blue-eyed boy. The dead were white except where the blood had sunk green on them and they were frozen with rigor mortis exactly as they had been when Tackett propped their heads up against a board front for photographs, so that they seemed to be raising up in their sleep; and they smelled worse than you'd think it possible, like the blast of bad air you'd get if you opened a junkyard icebox that was rank with spoiled chicken wings and vegetables and a rotting cat near the milk.

Undertaker W. H. Lape did some simple embalming and stole my binoculars off Bob. And some fortune hunter snuck in at noon and stripped every stitch of clothing off my brother. Then two clopping draft horses with mud-clumped hair at their fetlocks pulled a box wagon to the graveyard on Thursday afternoon. Orange kernels of corn jittered on the box planks and the spoke wheels crunched over gravel and the Dalton gang jostled with each bump—four dead men in buttoned shirt collars and blood-caked coats squeezed into four pinewood coffins.

A dozen men, including Chris Madsen, Henry Isham, and

Colonel Elliott, stood with hats in their hands at the burial while scoops of shoveled earth flopped black as Bibles on top of the coffins. The bent pipe we'd hitched our horses to was what they had instead of headstones until I purchased a simple granite slab with some of the income from my first movie.

I don't recall anything of October 7th and only snatches of the 8th when my family arrived by train from Kingfisher. Mom could only pat the bed covers near my sore leg and my brothers all were red-eyed but for Bill. Bill was hospital good cheer. He asked, "Where does it hurt the worst, Emmett?"

"It's miserable pain almost everywheres," I said. "I really can't separate it. The ache in my crotch, I guess."

He winked toward my brothers and laughed, saying, "Hell, that's just normal biology, Emmett. That's gonna bother you till you die."

Bill stayed on after the others left and straddled the split-bottom chair and stared at me and leaned to slap my face. "You stupid idiots. What in tarnashun am I going to do for a living? *Huh?*" He bit his lip and slapped my head again.

"Cut it out," I told him.

He said, "I'm glad they're dead. I am! You ruined me in California and now you've ruined me here and, by God, that's the end of it." He stood up and kicked the chair away and stalked out in his three-piece tweed suit.

On October 11th, I was slid onto a stretcher and transported in a locked Santa Fe express car to Independence, Kansas, with an escort of six deputies, Sheriff Callahan, Chief U. S. Marshal William Grimes, and twelve railroad detectives. My brother Bill accompanied me and sat on a safe smoking a cigarette that he stubbed out when I asked for a drag. On meeting Grimes, he shook the marshal's hand and said, "Extraordinary job of police work, sir. You had them every step of the way and they knew it. They got just what they deserved."

My trial was five months after the Coffeyville raid. My brother Bill hired a smart attorney named Joseph Fritch who pleaded me guilty to the second degree murder of George Cubine, and as he expected, Judge J. D. McCue of the Montgomery County District Court dismissed the other charges of bank robbery and murder. Because of my comparative youth, Fritch predicted ten to fifteen years, the minimum penalty for second degree, but the Dalton gang was too famous for that and I was sentenced to life imprisonment at the gloomy Kansas State Penitentiary in Lansing, which is halfway between Kansas City and Fort Leavenworth.

I was twenty-one years old and still on crutches when I hobbled into prison and a foul, stinking, four-by-eight cell. I wore a black-and-white striped uniform and cap and I was made a tailor in the prison, a trade I'm still good at, and I worked nights on a prison education, studying difficult books in the library until I could make the sentences out, copying down words I didn't know. I scrubbed the floor and walls of my jail cell with ammonia and kept it obsessively neat: a safety razor next to my shaving mug next to my hairbrush next to the pitcher. I spent my twenties and thirties as a stoic, devoting the last hour of each night to Bible study, and my only true entertainment was the mail from Miss Eugenia Moore.

My notes to her were brief, two or three sentences about what I'd heard of the outside, how prison was, how much I used to enjoy those nights at Big Jim Riley's ranch when we would smoke cheroot cigars in her blanket-hung room; but she'd respond with nine or ten pages about the past, putting down everything she could recall. At the end of one of her letters she wrote, "I keep wanting to ask if you're lonely, if you're unhappy, if there's anything you regret, but those seem such melancholy questions I'm a little ashamed of them. I suppose you *are* lonely, because I am. I'm lost without your brother Bob. I feel like a vacant house."

A letter I mailed to her was never answered and another I sent was returned, so I thought she was worn of me until I heard that she too was dead; that she'd walked out of a muffling snow and into a bank in Wichita, Kansas, and demanded the cash drawer from the teller. She got away but she was shot from her horse three miles from town at the start of a blizzard. And when the posse walked up to her she was coated in white except for the splash of her yellow hair and the snowflakes melting into her open brown eyes.

I don't know if I ever swallowed that story. It seemed a fabrication as likely as that empty grave she arranged for herself in Silver City, and though some have claimed the real Florence Quick was laid to rest in a plot in Cass County, Missouri, I think of her now as alive somewhere in Texas, teaching arithmetic to children, and married to a brakeman on the railroad.

And my information is just as scant about the Doolin-Dalton gang. I heard that my brother Bill had put his law books down and gathered, together with Bill Doolin, Bitter Creek Newcomb, and Pierce, one of the largest gangs that ever scavenged in the West. And in early 1893, they chose to announce the corporation by robbing a train at Wharton, just as we had. But soon Chris Madsen, Heck Thomas, and Bill Tilghman were assigned to head up a manhunt employing one hundred and fifty deputies, and the Doolin-Dalton gang didn't last long after that. They divided in March of 1894, my brother to wander into Texas where he picked up a scrub gang of his own, Doolin to stay on in the territories with a gang that was picked off one at a time by the law.

Chris Madsen shot down Ol Yountis at his shack in Orlando following a robbery at Spearville. After the Doolin gang robbed a Rock Island train at Dover, Bitter Creek Newcomb and Charlie Pierce hid in a pasture of rotted, barkless trees on the farm of Newcomb's brothers-in-law, the rustlers Bill, Dal, and John Dunn. But the brothers decided to cash in on the amnesty and money reward promised by a local marshal, and they drove a wagon to his office the next morning with the two bodies so shot up there were shotgun pellets imbedded in Pierce's and Newcomb's stocking feet.

And Bill Doolin was walking into a cornfield when Heck Thomas and a posse stood up in a ravine and Bee Dunn let go with a double-barreled twelve-gauge. Doolin broke through four rows of cornstalks keeling away from the posse, and then his dead body collapsed. They stripped Doolin's shirt off and sat him in a rocking chair and took photographs of him staring at the ceiling. The buckshot looked like pennies on his chest.

I would read what the newspapers said about my brother Bill and I wouldn't recognize him. He was shabby and filthy and he drank too much, and he might've been a little bit crazy. By April of 1894, my brother Bill had an accomplice-to-murder charge in addition to a previous warrant for the death of a deputy sheriff. Then, with his gang of three cowboys, my brother robbed the First National Bank in Longview, Texas. The take was barely two thousand dollars in ten and twenty dollar bills and slain were the city marshal and two business-men.

Bill Dalton escaped to Ardmore, Oklahoma, where his wife Jenny and the two children were renting the upstairs room of a farmhouse that nine mustached men in dark suits and vests surrounded on the morning of June 8th. Grasshoppers leeched to the possemen's pants legs and jumped off. The sun was already hot in a blue sky. Deputy Marshal Lindsay peered through a screen at the front stoop to see a girl in a leg-brace seated on a catalogue at the kitchen table, dunking sugared bread into milk. Then Bill was there with his hair mussed and his shirttails sloppy in his pants, putting a bowl in front of his daughter Grace and cutting up the poached egg in it. The girl leaned to look at the deputy marshal; then Bill looked that way too.

"Come on out with your hands up."

"Why don't you come in for coffee and we'll chat?"

Lindsay opened the screen door and Bill ducked next to the black stove and the posse in the backyard saw a drape thrown aside as Bill crouched out through the open kitchen window. They shot everything they could at him and window glass shattered and sash wood flew and bursts of paint flakes floated with gun smoke in the breeze as my brother jumped down, somehow unhurt. Bill ran toward a ravine but tripped on a rusted spade and he bent to catch the ground and then Marshal Loss Hart aimed a .44 caliber slug that slammed into Bill's kidney and exited big as a coffee can at his heart and my brother fell dead as a tire in the weeds, scattering grasshoppers.

He was displayed in a coffin covered with window glass at a mortician's parlor in Ardmore until he was badly decomposed. Spectators journeyed by train from everywhere and stereoscopic pictures were made and thousands of people crowded the street in front of the mortuary so they could file past and solemnly stare at the last of the notorious Daltons.

**22** Seven wardens oversaw my years at the Lansing penitentiary and I surprised them all with my quiet. There was a riot over bread pudding that I refused to participate in. There was a hullabaloo when some prisoners released all the cell doors and escaped up an elevator shaft, but I spent the night on my bunk in my private cell, reading *The Virginian.* My reward was that I became the first prisoner under sentence of life allowed jobs in town as a trustee. And in 1907, when Oklahoma became the forty-sixth state, I was pardoned after service of less than fifteen years by Kansas Governor E. W. Hoch.

I was thirty-five years old and gimped in the leg and I

needed work pretty bad, so I stayed with a family in Bartlesville working as a hired hand on local farms, chopping weeds
and baling hay and riding the spring-iron seat of a reaper. And
nights and Sundays I courted Julia Johnson just as I had as a
boy. I'd sit with her on a porch swing and play my Harpoon,
or I'd stroll downtown with her to see a nickelodeon film
about vaudeville or train robbery, and at noon she'd ride
through the corn rows on a mare and I'd sit against a fence
post in blue bib overalls, eating apple slices off a knife blade,
drinking lukewarm tea from a jar, grinning at my boots while
Julia talked.

Julia and I were married in Bartlesville in 1908 and two
years later I was hired as a special officer by the Tulsa police
department to scare off the worst of their badmen just by letting them know that one of the legendary Dalton boys was
around. Then my wife and I moved west to Los Angeles where
John Tackett and I filmed *Beyond the Law* and Julia and I
had picnics on the beach after Sunday church services, and
she'd lift her dress to wade out into the ocean while I sat on
the sand in my suit and tie and watched children pay nickels to
ride a horse in a roped circle next to the parked Ford Model
A's.

The movie got me script work in Hollywood and it resur-
rected my name and I traded off that as a real-estate broker
and building contractor in the California land rush. I hardly
needed to advertise. Smiling loan officers would stand up from
their desks whenever I walked into the bank and otherwise self-
possessed businessmen would sit enthralled at lunch while I
storied. I made more money on one Los Angeles suburban
development than I did in all those rustling and train-robbing
years in my past, and I deposited it in the construction of a
white stucco house much like you see among the parvenu
down in Argentina, with red tiles on the floor and a paddle fan
overhead in the billiards room and orange flowers big as a
child's face edging the pebbled driveway.

And not long ago my wife and I returned to Coffeyville,

Kansas, for a second honeymoon. John B. Tackett invited us back and the Chamber of Commerce provided tickets to a first class Pullman on the Union Pacific's Zephyr service east. So I spent three days at a club car window smoking cigarettes and staring out at badlands and hard-up farms with rusted machinery on cinder blocks, and at hired hands who would still stop their trucks and stand on the running boards to watch a train go by. Then we took the southbound Santa Fe and I sat in the morning breakfast car with Julia, gazing at Kansas wheat fields that were green as a child's green crayon. A porter rolled a luggage cart down the aisle and said, "Coffeyville, next stop." I poured coffee and slowly stirred sugar in with a spoon, and for some minutes Julia and I sat there in silence like a couple growing dead from a very long marriage, looking out the Santa Fe's windows at leaning barns and a rusted Model T next to a lug-wheeled tractor, then at a white water tower and grain elevators and the tin-roofed warehouses of Coffeyville.

She smiled across the table at me. 'Think your hometown's changed much?"

"Oh, I suppose. Seems like everywhere you look it's the twentieth century."

Then my wife and I stood on the platform between cars as passengers got off the train at the depot. A soldier in brown embraced his girlfriend, a mother with a pheasant feather in her hat straightened her boy's belt and tie, and a farmer in blue bib overalls stared at me from his bench. John Tackett sidled along the train in his white flannel suit, then discovered our Pullman and saw us and reached up to pump my hand. "Golly, it's great to see you two again! This is a red-letter day!"

He helped Julia down on the porter's step stool and then I climbed down to the step stool and cinders, using my left leg, and I was introduced to A. B. Macdonald of the Kansas City *Star,* a man my age in a gray serge suit and a camera case looped over his shoulder, his eyeglasses reflecting white in the sun. He asked, "Is this Julia, the sweetheart of your boyhood you talk so much about in your book?"

"This is she," I answered, patting her wrist like a doddering fool. "Did you ever read Longfellow's *Evangeline,* that wonderful story of how a woman followed after the man she loved, searching for him all her life, from girlhood to old age, and the beautiful words of the poem: 'Ye who believe in affection that hopes, and endures, and is patient, Ye who believe in the beauty and strength of woman's devotion, list to this mournful tradition.' Remember those lines? I committed them to memory when I was in the state prison. Well, all that Longfellow said of Evangeline's love and devotion I can say about Julia's. I owe all that I am to her."

My wife had the grace to seem flattered by that sentiment, and it was printed verbatim in the next edition of the *Star,* along with everything else I said during that long afternoon. A hotel limousine carried us to the Eldridge House, passing under a banner that welcomed my wife and me, that swelled and subsided with the winds. And we were shown to the Governor's Suite, where lunch was wheeled in on four wooden carts. My wife and Macdonald huddled together, discussing the schedule for that day and the next, Julia canceling the more rinky-dink affairs with a simple cross of her pen.

John Tackett dearly loved playing host, and he entertained us with stories through most of the meal. He said, "You know what I was ruminating about this morning? About how it was when you and me casted that movie about the raid." He turned towards Macdonald. "There must've been a hundred boys in audition, each of them scowling worse than the one before and shouting bandit talk as they waved two pistols around, and every one of them giving Emmett scared looks as he sat there in a theater seat putting check marks next to their names."

"Any stars in the bunch?"

Tackett ignored the question and said, "Afterwards Emmett and I would drink sherry and I'd work at convincing him about what a million-dollar idea it was. I'd say, 'Do you know how much money there is in these Westerns? Do you have even an inkling of how America craves stories like yours? You're going to be a rich man, Emmett.' "

"And he was right, wasn't he," said Macdonald.

I didn't answer, but Tackett winked and said, "I always was pretty savvy that way; just like his brother Bob."

That afternoon we were on tour. My wife and I sat in the back seat of Tackett's green La Salle and Macdonald sat in the front with a note pad, recording whatever was said as we rode slowly down the streets of a town that had radio shops and grocery stores and Tackett's two movie theaters where once there were houses and vegetable patches. A mailman walked down the street and mailboxes clinked. Boys swerved down a sidewalk on bicycles with balloons in the spokes. A woman rocked on the porch of her house, flapping her apron dry; a man stood in his yard with a garden hose, water trickling off the nozzle onto his shoes. Every once in a while someone would wave at Tackett's automobile and he'd acknowledge by lifting a finger off the steering wheel. He said, "This is the way they rode into town that morning, right in on Eighth Street."

Macdonald said, "I see."

Tackett said, "Along about here is where they found Dick Broadwell dead. His horse was standing over him and it reared up whenever anybody got close. I guess they couldn't pull the corpse away for a long time."

Macdonald turned in his seat to see me. "Is that true?"

"I really can't say. I was sort of distracted that morning."

Tackett continued, "Then on Saturday Dick Broadwell's kin came down from Hutchinson, Kansas, and demanded his remains, his horse, and the $92.40 the sheriff discovered in his braid wallet. That's why there's just the three men buried there now. Nobody ever came for Bill Powers. Name was probably an alias." Tackett looked at me in the rearview mirror. "Maybe we could show him the grave."

At Elmwood Cemetery I stopped first at my brother

Frank's gray stone monument and then strolled under the
shade trees to the potter's corner next to the railroad tracks.
The burial plot was marked by white-painted stones at each
corner, and my simple granite slab with three names chiseled
in it lay hidden in deep blue grass at the head of the common
graves. Tackett stole a red-flowered wreath from another plot
and Macdonald wanted to photograph me placing it near the
headstone, but instead I leaned against an elm tree and bent to
light a cigarette with a match, and when I lifted my head
Macdonald was standing across from me with his pencil in his
pocket. "You miss your brother Bob a lot, don't you."

"I miss all my brothers."

"But Bob especially?"

I squinted from the cigarette smoke. "I miss the past," I
said.


Julia and I had room service breakfast the next morning with
Tackett and Macdonald and three representatives from the
Chamber of Commerce who wouldn't let go of my hand once
they shook it, plus two other surprise visitors, Charley Gump
and Jack Long. Gump was seventy-seven years old, a dealer in
secondhand parts for motor cars, a lean, bald man with a dark
mustache and eyeglasses with black circle frames. He seemed
pleased as Punch just sitting with me on the sofa, and he was
quick to show off the mangled scar on his thumb that my dead-
eye brother gave him when he swung around at the First National Bank and blew his shotgun to smithereens. Then
blond Jack Long, a stout and cheerful man who was by then
in his fifties, spouted about leaning on the porch railing to
stare at the Condon bank until I punched the windowglass
with my rifle and yelled, "Get away from here, son, before you
get hurt." Then Tackett told the men, "It took three doctors
to dig all the buckshot out of Emmett's back. I stood over
Emmett, fanning him with a magazine during the whole
operation. He told everyone his name was Charles Dryden and

wouldn't admit his real name until they dragged the bodies of the gang upstairs so he could study their faces and allow they were dead."

I managed to smile at most of the stories but finally I stopped listening. I put on my bifocals and sat under a lamp with my legs crossed, and I saw my company only when I licked my thumb and happened to look over the top of my newspaper.

There were photographs in it of yesterday, of me with my hat in my hands and my head bowed, praying for the souls of my brothers, and another of me with John Tackett in the hotel dining room, examining the chamber of my pistol, and a third of Emmett Dalton astride a dark horse in the woods of Onion Creek, "where the raid was planned."

Julia was fastening a necklace in the bureau mirror; Macdonald stood next to my chair, rubbing a cigarette out. "Ready?"

And the Dalton party took the elevator down to the lobby where there was a large audience of applauding people, drugstore clerks and foundry men and secretaries in polka-dot scarves, and under the shade of the hotel's roof were gas station attendants and boys chewing gum and house painters in white coveralls, men in dark suits and gray felt hats, two schoolteachers with small schoolchildren, and flashbulbs going off when I waved my left hand.

I walked to the First National Bank just as I had at twenty and little boys tried to place their shoes on whatever bricks I stepped on. Maybe a thousand people gazed in awe as I stood at the doors of the Condon bank, my hand skating over the riddled wood, and gave my version of the Great Coffeyville Kansas Raid. Then I crossed Walnut Street just as my brother Grat had, recalling aloud the withering gunfire and wagon barricades and the smoke hanging at Isham's. I walked with a crowd shoved around me, adults and children gaping at the picket fence with pea vines on it where my brother Bob was killed. I scraped my heel in the cinders to indicate the place where I lay dying, and then I saw that the crowd had retreated, and there in the alley in black suits with red ribbons on their pockets were six survivors of those men who'd shot at me there forty-five years before. One sat in a wooden wheelchair; two leaned on canes; they shaded their eyes from the sun and grinned at me, and then they slunk up to shake my hand.

## A NOTE ON THE TYPE

The text of this book was set on the Linotype in a typeface called Baskerville. The face is a facsimile reproduction of types cast from molds made for John Baskerville (1706–75) from his designs. The punches for the revived Linotype Baskerville were cut under the supervision of the English printer George W. Jones. John Baskerville's original face was one of the forerunners of the type style known as "modern face" to printers—a "modern" of the period A.D. 1800.

Composed by The Maryland Linotype Composition Company, Inc., Baltimore, Maryland. Printed and bound by The Haddon Craftsmen, Inc. Scranton, Pennsylvania.

Typography and binding design by Virginia Tan.

Front and back endpaper maps by David Lindroth.

# Coffeyville

Baldwin's body

2.

3.

4.

5.

6.

Cubine
and Brown

Bob's position when he
killed Cubine and Brown

UNION STREET

1.

8.

9.

WALNUT STREET

7.

11.

12.

13.

14.

15.

EIGHTH STREET